Public Library San Francisco

English Prose Fiction

including translations

Public Library San Francisco

English Prose Fiction
including translations

ISBN/EAN: 9783337368722

Printed in Europe, USA, Canada, Australia, Japan

Cover: Foto ©Andreas Hilbeck / pixelio.de

More available books at **www.hansebooks.com**

SAN FRANCISCO

Free Public Library

ENGLISH PROSE FICTION
INCLUDING TRANSLATIONS.

SAN FRANCISCO:

June, 1897.

PREFATORY NOTE.

The last catalogue of English fiction was published in 1891. In addition to the customary alphabetical arrangement according to authors and titles, the works included in it were classified according to subject matter. The value of the catalogue for reference purposes was further enhanced by notes suggesting books for collateral reading. For such purposes, the catalogue of 1891 is of lasting value. Owing to the changes which have taken place in the contents of the fiction portion of the library, however, its usefulness as a record of available books has been much impaired. New books have been added and old ones have been worn out and removed from the shelves. Of the latter class, many being out of print have not been replaced. The necessity for a new guide to the available works of fiction becoming more and more pressing, this finding list has been prepared.

In order to facilitate delivery, the books have been re-numbered on a plan by which they will stand on the shelves in alphabetical order according to authors.

ENGLISH FICTION.

AUTHORS AND TITLES.

A., J. Y., *pseud. See* Ackerman, J. Y.
Abbé Birotteau. Balzac, H. de......*in* B198.32s
Abbé Constantin, L' Halévy, L...........H168.1
Abbé Tigrane. Fabre, F..................F123.1
Abbot, The. Scott, *Sir* W.................S431.1
Same..*in* S431.34
ABBOTT, C. C. A colonial wooing.........A130.1
ABBOTT, E. A. Flatland ; a romance of
many dimensions.......................A131.1
Abdallah. Laboulaye, E..................L124.1
A'BECKET, J. J. Song of the comforter.
27 pp. ....*in* S886.1
Abel Allnutt. Morier, J..................M855.1
ABOUT, E. The aunt's stratagem......*in* A156.3
King of the mountains..................A156.1
Man with the broken ear................A156.2
Mother of a marquise, and, The aunt's
stratagem...............................A156.3
Notary's nose.............................A156.4
Story of an honest man..................A156.5
About money and other things. Mulock,
D. M.......................................M960.1
Absentee. Edgeworth, M.............*in* E235.1
Same.......................................**E235.11
Same. 2 vols.............................E235.24-5
Accomplished gentleman. Sturgis, J....S935.1
ACHILLES TATIUS. Loves of Clitopho and
Leucippe..............................*in* S657.1
Achsah. Round, W. M. F..............R860.1
Across the chasm. Magruder, J.........M212.1
Actæon. Daintrey, L....................D134.1
"Acte." Westbury, H....................W523.1
ADAM, *Uncle,* (*pseud.* of C. A. Wetter-
bergh). Fatal chain. 40 pp........*in* B979.1 2
Hereditary goblet. 26 pp......*in* B979.1 3
ADAM, *Mme.* E. *See* Adam, J. L.
ADAM, J. L. A fascinating woman........A194.1
Adam and Eve. Parr, L..................Q258.1
Adam Bede. Eliot, G.....................E426.1
Adam Dickson. Mason, T.................M412.1

Adam Graeme of Mossgray, Memoirs, etc.,
of. Oliphant, M. O. W.................O475.32
Adam Johnstone's son. Crawford, F. M....
....C899.1
ADAMS, F. C. Manuel Pereira ; or, the sove-
reign rule of South Carolina...........A212.1
ADAMS, J. S. Town and country..........A213.1
ADAMS, M. Honorable surrender.........A215.1
ADAMS, N. Sable cloud ; a southern tale
with northern comments.................A216.1
ADAMS, W. T. *See* Optic, O., *pseud.*
Additional Christmas stories. Dickens,
C...................................*in* D548.52
ADEE, A. A. Life magnet. 30 pp....*in* S884.8
Adela Cathcart. MacDonald, G...........M135.1
Adèle. Kavanagh, J.....................K212.1
Adeline Mowbray. Opie, A............*in* O614.1
Adieu. 58 pp. Balzac, H. de.........*in* B198.41
Adirondack stories. Deming, P.,.........D382.1
Adirondack tales. v. 1. Murray, W. H.
H.......................................M984.1
Admiral's ward. Alexander, *Mrs*.........A374.2
Adolphe. Constant de Rebecque, H. B.....
......................................**C757.1
Adrift. Young, J. D.....................Y693.1
Adventure in the northwest territory. 25
pp...................................*in* T143.5
Same...............................*in* T143.5 '
Adventurer of the north. Parker, G......Q240.1
Adventures of a casket. Ménard, T......M535.1
Adventures of a Chinaman in China.
Verne, J.................................V531.1
Adventures of a widow. Fawcett, E......F278.1
Adventures of an aide-de-camp. Grant,
J.......................................G761.1
Adventures of an atom. 83 pp. Smollett,
T. G................................*in* **N938.21
Adventures of Baron Münchausen. Raspe,
R. E....................................**R226.1
Adventures of Caleb Williams. Godwin,

W.......... .... G592.1

Adventures of Captain Blake. Maxwell,
W. H..M465.1

Adventures of Captain Hatteras. 2 pts.
Verne, J..V531.2

Adventures of Captain Horn. Stockton,
F. R..S866.1

Adventures of Captain Mago. Cahun, L...
....C132.1

Adventures of Don Quixote. Cervantes
Saavedra, M. de.............................C419.1

Adventures of Hajji Baba in England.
Morier, J..M855.5

Adventures of Hajji Baba in Turkey, etc.
Morier, J..M855.2

Adventures of Harry Richmond. Mere-
dith, G...M559.1

Adventures of Joseph Andrews. Fielding,
H..F459.1

Adventures of Mr. Ledbury, and his friend
Jack Johnson. Smith, A..................S641.4

Adventures of Mr. Verdant Green. Bede,
C...B411.1

Adventures of Peregrine Pickle. Smollett,
T. G..S666.2

Adventures of Philip. Thackeray, W.
M...T363.1
Same T363.2

Adventures of Rob Roy. Grant, J.........G761.2

Adventures of Roderick Random. Smol-
lett, T. G...S666.3

Adventures of Sherlock Holmes. Doyle,
A. C..D754.1

Adventures of Telemachus. Fénelon, F.
de S. de la M....................................F332.1

Adventures of three Englishmen and three
Russians in southern Africa. Verne,
J..V531.3

Afghan knife. Sterndale, R. A..........S839.1

Afloat and ashore. Cooper, J. F...........C777.1
Same...*in* C777.36

Afraja. Mügge, T..................... ....M951.1

After dark, and other stories. Collins,
W...C713.1

After many days. Reid, C...................R353.1

After shipwreck. Owen, *Mrs.* J. A........O974.1

After the ball. 12 pp. Opie, A.........*in* O614.3

After twenty years, etc. Sturgis, J.........S935.3

Afterglow. Lathrop, G. P.....................L354.1

Aftermath. Allen, J. L........................A427.1

Against the stream. Charles, E. R........C476.1

Agamenticus. Tenney, E. P..................T298.1

Agatha Page. Henderson, I................H497.1

Agatha's husband. Mulock, D. M........M960.2

Agincourt. James, G. P. R..................J276.1

Agnes. Oliphant, M. O. W..................O475.1

Agnes Grey. Bronte, A....................*in* B871.2

Agnes Hilton. Hoffman, M. J.............H708.1

Agnes of Sorrento. Stowe, H. B...........S892.1

Agnes Surriage. Bynner, E. L.............B994.1

AGNEW, C. Peerless Cathleen.............A273.1

AGUILAR, G. Days of Bruce.................A283.1
Home influence.................................A283.2
Home scenes and heart studies...........A283.3
Mother's recompense : a sequel to Home
influence...A283.4
Vale of cedars ; or, the martyr...........A283.5
Woman's friendship...........................A283.6

AIDE, H. Carr of Carrlyon.................A288.1
Penruddocke.....................................A288.3
Voyage of discovery...........................A288.4

Aims and obstacles. James, G. P. R.....J276.41

AINSLIE, H., *pseud.* See Maitland, E.

AINSWORTH, W. H. Auriol ; or, the elixir
of life. (*Also*), A night's adventure
in Rome (1830)................................A297.1
Beau Nash ; or, Bath in the 18th cen-
tury...A297.2
Boscobel ; a tale of the year 1651........A297.3
Cardinal Pole ; or, the days of Philip
and Mary...A297.4
Constable of the tower.......................A297.5
Crichton...A297.6
Flitch of bacon ; or, the custom of Dun-
mow...A297.7
Guy Fawkes......................................A297.8
Jack Sheppard...................................A297.9
James the Second...............................A297.10
John Law, the projector......................A297.11
Lancashire witches : a romance of Pendle
forest...A297.12
Leaguer of Lathom. A tale of the civil
war in Lancashire...........................A297.13
Lord Mayor of London......................A297.26
Mervyn Clitheroe...............................A297.14
Miser's daughter : a tale....................A297.16
Night's adventure in Rome............*in* A297.1
Old St. Paul's : a tale of the plague and
the fire..A297.18
Ovingdean Grange... ....A297.19
Rookwood...A297.20
Saint James's ; or, the court of Queen
Anne...A297.21
The spendthrift..................................A297.22
Star-chamber....... ....A297.23
Tower of London................................A297.24
Windsor Castle..................................A297.25

Airy fairy Lilian. Duchess.................D829.1

AKERMAN, J. Y. [A., J. Y.] Tales of other days........ ....A314.1
Aladdin in London. Hume, F. W.........H920.1
ALARCÓN, P. A. de. Black eyes. 12 pp......
...............in H496.1
Tall woman. 34 pp...............in M690.1
Albert Lunel. 3 vols. Brougham, Lord H. P..............................B876.1
Albert Savarus. Balzac, H. de...............B198.1
Same..............in B198.44
Albert Travers, Fortunes of. Berrington, B. S..............................B533.1
Albrecht. Bates, A..............................B329.1
ALCOCK, D. The czar. A tale of the time of the first Napoleon.....................A354.1
Dark year of Dundee : a tale of the Scottish reformation. Also, Proctor's tithe A354.2
Geneviève ; or, the children of Port Royal..............................A354.3
Proctor's tithe........................in A354.2
Spanish brothers : a tale of the sixteenth century..............................A354.4
Under the southern cross.....................A354.5
ALCOTT, L. M. Hospital sketches...........A355.1
Independence : a centennial love story...
...............in A355.4
Modern Mephistopheles.....................A355.2
Moods..............................A355.3
Silver pitchers ; and, Independence.....A355.4
Work A355.5
Alderbrook. Chubbuck, E....................C559.1
ALDRICH, T. B. Marjorie Daw and other people. A365.3
Same and other stories.....................A365.4
Prudence Palfrey..............................A365.6
Queen of Sheba..............................A365.7
Two bites at a cherry, etc....................A365.9
—joint author. See Oliphant, M. O. W.
Alec Forbes. MacDonald, G...............M135.2
ALEXANDER, Mrs., (pseud. of A. F. Hector.)
Admiral's ward..............................A374.2
At bay..............................A374.4
By woman's wit..............................A374.7
The executor..............................A374.10
Fight with fate..............................A374.12
Forging the fetters, etc.....................A374.13
Found wanting..............................A374.14
The Freres..............................A374.15
Her dearest foe A374.17
Heritage of Langdale.....................A374.18
Look before you leap.....................A374.19
Maid, wife, or widow ?.....................A374.20
Mrs. Vereker's courier maid.........in A374.27

ALEXANDER, Mrs.—Continued.
Ralph Wilton's weird.....................A374.23
Snare of the fowler..............................A374.25
Valerie's fate. (Also) Mrs. Vereker's courier maid..............................A374.27
Woman's heart. A374.28
Wooing o't..............................A374.29
ALEXANDER, F. See Francesca, pseud.
ALEXIS, W. (pseud. of G. W. H. Häring).
Haus Preller : a legend of the Rhine falls..............................in T143.20
Alfgar the Dane. Crake, A. D...............C888.1
Alfrieda. Specht, E. E. H...............S741.1
Alhambra, The. Irving, W..............................I725.1
Alice. Lytton, E. G. E. L. Bulwer......L998.1
Alice Ashland. Neville, E..............................N523.1
Alice Learmont. Mulock, D. M......in M960.10
Alice Lorraine. Blackmore, R. D.........B629.1
Same..............................in B629.3
Alice Sherwin. M., C. J..............................M110.1
Alicia Warlock, and other stories. Collins, W..............................C713.2
Alide. Lazarus, E..............................L431.1
Aline. Gréville, H..............................G838.1
Alkahest, The. Balzac, H. de...............B198.2
All alone. Theuriet, A..............................T415.1
All in a garden fair. Besant, Sir W......B554.1
All in the dark. LeFanu, J. S...............L488.1
All sorts and conditions of men. Besant, Sir W..............................B554.2
All the dogs' fault. Connery, T. B.........C753.1
Allan Quatermain. Haggard, H. R......H146.1
ALLARDYCE, A. Edgar Wayne's escape. 62 pp..............................in T143.13
Pundrapore residency. 64 pp.........in T143.9
ALLEN, G. British barbarians.............A425.1
Duchess of Powysland.....................A425.4
Dumaresq's daughter.....................A425.5
For Maimie's sake..............................A425.7
General Passavant's will. 37 pp......in S887.1
In all shades..............................A425.9
Melissa's tour..............................in S885.9
Michael's crag..............................A425.11
Recalled to life..............................A425.12
This mortal coil..............................A425.14
What's bred in the bone..............................A425.16
ALLEN, J. L. Aftermath. Pt. 2 of " A Kentucky cardinal.".....................A427.1
Flute and violin and other Kentucky tales, etc..............................A427.3
John Gray : a Kentucky tale of the olden time A427.5
A Kentucky cardinal..............................A427.7
Summer in Arcady..............................A427.9

ALLEN, R. Miss Eaton's romance ; a story of the New Jersey shore..............A429.1

"All's dross but love." 64 pp. Lancaster, A. E..............L244.1

All's for the best. Arthur, T. S..........A791.1

Alma. Marshall, E. M367.1

Almayer's folly. Conrad, J..............C754.1

Almeria. 98 pp. Edgeworth, M........**E235.8

Same..............in E235.22

Same..............in E235.35

Almoran and Hamet. Hawkesworth, J.....
..............in **B232.26

Same..............in **N938.1

Alone. Harland, M..............H283.1

Alone in China, and other stories. Ralph, J..............R163.1

Aloys. Auerbach, B..............A918.1

Alroy. Disraeli, B..............D613.1

Altiora Peto. Oliphant, L..............O474.1

Alton Locke. Kingsley, C..............K553.1

Amazing marriage. 2 vols. Meredith, G..............M559.2

Amazon, The. Dingelstedt, F., Freiherr v..............D584.1

Amazon, The. Vosmaer, C..............V968.1

Amber gods and other stories. Spofford, H. P..............S762.1

Ambitious woman. Fawcett, E..........F278.2

Amelia. Fielding, H..............F459.2

Same..............in **N938.1

American, The. James, H., Jr..............J277.1

American baron. De Mille, J..............D381.1

American claimant. Twain, M..............T969.1

Same, and other stories, etc..............T969.8

American coin. By the author of "Aristocracy.".............A512.1

American girl in London. Cotes, S. J. D...
..............C843.1

American in Paris. Savidge, E. C.........S267.1

American politician. Crawford, F. M...C899.2

Améro, C., joint author. See Tissot, V.

AMES, L. T. Memoirs of a millionaire...A513.1

Amethyst. Coleridge, C. R..............C692.1

Amid the corn. By the author of "The evening and the morning." 3 vols......
..............A516.1

Among the hills. Poynter, E. F.........Q892.1

Among the northern hills. Prime, W. C....
..............Q942.1

Amorassan. Lewis, M. G..............in L675.1

Amos Judd. Mitchell, J. A..............M680.1

Amos Kilbright. Stockton, F. R.........S866.2

Ampthill Towers. Foster, A. J..............F754.1

Amulet, The. Conscience, H.............in C755.6

Amyas Egerton, cavalier. Hervey, M. H..............H579.1

Anaconda, The. 56 pp. Lewis, M. G......
..............in L675.1

Anastatius. 3 vols. Hope, T..........**H790.1

Ancestral footstep. Hawthorne, N....in H399.3

Ancient régime. 3 vols. James, G. P. R..............J276.2

ANDERDON, W. H. Antoine de Bonneval : a tale of Paris in the days of St. Vincent de Paul..............A543.1

ANDERSEN, H. C. The improvisatore...A544.1

Morten Lange: a Christmas story ; Man from Paradise..............in B979.1

O. T. a Danish romance..............A544.2

Only a fiddler..............A544.3

Two baronesses..............A544.4

Andersonville violets. Collingwood, H. W..............C710.1

Andreas Hofer. Mühlbach, L..............M952.1

Andreds-weald. Crake, A. D..............C888.2

ANDREWS, L. H. Marie..............A567.1

Andromeda. McLean, H. E..............M163.1

Ange Pitou. 2 vols. Dumas, A.........D886.2

Angèle's fortune. Theuriet, A..............T415.2

Angelina. Edgeworth, M..............in E235.18

Anglomaniacs, The. Harrison, C. C.....H318.1

Anie. Malot, H. H..............M257.1

Anna Karénina. Tolstoi, Count L. N....T654.1

Annals of a baby. Stebbins, S. B..........S811.1

Annals of a quiet neighbourhood. Mac-Donald, G..............M135.3

Annals of a sportsman. Turgénieff, I. S....
..............T936.1

Annals of the parish. Galt, J..............G179.1

Annan Water. Buchanan, R..............B918.1

Anne. Woolson, C. F..............W916.1

Anne Furness. Trollope, F. E.........T847.1

Anne Judge, spinster. 3 vols. Robinson, F. W..............R660.1

Anne of Geierstein. Scott, Sir W.........S431.2

Same..............in **S431.21

Anne Séverin. Craven, P. de la F........C898.1

Annie and her master. 79 pp.........in T143.14

Annie Kilburn. Howells, W. D..........H859.1

Annouchka. Turgénieff, I. S..............T936.2

Another study of woman. 62 pp. Balzac, H. de..............in B198.19

Same..............in B198.44

Another's crime. Hawthorne, J.........H398.1

ANSTEY, F., (pseud. of F. A. Guthrie).

Black poodle. 46 pp..............in S885.6

Same, and other stories..............A625.1

Fallen idol..............A625.3

ANSTEY, F.—*Continued.*
Giant's robe............................A625.5
Tinted Venus......................... ......A625.7
Vice versa ; or, a lesson to fathers. A625.9
——, *joint author. See* Matthews, B.
Antar. 4 vols. Tr. by T. Hamilton......H221.1
Anteros. Lawrence, G. A............. ....L421.1
Antiquary, The. Scott, *Sir* W.............S431.3
Same....................................**S431.4
Antoine de Bonneval. Anderdon, W. H....
....A543.1
Antoinette. 2 vols. Blyth, M. P.........B660.1
Antoinette. Ohnet, G......................O383.1
Antonia. Sand, G.........................S213.1
Antonina. Collins, W.....................C713.3
Antonio di Carara : a Paduan tale. 79
pp................................*in* T143.5
Same..............................*in* T143.5 *
Antony Brade. Lowell, R. T. S............L916.1
Ape, the idiot, and other people. Morrow,
W. C..................................M883.1
Aphrodite. Eckstein, E....................E195.1
Apostate, The. Daudet, E...............D239.1
Apotheosis of Mr. Tyrawley. Prescott, E.
L.....................................Q918.1
APPLETON, G. W. Frozen hearts.........A649.1
Apprentices to destiny. Long, L. A......L848.1
April hopes. Howells, W. D.............H859.2
APULEIUS, LUCIUS, *Madaurensis.* Works :
comprising the Metamorphoses ; or,
golden ass. The God of Socrates. The
Florida, and, His defence ; or, a dis-
course on magic. Added, A metrical
version of Cupid and Psyche, and, Mrs.
Tighe's Psyche : a poem in six cantos.
(*Bohn's Lib.*)........................A655.1
Arabella Stuart. 3 vols. James, G. P.
R......................................**J276.3
Arabesques. Greenough, S. D............G815.1
Arabian nights' entertainments...........A658.1
Same. Tr. from the Fr. of A. Galland...
.................................**N938.18
Same. Ed. by W. Hauff A658.1h
Same. Tr. by E. W. Lane. 2 vols.......
.....................................A658.1l
Same. Tr. by E. Foster.............*in* S892.14
ARBLAY, *Mme.* F. B. d' *See* Burney, F.
ARBOUVILLE, S. de B., *Countess* d' Chris-
tine: a Dutch story. 85 pp.........*in* T143.3
Same..............................*in* T143.3 ²
Village doctor. 77 pp..................*in* T143.3
Same..............................*in* T143.3 '
Archibald Malmaison. Hawthorne, J.....H398.2
Archie Lovell. Edwardes, A...............E254.1

Archipelago on fire. Verne, J.............V531.4
Ardath. Corelli, M.......................C797.1
Ardis Claverden. Stockton, F. R..........S866.3
Argonauts of North Liberty. Harte, B......
....H327.1
ARGYLE, A. Olive Lacey : a tale of the
Irish rebellion of 1798................A695.2
Ariadne. Ouida...........................O934.1
Aristocracy.............. ....A716.1
Arius, the Libyan. Kauns, N. C........K883.1
Armadale. Collins, W....................C713.4
Arminell. Gould, S. B....................G698.1
Armorel of Lyonesse. Besant, *Sir* W.....B554.4
Armourer of Paris. 83 pp. Smith, A......
....*in* S641.2
Armourer's prentices. Yonge, C. M......Y555.1
ARMSTRONG, L. Sergeant Gore. 30 pp...
....*in* S886.3
Army Portia. King, C.................*in* K523.21
Army tales. Winter, J. S................W785.1
Arne. Björnson, B.......................B625.1
Same...................................B625.1 '
ARNOLD, G. Why Thomas was discharged.
25 pp..............................*in* S884.5
Around a spring. Droz, G...............D793.1
Around the golden deep. Reeder, A. P.....
....R327.1
Around the world in eighty days. Verne,
J.......................................V531.5
ARROM, *Mrs.* C. Böhl de Faber. *See* Ca-
ballero, F., *pseud.*
ARTHUR, T. S. All's for the best.........A791.1
Latimer family, and other temperance
stories.................................A791.2
Mill and the tavern.....................A791.3
Orange blossoms........................A791.4
Strike at Tivoli mills ; and what came of
it......................................A791.5
Wife's engagement ring.................A791.6
Arthur. Sue, E..........................S944.1
Arthur Blane. Grant, J..................G761.3
Arthur Bonnicastle. Holland, J. G.....H735.1
Arthur Merton. Porter, D. D.............Q844.1
Arthur Mervyn. 2 vols. Brown, C. B......
....B879.1
Arthur O'Leary, Adventures of. Lever,
C......................................L658.1
Artists' wives. Daudet, A................D238.1
Arundel motto. Hay, M. C...............H413.1
Arvon. 2 vols. Charles, C. M...........C475.1
As Avon flows. Vince, H. S.............V767.1
As it may happen. Trebor................T785.1
As it was written. Harland, H..........H282.1
As 'tis in life. Delpit, A...............D363.1

Asaph. Cooley, A. K..................C774.1
Ascanio. Dumas, A..................D886.3
"Ask mamma." Surtees, R. S..........S962.1
Askaros Kassis the Copt. DeLeon, E....D346.1
Aslauga's knight. 42 pp. La Motte-Fou-
    qué, F. H. K. *Freiherr* de........*in* L235.1
Same ....*in* L235.6
Asmodeus. LeSage, A. R..............L622.1
Aspasia. 2 vols. Hamerling, R.........H214.1
Aspendale. Preston, H. W.........Q927.1
Aspern papers. James, H., *Jr*..........J277.2
Asphodel. Braddon, M. E..............B798.1
Assunta Howard, and other stories, etc.
    Salter, E.........................S177.1
Ass'ya. Turgénieff, I. S............*in* T936.12
ASTOR, W. W. Sforza : a story of Milan...
    ....A858.1
At a high price. Werner, E..........W492.1
At an old chateau. Macquoid, K. S......M173.1
At bay. Alexander, *Mrs.* A374.4
At fault. Smart, H..................S636.1
At her mercy. Payn, J...............Q345.1
At his gates. Oliphant, M. O. W.......O475.2
At last. Harland, M.................H283.2
At last. Kingsley, C................K553.2
At odds. Tautphœus, J. M. *Freiherrin*
    von T229.1
At the councillor's. Marlitt, E........W817.10
At the gate of the fold. Fletcher, J. S......
    ....F613.1
At the mercy of Tiberius. Wilson, A. J.
    E.................................W746.1
At the north pole. Verne, J.........V531.6
At the world's mercy. Warden, F.......W265.1
At ye Grene Griffin. Holt, E. S.......H758.1
Atelier du Lys. Roberts, M...........R646.1
Atheist's mass. 20 pp. Balzac, H. de......
    ....*in* B198.16
Same.............................*in* B198.34
Same.............................B198.42
ATHERTON, G. F. Before the gringo
    came..............................A868.1
    Los Cerritos.......................A868.2
    What dreams may come...............A868.3
    Whirl asunder......................A868.4
Attaché, The. Haliburton, T. C........H172.1
Attila. James, G. P. R................J276.4
Attorney, The. Irving, J. T..........I723.1
Aubert Dubayet. Gayarré, C..........G285.1
AUER, A. von., (*pseud. of* C. von Cosel.)
    It is the fashion..................A917.1
AUERBACH, B. Aloys.................A918.1
    The axe. 13 pp................*in* Z767.1
    Black forest village stories.......A918.2

AUERBACH, B.—*Continued.*
    Brigitta............................A918.3
    Convicts and their children.........A918.4
    The foresters......................A918.5
    German tales.......................A918.6
    Joseph in the snow.................A918.7
    Little barefoot....................A918.8
        Issued also as The barefoot maiden.
    Lorely and Reinhard................A918.9
    Master Bieland and his workmen......A918.10
    On the heights. 2 vols............A918.11
    Poet and merchant ; a picture of the
        times of Moses Mendelssohn.......A918.12
    Spinoza............................A918.13
    Villa on the Rhine. 2 vols........A918.14
        Issued also as Villa Eden.
    Waldfried A918.15
Aulnay Tower. Howard, B. W..........H848.1
Aunt Anne. Clifford, L. L..........C639.1
Aunt Ann's ghost story. 35 pp.......*in* T143.15
Aunt Diana. Carey, R. N.............C276.1
Aunt Johnie. Winter, J. S...........W785.2
Aunt Serena. Howard, B. W...........H848.2
Aunt's stratagem. 74 pp. About, E. *in* A156.3
Aurelian. 2 vols. Ware, W..........W273.1
Aurifodina. Peck, G. W............**Q366.1
Auriol. Ainsworth, W. H............A297.1
Aurora. Tincker, M. A...............T587.1
AUSTEN, J. Emma....................A933.1
    Mansfield Park.....................A933.2
    Northanger Abbey................*in* A933.5
    Same. (*Also*) Persuasion........A933.3
    Persuasion......................*in* A933.3
    Same...........................*in* A933.7
    Pride and prejudice................A933.4
    Same. (*Also*) Northanger Abbey....A933.5
    Sense and sensibility..............A933.6
    Same, and, Persuasion............A933.7
AUSTIN, J. G. Betty Alden...........A936.1
    David Alden's daughter, etc........A936.3
    Desmond hundred....................A936.4
    Dr. LeBaron and his daughters : a story
        of the old colony..............A936.5
    Mrs. Beauchamp Brown...............A936.7
    Nameless nobleman..................A936.8
    Nantucket scraps...................A936.9
    Standish of Standish...............A936.12
Austin Elliott. Kingsley, H..........K555.1
Austin Friars. Riddell, C. E. L......R543.1
Author of Beltraffio. James, H., *Jr*....J277.3
Author's love. Balch, E.............B174.1
Auld licht idyls. Barrie, J. M.......B275.1
Aurora Floyd. Braddon, M. E.........B798.2
Autobiography of a joint-stock company
    (limited). 66 pp..............*in* T143.11

Automaton ear, and other sketches. Mc-
Landburgh, F.............................M159.1
Avatar. Gautier, T.......................*in* G277.5
AVELINE, Alfred d' (*pseud. of A. H. C. van*
Hasselt.) Menshikoff, or, the peasant
prince....................................A948.1
Average woman, etc. Balestier, W........B184.1
Averil. Carey, R. N.....................C276.2
Awakening of Mary Fenwick. Whitby,
B W579.1
Axel and Anna. 41 pp. Bremer, F...*in* B836.2
Ayesha, the maid of Kars. Morier, J......
.... M855.3
Ayrshire legatees. Galt, J...............G179.1
AYTOUN, W. E. Congress and the Agape-
dome. 60 pp....................*in* T143.8
Emerald studs. 66 pp..............*in* T143.3
Same............................*in* T143.3 ²
Glenmutchkin railway. 44 pp.......*in* S885.8
Same............................*in* T143.1
Same............................*in* T143.1 ¹
How I became a yeoman. 55 pp.....*in* T143.1
Same............................*in* T143.1 ²
How I stood for the Dreepdaily burghs.
79 pp............................*in* T143.2
Same............................*in* T143.2 ²
How we got possession of the Tuileries.
89 pp... ....*in* T143.3
Same............................*in* T143.3 ¹
Norman Sinclair. 3 vols..................A990.1
Raid of Arnaboll. 75 pp..........*in* T143.8
Rapping the question : a tale of modern
magic. 45 pp....................*in* T143.15
The surveyor's tale. 48 pp........*in* T143.4
Same............................*in* T143.4 ²
Azarian. Spofford, H. P. S762.2
AZEGLIO, M. d'. Challenge of Barletta..A993.1
Aztec treasure-house. Janvier, T. A......J358.1
Babe, B. A. Benson, E. F................B474.1
Baboe Dalima. Perelaer, T. H...........Q437.1
Baby Rue. Clay, C. M...................C619.1
Baby's grandmother. Walford, L. B......W174.1
Bachelor maid. Harrison, C. C..........H318.2
Bachelor of Salamanca. 2 vols. ' LeSage,
A. R....................................L622.2
Bachelor of the Albany. Savage, M. W....
....S264.1
Bachelor's blunder. Norris, W. E........N861.1
Bachelor's Christmas, and other stories.
Grant, R................................G763.2
Bachelor's establishment. Balzac, H. de...
....B198.37s
Bachelor's surrender.......................B121.1
Bad lot. Cameron, E. S.................C182.1

Bad penny. Wheelright, J. T.............W566.2
Baffled conspirators. Norris, W. E........N861.2
BAGE, R. Man as he is not............**B232.48
Bagpipers, The. Sand, G..................S213.2
BAILEY, J. M. Mr. Phillips' goneness........
....B154.1
Bailiff's maid. Marlitt, E................W817.11
BAIN, F. W. Dmitri : a romance of old
Russia..................................B162.1
BAKER, W. M. (G. F. Harrington, *pseud.*)
Blessed Saint Certainty................B169.1
Colonel Dunwoddie, millionaire.........B169.2
Inside : a chronicle of secession.......B169.3
Making of a man.........................B169.4
Mose Evans.............................B169.5
New Timothy............................B169.6
Virginians in Texas.....................B169.7
Balaam and his master, and other sketches,
etc. Harris, J. C.......................H314.1
BALCH, E. An author's love ; being the
unpublished letters of Prosper Méri-
mée's 'Inconnue.'.......................B174.1
Balcony stories. King, G..................K527.1
BALESTIER, W. Average woman, etc......
....B184.1
Benefits forgot...........................B184.2
—*joint author. See* Kipling, R.
BALFOUR, C. L. Burnish family...........B185.1
Ball at Sceaux. Balzac, H. de...*in* B198.6² k
Ball of snow. Dumas, A...........*in* D886.4
Balsam-seller of Thurotzer. Gore, C......
....*in* G566.1 ¹
BALZAC, H. DE. Abbé Birotteau. Tr. by
C. Bell...........................*in* B198.32s
Translated also as Vicar of Tours.
Albert Savarus (*also* Paz *and* Madame
Firmiani) Tr. by K. P. Wormeley...B198.1
The Alkahest ; or, The house of Claës.
Tr. by K. P. Wormeley.................B198.2
Translated also as Quest of the Absolute.
Atheist's mass. Tr. by W. Wilson and
Count Stenbock................*in* B198.34
Same. Tr. by K. P. Wormeley.....*in* B198.16
Same, and other stories. Tr. by C. Bell.
Ed. by G. Saintsbury..................B198.42
    CONTENTS : Atheist's mass. Honorine.
Colonel Chabert. Commission in lunacy.
Pierre Grassou.
Bachelor's establishment. Tr. by C. Bell.
Ed. by G. Saintsbury..................B198.37s
Translated also as Two brothers.
Béatrix. Tr. by J. Waring. Ed. by G.
Saintsbury B198.3s
Same. Tr. by K. P. Wormeley..........B198.3

BALZAC, H. DE.—*Continued.*

Brotherhood of Consolation. Tr. by K.
P. Wormeley.....................................B198.4
Bureaucracy. Tr. by K.P. Wormeley... B198.5
Cat and battledore, and other tales. Tr.
by P. Kent. 3 vols. (vols. 2-3 only)...
....B198.6k
CONTENTS: The purse. The ball at Sceaux.
Madame Firmiani. A double family.
Catherine de' Medici. Tr. by K. P.
Wormeley....................................B198.7
César Birotteau. Tr. by E. Marriage. Ed.
by G. Saintsbury.........................B198.8s
Same. Tr. by K. P. Wormeley..........B198.8
The Chouans. Tr. by E. Marriage. Ed.
by G. Saintsbury..........................B198.9s
Same. Tr. by G. Saintsbury.............B198.9t
Same. Tr. by K. P. Wormeley..........B198.9
Country doctor. Tr. by E. Marriage.
Ed. by G. Saintsbury....................B198.10s
Same. Tr. by K. P. Wormeley........B198.10
Country parson. Tr. by E. Marriage.
Ed. by G. Saintsbury....................B198.40s
Translated also as Village rector.
Cousin Bette. Tr. by K. P. Wormeley...
....B198.11
Cousin Pons. Tr. by K. P.Wormeley..B198.12
A Cretin village ; A Breton town.......
....*in* Z.767.1 *
Daughter of Eve. Tr. by K. P. Wormeley...B198.13
Deputy of Arcis. Tr. by K. P. Wormeley...B198.43
Duchesse de Langeais ; with, An episode
under the Terror ; Illustrious Gaudissart ; A passion in the desert ; (*and*)
The hidden masterpiece. Tr. by K. P.
Wormeley....................................B198.14
Eugénie Grandet. Tr. by E. Marriage.
Ed. by G. Saintsbury...................B198.15s
Same. Tr. by K. P. Wormeley........B198.15
Fame and sorrow ; with, Colonel Chabert ; Atheist's mass ; La Grande Bretèche ; The purse ; La Grenadière. Tr.
by K. P. Wormeley.....................B198.16
Ferragus, chief of the Dévorants. (*Also*)
Last incarnation of Vautrin. Tr. by
K. P. Wormeley.........................B198.17
Gallery of antiquities. (*Also*) An old
maid. Tr. by K. P. Wormeley......B198.18
Gobseck. (*Also* Secrets of the Princesse de Cadignan ; Unconscious
comedians ; Another study of woman ;
Comedies played gratis.)...............B198.19

BALZAC, H. DE.—*Continued.*

La Grande Brèteche, and other stories.
Tr. by C. Bell............................B198.44
CONTENTS: A study of woman. Another
study of woman. La Grande Bretèche.
Peace in the house. Imaginary mistress.
Albert Savarus.
Great man of the provinces in Paris.
Tr. by K. P. Wormeley................B198.20
An historical mystery. Tr. by K. P.
Wormeley B198.21
Juana. (*Also* Adieu ; Drama on the seashore ; Red Inn ; The Recruit ; El
Verdugo ; Elixir of life ; Hated son ;
Maitre Cornélius.) Tr. by K. P.
Wormeley B198.41
Last incarnation of Vautrin..........*in* B198.17
Lesser bourgeoisie. Tr. by K. P. Wormeley..B198.22
Lily of the valley. Tr. by K. P. Wormeley..B198.23
Lost illusions. Tr. by K. P. Wormeley...
....B198.24
Louis Lambert. (*Also* Facino Cane *and*
Gambara). Tr. by K. P. Wormeley...
....B198.25
Lucien de Rubempré. Tr. by K. P.
Wormeley B198.26
Magic skin. Tr. by K. P. Wormeley...B198.27
Translated also as Wild ass's skin.
Marriage contract. (*Also* A double life ;
Peace of a home.) Tr. by K. P. Wormeley B198.28
Memoirs of two young married women.
Tr. by K. P. Wormeley.................B198.29
Modeste Mignon. Tr. by C. Bell. Ed.
by G. Saintsbury.........................B198.30s
Same. Tr. by K. P. Wormeley........B198.30
Old Goriot. Tr. by E. Marriage. Ed.
by G. Saintsbury.........................B198.31s
Translated also as Père Goriot.
An old maid................................*in* B198.18
The peasantry. Tr. by E. Marriage. Ed.
by G. Saintsbury.........................B198.35s
Translated also as Sons of the soil.
Père Goriot. Tr. by K. P. Wormeley...
....B198.31
Translated also as Old Goriot.
Pierrette, and, The Abbé Birotteau. Tr.
by C. Bell. Ed. by G. Saintsbury......
....B198.32s
Same. Tr. by K. P. Wormeley........B198.32
Quest of the absolute. Tr. by E. Marriage. Ed. by G. Saintsbury........B198.2s
Translated also as The Alkahest.

BALZAC, H. DE.—*Continued.*

Seraphita. (*Also*), Jesus Christ in Flanders (*and*) The exiles. Tr. by K. P. Wormeley..................................B198.33

Shorter stories. Tr. by W. Wilson and Count Stenbock..........................B198.34
  CONTENTS: Don Juan. Christ in Flanders. In the time of the terror. Madame de Dey's last reception (*La requisitionnaire*). A passion in the desert. Lost by a laugh. Gold (*Facino Cane*). Doomed to live (*El Verdugo*). An accursed house (*La grande Breteche*). The atheist's mass. A tragedy by the sea.

Sons of the soil. Tr. by K. P. Wormeley..................................B198.35
  Translated also as The peasantry.

Start in life, etc. Tr. by K. P. Wormeley..................................B198.36

Two brothers. Tr. by K. P. Wormeley...
..................................B198.37
  Translated also as Bachelor's establishment.

Ursula. Tr. by K. P. Wormeley......B198.38

Ursule Mirouet. Tr. by C. Bell. Ed. by G. Saintsbury...........................B198.38s
  Translated also as Ursula.

Vicar of Tours..........................*in* B198.32
  Translated also as Abbé Birotteau.

Village rector. Tr. by K. P. Wormeley..................................B198.40
  Translated also as Country Parson.

Wild ass's skin. Tr. by E. Marriage. Ed. by G. Saintsbury..................B198.27s
  Translated also as Magic skin.

BANDELIER, A. F. Delight makers........B214.1

BANGS, J. K. Rebellious heroine..........B216.3

Water ghost and others....................B216.4

—*and* Sherman, F. D. [*Two wags.*] New waggings of old tales..................B216.1

BANIM, J. Boyne water......................B217.1

The denounced; or, The last baron of Crana. *Also*, The conformists.........B217.2

Peter of the castle; and, The fetches.....
..................................B217.3

Rival dreamers....................*in* S885.4

—*and* M. Clough Fionn; or, the stone of destiny..........................*in* B217.5

Crohoore of the bill-hook..............*in* B217.6

Ghost-hunter and his family. (*Also*) Clough Fionn; or, the stone of destiny..................................B217.5

Peep o' day; and, Crohoore of the bill-hook..................................B217.6

BANIM, M. The croppy......................B218.1

Father Connell; a tale....................B218.2

Mayor of Wind-gap. *Also*, Canvassing.

BANIM, M.—*Continued.*
  (originally written by Miss Martin and ed. by J. Banim).....................B218.3

—*joint author.* See Banim, J.

Banished, The. Morier, J..................M855.4

Banned and blessed. Werner, E.........W817.32

Banshee, The ....*in* S885.4

Bar Harbor tales. Harrison, C. C....*in* H318.11

Barabbas. Corelli, M........................C797.3

Barbara. Braddon, M. E....................B798.3

Barbara Allan. Cleland, R......... ....C624.1

Barbara Dering. Rives, A...................R623.1

Barbara Heathcote's trial. Carey, R. N.
..................................C276.4

Barbara's history. Edwards, A. B........E261.1

BARBAULD, A. L., ed. The British novelists 50 vols......................................**B232.1-50
  CONTENTS:—vols. 1-8. Richardson, S: Clarissa; or, the history of a young lady.
  9-15. Richardson, S: History of Sir Charles Grandison.
  16-17. De Foe, D. The life and surprising adventures of Robinson Crusoe, of York, mariner.
  18. Fielding, H: History of the adventures of Joseph Andrews and his friend Mr. Abraham Adams.
  19-21. Fielding, H: The history of Tom Jones, a foundling.
  22. Reeve, C. The old English baron: a Gothic story.—Walpole, H., 4. *Earl of Orford.* The castle of Otranto: a Gothic story.
  23. Coventry, F. History of Pompey the little; or, the life . . . of a lap dog.—Goldsmith, O. The vicar of Wakefield.
  24-5. Lennox, C. R. The female Quixote; or, the fortunes of Arabella.
  26. Johnson, S: History of Rasselas, prince of Abissinia.—Hawkesworth, J: Almoran and Hamet: an oriental tale.
  27. Brooke, F. M. The history of Lady Julia Mandeville.—Inchbald, E. S. Nature and art.
  28. Inchbald, E. S. A simple story.
  29. Mackenzie, H. The man of feeling. (*And*) Julia de Roubigné.
  30-1. Smollett, T. The expedition of Humphry Clinker.
  32-3. Graves, R: The spiritual Quixote; or, the summer's ramble of Mr. Geoffry Wildgoose.
  34-5. Moore, J: Zeluco.
  36-7. Smith, C. T. The old manor house.
  38-9. Burney, F. Evelina; or, history of a young lady's introd. to the world.
  40-2. Burney, F. Cecelia; or, the memoirs of an heiress.
  43-4. Radcliffe, A. W. Romance of the forest. Interspersed with some pieces of poetry.
  45-7. Radcliffe, A. W. The mysteries of Udolpho. Interspersed with some pieces of poetry.
  48. Bage, R. Man as he is not; or, Hermsprong.
  49-50. Edgeworth, M. Belinda;—The modern Griselda.

Barchester Towers. Trollope, A............T846.1
BARDEEN, C. W. Roderick Hume........B245.1
BARING-GOULD, S. See Gould, S. Baring.
Barker's luck, and other stories. Harte,
     B...H327.40
BARLOW, J. Irish idylls.....................B258.3
     Kerrigan's quality B258.5
     Lost recruit......................................in S885.4
     Maureen's fairing, etc.......................B258.7
     Mrs. Martin's company, and other
         stories...B258.8
     Strangers at Lisconnel B258.9
Barnaby Rudge. Dickens, C...............D548.1
     Same..in D548.2
     Same..in D548.3
     Same..in D548.4
BARNARD, C. (J. Kingsford, pseud.) The
     soprano: a musical story B259.1
Barney Bradley. Carleton, W............in C281.7
Barney Branagan. Carleton, W.........in C281.3
Baron Münchausen, Adventures of. Raspe,
     R. E...**R226.1
Baron of Hertz. Labadye, A. de...........L112.1
Barque Future. Lie, J........................L716.1
BARR, A. E. Beads of Tasmer............B268.2
     Bernicia B268.3
     Border shepherdess: a romance of Esk-
         dale B268.4
     Bow of orange ribbon. A romance of
         New York...B268.5
     Christopher, and other stories.............B268.6
     Daughter of Fife B268.8
     Feet of clay......................................B268.10
     Jan Vedder's wife...............................B268.12
     Knight of the nets...............................B268.14
     Last of the Macallisters B268.15
     Lone house.......................................B268.16
     Master of his fate...............................B268.17
     Paul and Christina..............................B268.18
     Prisoners of conscience......................B268.23
     Remember the Alamo........................B268.19
     Rose with a hundred leaves................B268.20
     Singer from the sea B268.22
     Squire of Sandal-Side.......................B268.21
BARR, R. In the midst of alarms..........B269.1
     A woman intervenes............................B269.2
Barren honour. Lawrence, G. A............L421.2
BARRIE, J. M. Auld licht idylls.............B275.1
     Better dead.—My Lady Nicotine........B275.2
     Courting of T'nowhead's Bell. 30 pp. in S885.8
     Inconsiderate waiter. 21 pp.............in S885.6
     Is it a man?.....................................in S887.1
     Little minister.................................B275.5

BARRIE, J. M.—Continued.
     My lady Nicotine............. ....B275.7
     Same..in B275.2
     Sentimental Tommy B275.8
     When a man's single........................B275.9
     Window in Thrums B275.10
Barriers burned away. Roe, E. P........R699.1
BARRILI, A. G. Eleventh commandment
         ....B276.1
     Whimsical wooing B276.2
Barrington. Lever, C...........................L658.2
Barrington's fate. Hunt, M. R.............H942.1
BARRY, Rev. Dr.—New Antigone........B280.1
Barry Lyndon. Thackeray, W. M....in T363.10
     Same..T363.14
     Same..T363.15
BARTER, K. My trivial life and misfor-
     tunes..B283.1
BARTLETT, T. Heart stories B291.1
BARTOL, M. Honor May.........B292.1
Barton experiment. Habberton, J........H113.1
BASIL, pseud. See King, R. A.
Basil. Collins, W..................................C713.5
Bastonnais, The. Lesperance, J. L637.1
BATES, A. Albrecht......... ....B329.1
     Book o' nine tales...............................B329.2
     A lad's love.......................................B329.4
     The pagans.......................................B329.6
     Patty's perversities............................B329.7
     The Philistines B329.8
     Wheel of fire......................................B329.10
Bates's tour (personally conducted) 37 pp.
     ....in T143.13
Battle of Dryffe Sands..................in W750.8
Battle of the Moy; or, how Ireland gained
     her independence, 1892-1894.............B336.1
Battle summer. Harland, M... ....in H283.5
Battlement and tower. Rhoscomyl, O....R478.1
BAUER, K. See Detlef, K., pseud...........
Bay-path. Holland, J. G.....................H735.2
BAYLE, A. Thalia................................B358.1
BAYLY, A. E. See Lyall, E., pseud...........
BAYLOR, F. C. Claudia Hyde............B359.1
     On both sides.....................................B359.2
BEACONSFIELD, Earl of. See Disraeli, B.
Beads of Tasmer. Barr, A. E...... ....B268.2
Beatrice. Haggard, H. R.....................H146.2
Beatrice. Kavanagh, J.........................K212.2
Beatrice Boville, and other stories. Ouida.
     ....O934.2
Beatrice Cenci. Guerrazzi, F. D...........G934.1
Beatrice of Bayou Têche. Jones, A. I....J767.1
Béatrix. Balzac, H. de........................B198.3
Beau Nash. Ainsworth, W. H.............A297.2

Beauchamp. James, G. P. R..............J276.5
Beauchampe. Simms, W. G..............S592.1
Beauchamp's career. Meredith, G........M559.3
Beaumarchais. Brachvogel, A. E..........B796.1
BEAUMONT, F., and FLETCHER, J. Philaster: or, love lies bleeding. 24 pp...........
....in M875.1
BEAUMONT, M. Revenge of her race. in S885.7
BEAUREPAIRE, G. de. See Glouvet, J., pseud.
Beautiful Jim. Winter, J. S................ W785.3
Beauty and the beast; and tales of home.
Taylor, B...............................T238.1
Beauty draught. 42pp.....................in T143.5
Same..................................in T143.5 ¹
Beauty's daughters. Duchess............... D829.4
BEAZLEY, S. The Oxonians: sequel to
The roué....................................B386.1
The roué....................................B386.2
Bébée. Ouida..............................O934.3
BECKE, L. and JEFFERY, W. First Fleet
family....................................B394.1
BECKETT, Mrs. (—) See Griffith, C.
BECKFORD, W. Vathek: an Arabian tale.
....B396.1
Same...................................in S892.14
BECQUER, G. A. Maese Pérez, the organist....................................in M690.1
BEDE, C. (pseud. of E. Bradley.) Adventures of Mr. Verdant Green, an Oxford
freshman..................................B411.1
Issued also as The dude.
Nearer and dearer..........................B411.2
Bede's charity. Stretton, H..............S915.1
Beechcroft. Yonge, C. M...................Y555.2
BEECHER, E. W. B. From dawn to daylight; or, the simple story of a western
home.......................................B414.1
BEECHER, H. W. Norwood; or, village life
in New England............................B415.1
BEERS, H. A. Split zephyr; an attenuated
yarn spun by the fates. 53pp......... in S884.8
Beethoven. Rau, H........................R239.1
Before the dawn. Dulac, G................ D878.1
Before the gringo came. Atherton, G. F.
....A868.1
Beggar on horseback. Payn, J.............Q345.2
Beggars all. Dougall, L...................D731.1
Beginner, A. Broughton, R...............B877.1
Begum's daughter. Bynner, E. L.........B994.2
Behind closed doors. Green, A. K.......G795.1
Behind the arras. Neville, C. M..........N522.1
Behrens, B. See Heimburg, W., pseud....
Beleaguered city. Oliphant, M. O. W....O475.3
Belhaven tales. Harrison, C. C............H318.4

Belinda. Edgeworth, M....................E235.26
Same..............................**B232.49-50
Same. 2 vols....................in **E235.3-4
BELL, A., pseud. See Brontë, A............
BELL, C., pseud. See Brontë, C............
BELL, E., pseud. See Brontë, E............
BELL, L. Under side of things..............B433.1
BELL, M. Roanoke of Roanoke Hall.....B434.1
Bell of St. Paul's. Besant, Sir W......... B554.6
Bell-ringer of Angel's, and other stories.
Harte, B...................................H327.2
BELLAMY, C. J. Breton mills.............B436.1
Experiment in marriage..................B436.2
BELLAMY, E. Dr. Heidenhoff's process. B437.1
Looking backward 2000—1887........... B437.2
Lost. 20 pp.............................in S884.7
Miss Ludington's sister..................B437.3
Six to one.................................B437.4
Belle of Australia. Thomes, W. H........ T465.1
Belles and ringers. Smart, H.............. S636.2
Bells of Botreaux: a legend. 48 pp..... in T143.7
BELOT, A. Fedora; or, the tragedy in the
Rue de la Paix...........................B452.1
My good friend............................B452.3
Belteshazzar. Roe, E. R...................R700.1
Belton estate. Trollope, A.................T846.2
Ben Brace. Chamier, F.....................C448.1
BENEDICT, F. L. John Worthington's
name......................................B463.1
Miss Van Kortland........................B463.4
My daughter Elinor.......................B463.5
Price she paid............................B463.6
St. Simon's niece.........................B463.7
Benefits forgot. Balestier, W.............B184.2
Ben-Hur. Wallace, L......................W191.1
BENJAMIN, P. End of New York. 60 pp...
....in S884.5
Ben-na-groich. 32 pp.....................in T143.4
Same...................................in T143.4 ¹
BENNETT, E. Forest and prairie..........B471.1
Orphan's trials............................B471.3
BENSON, E. F. The Babe, B. A............B474.1
BENT, M. Chapter from an unknown life.
26 pp..................................in T143.24
Berber, The. Mayo, W. S..................M473.1
BERGER, F., pseud. See Sheppard, E. S.
BERINGTON, S. Signor Gaudentio di
Lucca...............................in **N938.21
Berkeley, the banker. Martineau, H......
....in **M385.2
Same. pt. 2...............................M385.1
Berkeleys and their neighbors. Seawell,
M. E.....................................S442.1
Bernard Lile. Clemens, J..................C625.1

BERNHARD, C. (*pseud. of* C. T. Heiberg).
    Aunt Francisca; Damon and Pythias...
    ....*in* B979.1 [2]
    The bankrupt. 32 pp.................*in* B979.1 [3]
    Cousin Carl.......................*in* B979.1 [1]
Bernicia.   Barr, A. E..............B268.3
Bernthal.   Mühlbach, L..................M952.3
BERRINGTON, B. S.   Fortunes of Albert
    Travers: a tale of the 18th century.....
    ....B533.1
BERRY, E. P.   Leah of Jerusalem: a story
    of the time of Paul....................B534.1
Bertram family.   Charles, E. R.........C476.2
Bertrams, The.   Trollope, A............T846.3
BESANT, *Sir* W.   All in a garden fair..... B554.1
    All sorts and conditions of men..........B554.2
    Armorel of Lyonesse....................B554.4
    Bell of St. Paul's..................... B554.6
    Beyond the dreams of avarice........... B554.7
    Camilla's last string..................*in* B554.16
    Children of Gibeon................... B554.9
    City of refuge........................ B554.10
    Dorothy Forster........................ B554.11
    Even with this..................... *in* B554.16
    For faith and freedom....................B554.13
    Herr Paulus: his rise, his greatness, and
        his fall.............................B554.15
    The holy rose.   (*Also*) Last mass.—In-
        ner house.—Even with this.—Camilla's
        last string..........................B554.16
    In deacon's orders, and other stories...B554.17
    Inner house............................*in* B554.16
    Same...................................B554.19
    Ivory gate.............................B554.18
    Katharine Regina.......................B554.21
    Same................................. *in* B554.30
    Last mass.............................*in* B554.16
    Master craftsman.................. ....B554.23
    Quarantine island.....................*in* S885.9
    Rebel queen.............................B554.26
    Revolt of man........................ B554.27
    St. Katherine's by the tower.............B554.28
    'Self or bearer'.......................*in* B554.30
    To call her mine.   (*Also*) Katharine Re-
        gina. (*And*) 'Self or bearer.'......... B554.30
    Verbena Camellia Stephanotis and other
        stories.............................B554.32
    World went very well then...............B554.33
    —and RICE, J.   By Celia's arbour......B554.37
    Case of Mr. Lucraft, and other tales...B554.38
    Chaplain of the fleet....................B554.39
    Golden butterfly....................... B554.40
    My little girl.....................B554.41
    Ready-money Mortiboy.................. B554.42

BESANT, *Sir* W.—*Continued.*
    Seamy side.............................B554.43
    This son of Vulcan......................B554.44
    'Twas in Trafalgar's bay, and other
        stories.............................B554.45
    With harp and crown.....................B554.46
BESCHE, C. G.   Strange surprising adven-
    tures of the venerable Gooroo Simple
    and his five disciples....................B555.1
Beside the bonnie brier bush.   Watson, J...
    ....W339.2
Bessie.   Kavanagh, J.................K212.3
Bessie Harrington's venture.   Mathews,
    J. A.................................M429.1
Bessie Lang.   Corkran, A.................C799.1
Bessie's fortune.   Holmes, M. J..........H751.1
Bessie Rane.   Wood, E. P................W874.1
Best of husbands.   Payn, J.............Q345.3
Bethesda.   Elbon, B....................E373.1
BETHUNE, A.   Ghost of Howdycraigs;—
    Ghost of Gairyburn..................*in* W750.6
    The warning........................*in* W750.8
    Young laird........................*in* W750.2
BETHUNE, J.   Bewildered student.......*in* W750.5
BETHUSY HUC, V., *Gräfin.   See* Reichen-
    bach, M. von, *pseud.*
Betrothed, The.   Manzoni, A.............M296.1
Betrothed, The.   Scott, *Sir* W.............S431.5
    Same...............................S431.6
    Same.............................*in* **S431.42
Betsy Thoughtless.   Haywood, E...*in* **N938.13
Better days.   Fitch, T., *and* A. M.........F546.1
Better dead.   Barrie, J. M..............B275.2
Better times.   Kirk, E. O...............K593.2
Betty Alden.   Austin, J. G..............A936.1
Between the lines.   King, C............K523.3
Between whiles.   Jackson, H. M..........J127.1
Beulah.   Wilson, A. J. E...............W746.2
Beyond the breakers.   Owen, R. D.......O976.1
Beyond the dreams of avarice.   Besant, *Sir*
    W.................................B554.7
Beyond the gates.   Phelps, E. S.......... Q539.1
Bianca.   Maturin, E...................M445.1
BIDWELL, J.   There's nothing in it........ B585.1
BIERCE, A.   Tales of soldiers and civilians.
    ....B588.1
Big Jack Small.   45 pp.   Gally, J. W. *in* G178.1
BIGLY, CANTELL A., *pseud. See* Peck, G. W.
BIGOT, *Mrs.* M. H. *See* Healy, M.
BIKELAS, D.   Loukis Laras.   Reminiscen-
    ces of a Chiote merchant during the
    Greek war of independence... ....B595.1
    Tales from the Ægean.....................B595.2
BIRD, *Capt.*   A dead man's vengeance
    44 pp.............................. *in* T143.23

BIRD, R. M. The infidel; or, the fall of Mexico. 2 vols..................B618.1
Nick of the woods : a tale of Kentucky...
....B618.2
Birds of prey. Braddon, M. E...........B798.4
Birth and education. Schwartz, M. S......S408.1
BISCHOFF, J. E. K. [K. von Bolanden.] Trowel or the cross, and other stories and sketches..............................B621.1
BISHOP, W. H. Choy Susan and other stories.................................B622.1
   CONTENTS: Choy Susan. The battle of Bunkerloo. Deodand. Braxton's new art. One of the thirty pieces. McIntyre's false face. Miss Calderon's german.
Detmold........................... B622.2
Golden justice.........................B622.4
House of a merchant prince...............B622.5
One of the thirty pieces. 40 pp.......in S884.1
Pound of cure.........................B622.7
Yellow snake.........................B622.9
BITZIUS, A. See Gotthelf, J., pseud.
Bivouac. Maxwell, W. H...................M465.2
BJÖRNSON, B. Arne.....................B625.1
  Same. (Also) The happy boy........B625.1²
  The betrothal. (Also) The wedding. Extr. from The bridal march.....in Z767.1²
Bridal march, and, One day..............B625.2
Captain Mansana, and other stories....B625.3
The fishing girl......................B625.4
Happy boy : a tale of Norwegian peasant life......................in B625.1²
Magnhild..........................B625.5
One day............................in B625.2
Railroad and the churchyard (etc). 54 pp..........................in G622.1
Synnöve Solbakken...................B625.6
BJURSTEN, J. Play of fate...............B626.1
BLACK, W. Briseis.....................B627.1
Daughter of Heth.....................B627.3
Donald Ross of Heimra.................B627.4
Green pastures and Piccadilly.............B627.6
Handsome Humes.....................B627.8
Highland cousins.....................B627.9
In far Lochaber.....................B627.11
In silk attire.......................B627.12
Judith Shakespeare...................B627.13
Kilmeny............................B627.15
MacLeod of Dare......................B627.17
Madcap Violet......................B627.18
Maid of Killeena, and other stories...B627.20
Monarch of Mincing-Lane................B627.21
Prince Fortunatus...................B627.23
Princess of Thule...................B627.24
Queen Tita's wager...................in S885.3

BLACK, W.—Continued.
Sabina Zembra.........................B627.27
Shandon bells........................B627.29
Strange adventures of a phaeton........B627.31
Sunrise............................B627.33
That beautiful wretch.................B627.35
Three feathers.......................B627.36
White heather.......................B627.38
White wings : a yachting romance.....B627.39
Yolande............................B627.43
Black : the story of a dog. Dumas, A...D886.6
Black arrow. Stevenson, R. L...........S848.1
Black baronet. Carleton, W...............C281.1
Black but comely. Melville, G. J. W...M530.1
  Same........................in **M530.32
Black diamonds. Jokai, M...............J745.1
Black dwarf. Scott, Sir W............in **S431.4
  Same...........................S431.7
  Same...........................S431.9
  Same..........................S431.10
  Same.......................in S431.48
Black Forest village stories. Auerbach, B..........................A918.2
Black gauntlet. Schoolcraft, M. H........S372.1
Black ice. Tourgée, A. W...............T727.1
Black list. Ewing, H...................E955.1
Black poodle. Anstey, F...............A625.1
Black prophet. Carleton, W...............C281.2
Black sheep. Yates, E..................Y317.1
Black tulip. Dumas, A..................D886.7
"Black Watch." Grant, J...............G761.27
BLACKALL, E. L. Superior to circumstances.............................B628.1
Won and not one.....................B628.2
BLACKMORE, R. D. Alice Lorraine.......B629.1
  Same.........................in B629.3
Christowell : a Dartmoor tale.............B629.2
  Same. (Also) Alice Lorraine..........B629.3
Clara Vaughan.......................B629.4
Cradock Nowell : a tale of the New Forest............................B629.5
Cripps, the carrier....................B629.6
Kit and Kitty.......................B629.8
Lorna Doone........................B629.9
Maid of Sker.......................B629.11
Mary Anerley : a Yorkshire tale........B629.12
Perlycross..........................B629.14
Remarkable history of Sir Thomas Upmore, Bart., M. P., formerly known as "Tommy Upmore."...............B629.15
Slain by the Doones, and other stories...
....B629.16
Springhaven : a tale of the great war....
....B629.17

Blanche Carey. Patricia...............Q314.1
Blanche, Lady Falaise. Shorthouse, J. H....
....S559.1
BLAND, T. A. Esau........................B642.1
Bleak House. Dickens, C................D548.6
Same. 2 vols.........................D548.5
Blemmertons, The. Nicholson, J. J.......N626.1
Blessed Saint Certainty. Baker, W. M....B169.1
BLESSINGTON, M. P. Gardiner, Countess of.
Country quarters.......................B648.1
BLICHER, S. S. Esben. 30 pp.........in B979.1 ³
Tale of Jutland. 34 pp.............in B979.1 ¹
Blind love. Collins, W................C713.6
Blind musician. Korolenko, V..........K845.1
Blindfold. Marryat, F.................M361.1
Blindpits. Taylor, E..................T240.1
Blithedale romance. Hawthorne, N......
....in H399.11
Same............................H399.16
Blockade of Phalsburg. Erckmann, E.,
and Chatrian, A....................E654.1
Blockade runners. Verne, J............V531.7
Same.........................in V531.15
Bloody chasm. De Forest, J. W........D315.1
Blossom-bud and her genteel friends.
Smith, J. P.........................S653.1
BLOT, T. (?) Man from Mars: his
morals, politics, and religion........B657.1
BLOW, Mrs. M. W. G. See Glascock M. W.
Blue banner. Cahun, L.................C132.2
Bluebeard's keys. 41 pp. Thackeray, A.
I....................................T362.1
Bluebell of Red-Neap. Parr, L.........Q258.2
Blue-stocking, A. Edwardes, A.........E254.2
Bluffton. Savage, M. J................S263.1
BLUNDELL, Mrs. F. See Francis, M. E., pseud.
BLUNT, M. Fate of the Georgiana. 71
pp...................................in S886.5
BLYTH, M. P. Antoinette: a tale of the
ancien régime. 2 vols................B660.1
BLYTHE, J. A. St. J. A lonely life......B661.1
Body and soul. Wilkins, G...........**W683.1
Bog-myrtle and peat. Crockett, S. R.....C938.2
BÖGH, E. Story of a story; Young Jens
Jensen; A patient.................in V629.1
BOGV, L. V. A common man............B675.1
BOISGILBERT, E., (pseud. of I. Donnelly).
Cæsar's column: a story of the twen-
tieth century.......................B683.1
Doctor Huguet......................B683.2
BOLANDEN, K. von, pseud. See Bischoff, J.
E. K.
BOLDREWOOD, R. (pseud. of T. A. Browne).
Crooked stick........................B687.3

BOLDREWOOD, R.—Continued.
Modern buccaneer....................B687.5
Robbery under arms: a story of life in
the bush and in the goldfields of Aus-
tralia..............................B687.7
Sealskin cloak......................B687.8
Squatter's dream....................B687.9
BOLTON, S. K. Present problem.........B694.1
Bonaventure. Cable, G. W.............C115.1
Bondman, The. Caine, H...............C135.1
"Bones and I." Melville, G. J. W......M530.2
Same.........................in **M530.35
BONIFACE, J. X. See Saintine, X. B., pseud.
BONNER, S. (Mrs. McDowell). Dialect
tales...............................B716.1
Suwanee river tales.................B716.2
Bonny Kate. Reid, C..................R353.2
Bonnybel Vane. Cooke, J. E...........C772.1
Bonnyborough. Whitney, A. D. T......W617.1
Book o' nine tales. Bates, A.........B329.2
Book of martyrs. Pratt, C. A.........Q901.2
Book of pity and of death. Loti, P.....L883.1
Book of Scottish story................B724.1
Book of snobs. Thackeray, W. M.......T363.3
Same.........................in T363.13
BOOTH, Mrs. E. M. J. von. See Rita, pseud.
Bootles' baby. Winter, J. S..........in W785.1
Border beagles. Simms, W. G..........S592.2
Border shepherdess. Barr, A. E.......B268.4
BORLASE, J. S. King of the conjurors....B735.1
Born coquette. Duchess...............D829.5
Born player. West, M.................W519.1
BORNEMANN, M. Madame Jane Junk and
Joe.................................B736.1
BORROW, G. Lavengro, the scholar—the
gypsy—the priest....................B737.1
The Romany Rye; a sequel to "Laven-
gro."...............................B737.2
BOSBOOM-TOUSSAINT, A. L. G. Major
Frances...........................in Z767.1 ²
Boscobel. Ainsworth, W. H............A297.3
Bostonians. James, H., Jr.............J277.4
Bothwell. Grant, J...................G761.4
BOUCICAULT, D., joint author. See Reade, C.
Boulderstone. Sime, W................S589.1
BOULGER, D. H. See Gift, T., pseud.
Bound by a spell. Conway, H..........C767.1
BOURDILLON, F. W. Nephelé............B769.3
BOURGET, P. Case of conscience. 15
pp...................................in R657.1
Pastels of men. 2d ser..............B772.6
Was it love?........................B772.9
Bourgonef. 89 pp...................in T143.19
Bow of orange ribbon. Barr, A. E.....B268.5

BOWLES, E. In the Camargue...............B787.1
BOWRING, Sir J., tr. The flowery scroll.
A Chinese novel. See Hwa tsien ki.
Bowsham puzzle. Habberton, J...........H113.2
BOWYER, J. T. Witch of Jamestown ; a
story of colonial Virginia...............B788.1
Boxes, The. 12 pp...................in T143.4
Same.............................in T143.4 ²
Boyar of the terrible. Whishaw, F......W576.3
BOYCE, J. See Peppergrass, P., pseud.
BOYD, A. Crown ward. 3 vols.............B789.1
BOYESEN, H. H. A daring fiction. 42
pp.............................in S884.10
Daughter of the Philistines...............B791.1
Falconberg.................................B791.2
Gunnar : a tale of Norse life............B791.3
Ilka on the hill-top, and other stories......
....B791.4
Light of her countenance.................B791.5
Mammon of unrighteousness............B791.6
Norseman's pilgrimage....................B791.7
The old Adam................................B791.8
Queen Titania, and other stories.........B791.9
Social strugglers...........................B791.10
Tales from two hemispheres..............B791.11
Vagabond tales.............................B791.12
BOYLE, F. A fetish city. 10 pp......in T143.19
Good hater.................................B792.1
BOYLSTON, P. John Charáxes : a tale of
the civil war in America.................B793.1
Boyne water. Banim, J....................B217.1
Boz, pseud. See Dickens, C.
Bracebridge Hall. Irving, W..............I725.2
BRACHVOGEL, A. E. Beaumarchais......B796.1
BRADDON, M. E. (Mrs. Maxwell.) Aspho-
del B798.1
Aurora Floyd..............................B798.2
Barbara....................................B798.3
Birds of prey..............................B798.4
Charlotte's inheritance...................B798.5
Cloven foot...............................B798.6
Court Royal...............................B798.7
The day will come.........................B798.8
Dead men's shoes..........................B798.9
Dead-sea fruit............................B798.10
The doctor's wife.........................B798.12
Fenton's quest............................B798.13
Hostages to fortune.......................B798.14
An Ishmaelite.............................B798.15
John Marchmont's legacy.................B798.16
Joshua Haggard's daughter...............B798.17
Lady Audley's secret......................B798.18
Lady's mile................................B798.19
Lovels of Arden...........................B798.20

BRADDON, M. E.—Continued.
Lucius Davoren............................B798.29
Issued also as Publicans and sinners.
Mohawks....................................B798.23
Mount Royal...............................B798.24
Only a clod...............................B798.26
Open verdict..............................B798.28
Publicans and sinners....................B798.29
Issued also as Lucius Davoren.
Ralph the bailiff, etc....................B798.30
Rupert Godwin.............................B798.31
Sir Jasper's tenant.......................B798.32
Strange world.............................B798.34
Strangers and pilgrims....................B798.35
Taken at the flood........................B798.36
To the bitter end.........................B798.37
Under the red flag........................B798.38
The Venetians.............................B798.39
Vixen B798.40
Weavers and weft..........................B798.41
Wyllard's weird...........................B798.42
BRADLEY, A. G. The doctor: an old Vir-
ginia fox hunter. 47 pp.............in T143.22
Mar'se Dab after the war. A Virginia
reminiscence. 39 pp................in T143.24
BRADLEY, E. See Bede, C., pseud.
BRADLEY, M. Pentock. 84 pp.......in T143.21
BRAGA, T., joint author. See Harding, V. E.
Bragelonne, the son of Athos. Dumas, A.
....D886.43
Same. 6 vols............................D886.44
BRAINERD, T. H., (pseud of M. T. Jarboe)
"Go forth and find."......................B814.1
Robert Atterbury B814.2
Brakespeare. Lawrence, G. A.............L421.3
Bramleighs of Bishop's Folly. Lever, C. L658.3
Bras d'acier. Bréhat, A. de..............B834.1
Brave lady. Mulock, D. M.............. M960.4
Bravo, The. Cooper, J. F.................C777.2
Same C777.3
Braxton's Bar. Daggett, R. M.............D125.1
Brazen android. O'Connor, W. D......in O196.2
Bread upon the waters. Mulock, D. M. M960.5
Same....................................in M960.10
Bread-winners, The. Hay, J.............. H412.1
Breaking a butterfly. Lawrence, G. A...L421.4
Bred in the bone. Payn, J................Q345.4
Breezie Langton. Smart, H...............S636.3
BREHAT, A. G. de. Bras d' acier; or, on
the gold path in '49......................B834.1
BREMER, F. Axel and Anna...........in B836.2
Brothers and sisters......................B836.1
A diary, The H—— family, Axel and
and Anna and other tales..............B836.2

BREMER, F.—*Continued.*
Same. *(Also)* Strife and peace.........B836.10
Father and daughter.........................B836.3
The II—— family ....*in* B836.2
The home. *(Also)* Strife and peace...B836.6
Midnight sun: a pilgrimage B836.7
The neighbours, (and other stories)......B836.8
Parsonage of Mora..........................B836.11
Issued also as Life in Dalecarlia.
The president's daughters B836.12
Same, pt. 2................................B836.12 ²
Strife and peace...........................*in* B836.6
Same..*in* B836.10
BRESCIANI, A. Lorenzo; or, the conscript.
....B842.1
Mathilda of Canossa, and Yoland of
Groningen B842.2
Ubaldo and Irene. 2 vols.................. B842.3
Bressant. Hawthorne, J....................H398.3
Breton maiden. 3 vols......................B844.1
Breton mills. Bellamy, C. J................B436.1
BREWSTER, A. H. M. St. Martin's sum-
mer B848.1
Brian Fitz-Count. Crake, A. D............. C888.3
Bricks without straw. Tourgée, A. W. T727.2
Bridal march, and other stories. Björnson,
B B625.2
Bride from the bush. Hornung, E. W. H816.1
Bride of Lammermoor. Scott, *Sir* W. S431.11
Same................................... S431.12
Same..................... .... S431.13
Same......................................*in* S431.48
Bride of the Nile. 2 vols. Ebers, G......E165.1
Bridegroom of Barna. 78 pp...... ...... *in* T143.6
Same......................................*in* T143.6 ²
BRIDGES, *Mrs. Col. See* Forrester, *Mrs.,
pseud.*
Bricry creek. Martineau, H..........*in* ** M385.3
Brigadier Frederick. Erckmann E., *and*
Chatrian, A..................................E654.2
BRIGHT, *Mrs.* M. A. *See* Lyndon, *pseud.*
Bright star of life. Farjeon, B. L..........F229.1
Brigitta. Auerbach, B......................A918.3
BRINK, *Mrs.* M. (di S.) ten. *See* Lenzen, M.
Briseis. Black, W...........................B627.1
British barbarians. Allen, G..............A425.1
British novelists (ed.) by Mrs. Barbauld.
50 vols.....................................**B232.1-50
Brittany and La Vendée. Souvestre, E....
....S729.1
BRITTON, J. J. Flight.......................B862.1
BROCK, F. E. G. Margaret's secret......B864.4
Broken columns. Dixon, J..................D620.1
Broken ring. Tompkins, E. K.............T662.1

Broken to harness. Yates, E..............Y317.2
BRONTË, A. (A. Bell, *pseud.*) Agnes
Grey.......................................*in* B871.2
Tenant of Wildfell Hall....................B869.1
BRONTË, C. *(Mrs Nicholls).* (C. Bell,
pseud.) Emma.........................*in* B870.3
Jane Eyre..................................B870.1
The professor..............................B870.2
Same. *(Also)* Emma. *(and)* Poems...B870.3
Shirley......................................B870.4
Villette.....................................B870.5
BRONTË, E. (E. Bell, *pseud.*) Wuthering
heights....................................B871.1
Same. *(Also)* Agnes Grey, by A.
Brontë.....................................B871.2
BROOKE, F. M. (M. Singleton, *pseud.*)
Lady Julia Mandeville...............**B232.27
BROOKE, H. Fool of quality. 2 vols......B872.1
BROOKE, W. Eastford.......................B873.1
Brooke and Brooke farm. Martineau,
H...*in* **M385.4
Brookes of Bridlemere. Melville, G. J.
W..M530.3
Same......................................**M530.4
BROOKS, E. S. Son of Issachar : a romance
of the days of Messias..................B875.1
BROOKS, N. Lost in the fog. 24 pp.
....*in* S884.4
Tales of the Maine coast..................B868.6
BROOKS, S. Gordian knot.................B874.1
Sooner or later.............................B874.2
Brooksmith. James, H., *Jr*..............*in* J277.8
Broom-squire. Gould, S. B................G698.2
BROSBÖLL, K. *See* Etlar, C., *pseud.*
Brother Jacob. Eliot, G..................*in* E426.9
Brother to dragons, etc. Rives, A........R623.2
Brotherhood of Consolation. Balzac, H.
de..B198.4
Brothers, The; or, a good conscience. 22
pp.......................................*in* B979.1 ³
Brothers, The. 2 vols. Herbert, H. W.....
....**H536.1
Brothers and sisters. Bremer, F..........B836.1
Brothers' bet. Flygare-Carlén, E. S......F648.1
Brothers Rantzau. Erckmann, E., *and*
Chatrian, A................................E654.3
BROUGHAM, H. P. *Lord Brougham and
Vaux.* Albert Lunel ; or, the chateau
of Languedoc............................**B876.1
Brought home. Stretton, H...............S915.2
BROUGHTON, R. A beginner..............B877.1
Cometh up as a flower....................B877.2
Good-bye sweetheart.....................B877.3
Joan.....................................*in* B877.4
Nancy. *(Also)* Joan......................B877.4

BROUGHTON, R.—*Continued.*
Not wisely but too well...................B877.5
Red as a rose is she.......................B877.6
Broughton house. Perry, B................Q463.1
BROWN, A. Meadow-grass...................B878.1
BROWN, A. R. Sir Mark...................B881.5
BROWN, C. B. Arthur Mervyn. 2 vols....B879.1
Clara Howard........................*in* B879.4
Edgar Huntly.............................B879.2
Jane Talbot..............................B879.3
Ormond. Clara Howard................B879.4
Wieland..................................B879.5
BROWN, H. D. Petrie estate...............B880.1
BROWN, V. My brother....................B882.1
BROWNE, T. A. *See* Boldrewood, R., *pseud.*
Brownlows. Oliphant, M. O. W............O475.5
BROWNSON, O. A. Spirit-rapper ; an auto-
biography B885.1
Brueton's bayou. Habberton, J...........H113.10
BRUNER, J. W. Free prisoners : a story of
California life..........................B894.1
BRUSH, C. C. Colonel's opera cloak......B912.1
Brushes and chisels. Serrao, T...........S488.1
BRYANT, J. D. Pauline Seward. 2 vols.....
....B915.1
Bryda. Field, *Mrs.* E. M................F452.1
BRYDGES, *Sir* S. E. Hall of Hellingsley.
3 vols..................................**B916.1
Tragic tales. 2 vols....................**B916.2
v. 1. Coningsby.
v. 2. Coningsby. Lord Brockenhurst.
Bubble fortune. Tytler, S.................T997.7
BUCHANAN, *Mrs.* H. J. *See* Jay, H.
BUCHANAN, R. Annan water...............B918.1
" Come, live with me, and be my love."..
....B918.2
God and the man..........................B918.3
Heir of Linne.........................*in* B918.7
A marriage by capture....................B918.8
Martyrdom of Madeline...................B918.4
Shadow of the sword.....................B918.5
Stormy waters............................B918.6
Same. (*Also*) Heir of Linne............B918.7
Buchholz family. 2 vols. Stinde, J.......S860.1
BUCKLAND, C. T. Pickle of salt : a tale of
the Indian monopoly. 16 pp.......*in* T143.24
Buffets. Doe, C. H.......................D649.1
Building of the city Beautiful. Miller, J....
....M649.1
BULWER-LYTTON, E. G. E. L. *See* Lytton.
BUNCE, O. B. Romance of the revolution;
true stories of the days of '76 ......'......B940.1

BUNGENER, L. Preacher and the king; or,
Bourdaloue in the court of Louis XIV.
.... B941.1
Priest and the Huguenot; or, persecu-
tions in the age of Louis XV. 2 vols. B941.2
BUNNER, H. C. Love in old cloathes.
17pp......................................*in* S884.4
Same, and other stories B942.1
The Midge...............................B942.2
More "short sixes."......................B942.3
Runaway Browns..........................B942.4
"Short sixes." B942.5
A woman of honor B942.6
Zadoc Pine, and other stories B942.7
—*joint author. See* Matthews, B.
BUNYAN, E. T., *joint author. See* Wag-
ner, H.
BUNYAN, J. Pilgrim's progress B943.1
Same....................................*in* S892.14
BURBURY, *Mrs.* E. J. *See* Burbury, S.
BURBURY, S. "The trust." 24 pp....... *in* S637.2
BURCH, H. E. Stella Rae................B947.1
BURDETT, C. Margaret Moncrieffe; the first
love of Aaron Burr B951.1
Issued also as The beautiful spy.
Bureaucracy. Balzac, H. de..............B198.5
Burgomaster's family. Müller, C.........M957.1
Burgomaster's wife. Ebers, G.............E165.2
Burial of the guns. Page, T. N........... Q133.1
BURKE, *Sir* B. Family romance; or,
episodes in the domestic annals of the
aristocracy B959.1
Burlesques. Thackeray, W. M...... ..... T363.4
Same...................................*in* T363.15
BURNAND, F. C. My health............ B963.1
My time and what I've done with it. B963.2
BURNETT, F. H. Earlier stories, 1st ser.:
Lindsay's luck ; Miss Crespigny ;
Theo....................................B964.3
Same 2d ser.: Kathleen Mavourneen;
Pretty Polly Pemberton..................B964.4
A fair barbarian B964.6
Haworth's B964.8
Kathleen Mavourneen...... .... *in* B964.4
Lady of quality B964.10
Lindsay's luck.........................*in* B964.3
Same B964.12
Louisiana................................ B964.13
Miss Defarge ....*in* H113.10
Miss Crespigny........................*in* B964.3
Same B964.14
Pretty Polly Pemberton..............*in* B964.4
Same B964.17
Pretty sister of José B964.18

BURNETT F. H.—*Continued.*
A quiet life....................................B964.19
Story of the Latin quarter. 30 pp...*in* S884.3
Surly Tim, and other stories............B964.21
That lass o' Lowrie's.......................B964.11
Theo...*in* B964.3
Through one administration.............B964.22
Vagabondia B964.23
 Issued also as Dolly.
BURNEY, F. (*Mme. d'Arblay*). Cecilia.
 3 vols...................................**B232.40-42
Evelina ; or, the history of a young lady's
 introduction to the world..............B965.1
Same. 2 vols..........................** B232.38-39
BURNHAM, C. L. Dearly bought.........B966.3
Miss Bagg's secretary: a West Point
 romance.......................................B966.5
Mistress of Beech Knoll....................B966.6
Next door......................................B966.8
" No gentlemen.".............................B966.9
The wise woman...........................B966.14
Young maids and old....................B666.15
Burnish family. Balfour, C. L............B185.1
Burnt million. Payn, J.....................Q345.5
BURRELL, A. Man with seven hearts, and
 other stories................................B969.1
BÜRSTENBINDER, E. *See* Werner, E., *pseud.*
BURTON, J. BLOUNDELLE- Denounced....
 .... B973.4
In the day of adversity....................B973.9
BURTON, *Mrs.* M. E. Don Angelo's stray
 sheep.......................................*in* T143.22
Fiddlers three. 41 pp..............*in* T143. 21
BURTON, R. F., *ed.* Vikram and the vam-
 pire ; or, tales of Hindu devilry......B974.1
BÜSCHING, J. G. G. History of Count Wal-
 ter and the Lady Helgunda ; Assassina-
 tion of the empress of Tartary, 1240...
 ....*in* R794.1 ²
Bushrangers. Thomes, W. H...............T465.2
BUSHBY, A. S., *tr.* The Danes, sketched by
 themselves. 3 vols....................B979.1 ¹·³
 CONTENTS: v. 1: Bernhard, C. Cousin
 Carl.—Ingemann, B. S. Doomed house ;
 Secret witness ; Felon's reverie.—Andersen,
 H. C. Morten Lange ; Man from Paradise.—
 Blicher, S. S. Tale of Jutland.—Baggesen, J.
 Agnete and the merman ; A waking dream.
 —Winther, C. The confessional.—Knorring,
 Baroness. The ancestress.
 v. 2: Etlar, C. Too old ; Shipwrecked
 mariner's treasure.—Bernhard, C. Aunt
 Francisca ; Damon and Pythias.—Adam,
 Uncle. Fatal chain.
 v. 3: Fair prospect.—Oehlenschloeger, A.
 Death and his victims.—Ingemann, B. S. All
 Souls' Day ; Aged rabbi ; Death ship. Holst,

BUSHBY, A. S.—*Continued.*
 H. P. Lisette's castles in the air.—Etlar, C.
 Twice sacrificed. —Storm, E. Herr Sinclair.
 —Bernhard, C. The bankrupt.—Adam, *Uncle.*
 Hereditary goblet ; The brothers.—Blicher,
 S. S. Esben.
BUSKEN-HUET, C. Gitje, 10 pp. Satur-
 day at the Hague, 4 pp. (*and*) Along
 the churchyard. 6 pp..............*in* Z767.1 ¹
But a Philistine. Townsend, V. F.........T751.1
But men must work. Carey, R. N...........C276.6
But yet a woman. Hardy, A. S............H268.1
BUTLER, *Lady* R. Jessie Cameron : a
 Highland story..............................B985.1
BUTLER, S. Erewhon ; or, over the
 range B986.1
BUTLER, W. A. Mrs. Limber's raffle......B987.1
BUTT, B. M. Miss Molly.....................B988.1
BUTTERWORTH, H. In old New Eng-
 land..B989.1
Button's inn. Tourgée, A. W...............T727.3
By a way she knew not. Robertson, M.
 M...R651.1
By and by. Maitland, E......................M231.1
By Celia's arbour. Besant, *Sir* W., *and*
 Rice, J......................................B554.37
By his own might. Hillern, W. von......H651.1
By proxy. Payn, J.............................Q345.6
By shore and sedge. Harte, B............H327.3
By still waters. Garrett, E. *and* R....G239.1
By the gate of the sea. Murray, D. C...M981.1
By the Tiber. Tincker, M. A...............T587.2
By the waters of Paradise. Crawford, F.
 M...*in* C899.24
By woman's wit. Alexander, *Mrs.*........A374.7
Bye-words. Yonge, C. M...................Y555.39
BYNNER, E. L. Agnes Surriage............B994.1
The begum's daughter.......................B994.2
Damen's ghost................................B994.3
Nimport...B994.4
Penelope's suitors............................B994.5
Tritons...B994.6
Zachary Phips.................................B994.7
—*joint author. See* Hale, L. P.

CABALLERO, F. (*pseud.* of C. Böhl de
 Faber Arrom). Gaviota—the sea-
 gull..C112.1
Old and the new...........................*in* Z767.1 ²
CABLE, G. W. Bonaventure : a prose pastoral
 of acadian Louisiana......................C115.1
Dr. Sevier.....................................C115.3
The Grandissimes : a story of creole
 life..C115.5
John March, southerner....................C115.7

CABLE, G. W.—*Continued.*
Madame Delphine............................C115.8
Old creole days................................C115.9
Strange true stories of Louisiana......C115.11
CADDELL, C. M. Nellie Netterville......C121.1
Wild times : a tale of the days of Queen
Elizabeth....................................C121.2
CADELL, *Mrs.* H. M. *See* Cadell, J.
CADELL, J. Ida Craven......................C122.1
Cæsar's column. Boisgilbert, E............B683.1
CAFFYN, *Mrs.* M. *See* Iota, *pseud.*
Caged lion. Yonge, C. M...................Y555.3
CAHAN, A. Yekl : a tale of the New York
Ghetto C131.1
CAHUN, L. Adventures of Captain Mago ;
or, a Phœnician expedition, B. C.
1000...C132.1
Blue banner ; or, the adventures of a
Mussulman, a Christian, and a pagan,
in the time of the crusades and Mongol
conquest C132.2
CAINE, H. The bondman...................C135.1
Capt'n Davy's honeymoon...................C135.2
The deemster.................................C135.3
The Manxman................................C135.6
The scapegoat...............................C135.9
Shadow of a crime...........................C135.10
Son of Hagar.................................C135.12
CAIRD, M. Romance of the moors........C136.1
Wing of Azrael...............................C136.2
Cakes and ale. Jerrold, D. W............*in* J566.3
Calbot's rival. 80 pp. Hawthorne, J...
....*in* H398.4
Calderon, the courtier. Lytton, E. G. E.
L. Bulwer-.............................*in* L998.14
Caleb Williams, Adventures of. Godwin,
W..*in* G592.1
CALHOUN, A. R. Kohala of Hawaii......C152.1
Called back. Conway, H...................C767.2
Called to account. Thomas, A..............T453.1
Callista. Newman, J. H...................N553.1
CALMETTES, F. Fisher girl of France...C163.1
Calmire C164.1
CAMBRIDGE, A. (*Mrs. Cross*). A humble
enterprise....................................C178.3
Little minx...................................C178.6
CAMERON, E. S. A bad lot...............C182.1
CAMERON, *Mrs.* H. L. *See* Cameron, E. S.
Cameron pride. Holmes, M. J............H751.2
Cameronians, The. Grant, J...............G761.5
Cameos. Corelli, M...........................C797.5
Camilla's last string. 16 pp. Besant,
Sir W...................................*in* B554.16

Camille. Dumas, A., *the younger*.........D885.1
Camors. Feuillet, O.........................F426.1
Camp on the Severn. Crake, A. D........C888.4
Campaigning with Crook, and stories of
army life. King, C.......................K523.5
Campaner Thal. 69 pp. Richter, J. P. F.
....R535.1
CAMPBELL, A. Autobiography of Willie
Smith; Rival nightcaps; Monk of St.
Anthony; The katherau; Monks of
Dryburgh.............................*in* W750.2
Curate of Govan; Countess of Cassilis;
Grace Cameron.......................*in* W750.8
Disasters of Johnny Armstrong; Countess
of Wistonbury; Donald Gorm....*in* W750.1
Floshend inn; The dream; Retribution;
Skean dhu............................*in* W750.7
Hawick spate; Lord of Hermitage; Curse
of Scotland; Barley bannock.....*in* W750.10
Laird of Lucky's How; Chatelard......
....*in* W750.5
Merchant's daughter; Doctor Dobbie;
Lady Rae.............................*in* W750.11
Penny wedding; Good man of Dryfield;
Leein Jamie Murdiston; Duncan
M'Arthur..............................*in* W750.4
Rattling, roaring Willie; Highland boy;
Snowstorm of 1825..................*in* W750.3
The recluse; A highland tradition;
Foundling at sea; The assassin; The
stone-breaker.........................*in* W750.9
Two comrades; The surtout; The moss-
trooper: The forger..................*in* W750.6
CAMPBELL, ARCHIBALD. Captain Mac-
donald's daughter.........................C186.1
CAMPBELL, *Sir* G. Dark stories from the
sunny south; or, legends of the Medi-
terranean..................................C187.1
Mysteries of the unseen...................C187.2
CONTENTS: The warning of the sword. A
day's shooting. What was it? The ghost at
the Proscenium. The Lady Isopel. 48, Fern-
valley Terrace, N.
Wild and weird; or, remarkable stories of
Russian life................................C187.3
CONTENTS: Nepimoff's father. The thief's
taper. The white wolf of Kostopchin. The
midnight skater.
CAMPBELL, H. Mrs. Herndon's income...
....C188.1
Roger Berkeley's probation...............C188.2
Unto the third and fourth generation...C188.3
CAMPBELL, J. G. E. H. D. S., *Marquis of
Lorne. See* Lorne, *Marquis of.*
CAMPBELL-PRAED, *Mrs. See* Praed, R.
Campbell-

Camps and quarters. Forbes, A., *and others*.................................F692.1
Can you forgive her? Trollope, A.........T846.4
Canadians of old. Gaspé, P. A. de....... G249.1
Cancelled will. Dupuy, E. A...............D945.2
CANNON, C. J. *See* Greenway, *Grandfather, pseud.*
Canolles. Cooke, J. E.........................C772.2
Canon's ward. Payn, J......... ....Q345.7
Canterbury tales. 2 vols. Lee, H........L478.1
Canterbury tales. Lee, S.......................L481.1
Canvassing. Martin, *Miss*.................*in* B218.3
Cape Cod folks. Greene, S. P. McL......G812.3
Capillary crime. Millet, F. D..............M653.1
Captain Blake. King, C.......................K523.6
Captain Blake, Adventures of. Maxwell, W. H...M465.1
Captain Carleton, Memoirs of. Defoe, D. ....*in* D314.4
Captain-general. Gordon, W. J.......... G664.1
Captain Jack, the scout. McKnight, C. M158.1
Captain Macdonald's daughter. Campbell, A... C186.1
Captain Mago, Adventures of. Cahun, L. C132.1
Captain Mansana, and other stories. Björnson, B....................................B625.3
Captain of the guard. Grant, J...... .....G761.6
Captain of the Janizaries. Ludlow, J. M. L945.1
Captain of the Polestar, and other tales. Doyle, A. C................................. D754.3
Captain Singleton, Life of. De Foe, D...D314.3
Capt'n Davy's honeymoon. Caine, H.....C135.2
Cardinal Pole. Ainsworth, W. H...........A297.4
Cardinal sin. Conway, H....... ....C767.3
Cardinal's daughter. Warfield, C. A.. ...W274.1
Career of a nihilist. Stepniak...............S838.1
CAREY, R. N. Aunt Diana.....................C276.1
Averil.. C276.2
Barbara Heathcote's trial...................C276.4
But men must work...... ....C276.6
Cousin Mona...... ....C276.8
Esther...C276.11
For Lilias...C276.13
Heriot's choice.................................C276.15
Little Miss Muffet.............................C276.17
Mary St. John..................................C276.19
Merle's crusade................................C276.20
Mistress of Brae Farm...... ....C276.21
Nellie's memories,............................C276.22
Not like other girls............................C276.23
Old, old story...................................C276.24

CAREY, R. N.—*Continued.*
Only the governess............................C276.25
Our Bessie.......................................C276.26
Queenie's whim................................C276.28
Robert Ord's atonement.................... C276.29
Search for Basil Lyndhurst.............. C276.31
Sir Godfrey's grand-daughters.......... C276.32
Uncle Max....................................... C276.34
Wee wifie.. C276.35
Wooed and married...........................C276.36
Carine: a story of Sweden. Enault, L...E561.1
Carissima, The. Malet, L................... M247.1
Carita. Oliphant, M. O. W................. O475.6
CARLÉN, *Mrs.* Flygare- *See* Flygare-Carlén, E. S.
CARLETON, W. Barney Branagan......*in* C281.3
Black baronet; or, the chronicles of Ballytrain................................. C281.1
Black prophet : a tale of Irish famine...C281.2
The clarionet; The dead boxer, and Barney Branagan...............................C281.3
Dead boxer................................ *in* C281.3
Emigrants of Ahadarra.................... C281.4
The evil eye; or, the black spectre.......C281.5
Fardorougha, the miser C281.6
Jane Sinclair, or, the fawn of Springvale, (and other stories).................C281.8
Same ; Neal Malone, and other tales...C281.7
Neal Malone............................*in* C281.7
Same................................ *in* S885.4
Poor scholar, and other tales of Irish life. C281.9
Tithe-proctor...... .... C281.10
Traits and stories of the Irish peasantry. 2 vols................................. C281.11
Same, 4 vols...................................C281.13
Same, 5 vols...................... .... **C281.12
Tubber Derg: or the red well; and other tales of Irish life...........................C281.14
Valentine M'Clutchy, the Irish agent C281.15
Willie Reilly, and his dear Coleen bawn. C281.16
CARLETON, *pseud. See* Coffin, C. C.
Carlotta's intended. Stuart, R. McE......S932.1
CARLYLE, T., *tr.* Tales by Musæus, Tieck, Richter. 2 vols......................C286.1-2
Carlyon's year. Payn, J.... ....Q345.8
CARPENTER, E. Your money or your life. C294.1
CARPENTER, E. J. Woman of Shawmut. C295.1
Carpenter, The. O'Connor, W. D..... *in* O196.2
Carr of Carrlyon. Aidé, H..................A288.1

CARROLL, L. (*pseud. of* C. L. Dodgson). A
  tangled tale...........................C319.1
CARRYL, C. E. Captain Black. 64 pp....
  ....*in* S886.5
CARY, A. Clovernook; or, recollections
  of our neighbourhood in the west.....C332.1
  Pictures of country life....................C332.2
Casa Braccio. 2 vols. Crawford, F. M......C899.3
Case of identity. Doyle, A. C.........*in* D754.21
Case of Mr. Lucraft, and other tales.
  Besant, *Sir* W., and Rice, J...........B554.38
Casella. Finley, M.........................F513.1
Casimir Maremma. Helps, *Sir* A........H484.1
Cassian. 2 vols. Gore, C.................G666.1ˑ²
Castelneau. James, G. P. R.............**J276.2
Casting away of Mrs. Lecks and Mrs. Ale-
  shine. Stockton, F. R..................S866.5
CASTLE, E. Consequences..................C352.1
Castle and town. Peard, F. M............Q359.1
Castle builders. Yonge, C. M...............Y555.4
Castle Daly. Keary, A....................K241.1
Castle Dangerous. Scott, *Sir* W........S431.14
  Same.........................*in* **S431.19
  Same.............................*in* S431.37
  Same.............................*in* S431.49
Castle Foam. French, H. W...............F874.1
Castle Hohenwald. Streckfuss, A.......W817.28
Castle in Spain. De Mille, J...............D381.2
Castle in the air. Ewing, H............E955.2
Castle Nowhere. Woolson, C. F.........W916.2
Castle of Ehrenstein. James, G. P. R...
  ....*in* J276.5
Castle of Otranto. Walpole, H.....*in* **B232.22
  Same.. ....W218.1
Castle of Roussillon. La Rochere, E....
  de...L328.1
Castle of the Carpathians. Verne, J......V531.8
Castle Rackrent. 86 pp. Edgeworth, M...
  ....*in* E235.1
  Same..................................**E235.2
  Same...................................E235.16
Castle Richmond. Trollope, A...........T846.5
CASTLETON, D. R. Salem: a tale of the
  seventeenth century...................C353.1
Cat and the cherub, and other stories. Fer-
  nald, C. B.............................F362.3
Cathedral courtship. Wiggin, K. D......W655.3
Catherine. Peard, F. M..................Q359.2
Catherine. Thackeray, W. M............T363.5
Catherine de' Medici. Balzac, H. de......B198.7
CATHERWOOD, M. H. Chase of Saint...
  Castin.....................................C363.2
  Lady of Fort St. John...................C363.4
  Little Renault........................*in* C363.8

CATHERWOOD, M. H.—*Continued*.
  Old Kaskaskia..........................C363.6
  Romance of Dollard...................C363.7
  Spirit of an Illinois town, and Little
    Renault C363.8
  Story of Tonty.........................C363.9
  White islander.........................C363.11
Caught in the net. Gaboriau, E...........G116.1
CAUNTER, H. Romance of history.
  India.......................................C374.1
Cause worth trying. 49 pp...........*in* T143.16
Cavalier, The. James, G. P. R............J276.7
Cavaliers, The. Keightley, S. R..........K273.1
Cavaliers of fortune. Grant, J...........G761.7
Cavalry life. Winter, J. S..........*in* W785.1
CAXTON, L. (*pseud. of* L. B. Comins). Hart-
  well farm.. ....C384.1
CAXTON, PISISTRATUS, *pseud*. *See* Lytton,
  E. G. E. L. Bulwer-
Caxtons, The. Lytton, E. G. E. L. Bul-
  wer-....................................L998.2
Cecil Castlemaine's gage, etc. Ouida.....O934.4
Cecil Dreeme. Winthrop, T...............W793.1
Cecilia. 3 vols. Burney, F..............**B232.40-2
Cecilia de Noël. Falconer, L.............F182.1
CENTLIVRE, S. The busybody. 32 pp...
  ....*in* M875.1¹
Century of gossip. Nash, W. G...........N253.1
Cerise. Melville, G. J. W................M530.5
  Same........................*in* **M530.16
Cerritos, Los. Atherton, G. F...........A868.2
CERVANTES SAAVEDRA, M. DE. Don
  Quixote C419.1
  Same....................................**N938.8
  Same. 2 vols...........................C419.2
  Galatea: a pastoral romance............. C419.3
  Wanderings of Persiles and Sigismunda;
    a northern story.......................C419.4
César Birotteau. Balzac, H. de...........B198.8
Césette. Pouvillon, E...................Q880.1
Chainbearer, The. Cooper, J. F...........C777.4
  Same....................................C777.5
Chaldean magician. Eckstein, E.........E195.2
Challenge of Barletta. Azeglio, M. d'...A993.1
CHAMBERLAIN, N. H. Sphynx in Aubrey
  parish.....................................C442.1
CHAMBERLAIN, P. B. Mistress of the
  house.....................................C443.1
CHAMBERS, J. (F. Somers, *pseud*.) Mad
  world and its inhabitants...............C444.1
CHAMBERS, R. W. A king and a few
  dukes C445.3
  Maker of moons, and other stories.....C445.5
  Red republic.............................C445.6

CHAMIER, F. Ben Brace; the last of Nelson's Agamemnons.........................C448.1
Saucy Arethusa...............................C448.2
Tom Bowling...................................C448.3
CHAMISSO, A. DE. Peter Schlemihl......C449.1
Chamois-hunter. Souvestre, E............S729.2
CHAMPFLEURY (pseud. of J. F. F. Husson-Fleury). Faience violin...................C451.1
CHAMPNEY, E. W. Heartbreak cameo...
  22 pp.................................in S884.6
Chance acquaintance. Howells, W. D...H859.5
Chance child. 51 pp. Garrett, E., and R...
  ....in G239.12
Chances and changes. Strutt, E......**S928.1
Chandos. Ouida O934.5
Change of air. Hope, A.....................H791.5
CHANLER, Mrs. A. R. See Rives, A.
CHANNING, G. E. House on the hilltop.
  60 pp.................................in S886.1
  Sister of a saint, and other stories......C458.1
Channings, The. Wood, E. P.............W874.2
Chantry House. Yonge, C. M...............Y555.5
Chap-book stories.............................C462.1
Chaplet of pearls. Yonge, C. M........... Y555.6
Chaplain of the fleet. Besant, Sir W. ,and
  Rice, J....................................... B554.39
CHAPLIN, H. W. (C. H. White, pseud.) Eli.
  38 pp.................................in S884.9
Five hundred dollars, and other stories
  of New England life.....................C464.1
Village convict. 25 pp.................. in S884.6
Charlemont. Simms, W. G.................S592.3
CHARLES, C. M. Arvon; or, the trials: a
  legend. 2 vols............................. C475.1
CHARLES, E. R. Against the stream. Story
  of a heroic age in England.............C476.1
Bertram family..... .... C476.2
Chronicles of the Schönberg-Cotta
  family........ .... C476.3
Conquering and to conquer. C476.4
Cripple of Antioch, and other scenes
  from the Christian life in early times.
  ....C476.5
Diary of Kitty Trevylyan. A story of the
  times of Whitefield and the Wesleys..C476.6
Draytons and the Davenants: a story of
  the civil wars.............................C476.7
Early dawn; or, sketches of Christian life
  in England in the olden time..........C476.8
Joan the maid, deliverer of France and
  England C476.9
Lapsed, but not lost.........................C476.10
Liberators of Holland ....in C476.11

CHARLES, E. R.—Continued.
Martyrs of Spain, and, The liberators of
  Holland.................................. C476.11
On both sides of the sea. A sequel to
  The Draytons and the Davenants... C476.12
Victory of the vanquished. A story of
  the first century.........................C476.14
Winifred Bertram and the world she
  lived in............................... C476.15
Charles Auchester. Sheppard, E. S........S549.1
Charles Lever. Gresley, W.............G831.1
Charles O'Malley. Lever, C.................L658.4
Charles Tyrrell. James, G. P. R..........J276.8
Charlie Kingston's aunt. Oliver, P...... O483.1
Charlotte Ackerman. Müller, O M959.1
Charlotte's inheritance. Braddon, M. E.
  .... B798.5
Charmed sea. Martineau, H.........in **M385.2
  Same........ .... M385.5
Charmouth Grange. Groves, J. P......... G884.1
Chase of Saint-Castin. Catherwood, M. H.
  .... C363.2
Château d'Or. Holmes, M. J.............. H751.3
Château Frissac. Logan, O.................. L831.1
Château Morville. Tr. by E. R............R110.1
CHATELAIN, C. DE P. DE. Dalecarlian conjuror's day book.......................**C492.1
CHATRIAN, A., joint author. See Erckmann, E.
CHATTERJEE, B. C. Poison tree: a tale of
  Hindu life in Bengal..................... C495.1
CHEADLE, W. B. My hunt of the silver
  fox. 29 pp..............................in T143.16
CHEAPE, D. Betsy Brown..............in T143.10
Chelsea householder. Lawless, E..........L418.1
CHENEY, E. D. Nora's return; a sequel
  to "The doll's house" of Henry Ibsen
  ....C518.1
CHENEY, J. V. The old doctor............C519.2
CHERBULIEZ, V. Count Costia............. C521.1
Jean Têterol's idea.........................C521.2
  Same (extract).........................in Z767.1
Meta Holdenis...... ....C521.3
Prosper.......................... .... C521.4
Romance of an honest woman............C521.5
Saints and sinners.......................... C521.6
Samuel Brohl and Company...............C521.7
The tutor's secret C521.8
With fortune made............................C521.10
Cherry and Violet. Manning, A.........M283.1
CHESEBRO', C. Foe in the household ... C524.1
CHESNEY, C. C. Fall of England? The
  battle of Dorking: reminiscences of a
  volunteer......................................C525.1
  Same........... ....in T143.8

Chevalier d'Harmental. Dumas, A....... D886.8
Chevalier de Maison Rouge. Dumas, A...D886.9
Chevalier of Pensieri-Vani. Fuller, H. B.
.... F968.1
Chevaliers of France. Herbert, H. W...H536.2
Chicot, the jester. Dumas, A............ D886.16
Chieu d'or. Kirby, W.............. .... K582.1
Chiffou's marriage. Gyp...... ....G997.1
CHILD, L.M. Philothea: a Grecian romance.
.................................,'......................... C536.1
Child and woman. Helm, C...... .... H478.1
Child of the cavern. Verne, J............ V531.39
Child of the century. Wheelwright, J. T.
.... W566.1
Child of the Jago. Morrison, A............M878.3
Child of the revolution. Roberts, M.. ...R646.2
Child wife. Reid, M................... ....R357.1
Childhood, boyhood, youth. Tolstoi, *Count*
L. N................... .... T654.2
Children of destiny. Seawell, M. E........S442.2
Children of Gibeon. Besant, *Sir* W......B554.9
Children of the abbey. Roche, R. M.....R673.1
Children of the Ghetto. Zangwill, I.......Z295.1
Children of the king. Crawford, F. M...C899.4
Children of the New Forest. Marryat,
Capt. F...M362.1
Children of the soil. Sienkiewicz, H.....S572.3
Children of the world. Heyse, P........H621.1
Children of to-morrow. Sharp, W.......S531.1
"Chimmie Fadden," etc. Townsend, E.
W..T747.1
Chinese tales. Gueullette, T. S......*in* **N938.5
Chita. Hearn, L.................................H436.1
Chosen few short stories. Stockton, F. R.
....S866.6
Chosen valley. Foote, M. H................F689.1
Chouans, The. Balzac, H. de...........B198.9
Choy Susan, etc. Bishop, W. H............B622.1
Chris. Norris, W. E...... ....N861.3
CHRISTIAN, S. Persis Yorke................ C555.1
Christian physiologist. Griffin, G........G851.1
Christian's mistake. Mulock, D. M......M960.6
Christie Johnstone. Reade, C.............R285.2
Same..R285.21
Same R285.22
Christie's faith. Robinson, F. W..........R660.2
Christina Chard. Praed, R. C-.............Q897.1
Christine. Curtis, L. J. C980.1
Christine. Sergeant, A....................S484.1
Christmas books. Dickens, C............D548.7
Same (with additional story) D548.13
Christmas books. Thackeray, W. M.....T363.6
Christmas eve and Christmas day. Hale,
E. E..H161.1

Christmas stories. Dickens, C........*in* D548.29 *
Christmas stories. Dickens, C............D548.53
Christmas stories. Holmes, M. J..........H751.4
Christmas wreck, and other stories. Stock-
ton, F. R....................................S866.7
Christopher, and other stories. Barr, A. E.
....B268.6
Christopher Tadpole. Smith, A............ S641.1
Christowell. Blackmore, R. D....... ...... B629.2
Same................................... .... B629.3
Christie Carew. Laffan, M........ ....L163.1
Chronicles of Count Antonio. Hope, A.H791.6
Chronicles of Dustypore. Cunningham,
H. S.....................................C973.1
Chronicles of the Schönberg-Cotta family.
Charles, E. R...........................C476.3
Chrysal. 4 vols. (in 2). Johnston, C... J723.1-2
CHUBBUCK, E. (*Mrs. Judson*). (Fanny
Forester, *pseud.*) Alderbrook.........C559.1
CHURCH, F. M. Ross- *See* Marryat, F.
Church and the king. Green, E. E...... G796.1
CHURTON, H., *pseud. See* Tourgée, A. W.
Cigarette-maker's romance. Crawford, F.
M..C899.5
Cinderella, and other stories. Davis, R. H.
....D264.3
Cinnamon and pearls. Martineau, H.
.... *in* **M385.6
Cinq-mars. Viguy, A. V. *comte* de V688.1
Ciphers. Kirk, E. O...........................K593.3
Circuit rider. Eggleston, E..................E294.1
Citizen Bonaparte, 1794-1815. Erckmann,
E., *and* Chatrian, A........................E654.4
Same..............................*in* E654.21
Citizen of Prague. Paalzow, H. W. von.
....Q111.1
Citoyenne Jacqueline. Tytler, S............T997.1
City and suburb. Riddell, C. E. L........R543.2
City of refuge. Besant, *Sir* W...........B554.10
Civil-service reform. Simpleton, *Major*..S612.1
CLACK, L. Our refugee household.. ....C583.1
Claire. By the author of "Vida"..........C585.1
Clara Howard. Brown, C. B...... ..... *in* B879.4
Clara Vaughan. Blackmore, R. D.........B629.4
Clarence. Harte, B............................H327.4
CLARETIE, J. The cigarette. 27 pp.....*in* R657.1
Monsieur le ministre...........................C591.1
Clarionet, The. 82 pp. Carleton, W.....C281.3
Clarissa Harlowe. Richardson, S......... R525.1
Same. 2 vols...................... ...... **N938.14-15
Same. 8 vols........................ ...... **B232.1-8
CLARK, *Mrs.* C. M. *See* Clay, C. M., *pseud.*
CLARK, F. T. In the valley of Havilah. C592.1

CLARK, J. F. Society in search of truth; or, stock gambling in San Francisco..C594.1
CLARKE, M. COWDEN- Girlhood of Shakespeare's heroines. 2 vols.............C599.1
A rambling story............................C599.2
CLARKE, R. S. *See* May, S., *pseud.*
Classic tales.......................................C615.1
  CONTENTS: Johnson, S. Rasselas; Goldsmith, O Vicar of Wakefield; Swift, J. Gulliver's travels; Sterne, L. Sentimental journey.
Claude Stocq. Reybaud, H. E. F......*in* H781.1
Claudia. Douglas, A. M.................D734.3
Claudia Hyde. Baylor, F. C..............B359.1
CLAVERS, *Mrs.* M., *pseud. See* Kirkland, C. M.
CLAY, C. M. (*pseud. of* C. M. Clark). Baby Rue..C619.1
CLAYTOR, G. Pleasant Waters: a story of southern life.................................C622.1
Cleg Kelly, arab of the city. Crockett, S. R.. C938.4
CLEGG, J. T. David's loom.................C623.1
CLELAND, R. Barbara Allan, the provost's daughter C624.1
CLEMENS, J. Bernard Lile: a romance of the Texas revolution and the Mexican war..C625.1
CLEMENS, S. L. *See* Twain, M., *pseud.*
Cleopatra. Ebers, G.........................E165.3
CLERK, A. M., *tr.* Ilam-en-Nas. Historical tales and anecdotes of the times of the early Khalifahs. Tr. from the Arabic.......................................C631.1
CLERK, *Mrs.* Godfrey. *See* Clerk, A. M.
Clever woman of the family. Yonge, C. M..Y555.7
Cliff-dwellers. Fuller, H. B..................F968.2
CLIFFORD, F. S. Romance of perfume lands.......................................C637.1
CLIFFORD, J. Overland tales.............C638.1
CLIFFORD, L. L. Aunt Anne............C639.1
Flash of summer............................C639.3
Love-letters of a worldly woman.........C639.5
Thomas. 28 pp...................*in* T143.19
CLIFFORD, *Mrs.* W. K. *See* Clifford, L. L.
Clifton picture. Coulson, G. J. A...........C855.1
Clipper of the clouds. Verne, J.............V531.9
Clique of gold. Gaboriau, E..............G116.2
Clockmaker, The. Haliburton, T. C......H172.2
Cloister and the hearth. Reade, C......R285.4
Cloister legends. Stewart, E. M...........S851.1
Cloud pictures. Underwood, F. H.........U363.1
Clough Fionn. Banim, J., *and* M......*in* B217.5
Cloven foot. Braddon, M. E................B798.6

Clovernook. Cary, A.........................C332.1
Club-book. Ed. by A. Picken................Q594.1
Coast of Bohemia. Howells, W. D.......H859.8
COBBAN, J. M. Julius Courtney; or, master of his fate..............................C653.1
A soldier and a gentleman..................C653.2
COBLEIGH, Tom, *pseud. See* Raymond, W.
COCKTON, H. George Julian..............C666.1
  Issued also as The prince.
The prince.................................C666.1
  Issued also as George Julian.
Stanley Thorn..............................C666.2
Sylvester Sound; the somnambulist....C666.3
Valentine Vox, the ventriloquist........C666.4
Cœlebs in search of a wife. More, H...M835.1
Same..M825.2
Cœur d'Alene. Foote, M. H...............F689.2
COFFIN, C. C. Daughters of the revolution and their times.............................C675.1
COFFIN, R. F. How old Wiggins wore ship. 12 pp...............................*in* S884.9
COGSWELL, F. H. The regicides...........C677.5
COLERIDGE, C. R. Amethyst; the story of a beauty..................................C692.1
COLERIDGE, S. H. Phantasmion, a fairy tale...................................... C693.1
Collaboration. James, H., *Jr*.........*in* J277.22
College girls. Goodloe, A. C..............G652.1
College theatricals. 38 pp.............*in* T143.1
Same...............................*in* T143.1 ?
Collegians, The. Griffin, G................G851.2
COLLINGWOOD, H. W. Andersonville violets: a story of northern and southern life..C710.1
COLLINS, F. C. *joint author. See* Collins, Mortimer.
COLLINS, M. Lord Vanecourt's daughter. 3 vols.....................................C711.1
COLLINS, MORTIMER. Fight with fortune..C712.1
Marquis and merchant....................C712.2
—*and* F. C. Frances.....................C712.4
COLLINS, R. U. *See* Reed, C., *pseud.*
COLLINS, W. After dark, and other stories...C713.1
Alicia Warlock, (a mystery,) and other stories...C713.2
  CONTENTS: Alicia Warlock. A sane madman. The fatal cradle: otherwise, the heartrending story of Mr. Heavysides. "Blow up with the brig!" A sailor story. The Queen's revenge. Fragments of personal experience. My black mirror. Sketches of character.—1. Mrs. Badgery. A case worth looking at. Memoirs of an adopted son.

COLLINS, W.—*Continued.*
Antonina; or, the fall of Rome............C713.3
Armadale...C713.4
Basil.. C713.5
Blind love.. C713.6
Dead secret.....................................C713.8
Evil genius.......................................C713.9
The frozen deep, and other tales... .....C713.11
Guilty river.... ....C713.13
Hide-and-seek........ ....C713.15
"I say No."; or the love letter answered.
....C713.16
The law and the lady.......................C713.18
Man and wife......... .... C713.21
Mr. Lismore and the widow............*in* S885.2
The moonstone..............................C713.23
New Magdalen.............................. C713.24
No name.... .... C713.25
Poor Miss Finch.............................C713.27
Queen of hearts.............................C713.28
Terribly strange bed. 43pp............*in* S885.10
Two destinies.................................C713.31
Woman in white.............................C713.34
—*joint author. See* Dickens, C.
COLLYER, J. Letters from Felicia to Char-
lotte....................................*in* **N938.23
Attributed also to Mrs. M. Collyer.
COLEMAN, G. Poor gentlemen. 29 pp. Heir
at law. 33 pp...........................*in* M875.1 ³
Colonel Carter of Cartersville. Smith, F. H.
....S647.2
Colonel Chabert. Balzac, H. de........*in* B198.16
Same ....*in* B198.42
Colonel Dunwoddie, millionaire. Baker,
W. M.....................................B169.2
Colonel Jack, Life of. De Foe, D..... *in* D314.3
Colonel Quaritch, V. C. Haggard, H. R.
....H146.3
Colonel Starbottle's client and other people.
Harte, B...................................H327.5
Colonel's Christmas dinner, etc. King, C.
....K523.7
Colonel's daughter. King, C......... ......K523.8
Colonel's opera cloak. Brush, C. C........B912.1
Colonial wooing. Abbott, C. C.. ....A130.1
Colonna the painter : a tale of Italy and
the arts....................................*in* T143.1
Same.....................................*in* T143.1 ¹
Color studies. Janvier, T. A J358.3
Columbia. Musick, J. R....................M987.1
Colville of 'the Guards.' Grant, J..........G761.8
COMBE, T. Question of love: a story of
Switzerland................................C729.1

Come forth. Phelps, E. S,, *and* Ward, H.
D..Q539.18
"Come, live with me, and be my love"
Buchanan, R...............................B918.2
Comedies of courtship. Hope, A......... H791.8
Comedies played gratis. 18 pp. Balzac,
H. de.....................................*in* B198.19
Comedy of sentiment. Nordau, M.. ......N828.1
Cometh up as a flower. Broughton, R... B877.2
Coming of Theodora. White, E. O...... W584.1
Coming race. Lytton, E. G. E. L. Bulwer-
....L998.3
Same.....................................L998.4
COMINS, L. B. *See* Caxton, L., *pseud.*
Commander Mendoza. Valera, J...........V162.1
Commission in lunacy. 85 pp. Balzac, H.
de.......................................*in* B198.42
Commodore's daughters. Lie, J............L716.2
Common man, A. Bogy, L. V...... .. ..B675.1
Commonplace, and other short stories.
Rossetti, C. G............ ....R829.1
Companions of Jehu. 2 vols. Dumas, A.
....D886.11
Complaining millions of men. Fuller, E.
....F966.1
Comtesse de Charny. 4 vols. Dumas, A.
....D886.12
Con Cregan, Confessions of. Lever, C.
....L658.5
Con O'Regan. Sadlier, M. A................S126.1
Condemned door. Du Boisgobey, F...... D816.1
Condensed novels. Harte, B...............H327.6
Same, etc...................................H327.7
Confederate chieftains. Sadlier, M. A...S126.2
Confession. Simms, W. G...................S592.4
Confessions of a clarionet player, and other
tales. Erckmann, E., *and* Chatrian,
A...E654.5
Confessions of a frivolous girl. Grant, R.
....G763.3
Confessions of a Thug. Taylor, M.........T244.1
Confessions of an odd-tempered man. 19
pp. Opie, A...............................*in* O614.3
Confessions of Claud. Fawcett, E.........F278.3
Confessions of Con Cregan. Lever, C.... L658.5
Confidence. James, H., *Jr.*...................J277.5
Conformists, The. Banim, J..............*in* B217.2
Coningsby. 2 vols. Brydges, *Sir* S. E.
....**B916.2
Coningsby. Disraeli, B........................D613.2
Connecticut Yankee in King Arthur's court.
Twain, M.....................................T969.2
CONNERY, T. B. All the dog's fault.......C753.1

CONOLLY, M. F. Tales of the east neuk of Fife: Castle of Crail; Legend of the Church of Abercrombie; Romance of the May..................................*in* W750.5
Same: Robbery at Pittenweem and the Porteous mob; Story of Charles Gordon and Christina Cunningham.........*in* W750.9
Conquering and to conquer. Charles, E. R. C476.4
CONRAD, J. Almayer's folly..................C754.1
CONSCIENCE, H. The amulet............*in* C755.6
Count Hugo of Craenhove..................C755.8
Same. (*Also*) Curse of the village......C755.1
Curse of the village.......................*in* C755.1
Fisherman's daughter..................*in* C755.10
Happiness of being rich. (*Also*) Ricketicketack. (*And*) Wooden Clara......C755.2
Lion of Flanders...............................C755.3
Ludovic and Gertrude. (*Also*) Young doctor........ ....C755.4
Merchant of Antwerp......................C755.5
Poor gentleman. (*Also*) The amulet.....C755.6
Ricketicketack...............................*in* C755.2
Tales of Flemish life.........................C755.7
Tales of old Flanders, (*viz.:*) Count Hugo of Craenhove, Wooden Clara, and The village innkeeper C755.8
Veva; or, the war of the peasants........C755.9
Village innkeeper...........................*in* C755.8
Same. (*Also*) Fisherman's daughter...C755.10
Wooden Clara..............................*in* C755.2
Same..*in* C755.8
Young doctor ....*in* C755.4
Conscript, The. Dumas, A..................D886.13
Conscript, The. Erckmann, E., *and* Chatrian, A..E654.6
Consequences. Castle, E....................C352.1
Conspirator, The. 2 vols. P., P. *Count.*.Q110.1
Conspirators, The. Dumas, A.................D886.8
Constable of France, etc. Grant, J........G761.9
Constable of the tower. Ainsworth, W. H. A297.5
Constance. Hawthorne, J...................H398.4
Constance Sherwood. Fullerton, *Lady* G. F971.1
CONSTANT DE REBECQUE, H. B. Adolphe **C757.1
Consuelo. Sand, G.............................S213.4
Contarini Fleming. Disraeli, B...........D613.4
Same. 2 vols................................**D613.3
Contraband. Melville, G. J. W-............M530.6
Same..**M530.7
Contrast, The. Edgeworth, M............**E235.7
Same..*in* E235.20

Convict, The..............................*in* W750.11
Convict, The. James, G. P. R..............J276.9
Convicts and their children. Auerbach, B. A918.4
CONWAY, H. (*pseud. of* F. J. Fargus.) Called back..C767.2
A cardinal sin...............................C767.3
Dark days.....................................C767.4
A family affair..............................C767.5
Living or dead..............................C767.6
CONWAY, M. D. Prisons of air..............C768.1
CONYNGHAM, D. Eunice Quince...........C769.1
CONYNGHAM, D. P. The O'Mahony: a tale of the rebellion of '98..............C770.1
COOK, D. Doubleday's children..............C771.1
COOKE, J. E. (Anas Todkill, *pseud.*) Bonnybel Vane...............................C772.1
Issued also as Henry St. John.
Canolles: the fortunes of a partisan of '81 ....C772.2
Doctor Vandyke............................C772.3
Fairfax: or the master of Greenway Court. C772.4
Henry St. John, Gentleman. A tale of 1774-'75...................... ....C772.1
Issued also as Bonnybel Vane.
Her Majesty the queen...................C772.6
Hilt to hilt; or days and nights on the banks of the Shenandoah in 1864.....C772.7
Leather stocking and silk. A story of the valley of Virginia............................C772.8
Mohun; or, the last days of Lee and his paladins..................................C772.9
My Lady Pokahoutas. A true relation of Virginia......................................C772.10
Out of the foam C772.11
Pretty Mrs. Gaston, and other stories..C772.12
Surry of Eagle's Nest......................C772.14
Virginia Bohemians.........................C772.15
Virginia comedians.........................C772.16
Youth of Jefferson; or, a chronicle of college scrapes at Williamsburg in Virginia, A. D. 1764........................C772.17
COOKE, R. T. Happy Dodd.................C773.1
Huckleberries gathered from New England hills...................................C773.2
Somebody's neighbors......................C773.3
The sphinx's children and other people's. C773.4
Steadfast......................................C773.5
COOLEY, A. K. Asaph: an historical novel. C774.1
COOLEY, W. F. Emmanuel: the story of the Messiah................................C775.1

COOLIDGE, S. (*pseud. of* S. C. Woolsey).
  For summer afternoons......................C776.1
COOPER, J. F. Afloat and ashore.........C777.1
  Same............ ....*in* C777.36
  The bravo C777.2
  Same. (Also) Mercedes of Castile......C777.3
  The chainbearer; or, the Littlepage man-
    uscripts C777.4
  Same. (Also) The redskins................ C777.5
  The crater. A tale of the Pacific.........C777.6
  Same. (Also) Miles Wallingford.........C777.7
  The deerslayer.................................C777.8
  Same. (Also) Last of the Mohicans.... C777.9
  Eve Effingham; or, home. A sequel to
    "Homeward bound."......................C777.13
    Issued also as Home as found.
  The headsman; or, the Abbaye des Vig-
    nerons......... ....C777.10
  Same................... ....*in* C777.12
  The Heidenmauer; or, the Benedictines.
    A legend of the Rhine...................C777.11
  Same. (Also) The headsman............C777.12
  Home as found. Sequel to "Homeward
    bound."........ ....C777.13
  Same.............. ....*in* C777.15
    Issued also as Eve Effingham.
  Homeward bound; or, the chase.. ......C777.14
  Same. (Also) Home as found..... ....C777.15
  Jack Tier; or, the Florida reef........... C777.16
  Same............. *in* C777.44
    Issued also as Rose Budd.
  Last of the Mohicans; or, a narrative of
    1757...C777.17
  Same............. ....*in* C777.9
  Leather stocking tales:
    The deerslayer C777.8
    Last of the Mohicans.......................C777.17
    The pathfinder........... ....C777.25
    The pioneers.............................C777.28
    The prairie...... ....C777.29
  Lionel Lincoln; or, the leaguer of Boston.
    ....C777.18
  Same. (Also) The wept of Wish-Ton-
    Wish...C777.19
  Mercedes of Castile; or, the voyage to
    Cathay.. ....C777.20
  Same................................*in* C777.3
  Miles Wallingford. Sequel to Afloat and
    ashore.......................................C777.7
  Same..........................*in* C777.21
    Issued also as Lucy Harding.
  The monikins....................................C777.22
  Same.............................*in* C777.46
  The oak openings; or, the bee-hunter...
    ....C777.23

COOPER, J. F.—*Continued.*
  Same. (Also) Satanstoe................C777.24
  The pathfinder; or, the inland sea......C777.25
  The pilot......................................C777.26
  Same. (Also) Red Rover..............C777.27
  The pioneers; or, the sources of the Sus-
    quehanna..C777.28
  The prairie....................................C777.29
  Precaution.....................................C777.30
  Same. (Also) Ways of the hour....C777.31
  Red Rover.....................................C777.32
  Same..*in* C777.27
  The redskins; conclusion of the Little-
    page manuscripts..........................C777.33
  Same..............................*in* C777.5
  Satanstoe; or, the Littlepage manu-
    scripts...C777.34
  Same.................................*in* C777.24
  Sea lions; or, the lost sealers.............C777.35
  Same. (Also) Afloat and ashore......C777.36
  The spy: a tale of the neutral ground...
    ....C777.37
  Two admirals..................................C777.38
  Same................................*in* C777.41
  The Water-witch...............................C777.39
  Same. (Also) Two admirals...........C777.41
  Ways of the hour..............................C777.40
  Same................................*in* C777.31
  Wept of Wish-Ton-Wish.................C777.42
  Same................................*in* C777.19
    Issued also as The borderers.
  Wing-and-Wing................................C777.43
    Issued also as Jack-o'-Lantern.
  Same. (Also) Jack Tier.............C777.44
  Wyandotté; or, the hutted knoll.........C777.45
  Same. (Also) The monikins..........C777.46
COOPER, *Mrs.* K. S. *See* Saunders, K.
COOPER, S. W. Three days; a midsum-
    mer love-story...............................C778.1
COPPÉE, F. Barrel organ. 11 pp......*in* R657.1
  Disillusion; or, the story of Amédée's
    youth...C785.1
  Ten tales......................................C785.2
  True riches....................................C785.3
Copperhead, The. Frederic, H...........F852.1
CORBETT, J. Fall of Asgard.................C790.3
  For God and gold...............................C790.4
  Kophetua the Thirteenth...................C790.5
Cord and creese. DeMille, J.................D381.3
CORELLI, M. Ardath............................C797.1
  Barabbas C797.3
  Cameos...C797.5
  Hired baby. 32 pp.....................*in* S885.6
  Mighty atom....................................C797.7

CORELLI, M.—*Continued.*
My wonderful wife.....................*in* C797.15
Romance of two worlds...................C797.9
Sorrows of Satan..........................C797.11
Soul of Lilith..............................C797.12
Thelma....................................C797.13
Vendetta. My wonderful wife.........C797.15
Wormwood...............................C797.16
Corinne. Staël-Holstein, A. L. G. N.
   Baronne de.............................S778.1
Corinthia Marazion. Griffith, C............G853.1
CORKRAN, A. Bessie Lang................C799.1
Corse de Leon. James, G. P. R.........J276.10
Corsican brothers. Dumas, A.......*in* D886.37 [2]
COSEL, C. von. *See* Auer, A. von, *pseud.*
Cossacks, The. Tolstoi, *Count L. N.*.......T654.3
COSTELLO, F. H. Master Ardick, buccaneer..................................C841.3
COTES, S. J. D. American girl in London..C843.1
   Daughter of to-day.........................C843.4
   His honor, and a lady.........................C843.8
   Simple adventures of a memsahib.....C843.14
   Social departure: how Orthodocia and I
   went round the world by ourselves..C843.16
   Vernon's aunt.........................C843.20
Cottar's daughter, The..............*in* W750.8
COTTIN, S. R. Elizabeth; or, the exiles of
   Siberia..............................*in* S892.14
   Matilda, princess of England. A romance
   of the crusades. 2 vols.....................C848.1
   The Saracen, a crusade romance. 4 vols.
   (in 2)..................................**C848.2
COUCH, A. T. Q. (Q, *pseud.*) Delectable
   duchy....................................C853.3
   Ia: a love story.............................C853.5
   The omnibus. 9 pp....................*in* S885.6
   Splendid spur: adventures of Mr. John
   Marvel, a servant of his late majesty,
   King Charles I., in 1642-3...............C853.10
   Wandering heath.........................C853.10
COULSON, G. J. A. Clifton picture.........C855.1
Counsel of perfection. Malet, L...........M247.2
Count Hugo of Craenhove. Conscience, H.
....C755.1
   Same.................................*in* C755.8
Count Kostia. Cherbuliez, V.................C521.1
Count Lucanor. Juan Manuel, *Prince*.....J912.1
Count Mirabeau. Mundt, T................M965.1
Count of Monte-Cristo. Dumas, A.........D886.15
Count Robert of Paris. Scott, *Sir W...* S431.17
   Same..................................**S431.19
Count Ulrich. Kingston, W. H. G.......K558.1
Counterparts. Sheppard, E. S...............S549.2
Countess de Charny. Dumas, A...........D886.12

Countess Erika's apprenticeship. Schubin,
   O...W817.25
Countess Eve. Shorthouse, J. H...........S559.2
Countess Gisela. Marlitt, E...............W817.12
Countess Irene. Fogerty, J...............F654.1
Countess Loreley. Menger, R............M544.1
Countess Muta. Montague, C. H.........M759.1
Countess of Pembroke's Arcadia. Sidney,
   Sir P..................................S569.1
Countess of Rudolstadt. Sand, G.........S213.5
Countess Radna. Norris, W. E............N861.4
Country by-ways. Jewett, S. O...........J593.3
Country doctor. Balzac, H. de...........B198.10
Country doctor. Jewett, S. O............J593.4
Country gentleman. Oliphant, M. O. W.
....O475.7
Country in danger. (1792.) Erckmann, E.,
   and Chatrian, A.........................E654.7
   Same..................................*in* E654.17
Country luck. Habberton, J..............H1113.3
Country of the pointed firs. Jewett, S. O.
....J593.19
Country parson. Balzac, H. de..........B198.40s
Country quarters. Blessington, *Countess of.*
....B648.1
COUPERUS, L. Ecstacy..................C857.1
   Eline Vere...............................C857.2
   Footsteps of fate..........................C857.3
Coupon bonds, etc. Trowbridge, J. T.....T863.1
Course of true love never did run smooth.
   Reade, C.................................R285.7
   Same..................................R285.8
Court of Charles IV. Perez Galdos, B....Q438.2
Court of Rath Croghan. O'Byrne, M. L..O138.1
Court Royal. Braddon, M. E............B798.7
Court Royal. Gould, S. B................G698.3
Courting and farming. Smith, J. P.......S653.3
Courting of Dinah Shadd, and other stories.
   Kipling, R................................K575.2
Courtship in 1720. Smart, H............S636.4
Courtship in 1860. Smart, H..........*in* S636.4
Courtship of Morrice Buckler. Mason, A.
   E. W.....................................M398.3
Cousin Bette. Balzac, H. de...........B198.11
Cousin Geoffry. Hook, T...............H781.1
Cousin John's property. 58 pp.........*in* T143.13
Cousin Marshall. Martineau, H.....*in* **M385.7
Cousin Maud. Holmes, M. J.............H751.5
Cousin Mona. Carey, R. N.............C276.8
Cousin Pons. Balzac, H. de...........B198.12
Cousin William. Hook, T...............H781.2
Cousins. Walford, L. B.................W174.2
COVENTRY, F. Pompey the little.. ...**B232.23
   Same..................................*in* **N938.19

COWLES, M. L. Redbauk....................C875.1

COWLEY, H. The belle's stratagem. 27 pp.
....................................in M875.1

COWPER, F. Christmas eve on a haunted hulk. 34 pp....................in T143.24

CRADDOCK, C. E. (pseud. of M. N. Murfree.) Despot of Broomsedge Cove.. C884.3
His vanished star..........................C884.5
In the clouds..............................C884.6
In the "stranger people's" country......C884.7
In the Tennessee mountains..............C884.8
Mystery of Witch-face mountain C884.10
Phantom of the foot-bridge.............C884.13
Prophet of the Great Smoky mountains.
....................................C884.14
Where the battle was fought............C884.16

Cradock Nowell. Blackmore, R. D.......B629.5

CRAIGIE, Mrs. P. W. See Hobbes, J. O., pseud.

CRAKE, A. D. Alfgar the Dane: a tale of the days of Edmund Ironside.........C888.1
The Andreds-weald: a tale of the Norman conquest.....................C888.2
Brian Fitz-Count..........................C888.3
Camp on the Severn: a tale of the tenth persecution in Britain.....................C888.4
Doomed city: a tale of the Anglo-Saxon conquest of Britain and the mission of Augustine C888.5
Edwy the fair: a tale of the days of Saint Dunstan..........................C888.6
Fairleigh Hall: a tale of Oxfordshire during the great rebellion.............C888.7
Last abbot of Glastonbury.................C888.8
The victor's laurel: a tale of school-life during the tenth persecution in Italy...
....................................C888.10

CRANE, A. M. See Seemüller, A. M.

CRANE, S. George's mother..............C891.1
Little regiment, and other episodes of the American civil war...................C891.4
Maggie: a girl of the streets............C891.2
Red badge of courage....................C891.3

Cranford. Gaskell, E. C...................G248.1

Crater, The. Cooper, J. F...............C777.6
Same.....................................C777.7

CRAVEN, Mme. A. See Craven, P. de la F.

CRAVEN, P. DE LA F. Anne Séverin......C898.1
Eliane...................................C898.2
Fleurange C898.3
A sister's story..........................C898.4

CRAWFORD, F. M. Adam Johnstone's son.....................................C899.1
American politician.......................C899.2
By the waters of Paradise............in C899.24
Casa Braccio. 2 vols.....................C899.3
Children of the king......................C899.4
Cigarette-maker's romance...............C899.5
Doctor Claudius..........................C899.6
Don Orsino. (Sequel to Sant' Ilario.)...C899.7
Greifenstein C899.8
Katharine Lauderdale. 2 vols...........C899.9
Khaled: a tale of Arabia................C899.10
Marion Darche............................C899.11
Marzio's crucifix.........................C899.12
Mr. Isaacs: a tale of modern India...C899.13
Paul Patoff...............................C899.14
Pietro Ghisleri..........................C899.15
The Ralstons. 2 vols. (Sequel to Katharine Lauderdale.).....................C899.16
Roman singer.............................C899.17
Sant' Ilario. (Sequel to Saracinesca)...
....................................C899.18
Saracinesca...............................C899.19
Tale of a lonely parish..................C899.20
Taquisara. 2 vols.........................C899.23
Three fates...............................C899.21
To leeward..............................C899.22
The upper berth; By the waters of Paradise C899.24
Witch of Prague.........................C899.26
With the immortals......................C899.27
Zoroaster...............................C899.29

CRAWFURD, O. World we live in.........C900.1

CRAYON, GEOFFREY, GENT., pseud. See Irving, W.

Crayon miscellany. No. 3. Irving, W. **I725.4

Craze of Christian Engelhart. Darnell, H. F.....................................D223.1

Cressy. Harte, B.........................H327.8

Crew of the "Dolphin." Stretton, H.....S915.3

Crew of the "Sam Weller." Habberton, J......................................H113.4

Crichton. Ainsworth, W. H...............A297.6

Crime and punishment. Dostoyevsky, F. M....................................D724.1

Crime of Henry Vane. Stimson, F. J.....S859.1

Crimson sign. Keightley, S. R...........K273.2

Crimson star. Wright, S. A...............W953.1

Cripple of Antioch. Charles, E. R......C476.5

Cripps, the carrier. Blackmore, R. D.....B629.6

CROCKETT, S. R. Bog-myrtle and peat...
....................................C938.2
Cleg Kelly, arab of the city.............C938.4
Galloway herd...........................C938.7

CROCKETT, S. R.—*Continued.*
Gray man...C938.8
"The heather lintie." 15 pp............*in* S885.8
Lilac sunbonnet......................................C938.9
Mad Sir Uchtred of the hills... ....C938.10
Men of the moss-hags........................C938.11
The play-actress................................C938.14
The raiders...C938.16
Stickit minister..................................C938.17
Crohoore of the bill-hook. Banim, J., *and*
M...*in* B217.6
CROKER, B. M. Some one else.............C943.1
CROLY, G. Marston: or, the soldier and
statesman. 3 vols..............................C944.1
Salathiel, the immortal.....................C944.2
Crooked places. Garrett, E.................G239.2
Crooked stick. Boldrewood, R............. B687.3
Croppy. Banim, M...............................B218.1
CROSBY, M. (M. Floyd, *pseud.*) Violin obli-
gato and other stories............. ....C949.1
Passages from the journal of a social
wreck. 23 pp...................................*in* S884.7
CROSS, *Mrs.* M. A. E. *See* Eliot, G., *pseud.*
Crotchet Castle. Peacock, T. L....... ......Q356.1
CROWE, C. Night side of nature; or, ghosts
and ghost seers....................... ....C953.1
Story of Martha Guinnis and her son.
....*in* J737.1
Same...*in* T559.1
Crown from the spear. Hamilton, C. V. D.
....H218.1
Crown of straw. Upward, A...................U688.3
Crown of thorns. Loughead, F. H......*in* L887.1
Crown ward. 3 vols. Boyd, A...............B789.1
Crow's nest. Harrison, C. C...... ...... *in* H1318.4
Crucifix of Baden, and other stories.......C955.1
Cruciform mark. Stephens, R...............S835.1
CRUGER, *Mrs.* J. G. S. *See* Gordon, J.,
pseud.
Cruikshank at home...........................C957.1
Cruise of the Midge. Scott, M..............S428.1
Crusade of the Excelsior. Harte, B......H327.9
Crusoe in New York, and other tales. Hale,
E. E..H161.2
Crust and the cake. Garrett, E............G239.3
Cryptogram, The. De Mille, J..............D381.4
Cryptogram, The. Verne, J............*in* V531.19
Cuckoo in the nest. Oliphant, M. O. W....
....O475.8
Cudjo's cave. Trowbridge, J. T..............T863.2
CUDLIP, *Mrs.* A. H. T. *See* Thomas, A.
CUDLIP, *Mrs.* PENDER. *See* Thomas, A.
Culture. Furney, E. E..........................F989.1

Cumberland vendetta, and other stories.
Fox, J., *Jr*..F792.1
CUMMING, C. F. GORDON- "Unfathomed
mysteries." 45 pp.........................*in* T143.24
CUMMINS, M. S. El Fureidis................C970.1
The lamplighter.................................C970.2
Mabel Vaughan.................................C970.3
CUNNINGHAM, A. Gowden Gibbie.....*in* Q594.1
Lord Roldan.......................................C971.1
CUNNINGHAM, G. C., *ed.* Foreign tales
and traditions, chiefly from the fugitive
literature of Germany. 2 vols.........C972.1
CUNNINGHAM, H. S. Chronicles of Dusty-
pore: a tale of modern Anglo-Indian
society..C973.1
Cup of trembling, and other stories. Foote,
M. H..F689.3
Cupid and the sphinx. Flemming, H...F599.1
Cupid on crutches. Wood, A. B..........W873.1
Curate and the rector. Strutt, E............S928.2
Curate in charge. Oliphant, M. O. W...O475.9
CURRAN, J. E. Miss Frances Merley......C976.1
CURRIER, E. C. Hubbub......................C978.1
Curse of Carne's Hold. Henty, G. A.....H527.1
Curse of Everleigh. Pierce, H. C.........Q616.1
Curse of Koshiu. Wingfield, L.............W771.1
Curse of the village. Conscience, H......C755.1
CURTIS, G. W. Prue and I....................C979.1
Trumps..C979.2
CURTIS, L. J. Christine.......................C980.1
CUSHING, P. (*pseud. of* R. A. Wood). A
bud that lived. 30 pp.............*in* T143.23
CUTHBERTSON, *Misses.* Forest of Montal-
bano. 4 vols..............................**C988.1
CUTHELL, E. E., *joint author. See* Foster,
A. J.
CUTLER, M. C. Philip: a story of the first
century...C989.1
Cyrilla. Tautphoeus, J. M. *Freiherrin*
von..T229.2
Czar, The. Alcock, D............................A354.1
Dacre. Morley, F. T. Parker, *Countess*
of..**M864.1
DAGGETT, R. M. Braxton's Bar; a tale of
pioneer life in California.................D125.1
DAHLGREN, M. V. Lights and shadows of
a life..D130.1
DAHN, F. Felicitas..............................D131.1
DAINTREY, L. Actaeon.......................D134.1
Daisy. Warner, S................................W284.1
Daisy Burns. Kavanagh, J...................K212.4
Daisy chain. Yonge, C. M...................Y555.8
Daisy Thornton. Holmes, M. J.........*in* H751.6

Dalbroom folks. 2 vols. Smith, J.........S651.1
Dalecarlian conjurer's day-book. Chate-
  lain, C. de P. de.....................**C492.1
Dally. Pool, M. L.........................Q821.4
DALTON, W. Phaulcon the adventurer...D152.1
Daltons, The. Lever, C......................L658.6
  Same...................................L658.7
DAMANT, M. Peggy Thornhill: a tale of
  the Irish rebellion..................D155.1
Dame Care. Sudermann, H................S943.5
Dame de Monsoreau. 2 vols. Dumas,
  A.................................D886.16
Damen's ghost. Bynner, E. L..............B994.3
Damnation of Theron Ware. Frederic,
  H.....................................F852.2
Damsel of Darien. Simms, W. G........**S592.5
Danes, The, sketched by themselves.
  Stories tr. by Mrs. Bushby. 3 vols....B979.1
DANIEL, J. W. Girl in checks; or, the
  mystery of the mountain cabin.......D184.1
Daniel Deronda. 2 vols. Eliot, G..........E426.2
DANILEVSKI, G. P. Princess Tarakon-
  ava D187.1
Danites in the Sierras. Miller, J..........M649.2
Danvers papers. Yonge, C. M.........*in* Y555.16
Daphne. Rita...............................R598.1
Dare. Glascock, M. W.....................G548.1
Darien. 3 vols. Warburton, E. B. G...W254.1
Dark colleen. Jay, H......................J421.1
Dark days. Conway, H.....................C767.4
Dark stories from the sunny south. Camp-
  bell, *Sir* G............................C187.1
Dark year of Dundee. Alcock, D.........A354.2
Darkness and dawn. Farrar, F. W........F242.1
Darkness and daylight. Holmes, M. J...H751.7
DARMESTETER, *Mrs.* A. M. F. *See* Robin-
  son, A. M. F.
DARNELL, H. F. Craze of Christian En-
  gelhart...............................D223.1
Darnley. James, G. P. R...................J276.11
Darryll Gap. Townsend, V. F.............T751.2
DASENT, G. W., *tr.* Story of Gisli the out-
  law **D229.1
DAUDET, A. Artists' wives.................D238.1
  Issued also as Wives of men of genius.
  The immortal; or, one of the "Forty."...
  ....D238.3
  Issued also as One of the "Forty."
  Indret; The vice (and) The machines.
  (*Extr. from* Jack.).................*in* Z767.1
  Jack.................................D238.4
  Kings in exile.......................D238.5
  Numa Roumestan....................D238.8

DAUDET, A.—*Continued.*
  Port Tarascon, the last adventures of the
    illustrious Tartarin....................D238.9
  Robert Helmont: diary of a recluse 1870-
    1871...............................D238.10
  Sappho: Parisian manners...............D238.11
  Sidonie. (*Fromont jeune et Risler*
    ainé.)...............................D238.12
  Stories of Provence....................D238.13
  Tartarin of Tarascon...................D238.14
  Tartarin on the Alps...................D238.15
  Wives of men of genius................D238.16
  Issued also as Artists' wives.
DAUDET, E. The apostate D239.1
Daughter of an empress. Mühlbach, L...M952.4
Daughter of Bohemia. Reid, C... ....R353.3
Daughter of Eve. Balzac, H. de..........B198.13
Daughter of Eve. Kirk, E. O..............K593.4
Daughter of Fife. Barr, A. E.............B268.8
Daughter of Heth. Black, W.............B627.3
Daughter of night. Fullom, S. W........F972.1
Daughter of silence. Fawcett, E..........F278.4
Daughter of the Philistines. Boyesen, H. H.
  ....B791.1
Daughter of the tenements. Townsend, E.
  W...................................T747.2
Daughter of to-day. Cotes, S. J. D........C843.4
Daughters of the revolution and their times.
  Coffin, C. C.........................C675.1
Davault's mills. Jones, C. H..............J774.1
Davenport Dunn. 2 vols. Lever, C........L658.8
David Alden's daughter, etc. Austin, J. G.
  ....A936.3
David Balfour. Stevenson, R. L...........S848.2
David Copperfield. Dickens, C............D548.14
David Elginbrod. MacDonald, G........M135.4
David Grieve, History of. Ward, M. A. A.
  .... W261.3
David Lloyd's last will. Stretton, H......S915.4
David Lorimer.........................*in* W750.11
David Simple. Fielding, S...........*in* **N938.9
David's loom. Clegg, J. T...............C623.1
DAVIS, A. J. Tale of a physician..........D260.1
DAVIS, H. R. In sight of the goddess... D261.1
DAVIS, L. C. A stranded ship.............D262.1
DAVIS, M. E. M. Under the man-fig....D265.5
DAVIS, *Mrs.* R. H. Balacchi brothers. 25 pp.
  ....*in* S884.1
  Doctor Warrick's daughters.............. D263.1
  Frances Waldeaux.....................D263.6
  John Andross........................D263.5
  Margret Howth.......................D263.2
  Silhouettes of American life.............D263.3
  Tirar y Soult. 48 pp.................*in* S886.6
  Waiting for the verdict................D263.4

DAVIS, R. H. Cinderella, and other stories.
.... D264.3
The exiles, and other stories.............D264.5
Gallegher and other stories.............D264.7
Princess Aline...............................D264.10
Van Bibber and others........ ....D264.12
DAVIS, R. S. See Trebor, pseud.
DAVISON, C. S. How I sent my aunt to
Baltimore. 21 pp.....................in S886.4
DAWES, R. Nix's mate: an historical ro-
mance of America D270.1
Dawn. Haggard, H. R.....................H146.4
DAWSON, E. F. An itinerant house and
other stories.................................D271.3
DAWSON, W. J. London idylls...............D272.4
Story of Hannah...........................D272.7
Day and night stories. Sullivan, T. R... S952.1
Day at Laguerre's, and other days. Smith,
F. H...S647.3
Day of fate. Roe, E. P....................R699.2
Day of their wedding. Howells, W. D.. H859.9
Day will come, The. Braddon, M. E..... B798.8
Days of auld lang syne. Watson, J... ...W339.5
Days of Bruce. Aguilar, G............A283.1
Days of Lamb and Coleridge. Lord, A. E.
....L866.1
Days of yore. 2 vols. Tytler, S...............T997.2
Day's pleasure, etc. Howells, W. D.....H859.10
Day's ride. Lever, C.....................in L658.7
Same..L658.9
Dayspring. Marshall, E....................M367.2
Dead boxer. Carleton, W................ in C281.3
Same ....in C281.8
Dead marquise. Kip, L.................. K572.1
Dead men tell no tales. Sala, G. A........S159.1
Dead men's shoes. Braddon, M. E........B798.9
Dead-sea fruit. Braddon, M. E...........B798.10
Dead secret. Collins, W....................C713.8
Dead sin, and other stories. Garrett, E.
.... G239.4
Dead tryst. Grant, J..........................G761.10
Dean's daughter. Veitch, S. F. F... ...V429.1
Dean's watch. Erckmann, E., and Chat-
rian, A.................................. ...in E654.2
Dearest. Forrester, Mrs............... ....F730.1
Dearly bought. Burnham, C. L...... ....B966.3
Death of the laird's Jock. Scott, Sir W.
....in S431.15
Same.................................. ...in S431.51
Same................................. in **S431.19
Death trust. Halstead, A. L..............H197.1
Debit and credit. Freytag, G..........F895.1
"December roses." Praed, R. C-..........Q897.2

Deemster, The. Caine, H.................C135.3
Deephaven. Jewett, S. O.................J593.5
Deerbrook. Martineau, H..................M385.8
Deerslayer, The. Cooper, J. F..... .... C777.8
Same..C777.9
DEFOE, D. Works. 3 vols................D314.3-5
  1. Captain Singleton. Colonel Jack.
  2. Memoirs of a cavalier. Captain Carleton.
     Dickory Cronke, etc.
  7. Robinson Crusoe.
Robinson Crusoe...........................D314.5
Same..............................in **N938.4
Same.............................. ....in S892.14
Same, illus. by Cruikshank............**D314.5
Same. 2 vols................. ....**B232.16-17
DE FOREST, J. W. Bloody chasm... ......D315.1
Issued also as The oddest of courtships.
Brigade commander....................... in S884.8
Inspired lobbyist. 35 pp................in S884.4
Irene, the missionary...................D315.2
Kate Beaumont.............................D315.3
Playing the mischief......................D315.5
Wetherel affair............................D315.6
DE KAY, C. Manmat'ha. 24 pp......in S884.10
DELAND, M. John Ward, preacher........D337.3
Mr. Tommy Dove, and other stories.....D337.5
Philip and his wife.................... ....D337.7
Sidney... D337.9
Delaware. James, G. P. R.................J276.12
Delectable duchy. Couch, A. T. Q........C853.3
DE LEON, E. Askaros Kassis, the Copt: a
romance of modern Egypt.. ....D346.1
Delight makers. Bandelier, A. F............B214.1
DELITZSCH, F. José and Benjamin: a tale
of Jerusalem in the time of the Herods.
.... D355.1
DELLENBAUGH, F. S. A singular case.
.... in T143.21
De l'Orme. James, G. P. R.................J276.13
DELPIT, A. As 'tis in life...................D363.1
Deluge, The. 2 vols. Sienkiewicz, H.....S572.4
Demerara. Martineau, H....................M385.9
Same.............................in **M385.10
DE MILLE, J. American baron.............D381.1
Castle in Spain..............................D381.2
Cord and creese............................D381.3
The cryptogram.............................D381.4
Dodge Club...................................D381.5
Lady of the ice..............................D381.6
Lily and the cross: a tale of Acadia....D381.7
Living link....................................D381.8
Open question................................D381.9
Democracy. King, C.........................K524.1
De Molai. Flagg, E..........................F574.1

DEMING, P. Adirondack stories........... D382.1
Tompkins and other folks................D382.2
Demon of Cawnpore. Verne, J......... V531.35 '
Same.....................................in V531.35
DEMPSTER, C. L. Ninette: an idyll of
Provence.....................................D389.1
Dene Hollow. Wood, E. P..................W874.3
Denis Duval. Thackeray, W. M.........in T363.5
Same....................................T363.7
DENISON, M. A. Mr. Peter Crewitt...... D396.1
That husband of mine........ ....D396.2
Denounced. Banim, J......................... B217.2
Denounced. Burton, J. B-..................B973.4
Denzil Quarrier. Gissing, G................G535.1
De profundis. Gilbert, W..................G466.1
Deputy of Arcis. Balzac, H. de..........B198.43
DEQUET, A. Theodore, conte de la vie
littéraire. 18 pp.....................in H496.1
DERING, R. G. Giraldi; or, the curse of
love.................................D433.1
Derrick Vaughan, novelist. Lyall, E.....L981.3
Derval Hampton. Grant, J..................G761.11
Desert of ice. Verne, J..................V531.13
Deserter, The. King, C....................K523.9
Desmond hundred. Austin, J. G..........A936.4
Desperate remedies. Hardy, T............H272.3
Despot of Broomsedge cove. Craddock, C.
E..................................C884.3
Destiny. Ferrier, S. E......................F391.1
Destruction of Gotham. Miller, J.........M649.3
Desultory man. James, G. P. R............J276.14
DETLEF, K. (pseud. of K. Bauer). Valen-
tine, the countess.......................D481.1
Detmold. Bishop, W. H....................B622.2
De Vane. Hilliard, H. W....................H654.1
De Vere. Ward, R. P.......................W262.1
Devereux. Lytton, E. G. E. L. Bulwer-...
....L998.5
Devil-puzzlers, and other sketches. Per-
kins, F. B................................Q448.1
Devil upon two sticks, etc. Le Sage, A.
R..................................in **N938.2
Same....................................L622.1
Devil's Ford. Harte, B................in H327.23
Devil's frills: a Dutch illustration of the
water cure. 29 pp.....................in T143.14
Dialect tales. Bonner, S......................B716.1
Diana. Warner, S..........................W284.2
Diana Carew. Forrester, Mrs..............F730.2
Diana, Lady Lyle. 3 vols. Dixon, W.
H..................................D621.1
Diana of the crossways. Meredith, G...M559.4
Diana's livery. McGlasson, E. W.........M146.1
Diane Coryval..............................D538.1

Diary, A. Bremer, F...........................B836.2
Same.....................................in B836.10
Diary of a superfluous man. Turgénieff,
I. S................................in T936.7
Diary of a woman. Feuillet, O............F426.2
Diary of an old doctor. Maitland, J. A...
....M232.1
Diary of Kitty Trevylyan. Charles, E.
R..................................C476.6
Dick Netherby. Walford, L. B............W174.3
Dick Sands. Verne, J......................V531.11
DICKENS, C. Additional Christmas stor-
ies...............................in D548.52
American notes.........................in D548.13
Same..................................in D548.20
Same..................................in D548.25
Barnaby Rudge : a tale of the riots of
'eighty.................................D548.1
Same, and, Hard times.....................D548.2
Same. (Also) Sketches. Pt. 2.........D548.3
Same. (Also) Tale of two cities. (And)
Hard times.............................D548.4
Bleak House. 2 vols.....................D548.5
Same. (Also) A child's history of Eng-
land..................................D548.6
Christmas books........................D548.7
Same (with additional story). (Also)
Pictures from Italy and American
notes................................ D548.13
Christmas stories.......................D548.53
Same. (another collection).........inD548.29 [2]
David Copperfield.........................D548.14
Dombey and son..........................D548.16
Same. (Also) Uncommercial traveller...
....D548.17
Edwin Drood............................D548.28
Same..................................in D548.50
Same, and other stories...................D548.29
Same. (Also) Reprinted pieces. (And)
Christmas stories.......................D548.29 [2]
George Silverman's explanation. 29 pp...
....in D548.29 [2]
Great expectations.........................D548.19
Same..................................in D548.38
Same, and, Hard times.....................D548.21
Same. (Also) Pictures from Italy. And
American notes.........................D548.20
Hard times.............................in D548.2
Same..................................in D548.2 [2]
Same..................................in D548.4
Same..................................in D548.21
Holiday romance........................in D548.29 [2]
Little Dorrit............................D548.22
Same. (Also) Oliver Twist...............D548.23

DICKENS, C.—*Continued.*
Martin Chuzzlewit............................D548.24
Same. (*Also*) American notes, and Pictures from Italy............................D548.25
Master Humphrey's clock..................D548.26
Same....................................*in* D548.29
Same....................................*in* D548.29 º
Same....................................*in* D548.33
Mudfog papers...............................D548.27
Nicholas Nickleby...........................D548.30
Same. (*Also*) Old curiosity shop........D548.31
Old curiosity shop........ ....*in* D548.31
Same. (*Also*) Master Humphrey's clock.
.... D548.33
Same. (*Also*) Reprinted pieces D548.35
Oliver Twist.............. ....*in* D548.23
Same...D548.37
Same. (*Also*) Great expectations...... D548.38
Same. (*Also*) Uncommercial traveller.D548.39
Our mutual friend............................ D548.40
Pickwick papers.............................D548.42
Same. (*Also*) Sketches by Boz...........D548.44
Pictures from Italy.....................*in* D548.13
Same....................................*in* D548.20
Same....................................*in* D548.25
Readings condensed by himself........ D548.45
Reprinted pieces......................*in* D548.29 º
Same .... *in* D548.35
Same...................................*in* D548.35 º
Same. (*Also*) Lazy tour of two idle apprentices.............................. D548.46
Sketches by Boz................. ....*in* D548.44
Same...D548.47
Same. (*Also*) Tale of two cities.. ... .D548.48
Same. Pt. 2...............................*in* D548.3
Tale of two cities.............. ....*in* D548.4
Same...................................*in* D548.48
Same...D548.49
Same. (*Also*) Edwin Drood...............D548.50
Uncommercial traveller.................*in* D548.17
Same....................................*in* D548.39
Same....................................... D548.51
Same, and additional Christmas stories.
....D548.52
Same. (*Also*) Child's history of England.
....D548.54
Pierce, G. A. *and* Wheeler, W. A. The
Dickens dictionary........... ....D548.55
DICKENS, M. A. Mist of error. D549.1
Dickory Cronke. Defoe, D..............*in* D314.4
Dictator, The. McCarthy, J..... ....M122.1
Did she love him? Grant, J......... ....G761.13
DIEHL, A. M. Dr. Paull's theory...........D560.1

Digby Grand. Melville, G. J. W-.........M530.8
Same......................................**M530.9
DILLWYN, E. A. Jill and Jack......D580.1
Dimitri Roudine. Turgénieff, I. S........T936.3
DINGELSTEDT, F. *Freiherr* von. The
amazon............................. D584.1
Dinna forget. Winter, J. S.................W785.5
Diothas, The. Thiusen, I...................T449.1
Diplomat's diary. Gordan, J..............G663.1
Disillusion. Coppée, F.......................C785.1
Disk, The. Robinson, E. A., *and* Wall, G.
A.................................. R658.1
Disowned, The. Lytton, E. G. E. L. Bulwer-........... ... . I.998.6
DISRAELI, B. *Earl of Beaconsfield.* Alroy;
(*Also*) Ixion in heaven ; The infernal
marriage; (*and*) Popanilla.............D613.1
Contarini Fleming. 2 vols..............**D613.3
Same. (*Also*) Rise of Iskander...... .....D613.4
Coningsby; or, the new generation......D613.2
Endymion. D613.5
Henrietta Temple..........................D613.7
Ixion in heaven.......................*in* D613.1
Infernal marriage..................... *in* D613.1
Lothair..D613.8
Popanilla................................*in* D613.1
Rise of Iskander........................*in* D613.4
Sybil; or, the two nations................. D613.10
Same. (*Also*) Venetia........ ....D613.11
Tancred; or, the new crusade...........D613.12
Venetia..............................*in* D613.11
Same....................................... ....D613.13
Vivian Gray..................................D613.14
The young duke.............................D613.16
Same. (*Also*) Count Alarcos...........D613.15
Disturbing element. Yonge, C. M........Y555.9
Dita. Majendie, *Lady* M......................M233.1
Divided lives. Fawcett, E...................F278.5
DIXON, E. H. Story of a modern woman...
....D619.1
DIXON, J. Broken columns..................D620.1
DIXON, W. H. Diana, Lady Lyle. 3 vols...
....D621.1
Ruby Grey. 3 vols...........................D621.2
Djambek the Georgian. Suttner, A. G.
von...S967.1
Dmitri. Bain, F. W.............................B162.1
Doctor Breen's practice. Howells, W. D...
....H859.11
Dr. Caldwell. Roe, E. R....................R700.2
Doctor Claudius. Crawford, F. M........C899.6
Doctor Congalton's legacy. Johnston, H...
....J725.1
Dr. Faustus.................................*in* R794.1 ¹

Dr. Goethe's courtship. Müller, O........M959.2
Doctor Grimshawe's secret. Hawthorne,
N...H399.1
Dr. Heidenhoff's process. Bellamy, E...B437.1
Doctor Hildreth. White, A. L..............W582.1
Doctor Huguet. Boisgilbert, E.............B683.2
Doctor Jacob. Edwards, M. B-.............E267.1
Dr. Janet of Harley street. Kenealy, A...
....K334.1
Dr. Jekyll and Mr. Hyde, Strange case of.
Stevenson, R. L....................in S848.7
Same...S848.11
Doctor Johns. 2 vols. Mitchell, D. G....M679.1
Dr. LeBaron and his daughters. Austin, J.
G..A936.5
Dr. Paull's theory. Diehl, A. M...........D560.1
Dr. Rameau. Ohnet, G....................O383.2
Dr. Sevier. Cable, G. W..................C115.3
Doctor Thorne. Trollope, A...............T846.7
Doctor Vandyke. Cooke, J. E..............C772.3
Dr. Wainwright's patient. Yates, E......Y317.3
Doctor Warrick's daughters. Davis, Mrs.
R. H...D263.1
Doctor Zay. Phelps, E. S...................Q539.2
Doctor's family. Oliphant, M. O. W.......
....in O475.51
Doctor's wife. Braddon, M. E..............B798.12
Dodd, A. B. Glorinda....................D639.1
Dodd, W. The sisters.................in **N938.5
Dodd family abroad. 2 vols. Lever, C....L658.10
Dodge, M. A. See Hamilton, G., pseud.
Dodge, M. M. Theophilus and others....D645.1
Dodge Club. De Mille, J..................D381.5
Dodgson, Rev. C. L. See Carroll, L., pseud.
Doe, C. H. Buffets........................D649.1
Dog fiend. Marryat, Capt. F............M362.2
Doing and dreaming. Garrett, E..........G239.5
Doings of Raffles Haw. Doyle, A. C.....D754.5
Dole, N. H. Not angels quite.............D663.3
On the point..............................D663.4
Dollars and cents. Warner, A. B.........W279.1
Dollie and the two Smiths. 35 pp.....in T143.2
Dolliver romance. Hawthorne, N..........H399.3
Same....................................in H399.3 2
Same, and other pieces...................H399.2
Dolly dialogues. Hope, A................H791.10
Dolores. Forrester, Mrs...................F730.3
Dombey & Son. Dickens, C.............D548.16
Same..D548.17
Don Braulio. Valera, J....................V162.2
Don Gesualdo. Ouida...................in O934.10
Don John. Ingelow, J.....................I464.1
Don Orsino. Crawford, F. M.............C899.7

Don Quixote. Cervantes Saavedra, M. de
....C419.1
Same...**N938.8
Same. 2 vols..............................C419.2
Don Quixote, Continuation of. Fernandez
de Avellaneda, A.................in **N938.16
Doña Luz. Valera, J........................V162.3
Doña Perfecta. Perez Galdos, B...........Q438.1
Donal Grant. Mac Donald, G.............M135.5
Donald Marcy. Phelps, E. S..............Q539.3
Donald Ross of Heimra. Black, W........B627.4
Donaldson, P., joint editor. See Ridgely,
J. L.
Donnelly, I. See Boisgilbert, E., pseud.
Donnet, L. Notary's daughter...........D686.1
Donovan. Lyall, E........................L981.4
Doomed city. Crake, A. D................C888.5
Dora Deane. Holmes, M. J................H751.8
Doran, J. Zanthon.......................D693.1
Doreen, the story of a singer. Lyall, E..L981.5
Dorothea; or, a ray of the new light. 3 vols.
....**D715.1
Dorothy, and other Italian stories. Wool-
son, C. F...................................W916.3
Dorothy Forster. Besant, Sir W.........B554.11
Dorothy Fox. Parr, L.....................Q258.5
Dorothy's vocation. Green, E. E.........G796.2
Dorrington, E., pseud. (?) English hermit.
....in **N938.21
Dorsey, A. H. Oriental pearl; or, the
Catholic emigrants........................D718.2
Dostoyevsky, F. M. Crime and punish-
ment..D724.1
Poor folk...................................D724.2
Double family. Balzac, H. de........in B198.63 k
Double life. 97 pp. Balzac, H. de...in B198.28
Double wedding. Warfield, C. A..........W274.2
Doubleday, T. The murderer's last night.
22 pp..................................in T143.4
Same..................................in T143.4 1
Doubleday's children. Cook, D............C771.1
Dougall, L. Beggars all..................D731.1
The mermaid..............................D731.2
What necessity knows.....................D731.3
Douglas, A. M. Claudia..................D734.3
Floyd Grandon's honor....................D734.5
Foes of her household.....................D734.6
Fortunes of the Faradays..................D734.7
From hand to mouth.......................D734.8
Heirs of Bradley house....................D734.10
Home nook.................................D734.11
Hope mills.................................D734.12
In the king's country......................D734.13
In trust....................................D734.14

DOUGLAS, A. M.—*Continued.*
Lost in a great city............ .... D734.16
Lyndell Sherburne..............................D734.18
Mistress of Sherburne........................D734.35
Modern Adam and Eve in a garden...D734.19
Nelly Kinnard's kingdom.................D734.20
Old woman who lived in a shoe.........D734.21
Issued also as There's no place like home.
Osborne of Arrochar........................D734.22
Out of the wreck.................. ....D734.23
Seven daughters...............................D734.24
Sherburne cousins......... ....D734.25
Sherburne house..............................D734.26
Sherburne romance...........................D734.27
Stephen Dane............ .... .D734.28
Sydnie Adriance..............................D734.29
Whom Kathie married..................... D734.32
Woman's inheritance........... ....D734.34
DOUGLAS, E., *pseud. See* Burnham, C. L.
DOUGLAS M. (*pseud. of* A. D. G. Robinson).
Peter and Polly.................................D735.1
DOUGLAS, R. K. Chinese girl graduate.
....*in* S885.7
A matrimonial fraud ; adapted from a
chapter of a Chinese novel. 31 pp...T143.19
The twins.............................*in* T143.22
Within his danger : a tale from the
Chinese. 51 pp......................*in* T143.20
Douglas Duane. Fawcett, E.. ....*in* H398.18
DOUGLAS, *Mrs.* R. D. Romance at the anti-
podes...D737.1
Dove in the eagle's nest. Yonge, C. M...Y555.10
Down-easters. Neal, J..........................**N341.1
Downward path. Gaboriau, E.................G116.4
DOYLE, A. C. Adventures of Sherlock
Holmes.................................... ....D754.1
Case of identity...........................*in* D754.21
Captain of the Polestar, and other tales.
....D754.3
Doings of Raffles Haw.......... ....D754.5
Exploits of Brigadier Gerard............. D754.7
Firm of Girdlestone........... ....D754.8
Great shadow............... ....D754.9
Memoirs of Sherlock Holmes............D754.11
Micah Clarke................................D754.12
My friend the murderer...................D754.13
Mystery of Sassassa Valley........ ......*in* S885.1
The parasite..................................D754.15
Raffles Haw. (*Also*) A study in scarlet D754.16
The refugees........ ....D754.17
Rodney Stone...............................D754.19
Round the red lamp........................D754.18
Scandal in Bohemia..................... *in* D754.21
Sherlock Holmes, Adventures of.........D754.1

DOYLE, A. C.—*Continued.*
Same, Memoirs of................. ....D754.11
Sign of the four.... .... D754.20
Same. (*Also*) Scandal in Bohemia. *(And)*
Case of identity...................... ....D754.21
Stark Munro letters..........................D754.22
Study in scarlet.............................*in* D754.16
White company........ ....D754.25
DRACHMANN, H. Paul and Virginia of a
northern zone.......... ....D757.1
Dragon's teeth. Queiros, E. de............Q993.1
DRAKE, J. In old St. Stephen's............D761.1
Metropolitans........................ ....D761.4
Drama in Dutch. Z., Z............ ....Z111.1
Drama of the seashore. 27 pp. Balzac, H.
de.......................... *in* B198.34
Same...................................... ...*in* B198.41
Drayton. Shreve, T. H................ ....S561.1
Draytons and Davenants. Charles, E. R.
....C476.7
Dream and a forgetting. Hawthorne, J...
.... H398.5
Dream-Charlotte. Edwards, M. B~.........E267.2
Dream life. Mitchell, D. G..................M679.2
Dream life and real life. Schreiner, O...S378.1
Dream of John Ball. Morris, W..........M877.4
Dreamer, A. Wylde, K.....................W982.1
Dreamer of dreams. Nicholson, J. S.....N627.1
Dreams. Schreiner, O................... ......S378.2
Dred. Stowe, H. B...........................S892.2
DREW, C. Lutaniste of St. Jacobi's.......D776.1
DREY, S. Lights and shadows of the
soul...D778.1
Drift from Redwood Camp. 43 pp. Harte,
B..*in* H327.27
Drift from two shores. Harte, B.........H327.11
Drift-wood. Longfellow, H. W.........*in* L853.1
DROZ, G. Around a spring..................D793.1
DRYSDALE, W. Princess of Montserrat...
....D808.1
DUBOIS, C. Madame Agnes.................D813.1
DU BOISGOBEY, F. Condemned door.....D816.1
Lost casket.................... ....D816.2
Issued also as The severed hand.
Sealed lips.....................................D816.4
Severed hand................................D816.2
Issued also as The lost casket.
DU BOIS-MELLY, C. History of Nicolas
Muss : an episode of the massacre of
St. Bartholomew..............................D814.1
DU CHAILLU, P. B. Ivar the viking......D826.5
DUCHESS. (*pseud. of* M. Hungerford).
Airy fairy Lilian..............................D829.1
Beauty's daughters.........................D829.4
Born coquette...............................D829.5

DUCHESS.—*Continued.*
Faith and unfaith..............................D829.7
Lady Branksmere.............................D829.9
Little Irish girl (and other stories)....D829.10
Loys, Lord Berresford, and other tales...
....D829.11
Mrs. Geoffrey..................................D829.12
Molly Bawn.....................................D829.13
Phyllis...D829.15
Portia..D829.16
Three Graces...................................D829.18
Duchess Frances. 2 vols. Tytler, S......T997.3
Duchess of Powysland. Allen, G..........A425.4
Duchess of Rosemary Lane. Farjeon, B.
L...F229.2
Duchesse de Langeais. Balzac, H. de...
....B198.14
DUDEVANT, *Mme.* A. L. A. D. *See* Sand,
G., *pseud.*
Duellists, The : a tale of the "Thirty years'
war." 28 pp.............................*in* T143.5
Same...................................*in* T143.5 [2]
Duffels. Eggleston, E...........................E294.2
Duke of Albany's Own Highlanders.
Grant, J...G761.14
Duke of Monmouth. Griffin, G............G851.3
Duke's dilemma. 52 pp..................*in* T143.2
Same......................................*in* T143.2 [2]
Duke's motto. 96 pp. Féval, P.........**F428.1
Dukesborough tales. Johnston, R. M.....J733.3
DULAC, G. Before the dawn : a story of
Paris and the Jacquerie..................D878.1
Dulcie Carlyon. Grant, J....................G761.15
Dumaresq's daughter. Allen, G............A425.5
DUMAS, A. D. Ange Pitou. 2 vols. Sequel
to Queen's necklace.........................D886.2
Issued also as Six years later; Taking the
Bastile. *For continuation see* Comtesse de
Charny.
Ascanio. 2 vols...................................D886.3
Ball of snow.......................................D886.4
Black: the story of a dog...................D886.6
Black tulip..D886.7
Bragelonne, the son of Athos; or, "ten
years later." Being the conclusion of
"Twenty years after."....................D886.43
Same. 6 vols.....................................D886.44
Issued also as Vicomte de Bragelonne.
Sometimes published in three parts as Brage-
lonne, The iron mask, Louise La Vallière.
Chevalier d'Harmental........................D886.8
Issued also as The conspirators. *For con-
tinuation see* The regent's daughter.
Chevalier de Maison Rouge : a tale of
the reign of terror. Sequel to "Com-
tesse de Charny.".............................D886.9

DUMAS, A. D.—*Continued.*
Chicot, the jester. Sequel to "Mar-
guerite de Valois.".........................D886.16
Issued also as La dame de Monsoreau;
Diana of Meridor. *For continuation see* The
forty-five.
Companions of Jehu. 2 vols...........D886.11
Issued also as Roland Montreval. *For con-
tinuation see* The whites and the blues.
Comtesse de Charny. Sequel to Ange
Pitou. 4 vols.................................D886.12
Issued also as Countess de Charny. *For
continuation see* Chevalier de Maison Rouge.
The conscript. *(Conscience l'innocent.)*...
....D886.13
The conspirators; or, the chevalier d'Har-
mental...D886.8
Issued also as Chevalier d'Harmental. *For
continuation see* The regent's daughter.
Corsican brothers......................*in* D886.37 [2]
Count of Monte-Cristo.....................D886.15
Countess de Charny. Sequel to Ange
Pitou...D886.12
Issued also as Comtesse de Charny. *For
continuation see* Chevalier de Maison Rouge.
Dame de Mousoreau. Sequel to Mar-
guerite de Valois. 2 vols...........D886.16
Issued also as Chicot the jester; Diana of
Meridor. *For continuation see* The forty-
five.
D'Artagnan romances. 3 pts.
1. Three musketeers. 2 vols............D886.39
2. Twenty years after. 2 vols............D886.40
3. Vicomte de Bragelonne. 6 vols........D886.44
The forty-five. Sequel to La dame de
Monsoreau. 2 vols.....................D886.19
Issued also as The forty-five guardsmen.
Half brothers.....................................D886.20
Issued also as The Iron hand.
Ingénue..D886.21
The iron mask...................................D886.22
Pt. 2 of Vicomte de Bragelonne.
Isabel of Bavaria...........................D886.23
Joseph Balsamo..............................D886.30 [2]
Pt. 1 of Memoirs of a physician.
Love and liberty: a narrative of the
French revolution of 1792..............D886.27
Margaret de Valois...........................D886.29
Issued also as Margaret of Navarre;
La Reine Margot. *For continuation see*
Chicot the jester.
Marie Antoinette romances. 5 pts.
1. Memoirs of a physician. 3 vols............D886.30
2. Queen's necklace. vols...........................D886.35
3. Ange Pitou. 2 vols. D886.2
4. Comtesse de Charny. 4 vols............D886.12
5. Chevalier de Maison-Rouge....................D886.9
Memoirs of a physician......................D886.30
*The two parts of this romance are sometimes pub-
lished separately as* Joseph Balsamo *and* Andrée
de Taverney.

DUMAS, A. D.—*Continued.*
Memoirs of a physician ser. *See* Marie
   Antoinette romances.
Mohicans of Paris...................... ....D886.31
   Last part issued as The horrors of Paris. Con-
   tin. and conclusion Salvator.
Nanon; or, women's war......... ....D886.45
   Issued also as War of women.
Napoleon romances. 2 pts.
   1. Companions of Jehu. 2 vols........ ....D886.11
   2. Whites and the blues. 2 vols..................D886.47
Olympe de Clèves. 2 vols...... ....D886.33
Page of the duke of Savoy. 2 vols......D886.34
   Issued also as Emmanuel-Philibert.
Queen's necklace. Sequel to "Memoirs
   of a physician.".....................D886.35
   For continuation see Ange Pitou.
The regent's daughter. Sequel to Chev-
   alier d'Harmental......... ....D886.36
She-wolves of Machecoul. *(Also)* The
   Corsican brothers. 2 vols............... D886.37
Sultanetta.................... ....*in* D886.4
Taking the Bastile. Sequel to "The
   queen's necklace."...........................D886.2
   Issued also as Ange Pitou.
Tales of the Caucasus : Ball of snow, and
   Sultanetta.......... ....D886.4
Three guardsmen.......................⌐.....D886.39
   Issued also as Three Musketeers.
   For continuation see Twenty years after.
Three guardsmen ser. *See* D'Artagnan
   romances.
Three musketeers. 2 vols.................. D886.39
   Issued also as Three guardsmen.
   For continuation see Twenty years after.
Twenty years after. Sequel to The three
   guardsmen D886.40
   For continuation see Vicomte de Bragelonne.
Two Dianas......... ....D886.41
Valois romances. 3 pts.
   1. Margaret de Valois. 2 vols...............⌐...D886.29
   2. La Dame de Monsoreau. 2 vols...............D886.16
   3. The forty-five. 2 vols........D886.19
Vicomte de Bragelonne. 6 vols.......D886.44
War of women. 2 vols............. ....D886.45
   Issued also as Nanon.
Whites and the blues. (Sequel to com-
   panions of Jehu.) 2 vols.................D886.47
DUMAS, A., *the younger.* Camille........D885.1
DuMAURIER, G. Peter Ibbetson D887.1
Trilby...D887.2
Dun, The. Edgeworth, M.................**E235.9
Same.. ....*in* E235.21
Same...*in* E235.34
DUNCAN, S. J. *See* Cotes, S. J. D.
Dunderviksborg and other tales. (Ed. by)
   F. C. Henderson.................................H496.1

DUNLAP, W. Thirty years ago; or, the
   memoirs of a water-drinker. 2 vols....D921.1
DUNNING, C. (*pseud. of* C. D. Wood) A
   step aside...D924.1
Dunraven ranch. King, C..............*in* K523.25
DUPREE, F. Married by proxy..............D942.1
DUPUY, E. A. Cancelled will......... .....D945.2
Huguenot exiles D945.4
Michael Rudolph.............. ....D945.5
DURAND, A. M. C. H. *See* Gréville, H.,
   pseud.
Dusantes, The. Stockton, F. R..........…..S866.10
Dutchman's fireside. Paulding, J. K......Q325.1
DUTHEIL, E. *See* La Rochere, E. de, *pseud.*
Dynamiter. Stevenson, R. L., *and* F. V.
   .... S848.17
Dynevor terrace. Yonge, C. M............Y555.11
DZIEWICKI, M. H. Airy nothing. 42 pp.
   ....*in* T143.24
Earl of Mayfield.....................................E126.1
EARLE, A. R. Her great ambition E127.1
Earl's promise. Riddell, C. E. L..........R543.3
Early dawn. Charles, E. R..............C476.8
Earnest trifler. Sprague, M. A.......... ......S766.1
Earth trembled. Roe, E. P.................R699.3
Earth's enigmas. Roberts, C. G. D........R643.1
East and west. Hale, E. E.... ....H161.18
East Angels. Woolson, C. F...... ....W916.4
East Lynne. Wood, E. P................... ....W874.4
Easter trip of two ochlophobists........*in* T143.15
Eastern sketches. Harte, B............. *in* H327.34
Eastford. Brooke, W...........................B873.1
Ebb-tide. Reid, C.................................R353.4
Ebb tide. Stevenson, R. L., *and* Osbourne,
   L............... ....S848.14
EBERHARDT, (—) The bet. Treachery its
   own betrayer..........................*in* R794.1 "
EBERS, G. Bride of the Nile. 2 vols......E165.1
Burgomaster's wife.............................E165.2
Cleopatra...... ....E165.3
Egyptian princess.................................E165.4
   Issued also as Daughter of an Egyptian king.
The elixir, and other tales..................E165.5
The emperor. 2 vols..........................E165.6
Homo sum...E165.8
In the fire of the forge: a romance of old
   Nuremberg. 2 vols......................E165.9
Joshua: a tale of Biblical times.....E165.10
Margery: a tale of old Nuremberg. 2
   vols...E165.11
   Issued also as Gred of Nuremberg.
A question..E165.12
Serapis..E165.13
The sisters...E165.14

EBERS, G.—*Continued.*
A thorny path. (Per aspera), 2 vols...
....E165.15
Uarda : a romance of ancient Egypt. 2
vols..E165.16
A word only a word.........................E165.17
Echo of passion. Lathrop, G. P............L354.2
ECKSTEIN, E. Against the stream. 29 pp.;
Boarding school girls. 28 pp.; Visit to
the lockup. 26 pp......................*in* S331.1
Aphrodite: a romance of ancient Hellas...
....E195.1
Cards for four. 26 pp................*in* H496.1
Chaldean magician: an adventure in
Rome in the reign of the emperor
Diocletian....................................E195.2
Monk of the Aventine.....................E195.3
Nero: a romance. 2 vols..................E195.4
Prusias: a romance of ancient Rome un-
der the republic. 2 vols.................E195.5
Quintus Claudius: a romance of imperial
Rome. 2 vols...............................E195.6
Ecstasy. Couperus, L.......................C857.1
EDDY, J. A dinner-party. 48 pp.......*in* S884.2
Edelweiss of the Sierras, etc. Harrison,
C. C...H318.5
EDEN, E. Semi-detached house............E221.1
Edgar Huntly. Brown, C. B................B879.2
EDGEWORTH, M. Tales and miscellaneous
pieces. 14 vols......................**E235.2-15
  CONTENTS: 1. Castle Rackrent.—Essay on
  Irish bulls.—Modern Griselda..................E235.2
  2.-3. Belinda............................E235.3-4
  4. Essay on self-justification.—Leonora.—
  Letters of Julia and Caroline, *etc*..................E235.5
  5. Lame Jervas.—Limeric gloves.—Lot-
  tery.—Manufacturers.—Murad the unlucky.—
  Out of debt out of danger.—Rosanna.—The
  will..E235.6
  6. Contrast.—Dramas; (*viz*: Love and
  law.—Rose, thistle, and shamrock.)—Grateful
  negro.—To-morrow...................... E235.7
  7. Almeria.—Ennui........................E235.8
  8. The dun.—Madame de Fleury.—Manœuvring....................................E235.9
  9. Emilie de Coulanges.—Vivian............E235.10
  10. The absentee..........................E235.11
  11-12. Patronage...........................E235.12-3
  13. Harrington.—Ormond....................E235.14
  14. Ormond; *concluded*....................E235.15
Tales and novels. 18 vols..............E235.16-32
  CONTENTS: 1. Castle Rackrent.—Essay on
  Irish bulls.—Essay on self-justification.........E235.16
  2-3. Moral tales. 2 vols, (*viz*., v. 1: Forester.—The Prussian vase.—The good aunt.—v.
  2: Angelina.—The good French governess.—
  Mademoiselle Panache.—The knapsack.)...
  ....E235.17-18

EDGWORTH, M.—*Continued.*
  4-5. Popular tales. 2 vols. (*viz*.: v. 1:
  Lame Jervas.—The will.—The Limerick
  gloves.—Out of debt out of danger.—The
  lottery.—Rosanna. v. 2: Murad, the unlucky.—The manufacturers.—The contrast.—
  The grateful negro.—To-morrow............E235.19-20
  6-10. Tales of fashionable life. 5 vols. (*viz*:
  v. 1: Ennui.—The dun.—v. 2: Manœuvring.—
  Almeria.—v. 3: Vivian.—vols. 4-5: The absentee.—v. 5 *Also*, Madame de Fleury.—
  Emilie de Coulanges.—Modern Griselda)...E235.21-5
  11-12. Beluda. 2 vols......................E235.26
  13. Leonora.—Letters on various subjects...
  ....E235.27
  14-16. Patronage. 3 vols. v. 3. *Also*
  Comic dramas (*viz*: Love and law.—The
  rose, thistle and shamrock.)..................E235.28-30
  17. Harrington.—Thoughts on bores........E235.31
  18. Ormond..................................E235.32
The absentee................................*in* E235.1
Almeria....................................*in* E235.35
Belinda. (*Also*) Modern Griselda. 2
vols....................................**B232.49-50
Castle Rackrent, and, The absentee.....E235.1
The dun..................................*in* E235.34
Emilie de Coulanges....................*in* E235.33
Ennui, and, Emilie de Coulanges......E235.33
Madame de Fleury.....................*in* E235.34
Manœuvring.............................*in* E235.35
Same. (*Also*) Madame de Fleury. (*And*)
The dun....................................E235.34
Modern Griselda. 82 pp............*in* **B232.50
Vivian. (*Also*) Almeria. (*And*) Manœuv-
ring. E235.35
Edina. Wood, E. P...........................W874.5
Edith Lyle. Holmes, M. J...................H751.9
Edleen Vaughan. Sylva, C..................S985.1
Edmond Dantès. Sequel to Alexander
Dumas' The Count of Monte-Cristo...
....E243.1
Edna Browning. Holmes, M. J..........H751.10
Edward. 2 vols. Moore, J..................M822.1
Same. 4 vols...........................**M822.2
EDWARDES, A. Archie Lovell.............E254.1
A blue-stocking.............................E254.2
Leah: a woman of fashion..................E254.3
Ought we to visit her?.....................E254.4
Pearl-powder...............................E254.6
Point of honor.............................E254.7
Susan Fielding.............................E254.8
Vagabond heroine...........................E254.9
Vivian the beauty..........................E254.10
EDWARDS, A. B. Barbara's history.......E261.1
Four-fifteen express.................*in* S885.2
Hand and glove.............................E261.2
Same.................................*in* E261.4

EDWARDS, A. B.—*Continued.*
Miss Carew...................................E261.3
Same. (*Also*) My brother's wife. (*And*)
Hand and glove..........................E261.4
My brother's wife....................*in* E261.4
EDWARDS, A. *See* Edwardes, A.
EDWARDS, B. Rachel Noble's experience...................................E263.1
EDWARDS, C. Di Vasari: a tale of Florence. 95 pp...........................*in* T143.4
Same...*in* T143.4 ²
EDWARDS, H. S. Sons and fathers....E265.2
Two runaways and other stories.........E265.1
EDWARDS, M. BETHAM- Doctor Jacob...E267.1
Dream-Charlotte..........................E267.2
North country comedy...................E267.3
The Sylvestres; or, the outcasts.........E267.4
Edwin Brothertoft. Winthrop, T.........W793.2
Edwin Drood. Dickens, C.................D548.28
Same..D548.29
Same..D548.29 ²
Same...*in* D548.50
Edwy the fair. Crake, A. D...............C888.6
EGERTON, F., *Earl of Ellesmere.* Dramatic scenes founded on Victor Hugo's Hernani..................................*in* Q594.1
EGGLESTON, E. Circuit rider.............E294.1
Duffels......................................E294.2
End of the world..........................E294.3
Faith doctor: a story of New York......E294.4
The Graysons: a story of Illinois......E294.5
Hoosier school-master...................E294.6
Mystery of Metropolisville...............E294.7
Roxy...E294.8
EGGLESTON, G. C. Man of honor.........E295.1
—and, Marbourg, D. Juggernaut: a veiled record....................................E295.2
Eglantine. Tabor, E......................T114.1
Egoist, The. Meredith, G................M559.5
Egyptian princess. Ebers, G...........E165.4
Eichhofs, The. Reichenbach, M. von...
....W817.23
Eight days. Forrest, R. E...............F729.1
'89. Henry, E.............................H521.1
Ekkehard. Scheffel, J. V. von.........S317.1
El Fureidis. Cummins, M. S.............C970.1
ELBON, B. (*pseud. of* L. B. Halstead).
Bethesda....................................E373.1
Elect lady. MacDonald, G...............M135.6
Elective affinities. Goethe, J. W. v....*in* G599.2
Eleventh commandment. Barrili, A. G..B276.1
Eliane. Craven, P. de La F...............C898.2
Eline Vere. Couperus, L.................C857.2
ELIOT, A. From four to six. 39 pp.....*in* S886.2
White birches............................E425.1

ELIOT, G. (*pseud. of* M. A. E. Cross) Adam Bede.......................................E426.1
Brother Jacob............................*in* E426.9
Daniel Deronda. 2 vols..................E426.2
Felix Holt, the radical..................F426.3
Lifted veil.................................*in* E426.9
Middlemarch: a study of provincial life.
....E426.4
Mill on the Floss.........................E426.6
Romola......................................F426.7
Scenes of clerical life..................E426.10
Same, and, Silas Marner................E426.8
Silas Marner..............................*in* E426.8
Same. The lifted veil, and Brother Jacob. (*Also*) poetical works........E426.9
Elixir and other tales. Ebers, G........E165.5
Elixir of life. 30 pp. Balzac, H. de...*in* B198.41
Elizabeth, *Queen of Roumania.* See Sylva, C., *pseud.*
Elizabeth. Nathusius, M. von.........N276.1
Elizabethines, The. 38 pp. Gore, C. *in* G666.1 ²
Ella of Garveloch. Martineau, H...*in* **M385.10
Ellen Duncan. Carleton, W............*in* C281.8
Ellen Middleton. Fullerton, *Lady* G....F971.2
ELLINWOOD, M. Year at Poplar Row... E464.1
ELLIOT, F. The Italians.................E465.1
Romance of old court-life in France... E465.2
ELLIOTT, *Mrs.* M. H. *See* Howe, M.
ELLIOTT, S. B. Jerry....................E467.2
John Paget..................................E467.3
ELLIS, S. S. Hearts and homes. 3 vols...E473.2
Home; or, the iron rule.................E473.3
Pique: a tale of the English aristocracy.
....E473.4
Elsa. Hogbin, A. C.....................H715.1
Elsie Venner. Holmes, O. W...........H752.1
Elsket. Page, T. N......................Q133.4
Elster's folly. Wood, E. P..............W874.6
Elves, The. Tieck, L....................T559.1
Emanuel. Pontoppidan, H.............Q818.1
Embarrassments. James, H. *Jr*.......J277.6
Emerald gems: a chaplet of Irish fireside tales.....................................E536.1
EMERY, E. B. Queens....................E537.1
EMERY, S. A. Three generations........F538.1
Emigrants of Ahadarra. Carleton, W ...C281.4
Emilie de Coulanges. Edgeworth, M..**E235.10
Same...*in* E235.25
Same..E235.33
Emma. Austen, J.........................A933.1
Emma. Brontë, C........................*in* B870.3
Emmanuel. Cooley, W. F...............C775.1
Emperor, The. 2 vols. Ebers, G........E165.6

Empress Josephine. Mühlbach, L........M952.5
Empty heart. Harland, M.................H283.3
ENAULT, L. Carine: a story of Sweden
....E561.1
Enchanter Faustus and Queen Elizabeth.
12 pp............................ ....in T143.1
Same.....................................in T143.1 [2]
End of the world. Eggleston, E..........E294.3
Endymion. Disraeli, B.................D613.5
ENGEL, M. E. The anti-speculator. Toby
Witt. Lady Elizabeth Hill.......in R794.1 [4]
English at the north pole. Verne, J.. in V531.2
Same.................................... ....V531.12
English hermit. Dorrington, E... in **N938.21
English orphans. Holmes, M. J......... H751.11
ENNERY, A. P. d' See D'Ennery, A. P.
Ennui. Edgeworth, M.. ....in **E235.8
Same.................................. in E235.21
Same...................................in E235.33
Entail, The. Galt, J.................G179.2
Entailed hat. Townsend, G. A..............T748.1
Episode under the Terror. Balzac, H. de
....in B198.14
Same.......................................in B198.34
ERCKMANN, E. and Chatrian, A. Block-
ade of Phalsburg: an episode of the
empire.................................E654.1
Brigadier Frederick. (Also) The dean's
watch. (And) Invisible eye..............E654.2
Brothers Rantzau.......................E654.3
Citizen Bonaparte, 1794-1815: the story
of a peasant.................................. E654.4
Same..................................E654.21
Confessions of a clarionet player, and
other tales.....................................E654.5
The conscript: a story of the French war
of 1813.................................E654.6
Country in danger. E654.7
Same...................................in E654.17
The dean's watch...... ....in E654.2
Friend Fritz: a tale of the banks of the
Lauter. E654.9
Illustrious Dr. Mathéus...... ....E654.10
Invasion of France in 1814: comprising
the night march of the Russian army
past Phalsburg............................E654.11
Invisible eye...........................in E654.2
Madame Thérèse; or, the volunteers of
'92.................................. ....E654.12
Man of the people: a tale of 1848. 2
vols.................................. .... E654.13
The plébiscite; or, a miller's story of the
war.................................E654.14
Issued also as A miller's story of the war.
Story of the plébiscite.

ERCKMANN, E. and Chatrian, A.—Continued.
Polish Jew, (the original work upon
which the play of "The bells" is found-
ed,) and other tales.................. ......E654.15
States general, (1789)...... ....E654.16
Same, and, The country in danger. ...E654.17
Waterloo. Sequel to The conscript of
1813.................................. ....E654.19
Year one of the republic—1793.........E654.20
Same, and, Citizen Bonaparte E654.21
Brewhou. Butler, S.................... .....B986.1
Eric Brighteyes. Haggard, H. R.........H146.5
Erlach Court. Schubin, O.................W817.26
Ernest Maltravers. Lytton, E. G. E. L.
Bulwer-....................................L998.7
Ernestine. 2 vols. Hillern, W. von......H651.2
Errant wooing. Harrison, C. C............H318.6
Ersilia. Poynter, E. F....................Q892.2
ERSKINE, Mrs. T. Wyncote.................E735.1
Esau. Bland, T. A...........................B642.1
Escape from the tower. Marshall, E.....M367.3
Escaped from Siberia. Tissot, V. and
Améro, C..................................T616.1
ESCRICH, E. P. Martyr of Golgotha. 2
vols..................................E746.1
ESLER, E. R. Way they loved at Grim-
pat E763.5
Essay on Irish bulls. Edgeworth, M...
....in **E235.2
Same.. ....in E235.16
Essay on self-justification. Edgeworth,
M......................................in **E235.5
Same.................................in E235.16
Estevan. Musick, J. R.........................M987.2
Esther. Carey, R. N......................C276.11
Ethelyn's mistake. Holmes, M. J......H751.12
Ethne. Field, Mrs. E. M.....................F452.2
Etidorhpa. Lloyd, J. U....................L793.1
ETLAR, C. (pseud. of K. Brosböll).
Priest's lamb. Repaid. White stone.
Aunt Bodil. What a woman never
forgets. A masquerade. Who can
one depend on? Whitsuntide at Ti-
birke..in V629.1
Too old .Shipwrecked mariner's treas-
ure..in B979.1 [2]
Twice sacrificed. 48 pp...............in B979.1 [3]
Etna Vandemir. Hancock, S. J...........H235.1
Ettrick shepherd, pseud. See Hogg, J.
Eugene Aram. Lytton, E. G. E. L. Bul-
wer-...L998.8
Eugénie Grandet. Balzac, H. de.........B198.15

Eunice Lathrop, spinster. Noble, A. L...
....N747.1
Eunice Quince. Conyngham, D............C769.1
European slave life. Hackländer, F. W...
....H122.1
Europeans. James, H., Jr....................J277.7
Eustace diamonds. Trollope, A............T846.9
Eutaw. Simms, W. G......................S592.6
Eva St. Clair. James, G. P. R.....J276.15
Evan Harrington. Meredith, G...........M559.6
EVANS, A. J. See Wilson, A. J.
Eve. Gould, S. B-.........................G698.4
Eve Effingham. Cooper, J. F............C777.13
Evelina. Burney, F.........................B965.1
Same. 2 vols....................**B232.38-9
Even with this. 22 pp. Besant, Sir W...
....in B554.16
Evenings at Haddon Hall..................E935.1
Every inch a soldier. Winter, J. S......W785.7
Eve's ransom. Gissing, G.................G535.2
Evil eye. Carleton, W....................C281.5
Evil genius. Collins, W...................C713.9
Evolution of "Dodd." Smith, W. H.....S664.1
EWALD, H. F. Treasure of Kjœrsholm.
Olufsborg........................in V629.1
EWING, H. Black list.....................E955.1
Castle in the air........................E955.2
Executor, The. Alexander, Mrs.........A374.10
Exeter Hall. McDonnell, W...............M136.1
Exiles, The. 46 pp. Balzac, H. de...in B198.33
Exiles, and other stories. Davis, R. H...
....D264.5
Exile's romance. Keyser, A................K445.1
Expatriation. By the author of "Aris-
tocracy.".....................................E964.1
Experiment in altruism. Sherwood, M...S553.3
Experiment in marriage. Bellamy, C. J..B436.2
Expiated. Prior, H. I......................Q948.1
Expiation. Thanet, O T367.3
Exploits of Brigadier Gerard. Doyle, A. C.
....D754.7
EXPLORABILIS, pseud. See Haywood, E.
Eyes like the sea. Jokai, M...............J745.3
FABER, C. Fickle fortune.................F115.1
Fabiola. Wiseman, N. P. S................W814.1
Fables. Stevenson, R. L.................S848.18
FABRE, F. Abbé Tigrane: candidate for
the papal chair............................F123.1
Face illumined. Roe, E. P.................R699.4
Facino Cane. 22 pp. Balzac, H. de.....in B198.25
Same................................in B198.34
Fadette. Sand, G...........................S213.6
Faience violin. Champfleury...............C451.1

Fainalls of Tipton. Johnson, V. W. J695.1
Fair barbarian. Burnett, F. H..... ......B964.6
Fair emigrant. Mulholland, R...... ......M956.1
Fair god. Wallace, L........................W191.2
Fair Harvard. Washburn, W. T..........W315.1
Fair maid of Perth. Scott, Sir W.........S431.20
Same..**S431.21
Same..in S431.31
Fair prospect. 12 pp. B979.1 3
Fair Puritan. Herbert, H. W...........H536.3
Fair women. Forrester, Mrs..............F730.4
Fairer than a fairy. Grant, J..............G761.16
FAIRFAX, L. R. Misfortunes of bro' Thomas
Wheatley. 25 pp..... ....in S884.6
Fairfax. Cooke, J. E.......................C772.4
FAIRLEIGH, F., pseud. See Smedley, F. E.
Fairleigh Hall. Crake, A. D...............C888.7
Faith and unfaith. Duchess............D829.7
Faith doctor. Eggleston, E...... ....E294.4
Faith Gartney's girlhood. Whitney, A. D.
T..W617.2
FAITHFULL, E. A reed shaken with the
wind..F174.1
Falcon family. Savage, M. W............S264.2
Falconberg. Boyesen, H. H...............B791.2
FALCONER, L. (pseud. of M. Hawker.)
Cecilia de Noël............................F182.1
Falkland. Lytton, E. G. E. L. Bulwer-...
....in L998.4
Fall of Asgard. Corbett, J................C790.3
Fall of Damascus. Russell, C. W.........R960.1
Fall of England? Chesney, C. C..........C525.1
Fallen idol. Anstey, F.....................A625.3
False coin or true? Moutrésor, F. F......M811.1
False or true. 19 pp. Opie, A.........in O614.3
Falsely accused: a criminal trial in Nürn-
berg, 1790...............................in T143.9
Fame and sorrow. 91 pp. Balzac, H. de...
....B198.16
Family affair. Conway, H.................C767.5
Family feud. Harder, L....................W817.2
Family fortunes. Garrett, E. and R...
....G239.6
Family romance. Burke, Sir B............B959.1
Famous victory...............................F198.1
FANE, V. (pseud. of M. M. L. Singleton.)
Story of Helen Davenant.................F211.1
Fanshawe. Hawthorne, N.................H399.3
Same..in H399.3 2
Far above rubies. Riddell, C. E. L.......R543.4
Far from the madding crowd. Hardy, T...
....H272.5
Far from to-day. Hall, G..................H176.1
Fardorougha, the miser. Carleton, W...C281.6

FARGUS, F. J. *See* Conway, II., *pseud.*
FARINA, S. Separation......................*in* Z767.1 ¹
Farina. Meredith, G....................*in* M559.12
FARJEON, B. L. Bright star of life. (*Also*)
   Nine of hearts............................F229.1
   Duchess of Rosemary Lane................F229.2
   For the defence. (*Also*) Story of Jael.
    By S. Baring-Gould........................F229.3
   Gautran. (*Also*) Little Make-Believe...
    ....F229.4
   Great Porter Square.......................F229.5
   Grif: a story of Australian life.............F229.6
   Jessie Trim................................F229.7
   The last tenant............................F229.10
   Little Make-Believe.....................*in* F229.4
   London's heart.............................F229.11
   Love's victory.............................F229.12
   Nine of hearts.........................*in* F229.1
   Same......................................F229.13
   Shadows on the snow: a Christmas
    story................................. F229.14
   Something occurred.........................F229.15
   Toilers of Babylon.........................F229.16
FARQUHAR, G. Beaux stratagem. 30 pp....
   ....*in* M875.1 ¹
FARQUHARSON, M., *pseud.* See Finley, M.
FARRAR, F. W. Darkness and dawn.....F242.1
   Gathering clouds..........................F242.2
Farrers of Budge-Row. Martineau, H......
   ....*in* M385.11
FARRINGTON, M. V. Fra Lippo Lippi: a
   romance...................................F246.1
Fascinating woman. Adam, J. L...........A194.1
Fashionable sufferer. Hoppin, A.......H798.1
Fatal repast. 20 pp.....................*in* T143.5
   Same...............................*in* T143.5 ²
Fate, The. James, G. P. R...........*in* J276.41
Fate of Mansfield Humphreys. White, R.
   G.......................................W587.1
Fated to be free. Ingelow, J...............I464.2
Father and daughter. Bremer, F..........B836.3
Father Connell. Banim, M...............B218.2
Father Oswald.............................F252.1
Fathers and sons. Hook, T...............H781.3
Fathers and sons. Turgénieff, I. S.........T936.4
Faustine. Rita...........................R598.2
FAWCETT, E. Adventures of a widow...F278.1
   An ambitious woman.......................F278.2
   Confessions of Claud......................F278.3
   Daughter of silence.......................F278.4
   Divided lives.............................F278.5
   Douglas Duane........................*in* H398.18
   Gentleman of leisure......................F278.7
   Heir to millions..........................F278.8

FAWCETT, E.—*Continued.*
   Her fair fame.............................F278.9
   House at High Bridge......................F278.10
   How a husband forgave.....................F278.11
   A man's will..............................F278.12
   Miriam Balestier..........................F278.13
   New Nero..................................F278.15
   Olivia Delaplaine.... ....F278.14
   Tinkling cymbals..........................F278.16
FAY, T. S. Norman Leslie. 2 vols.....**F282.1
Fearful responsibility, and other stories.
   Howells, W. D........................H859.13
Fedora. Bélot, A..........................B452.1
Feet of clay. Barr, A. E..................B268.10
FEILING, C. A., *joint tr.* See Oxenford, J.
Felicia. Murfree, F. N. D...............M975.1
Felicitas. Dahn, F........................D131.1
Felix Holt, the Radical. Eliot, G.........E426.3
Fellowe and his wife. Howard, B. W., *and*
   Sharp, W.................................H848.7
Felon's reverie. 22 pp...................*in* B979.1 ¹
Female nihilist. Stepniak...............S838.2
Female Quixote. Lennox, C. R...*in* **N938.12
   Same. 2 vols.......................**B232.24-5
FÉNELON, F. DE S. DE LA M. Tele-
   machus.................................. F332.1
   Same.................................*in* **N938.17
   Same. Tr. by J. Hawkesworth.........F332.1h
Fenian alarm. 47 pp.....................*in* T143.16
FENN, G. M. Antony Grace..............F334.8
   Master of ceremonies......................F334.1
   Morgan's horror...........................F334.2
   Nurse Elisia..............................F334.3
   One maid's mischief.......................F334.4
   Poverty Corner............................F334.5
   Rosery folk...............................F334.6
   "Ship ahoy!"..............................F334.7
   Sweet Mace: a Sussex legend of the iron
    times..................................F334 9
   The vicar's people.........................F334.11
   Witness to the deed...... ....F334.12
Fenton's quest. Braddon, M. E...........B798.13
Ferdinand, Count Fathom. Smollett, T.
   G....................................*in* **N938.7
FERGUSON, *Sir* S. (Michael Heffernan,
   pseud.) Father Tom and the Pope...
   ....*in* T143.2
   Same ....*in* T143.2 ¹
   Gascon O'Driscoll.....................*in* T143.19
   Wet wooing: a narrative of ninety-eight.
    65 pp.................................*in* T143.4
   Same..............................*in* T143.4 ¹
FERGUSON, V. M. Music hath charms...F353.1

FERN, F. (pseud. of S. P. W. Parton.) Ruth Hall: a domestic tale.....................F361.1
FERNALD, C. B. The cat and the cherub, and other stories.....................F362.3
FERNANDEZ DE AVELLANEDA, A. (pseud.) Continuation of Don Quixote...in **N938.16
FERNANDEZ Y GONZALEZ, M. Hermesenda; or, bishop, husband, and king... ....F363.1
Ferne Fleming. Warfield, C. A..........W274.3
Ferragus, chief of the Dévorants. Balzac, H. de.....................B198.17
FERRIER, S. E. Destiny; or, the chief's daughter.....................F391.1
The inheritance.....................F391.2
Marriage.....................F391.3
　　Note.—Miss Clavering contributed a few pages: the 'History of Mrs. Douglas.'
Ferry on the Danube. 23 pp. Gore, C... ....in G666.1 ²
Festival of the Three Kings. 30 pp. Gore, C.....................in G666.1 ³
Fetches, The. Banim, J.....................in B217.3
Feud of Oakfield creek. Royce, J.........R890.1
FEUILLET, O. (Désiré Hazard.) Camors... ....F426.1
　　Issued also as Count de Camors.
Diary of a woman.....................F426.2
　　Issued also as Woman's journal.
Julia de Trécœur.....................in Z767.1
Madame de Maurescamp: a story of Parisian life.....................F426.3
Romance of a poor young man.........F426.4
FÉVAL, P. The duke's motto; or, the little Parisian. 96 pp.....................**F428.1
Few words on social philosophy. 33..........
pp.....................in T143.6
Same.....................in T143.6 ²
Fickle fortune. Faber, C.....................F115.1
FIELD, Mrs. E. M. Bryda: a story of the Indian mutiny.....................F452.1
Ethne: being a truthful historie of the great and final settlement of Ireland by Oliver Cromwell.....................F452.2
FIELD, E. Holy cross, and other tales... ....F453.2
The house.....................F453.1
Second book of tales.....................F453.3
FIELD, H. Glitter and gold.....................F454.1
FIELD, M. ? Secret of Fontaine-la-Croix... ....F455.1
Field of ice. Verne, J.....................in V531.2
Same.....................V531.13

FIELDING, H. Amelia.....................F459.2
Same.....................in **N938.1
Jonathan Wild the Great.............in **N938.9
Same; and, A journey from this world to the next, etc.....................F459.3
Joseph Andrews.....................**B232.18
Same.....................F459.1
Same.....................in **N938.1
Journey from this world to the next... ....in F459.3
Same.....................in **N938.12
Tom Jones.....................F459.4
Same.....................in **N938.3
Same. 3 vols.....................**B232.19-21
FIELDING, S. David Simple.........in **N938.9
Ophelia.....................in **N938.19
FIFE, M. B. In Glenoran.....................F469.1
Fifty years, three months, two days. Wolff, J.....................W857.1
Fight with fate. Alexander, Mrs.........A374.12
Fight with fortune. Collins, M.............C712.1
Figs and thistles. Tourgée, A. W.........T727.4
File No. 113. Gaboriau, E.....................G116.5
FILLEUL, M. Pendower: a story of Cornwall in the time of Henry the Eighth... ....F485.1
Final war. Tracy, L.....................T761.3
FINDLATER, J. H. Green graves of Balgowrie.....................F494.3
FINLEY, M. (M. Farquharson, pseud.) Casella.....................F513.1
Signing the contract and what it cost... ....F513.2
Thorn in the nest.....................F513.3
Wanted—a pedigree.....................F513.4
Fior d'Aliza. Lamartine, A. de.............L217.1
Firm of Girdlestone. Doyle, A. C.........D754.8
First and last crime. 25 pp.............in T143.6
Same.....................in T143.6 ¹
First and last kiss. 37 pp.............in T143.5
Same.....................in T143.5 ²
First family of Tasajara. Harte, B......H327.13
First fam'lies of the Sierras. Miller, J.... ....M649.4
First Fleet family. Becke, L., and Jeffery, W.....................B394.1
First love & last love. Grant, J.........G761.17
First person singular. Murray, D. C.....M981.2
First violin. Fothergill, J.....................F761.1
Fisher girl of France. Calmettes, F......C163.1
Fisherman's daughter. Conscience, H... ....in C755.10
Fishing girl. Björnson, B.....................B625.4
FITCH, A. M., joint author. See Fitch, T.

FITCH, T., *and* A. M. Better days.........F546.1

Fitzboodle papers. Thackeray, W. M...
.....................................*in* T363.16

Five hundred dollars, etc. Chaplin, H....
W..C464.1

Five hundred majority. Hume, J. F.......H921.1

Five weeks in a balloon. Verne, J.......V531.14

Flag on the mill. Sleight, M. B............S632.1

FLAGG, E. De Molai: the last of the military grand masters of the order of Templar Knights.........................F574.1

Flaminia and other stories..................F579.1

FLAMMARION, C. Omega....................F581.1

Urania..F581.2

Flash of summer. Clifford, L. L............C639.3

Flatland. Abbott, E. A......................A131.1

FLEMING, G. (*pseud. of* J. C. Fletcher.)
Head of Medusa.............................F597.1

Kismet..F597.2
Issued also as A Nile novel.

Mirage F597.3

Vestigia F597.4

FLEMMING, H. (*pseud. of* H. H. McClellan). Cupid and the sphinx............F599.1

FLETCHER, J., *joint author. See* Beaumont, F.

FLETCHER, J. C. *See* Fleming, G., *pseud.*

FLETCHER, J. S. At the gate of the fold...
....F613.1

Mistress Spitfire: episodes in the revolution 1642-1644...........................F613.3

When Charles the First was king........F613.4

Fleurange. Craven, P. de La F...........C898.3

FLEURY, J. F. F. HUSSON- *See* Champfleury, *pseud.*

Flight. Britton, J. J........................B862.1

Flip. Harte, B...............................H327.14

Flirtation Camp. Van Dyke, T. S........V248.1

Flitch of bacon. Ainsworth, W. H.......A297.7

Flitters, Tatters, and the Counsellor, etc. Laffan, M...................................L163.2

Floating beacon. 36 pp.....................*in* T143.1

Same...*in* T143.1 ¹

Floating city. Verne, J......................V531.15

Flood and field. Maxwell, W. H..........M465.3

Florence Macarthy. Morgan, *Lady* S. O.
....M850.1

Florida pirate 48 pp.........................*in* T143.5

Same...*in* T143.5 ¹

Flotsam. Merriman, H. S....................M571.3

Flower de Hundred. Harrison, C. C......H318.7

Flower, fruit and thorn pieces. Richter, J. P. F................................R535.2

Flower that grew in the sand, and other stories. Higginson, E..................H636.3

Flowery scroll. Hwa Tsien Ki.............H991.1

FLOYD, M., *pseud. See* Crosby, M.

Floyd Grandon's honor. Douglas, A. M.
....D734.5

Flute and violin, etc. Allen, J. L.........A427.3

FLYGARE-CARLÉN, E. S. The brothers' bet..F648.1

The guardian. 3 vols.......................F648.2

The smugglers........................*in* Z767.1 ¹

Flying Dutchman. Russell, W. C.........R968.3

Flying mail. 36 pp. Goldschmidt, M. A.
....G622.1

Foe in the household. Chesebro', C......C524.1

Foes in ambush. King, C....................K523.11

Foes of her household. Douglas, A. M..D734.6

FOGERTY, J. Countess Irene..............F654.1

Folle-farine. Ouida........................O934.6

Folly and fresh air. Phillpotts, E.........Q565.1

Folly of Eustace, and other stories. Hichens, R. S...................................H626.3

Fontluce. Tinseau, L. de..................*in* T592.1

Fool of nature. Hawthorne, J..............H398.7

Fool of quality. 2 vols. Brooke, H.......B872.1

Fool's errand. Tourgée, A. W.............T727.5

Same...T727.6

FOOTE, M. H. Chosen valley.............F689.1

Cœur d'Alene.................................F689.2

Cup of trembling, and other stories.....F689.3

Friend Barton's concern. 54 pp.......*in* S884.4

In exile, and other stories................F689.5

John Bodewin's testimony.................F689.6

The Led-horse claim.........................F689.8

Footsteps of fate. Couperus, L.............C857.3

"For a dream's sake." Martin, M. E......M382.1

For a mess of pottage. Lyon, S............L991.1

For each and all. Martineau, H...*in* **M385.12

For faith and freedom. Besant, *Sir* W. B554.13

For fifteen years. Ulbach, L................U362.1

For God and gold. Corbett, J..............C790.4

For her dear sake. Hay, M. C.............H413.2

For her sake. Roy, G.......................R888.1

For life and love. Savage, R. H...........S265.1

For Lilias. Carey, R. N....................C276.13

For love and life. Oliphant, M. O. W...O475.11

For Maimie's sake. Allen, G..............A425.7

For summer afternoons. Coolidge, S......C776.1

For the defense. Farjeon, B. L............F229.3

For the major. Woolson, C. F.............W916.5

For the right. Franzos, K. E...............F837.1

For the white rose of Arno. Rhoscomyl, O..R478.5
Forayers, The. Simms, W. G................S592.7
FORBES, A., *and others*. Military sketches and stories; camps and quarters........F692.1
FORD, P. L. Honorable Peter Stirling...F711.1
Foregone conclusion. Howells, W. D...H859.14
Foreign tales and traditions. Ed. by G. C. Cunningham. 2 vols........ ....C972.1
Forest and prairie. Bennett, E............B471.1
Forest days. James, G. P. R.................J276.16
Forest life. 2 vols. Kirkland, C. M......K598.1
Forest of Montalbano. 4 vols. Cuthburtson, *Misses*....................................**C988.1
FORESTER, F., *pseud. See* Chubbuck, E.
FORESTER, Frank, *pseud. See* Herbert, H. W. Forester. Edgeworth, M........*in* E235.17
Foresters, The. Auerbach, B.................A918.5
Forewarned, forearmed. 30 pp. Riddell, C. E. L.....................................*in* R543.5
Forge in the forest. Roberts, C. G. D....R643.3
Forging the fetters. Alexander, *Mrs*... A374.13
FORNEY, J. W. New nobility: a story of Europe and America........................F727.1
FORREST, R. E. Eight days.. ....F729.1
Forest House. Holmes, M. J........ ....H751.13
Forest-Race romance. 53 pp.............*in* T143.4
Same....................................*in* T143.4 ²
FORRESTER, *Mrs.* (*pseud. of* Mrs. Bridges.)
Dearest..F730.1
Diana Carew....................................F730.2
Dolores..F730.3
Fair women..................... .....F730.4
I have lived and loved.............. ....F730.5
Mignon....................... ....F730.6
My lord and my lady........ ....F730.7
Omnia vanitas..................................F730.8
Once again F730.12
Rhona........................ ....F730.9
Roy and Viola..................................F730.10
Viva..F730.11
Forsaken inn. Green, A. K................G795.2
FORSTER, E., *tr.* Tales from the Arabian nights' entertainments................*in* S892.14
Fortunate country maid. Mouhy, C. de F. *Chevalier* de........................*in* **N938.7
Fortunes of Albert Travers. Berrington, B. S.....................................B533.1
Fortunes of Glencore. Lever, C......... L658.11
Fortunes of Harry Racket Scapegrace. Smedley, F. E..................................S637.1
Fortunes of Hector O'Halloran. Maxwell, W. H.......................................M465.4
Fortunes of Margaret Weld. Gardner, S. M. H..................... ....G229.1

Fortunes of Nigel. Scott, *Sir* W.........S431.22
Same..................................**S431.23
Same......................................S431.24
Fortunes of Rachel. Hale, E. E..........H161.3
Fortunes of the Colville family. Smedley F. E..................................S637.2
Fortunes of the Faradays. Douglas, A. M. D734.7
Fortunes of the Scattergood family. Smith, A..................................S641.2
Forty-five. 2 vols. Dumas, A...... .....D886.19
FOSTER, A. J. Ampthill Towers...........F754.1
—*and* Cuthell, E. E. Robber baron of Bedford Castle................................F754.2
FOTHERGILL, J. First violin.................F761.1
Healey.......................................F761.2
Kith and kin.................................. F761.3
Made or marred....................*in* F761.4
"One of three," and Made or marred.. F761.4
Probation.......................................F761.6
The Wellfields...............................F761.7
Foul play. Reade, C., and Boucicault, D. R285.33
Found at Blazing Star. 84 pp. Harte, B. ....*in* H327.14
Found dead. Payn, J...... ....Q345.9
Found wanting. Alexander, *Mrs*........A374.14
Four destinies. Gautier, T....................G277.2
Four meetings. 42 pp. James, H., *Jr.*.*in* J277.3
Four seasons. La Motte-Fouqué, F. H. K. *Freiherr* de...................................L235.1
Fourteen to one. Phelps, E. S..............Q539.4
Fox, E. Gemini.................................F791.1
Fox, J., *Jr.* Cumberland vendetta, and other stories.................................F792.1
Fra Lippo Lippi. Farrington, M. V...... F246.1
Fragoletta. Rita................................R598.3
Framley parsonage. Trollope, A..........T846.10
Frances. Collins, M., *and* F. C.............C712.4
Frances Waldeaux. Davis, *Mrs.* R. H...D263.6
FRANCESCA (*pseud. of* F. Alexander). Story of Ida.....................................F815.1
FRANCILLON, R. E. A dog without a tail. 38 pp...................................*in* T143.12
Grace Owen's engagement.............*in* T143.8
Left-handed Elsa...... ....*in* T143.18
Story of Eulenburg...... ....*in* T143.14
Under Slieve-Ban..............................F817.1
Zelda's fortune.................................F817.2
—*and* Senior, W. Golden flood............F817.3
FRANCIS, M. E. (*pseud. of* Mrs. F. Blundell). Story of Dan................F819.1
In a north country village.................. F819.2

FRANCO, J. J. Tigranes: a tale of the days of Julian the Apostate..................F825.1
Frank Fairlegh. Smedley, F. E...........S637.3
Frank Forester's sporting scenes, etc. 2 vols. Herbert, H. W...............H536.6
Frank Hilton. Grant, J............ G761.18
Frank Mildmay. Marryat, *Capt*. F.......M362.3
Same.........................M362.4
Frank Sinclair's wife. Riddell, C. E. L.
...............................R543.5
Frank Warrington. Harris, M. C......... H315.1
Frankenstein. Shelley, M. W........S545.1
FRANZOS, K. E. For the right..........F837.1
Jews of Barnow..................F837.2
FRASER, *Mrs*. The cousins ....*in* J737.1
Same..................... *in* T559.1
FRASER, J. *See* Tasma, *pseud*.
FRASER-TYTLER, C. C. *See* Tytler, C. C. F-
Frau Wilhelmine. Stinde, J..................S860.2
FREDERIC, H. Brother Sebastian's friendship. 20 pp...................*in* S884.6
The copperhead....................F852.1
Damnation of Theron Ware..................F852.2
In the sixties....................F852.3
In the valley....................F852.4
The Lawton girl....................F852.5
March hares..................F852.6
Marsena, and other stories of the wartime...................F852.7
Seth's brother's wife...................F852.8
Frederick the Great and his court. Mühlbach, L...........................M952.6
Frederick the Great and his family. Mühlbach, L..........................M952.7
Free Joe, and other Georgian sketches. Harris, J. C...............H314.3
Free lances. Reid, M...........R357.2
Free prisoners. Bruner, J. W......... B894.1
Freeland. Hertzka, T...................H576.1
FREEMAN, *Mrs*. A. M. Somebody's Ned.
...............................F855.1
Freischutz, Der. 27 pp...................*in* C972.1 ²
FRENCH, A. *See* Thanet, O., *pseud*.,
FRENCH, H. W. Castle Foam: a Russian story...................F874.1
The only one...................F874.2
French wines and politics. Martineau, H.
...............................*in* **M385.12
Freres, The. Alexander, *Mrs*...............A374.15
FREYTAG, G. Debit and credit..........F895.1
German professor ....*in* Z767.1 ²
Lost manuscript...................... F895.4
Our forefathers. 2 vols. 1. Ingo. 2. Ingraban...................F895.2-3

Fridolin's mystical marriage. Wilbrandt, A. von...............W665.1
FRIEDRICH, B. H. *See* Raimund, G., *pseud*.
Friend Fritz. Erckmann, E. *and* Chatrian, A....................E654.9
Friends. Phelps, E. S...................Q539.5
Friends of Bohemia. 2 vols. Whitty, E.M. W627.1
Friendship. Ouida...................O934.8
FRIIS, J. A. Lajla: a tale of Finmark....F913.1
FRITH, W. In search of quiet..............F920.1
From an island. Thackeray, A. I......*in* T362.5
From dawn to daylight. Beecher, E. W. B.
...............................B414.1
From dusk to dawn. Woods, K. P........W895.1
From flag to flag. Ripley, E. McII......R589.1
From hand to hand. Raimund, G......W817.21
From hand to mouth. Douglas, A. M...D734.8
From jest to earnest. Roe, E. P..........R699.5
From my youth up. Harland, M.........H283.4
From one generation to another. Merriman, H. S..................M571.4
From shadow to sunlight. Lorne, *Marquis of*...................L875.1
From the earth to the moon. Verne, J...
...............................V531.16
From the memoirs of a minister of France. Weyman, S. J...................W549.3
From the ranks. King, C..............*in* K523.9
Front yard, and other Italian stories. Woolson, C. F...................W916.6
FROUDE, J. A. Nemesis of faith.........F942.1
Two chiefs of Dunboy: an Irish romance of the last century...................F942.2
Frozen deep, and other tales. Collins, W...
...............................C713.11
Frozen hearts. Appleton, G. W..........A649.1
Frozen pirate. Russell, W. C..............R968.4
Fulham Lawn. Thackeray, A. I......*in* T362.2
FULLER, A. Peak and prairie...............F965.1
Pratt portraits sketched in a New England suburb...................F965.2
Venetian June F965.3
FULLER, E. Complaining millions of... men...................F966.1
FULLER, F. A. *See* Victor, F. A. F.
FULLER, G. A. Pennimans; or, the triumph of genius...................F967.1
FULLER, H. B. Chevalier of Pensieri-Vani...................F968.1
Cliff-dwellers...................F968.2
With the procession...................F968.3
FULLERTON, *Lady* G. Constance Sherwood: an autobiography of the 16th century...................F971.1

FULLERTON, *Lady J.—Continued.*
Ellen Middleton...............................F971.2
Lady-bird...F971.3
FULLOM, S. W. Daughter of night......F972.1
Fur country. 2 pts. Verne, J...........V531.17
FURMAN, L. S. Stories of a sanctified
   town F986.1
FURNEY, E. E. Culture....................F989.1
G., *Rev.* W. Farewell to a place on the
   borders ....*in* W750.12
G. T. T. Hale, E. E..............................H161.4
GABORIAU, E. Amateur detective...*in* Z767.1 [2]
Caught in the net.............................G116.1
Clique of gold...................................G116.2
   Issued also as Gilded clique.
Downward path................................G116.4
File No. 113......................................G116.5
Marriage at a venture.......................G116.6
   Issued also as Chance marriage.
Monsieur Lecoq. 2 pts.....................G116.7
Mystery of Orcival............................G116.8
Other people's money.......................G116.9
Within an inch of his life.............G116.11
Gabriel Conroy. Harte, B.................H327.15
Gabrielle. McCarty, L.......................M123.1
GAGE, C. S. Mr. Bixby's Christmas visitor.
   12 pp.....................................*in* S884.9
Gala-days. Hamilton, G.....................H220.2
Galama. Liefde, J. B. de...................L719.1
Galatea. Cervantes Saavedra, M. de......C419.3
GALDOS, B. P. *See* Perez Galdos, B.
GALLAND, A., *tr.* Arabian nights enter-
   tainments...........................*in* **N938.18
Gallegher and other stories. Davis, R.
   H..D264.7
Gallery of antiquities. Balzac, H. de...B198.18
Galloping Dick. Watson, H. B. M......W338.1
Galloway herd. Crockett, S. R............C938.7
GALLY, J. W. Sand; and, Big Jack
   Small G178.1
GALT, J. Annals of the parish, and, The
   Ayrshire legatees..........................G179.1
Ayrshire legatees....................*in* G179.1
Book of life;—Fatal whisper;—Haddad-
   Ben-Ahab;—The painter;— Unguarded
   hour..................................*in* Q594.1
The entail..G179.2
The member.......................................G179.3
Same.....................................*in* G179.6
The radical...G179.5
Same.....................................*in* G179.6
Provost, and other tales..................G179.4
The reform: being The member and The
   Radical G179.6

GALT, J.—*Continued.*
Sir Andrew Wylie of that ilk...........G179.7
Wearyful woman. 10 pp..............*in* T143.2
Same...............................*in* T143.2 [1]
Gambara. 86 pp. Balzac, H. de...*in* B198.25
Garden of women. Tytler, S...............T997.4
GARDENER, H. H. Is this your son, my
   lord?..G218.1
Pray you sir, whose daughter?...........G218.2
Pushed by unseen hands...................G218.3
Unofficial patriot...............................G218.4
GARDINER, M. P., *Countess of Blessington.*
   See Blessington, *Countess of.*
GARDNER, S. M. H. Fortunes of Mar-
   garet Weld.......................................G229.1
GARLAND, H. Jason Edwards............G233.1
Main-travelled roads.........................G233.2
Prairie folks.......................................G233.3
Rose of Dutcher's Coolly G233.4
Spoil of office: a story of the modern
   west.......................................G233.5
GARRETT, E., *pseud. See* Garrett, E., *and*
   R.
GARRETT, E., *and* R. (*pseud. of* I. F.
   Mayo). By still waters........ ....G239.1
A chance child............................*in* G239.12
Crooked places.................................G239.2
Crust and the cake...........................G239.3
Dead sin, and other stories......... ......G239.4
Doing and dreaming. *(Also)* A real lady.
   ....G239.5
Family fortunes.................................G239.6
Gold and dross..................................G239.7
House by the works...........................G239.8
John Winter.......................................G239.9
Occupations of a retired life.............G239.10
Premiums paid to experience............G239.11
Quiet Miss Godolphin; and, A chance
   child G239.12
A real lady...................................*in* G239.5
White as snow...................................G239.13
Garrison gossip. Winter, J. S.............W785.9
Garth. Hawthorne, J.......................H398.8
GASKELL, E. C. Cranford........ ....G248.1
Same, etc...G248.4
Lizzie Leigh and other tales........ ...G248.2
Mary Barton, and other tales... ....G248.3
North and south................................G248.5
Phyllis.......................... ....G248.6
Right at last, and other tales.. ....G248.7
Sylvia's lovers...................................G248.8
GASPÉ, P. A. de. The Canadians of old. G249.1
Gaston de Latour. Pater, W...........Q295.1

Gates ajar. Phelps, E. S...............Q539.6
Gates between. Phelps, E. S.........Q539.7
Gathering clouds. Farrar, F. W...........F242.2
GAUTIER, J. (*Mme. Mendès*). The usurper:
an episode in Japanese history.........G276.1
GAUTIER, T. Four destinies............G277.2
Romance of a mummy.....................G277.3
Spirite...................................G277.4
Thousand and second night. 34 pp.. *in* R657.1
—and Mérimée, P. Tales before supper..G277.5
CONTENTS.—Introduction. (Sketch of T. Gautier) by E. Saltus.—Avatar, by T. Gautier.—Venus of Ille, by P. Mérimée.
Gautran. Farjeon, B. L................F229.4
Gaviota, La,—the sea-gull. Caballero, F.
....C112.1
GAYARRÉ, C. Aubert Dubayet; or, the two
sister republics. (Sequel to "Fernando
de Lemos.").............................G285.1
Gayworthys, The. Whitney, A. D. T...W617.3
Gemini. Fox, E..........................F791.1
General Bounce. Melville, G. J. W.....M530.10
Same............................ **M530.11
Geneviève. Alcock, D....................A354.3
GENLIS, S. F. *Comtesse* de. Madamoiselle
de La Fayette: an hist. novel of the
court of Louis XIII..................**G332.2
Gentle belle. Reid, C...................R353.5
Gentle savage. King, E..................K526.1
Gentleman of France. Weyman, S. J...W549.4
Gentleman of leisure. Fawcett, E........F278.7
Gentleman of the old school. James, G. P.
R...................................J276.17
Gentleman Upcott's daughter. Raymond,
W....................................R273.1
Gentleman vagabond and some others.
Smith, F. H............................S647.5
Genuine girl. Lincoln, J. G.............L737.1
Geoffry Hamlyn, Recollections of. Kingsley, H...............................K555.9
Geoffrey Hampstead. Jarvis, T. S........J385.1
Geoffrey the knight. Jaufre, *Chevalier.*
.....................................J413.1
George Geith of Fen Court. Riddell, C. E.
L...................................R543.6
George Julian. Cockton, H...............C666.1
George Silverman's explanation. 29 pp.
Dickens, C...................*in* D548.29 ²
George's mother. Crane, S...............C891.1
Georgia scenes. Longstreet, A. B........L857.1
Georgina's reasons. James, H. *Jr*......*in* J277.3
Georgy Sandon. Ogle, A...................O353.1
Gerald Estcourt. Marryat, F............M361.2
Gerald Ffrench's friends. Jessop, G. H....
.....................................J585.1
GERARD, D. Orthodox...................G356.1
Rich Miss Riddell....................G356.2
—joint author. *See* Gerard, E.
GERARD, E. (*Mrs. von Laszowski*) and, D.
A sensitive plant....................G357.1
Gerda. Schwartz, M. S..................S408.2
German emigrants. Goethe, J. W. v...*in* G599.2
German novelists. Tr. by T. Roscoe......R794.1
German tales. Auerbach, B................A918.6
Gerund de Campazas, History of the famous
preacher. 2 vols. Isla, J. F..........I821.1
Gervase Skinner. Hook, T................H781.4
Ghetto tragedies. Zangwill, I...........Z295.3
Ghost, The. 78 pp. O'Connor, W. D...O196.1
Same..............................*in* O196.2
Ghost-hunter and his family. Banim, J.
and M.............................B217.5
Ghost of Dred Power. McClelland, M.
G..................................*in* M126.1
Giannetto. Majendie, *Lady* M...........M233.2
Giant raft. 2 pts. Verne, J.............V531.19
Giant's robe. Anstey, F.................A625.5
GIBBON, C. Golden shaft................G439.1
GIBERNE, A. The rector's home...........G445.1
Gideon Fleyce. Lucy, H. W..............L943.1
GIFT, T. (*pseud. of* D. H. Boulger.) Pretty
Miss Bellew........................G458.2
Gil Blas. Le Sage, A. R................L622.3
Same............................*in* **N938.4
GILBERT, W. De profundis...............G466.1
Gilbert Gurney. Hook, T................H781.5
Gilded age. Twain, M. *and* Warner, C.
D..................................T969.7
Gilead Guards. Scott, *Mrs.* O. W........S429.1
GILLESPIE, T. Gleanings of the covenant.
1–9: Grandmother's narrative; Covenanter's march; Peden's farewell sermon; Persecution of the M'Michaels;
Rescue at Enterkin; Fatal mistake;
Bonny Mary Gibson; Eskdale-muir
story; Douglas tragedy.............*in* W750.8
Same, 10–17: Sergeant Wilson; Helen
Palmer; Cairny cave of Gavin Muir;
Porter's Hole; James Renwick; Old
Isbel Kirk; The curlers; Violated coffin..............................*in* W750.9
Same, 18–23: Kinaldy; Trials of the
Rev. Samuel Austin; John Govan's
narrative; "Old Bluntie;" Thomas
Harkness of Lockerben; Shoes reversed.............................*in* W750.10

GILLESPIE, T.—*Continued.*
Same, Early days of a friend of the covenant..................................*in* W750.11
Same, Last scrap........................*in* W750.12
Professor's tales: Family incidents; Home and the gipsy maid; The return...*in* W750.4
Same, Last of the pedlars............*in* W750.3
Same, Mountain storm; Fair maid of Cellardykes; Convivialists; Philips Grey..................................*in* W750.1
Same, Natural history of idiots; The enthusaast; Trees and burns; Kirkyards................................*in* W750.7
Same, Phœbe Fortune; Early recollections of a son of the hills; Suicide's grave.......................................*in* W750.2
Same, Social man; The wedding.....*in* W750.6
Same, Three brethren; Mistake rectified; Dura Den; Peat-casting time; The medal.....................................*in* W750.5
GILLIAM, E. W. 1791: a tale of San Domingo................................G480.1
GILLIES, R. P. Thurston tales. 2 vols..**G481.1
GILLMORE, P. Travel, war, and shipwreck...........................G482.1
GILMORE, J. R. *See* Kirke, E., *pseud.*
Gipsy, The. James, G. P. R..............J276.18
Giraldi. Dering, R. G.................D433.1
Girl he married. Grant, J............G761.19
Girl in checks. Daniel, J. W...........D184.1
Girlhood of Shakespeare's heroines. 2 vols. Clarke, M. C.................C599.1
Girls of Feversham. Marryat, F............M361.3
GISSING, G. Denzil Quarrier.............G535.1
Eve's ransom...........................G535.2
In the year of jubilee....................G535.3
Odd women...............................G535.4
Gladiators, The. Melville, G. J. W-....M530.12
Same........................... **M530.13
GLASCOCK, M. W. (*Mrs. Blow*). Dare...G548.1
Glimpse of the world. Sewell, E. M....S516.1
Glitter and gold. Field, H.................F454.1
GLOERSEN, K. Mighty hunter. 4 pp..*in* V629.1
"Gloria victis." Schubin, O.............S384.2
Glorinda. Dodd, A. B.......................D639.1
GLOUVET, J. DE (*pseud. of* G. de Beaurepaire). The woodman................G564.1
Gloverson and his silent partners. Keeler, R..K264.1
GLÜMER C. von. A noble name. Tr. by A. L. Wister.........................W817.1
"Go forth and find." Brainerd, T. H.....B814.1

GOBINEAU, J. A. *Comte* de. Romances of the east. G575.1
Typhaines Abbey: a tale of the twelfth century...............................G575.2
Gobseck. 94 pp. Balzac, H. de....B198.19
God and the man. Buchanan, R..........B918.3
God in the car. Hope, A.................H791.13
Godfrey Morgan. Verne, J...........V531.20
Godolphin. Lytton, E. G. E. L. Bulwer-....................................L998.9
God's fool. Maartens, M.................M111.3
Gods, some mortals and Lord Wickenham. Hobbes, J. O........................H682.1
Godson of a marquis. Theuriet, A.....T415.4
GODWIN, W. Adventures of Caleb Williams..................................G592.1
St. Leon: a tale of the sixteenth century. 4 vols...............................G592.2
GOETHE, J. W. VON. Novels and tales...G599.2
CONTENTS: Elective affinities. Sorrows of Werther. German emigrants. Good women. A tale.
New Paris. 11 pp.....................*in* O983.1
Sorrows of Werter......................*in* G599.2
Same.................................**G599.3
Wilhelm Meister's apprenticeship.........G599.4
Same, and Travels. 2 vols.............G599.4¹⁻²
Wilhelm Meister's travels.................G599.5
Same.................................*in* G599.4²
Gœthe and Schiller. Mühlbach, L........M952.8
GOGOL, N. V. St. John's eve, and other stories.................................G613.1
Taras Bulba.............................G613.2
Tchitchikoff's journeys; or, dead souls. 2 vols..................................G613.3
Issued also as Dead souls.
Gold and dross. Garrett, E.............G239.7
Gold and name. Schwartz, M. S.....S408.3
Gold Elsie. Marlitt, E...................W817.13
Gold hunter's adventures. Thomes, W. H. T465.3
Gold hunters in Europe. Thomes, W. H. T465.4
Gold of Chickaree. Warner, S., *and* A. B...................................W284.11
Gold-worshippers. Robinson, J.........R662.2
Golden age. Grahame, K................G743.1
Golden butterfly. Besant, *Sir* W., *and* Rice, J...............................B554.40
Golden Dog. Kirby, W...................K582.1
Golden flood. Francillon, R. E., *and* Senior, W..............................F817.3
Golden Hope. Russell, W. C...........R968.5
Golden house. Warner, C. D............W280.1

Golden justice. Bishop, W. H...............B622.4
Golden Lion of Granpere. Trollope, A...
....T846.11
Golden shaft. Gibbon, C....................G439.1
Golden wedding, and other tales. Stuart,
R. McE..................................S932.2
Goldmakers' village. Zschokke, H........Z923.1
GOLDSCHMIDT, M. A. The flying mail.
(From the Danish.) 36 pp. (*Also*)
Old Olaf by M. Thoresen. 46 pp.
(*And*) Railroad and the churchyard,
(*etc.*) by B. Björnson. 54 pp.........G622.1
Wind as post office. 14 pp.............*in* V629.1
GOLDSMITH, C., *pseud. See* Smith, J. P.
GOLDSMITH, M. Rabbi and priest.........G624.1
GOLDSMITH, O. She stoops to conquer. 34
pp..............................*in* M875.1 ²
Same.................................**B232.23
Vicar of Wakefield.........................G625.1
Same...............................*in* C615.1
Same.............................*in* **N938.2
Same.............................*in* S892.14
Same. (*Also*) The traveller (*And*) The
deserted village.........................G625.2
Same. (*Also*) Paul and Virginia.......G625.3
GOOCH, *Mrs.* F. P. Miss Mordeck's father...
....G645.1
Good aunt. Edgeworth, M.........*in* E235.17
Good French governess. Edgeworth, M...
....*in* E235.18
Good for nothing. Melville, G. J. W-...M530.14
Same...........................*in* **M530.13
Good hater. Boyle, F....................B792.1
"Good luck!" Werner, E..................W492.2
Good stories. Reade, C..................R285.9
Good women. 22 pp. Goethe, J. W. v...
....*in* G599.2
Good-bye sweetheart. Broughton, R......B877.3
GOODLOE, A. C. College girls.............G652.1
GOODMAN, E. J. Too curious..............G653.1
GOODWIN, M. W. Head of a hundred: be-
ing an account of an officer in the
colony of Virginia....................G657.4
White aprons............................G657.1
Gooroo Simple, Strange adventures of the
venerable. Besche, C. G..............B555.1
Gordian knot. Brooks, S.................B874.1
GORDON, *Mrs.* Sir Gervase Grey. 3 vols.
(in 2)....................................G662.1
GORDON, A. C. Flandroe's mogul. 47
pp....................................*in* S886.4
GORDON, J. (*pseud. of* J. G. S. Cruger). A
diplomat's diary....................G663.1
Marionettes G663.3

GORDON, J.—*Continued.*
Poppaea...............................G663.4
A puritan pagan.......................G663.5
A successful man......................G663.7
GORDON, W. J. Captain-general: the at-
tempt of the Dutch to colonize New
Holland..............................G664.1
Gordonhaven: scenes and sketches of fisher
life in the north....................G665.1
GORE, C. G. Hungarian tales. 3 vols...G666.1
Maid of honour. 16 pp..............*in* J737.1
Same.............................*in* T559.1
GOTTHELF, J. (*pseud. of* A. Bitzius.)
Wealth and welfare. 2 vols..........G685.1
GOTTSCHALCK, C. F. Popular traditions and
tales of the Germans. 89 pp......*in* R794.1 ²
GOULD, J. T. *See* Lincoln, J. G.
GOULD, S. BARING- Alexander Nesbitt, ex-
schoolmaster. 44 pp................*in* T143.19
Arminell...............................G698.1
The broom-squire......................G698.2
Court Royal...........................G698.3
Eve....................................G698.4
Last words of Joseph Barrable. 48 pp....
...............................*in* T143.21
Little Tu'penny........................G698.6
Mrs. Curgenven of Curgenven. G698.7
The Pennycomequicks...................G698.9
Story of Jael......................*in* F229.3
Urith: a tale of Dartmoor..............G698.11
Governor's garden. Rivers, G. R. R......R622.1
Gowrie. James, G. P. R. J276.19
Grace Lee. Kavanagh, J K212.5
Grace Seymour. 2 vols.................**G729.1
Grace Willoughby. Maxwell, W. H......M465.5
GRAFIGNY, F. DE. Letters of a Peruvian
Princess, with the sequel..........*in* **N938.9
GRAHAM, E., *pseud. See* Molesworth, M. L.
GRAHAM, J. W. Nemra: a tale of ancient
Rome.................................G740.1
GRAHAM, M. C. Stories of the foothills..G741.1
GRAHAME, K. The golden age...........G743.1
GRAND, S., *pseud.* Heavenly twins......G751.1
Ideala G751.2
Singularly deluded....................G751.3
Grande Bretèche. 44 pp. Balzac, H. de...
.................................*in* B198.16
Same...........................*in* B198.34
Same...........................*in* B198.44
Grandee, The. Valdés, A. P...........V145.3
Grandissimes, The. Cable, G. W.........C115.5
Grania. Lawless, E....................L418.2

GRANT, J. Adventures of an aide-de-camp..G761.1
Arthur Blane...G761.3
The "Black Watch"........................G761.27
Bothwell; or, the days of Mary queen of Scots G761.4
The Cameronians...............................G761.5
Captain of the guard........................G761.6
Cavaliers of fortune.........................G761.7
Colville of 'the Guards'..................G761.8
Constable of France, and other military historiettes G761.9
Dead tryst. (Also) Haunted life......G761.10
Derval Hampton.............................G761.11
Did she love him?............................G761.13
Duke of Albany's Own Highlanders...G761.14
Dulcie Carlyon................................G761.15
Fairer than a fairy...........................G761.16
First love & last love: a tale of the Indian mutiny......................................G761.17
Frank Hilton......................................G761.18
Girl he married................................G761.19
Harry Ogilvie...................................G761.20
Haunted life.............................in G761.10
Jack Chaloner..................................G761.21
Jack Manly.......................................G761.22
Jane Seton..G761.23
King's Own Borderers......................G761.24
Lady Wedderburn's wish: a tale of the Crimean war..............................G761.25
Laura Everingham............................G761.26
Letty Hyde's lovers..........................G761.28
Lord Hermitage.................................G761.29
Lucy Arden.......................................G761.30
Mary of Lorraine G761.31
Miss Cheyne of Essilmont................G761.32
Morley Ashton.................................G761.33
Oliver Ellis.......................................G761.34
One of "The six hundred".................G761.35
Only an ensign: a tale of the retreat from Cabul..G761.36
Phantom regiment............................G761.37
Philip Rollo......................................G761.38
Playing with fire: a story of the Soudan war G761.39
Queen's cadet, and other tales..........G761.40
Rob Roy...G761.2
Romance of war; or, the Highlanders in Spain G761.41
Issued also as Guerrilla chief.
Ross-shire Buffs, and other stories......G761.42
Royal Highlanders; or, the Black Watch in Egypt.......................................G761.43
Royal regiment, and other novelettes..G761.44

GRANT, J.—Continued.
Scots brigade, and other tales..........G761.45
Scottish cavalier..............................G761.46
Scottish soldiers of fortune..............G761.47
Second to none G761.48
Secret dispatch.................................G761.49
Shall I win her?...............................G761.50
Six years ago....................................G761.51
Under the red dragon.......................G761.52
Vere of "Ours"................................G761.53
Violet Jermyn..................................G761.54
White cockade..................................G761.55
Yellow Frigate..................................G761.56
GRANT, M. M. Sun-maid.................G762.1
GRANT, R. Bachelor's Christmas, and other stories...................................G763.2
Confessions of a frivolous girl..........G763.3
Mrs. Harold Stagg............................G763.5
Opinions of a philosopher.................G763.7
Reflections of a married man............G763.9
—and others. The king's men.........G763.12
GRAS, F. Reds of the midi.................G767.1
Grateful negro. Edgeworth, M..........**E235.7
Same...in E235.20
GRATTAN, T. C. Heiress of Bruges........G771.1
GRAVES, R. Spiritual Quixote. 2 vols...
....**B232.32-3
Graveyard flower. Hillern, W. von........H651.3
GRAY, A. Periwinkle: an autobiography...
.... G778.1
GRAY, M. (pseud. of M. G. Tuttiet). In the heart of the storm.......................G781.5
Innocent imposter, etc......................G781.6
Last sentence....................................G781.9
Reproach of Annesley......................G781.12
Silence of Dean Maitland................G781.14
Unexpected fare. 47 pp...............in T143.22
Gray man. Crockett, S. R.................C938.8
Graysons, The. Eggleston, E.............E294.5
GRAZIANI, G. MAGHERINI- See Magherini-Graziani, G.
Graziella. Lamartine, A. de...............L217.2
Great Amherst mystery. Hubbell, W...H876.1
Great earthquake at Lisbon. 38 pp...in T143.18
Great expectations. Dickens, C..........D548.19
Same.. D548.20
Same.. D548.21
Same...in D548.38
Great Hoggarty diamond, History of Samuel Titmarsh and the. Thackeray, W. M...............................in T363.7
Great man of the provinces in Paris. Balzac, H. de....................................B198.20
Great match, etc. Smith, M. P. W........S655.1

Great Porter Square. Farjeon, B. L......F229.5
Great shadow. Doyle, A. C................D754.9
Great war syndicate. Stockton, F. R....S866.12
Greater glory. Maartens, M................M111.4
Greatest heiress in England. Oliphant, M.
    O. W.................................O475.12
Greek romances. Tr. by R. Smith.......S657.1
GREEN, A. D. *See* Douglas, M., *pseud.*
GREEN, A. K. (*Mrs. Rohlfs*). Behind
    closed doors............................G795.1
Forsaken inn................................G795.2
Hand and ring...............................G795.3
Leavenworth case...........................G795.4
Matter of millions..........................G795.5
Mill mystery.................................G795.6
Strange disappearance......................G795.7
Sword of Damocles..........................G795.8
GREEN, E. E. Church and the king: a
    tale of the days of Henry VIII........G796.1
Dorothy's vocation..........................G796.2
Stronger will...............................G796.3
GREEN, W. S. Sacrifice; or, the living
    dead....................................G798.1
Green book. Jokai, M......................J745.4
Green gate. Wichert, E....................W817.34
Green graves of Balgowrie. Findlater, J.
    H.......................................F494.3
Green mountain boys. Thompson, D. P....
    ....T470.1
Green pastures and Piccadilly. Black,
    W..B627.6
Green ray. Verne, J.......................V531.21
GREENE, S. P. McL. Cape Cod folks.....G812.3
Leon Pontifex...............................G812.6
Towhead, the story of a girl..............G812.9
Vesty of the Basins.........................G812.11
GREENOUGH, *Mrs. R. S. See* Greenough,
    S. D.
GREENOUGH, S. D. Arabesques: Monarè;
    Apollyona; Domitia; Ombra............G815.1
In extremis.................................G815.2
GREENWAY, *Grandfather* (*pseud. of* C. J.
    Cannon). Ravellings from the web of
    life....................................G816.1
GREG, P. Guy Neville's ghost. 38 pp....
    ....*in* T143.15
Greifenstein. Crawford, F. M.............C899.8
Grenadière, La. 36 pp. Balzac, H. de....
    ....*in* B198.16
GRESLEY, W. Charles Lever; or, the man
    of the nineteenth century..............G831.1
Gretchen. Holmes, M. J....................H751.14

GRÉVILLE, H. (*pseud. of* A. M. C. H. Du-
    rand). Aline............................G838.1
Guy's marriage.............................G838.3
Mam'zelle Eugénie..........................G838.4
Markof, the Russian violinist.............G838.5
Princess Oghérof...........................G838.7
Sylvie's betrothed.........................G838.8
Trials of Raïssa...........................G838.9
Xénie's inheritance........................G838.10
GREY, E. C. Trials of life. 2 vols.....**G842.3
GREY, H. Key to the Waverley novels, in
    chronological sequence, with index of
    the principal characters. Rev. ed....S431.57
Greyslaer. 3 vols. Hoffman, C. F......H709.1
GRIER, S. C. Uncrowned king............G848.5
Grif. Farjeon, B. L.......................F229.6
GRIFFIN, G. Christian physiologist......G851.1
Collegians: a tale of Carryowen.........G851.2
Duke of Monmouth..........................G851.3
The invasion...............................G851.4
The rivals, and, Tracy's ambition......G851.5
Tales of the Munster festivals..........G851.6
Same. 2d ser............................G851.7
Talis qualis; or, tales of the jury-room...
    ....G851.8
Tracy's ambition..........................*in* G851.5
Same.....................................G851.9
GRIFFITH, C. (*Mrs. Beckett*). Corinthia
    Marazion................................G853.1
Victory Deane..............................G853.2
Griffith Gaunt. Reade, C.................R285.10
GRIFFITHS, A. Lola: a tale of Gibraltar...
    ....G855.1
GRIMM, J. L., *and* W. K. Specimens from
    the Kinder- and Haus-Märchen...*in* R794.1 ²
Grip. Winter, J. S........................W785.10
Grisly Grisell. Yonge, C. M.............Y555.12
GROGAN, M. *See* Mackenzie, E., *pseud.*
GROOME, F. H. Kriegspiel: the war-
    game...................................G876.1
GROSSI, T. Marco Visconti...............G878.1
"Ground arms!" Suttner, B. *Freiherrin*
    von.....................................S966.1
Group of noble dames. Hardy, T........H272.6
GROVES, J. P. Charmouth Grange........G884.1
Grumbler, The. Pickering, E.............Q595.2
Gryll Grange. 2 vols. Peacock, T. L...Q356.2
Guardian, The. 3 vols. Flygare-Carlén,
    E. S....................................F648.2
Guardian angel. Holmes, O. W.........H752.2
Guenn. Howard, B. W.....................H848.3
GUÉNOT, C., *Abbé.* Vengeance of a Jew...
    ....G926.1
GUÉNOT, H. Moor of Granada.............G927.1

Guerndale. Stimson, F. J.....................S859.2

GUERRAZZI, F. D. Beatrice Cenci.........G934.1

Manfred; or, the battle of Benevento...G934.2

Guest at the Ludlow. Nye, E. W........N994.1

GUEULLETTE, T. S. Chinese tales...*in* **N938.5

Tartarian tales; or, a thousand and one
quarters of hours....................*in* **N938.19

Guild court. Macdonald, G................M135.7

Guilt and innocence. Schwartz, M. S.....S408.4

Guilty, or not guilty.........................*in* W750.3

Guilty river. Collins, W.....................C713.13

GUINEY, L. I. Lovers' Saint Ruth's, and
three other tales.....................G964.3

GULLIVER, L., *pseud. See* Swift, J.

Gulliver's travels. Swift, J............*in* **N938.9

Same.....................................S976.1

Gunnar. Boyesen, H. H.....................B791.3

GUNSAULUS, F. W. Monk and knight. 2
vols.....................................G976.1

GUNTER, A. C. Mr. Barnes of New York..
....G977.9

Mr. Potter of Texas.........................G977.10

That Frenchman! G977.11

Gurney married. Hook, T..................H781.6

GUTHRIE, F. A. *See* Anstey F., *pseud.*

Guy Deverell. Le Fanu, J. S..............L488.2

Guy Fawkes. Ainsworth, W. H..........A297.8

Guy Livingstone. Lawrence, G. A.........L421.5

Guy Mannering. Scott, *Sir* W.............S431.25

Same....................................S431.26

Same.................................*in* **S431.53

Guy Rivers. Simms, W. G.................S592.8

Guy Waterman. 3 vols. Saunders, J....S257.1

Guy's marriage. Gréville, H..............G838.3

Gwendoline's harvest. Payn, J............Q345.10

GYP *(pseud. of* S. G. M. A., *Comtesse* de
Martel de Janville). Chiffon's marriage.................................G997.1

Gypsy Christ, and other tales. Sharp, W...
....S531.4

H., J. Laird of Darnick Tower.........*in* W750.4

H—— family. Bremer, F..................*in* B836.2

HABBERTON, J. Barton experiment......H113.1

Bowsham puzzle...........................H113.2

Brueton's bayou. *(Also)* Miss Desarge...
By F. H. Burnett.....................H113.10

Country luck...............................H113.3

Crew of the "Sam Weller"................H113.4

Helen's babies.............................H113.5

Jericho road................................H113.6

Little Guzzy, and other stories...........H113.7

Mrs. Mayburn's twins......................H113.8
Issued also as Just one day.

Scripture club of Valley Rest.............H113.9

HACKLÄNDER, F. W. European slave life...
....H122.1

The volunteer............................*in* Z767.1 [1]

HAGG, W. J. Woman the stronger........H145.1

HAGGARD, H. R. Allen Quatermain.....H146.1

Beatrice....................................H146.2

Colonel Quaritch, V. C....................H146.3

Dawn..H146.4

Eric Brighteyes............................H146.5

Heart of the world........................H146.6

"Jess".....................................H147.7

King Solomon's mines......................H146.8

Long odds.................................*in* S885.1

Maiwa's revenge............................H146.9

Mr. Meeson's will.........................H146.10

Montezuma's daughter......................H146.11

Nada the lily.............................H146.12

She...H146.13

Witch's head..............................H146.14

The wizard H146.15

—*and* Lang, A. World's desire...........H146.17

Hajji Baba in England. Morier, J........M855.5

Hajji Baba in Turkey, etc. Morier, J.....M855.2

HALE, E. E. Christmas eve and Christmas
day H161.1

Crusoe in New York, and other tales...H161.2

East and west............................H161.18

Fortunes of Rachel........................H161.3

G. T. T.; or, the wonderful adventures
of a pullman.............................H161.4

His level best, and other stories.........H161.5

How they lived in Hampton...............H161.6

In His name: a story of the Waldenses...
....H161.7

Ingham papers.............................H161.8

Man without a country, and other tales...
....H161.9

Mr. Tangier's vacations...................H161.11

Mrs. Merriam's scholars..................H161.10

My friend the boss........................H161.12

Our Christmas in a palace................H161.13

Our new crusade: a temperance tale...H161.14
Issued also as Good time coming.

Philip Nolan's friends....................H161.15

Ten times one is ten......................H161.16

Ups and downs............................H161.17

HALE, L. P., *and* Bynner, E. L. Uncloseted
skeleton.............. ....H162.1

HALÉVY, L. L'abbé Constantin...........H168.1

Half brothers. Dumas, A..................D886.20

Half-hours with foreign novelists. 2 vols.
Zimmern, H., *and* A................Z767.1

HALIBURTON, T. C. (Sam Slick, *pseud.*)
The attaché; or, Sam Slick in Eng-
land H172.1
The clockmaker...............................H172.2
Letter-bag of the Great Western.........H172.3
Season-ticket...................................H172.4
HALL, A. M. Last in the lease. 20 pp....*in* S637.2
Sketches of Irish character.................H179.1
HALL, C. W. Twice taken...................H174.1
HALL, G. Far from to-day H176.1
HALL, J. Legends of the West.............H177.1
Hall of Hellingsley. 3 vols. Brydges, *Sir
S. E.*..**B916.1
HALPINE, C. G. Life and adventures, etc.,
of private Miles O'Reilly..................H195.1
HALSEY, C. Two of us........................H196.1
HALSTEAD, A. L. The death trust.........H197.1
HALSTEAD, L. B. *See* Elbon, B., *pseud.*
Halves. Payn, J...............................Q345.11
HAMERLING, R. Aspasia: a romance of
ancient Hellas. 2 vols....................H214.1
HAMERTON, P. G. (A. Segrave, *pseud.*)
Her picture.....................................H215.1
Marmorne.......................................H215.2
Wenderholme: a story of Lancashire and
Yorkshire......................................H215.3
HAMILTON, A. K. Mildred's cadet........H217.1
One of the Duanes............................H217.2
HAMILTON, C. V. D. Crown from the
spear...H218.1
HAMILTON, G. (*pseud. of* M. A. Dodge).
Gala-days.......................................H220.2
HAMILTON, K. W. The parson's proxy...
....H219.1
HAMILTON, T., *tr.* Antar: a Bedoueen ro-
mance. 4 vols................................H221.1
HAMLEY, C. Light on the hearth...*in* T143.11
Wassail..*in* T143.12
HAMLEY, *Sir* E. B. Lady Lee's widow-
hood...H223.1
Last French hero. 55 pp..............*in* T143.10
Lazaro's legacy: a tale of the siege of
Gibraltar. 64 pp.......................*in* T143.1
Same..*in* T143.1 ²
Legend of Gibraltar. 67 pp..........*in* T143.1
Same..*in* T143.1 ¹
Recent confession of an opium-eater. 23
pp. Shakespeare's funeral. 65 pp..*in* T143.7
HAMLEY, W. G. Magnetic mystery. 58
pp...*in* T143.20
Medium of last century...............*in* T143.22
HAMLIN, M. C. W. Legends of le Dé-
troit...H224.1

Hammer and anvil. Spielhagen, F........S755.1
Hammersmith. Severance, M. S.........S498.1
HAMMOND, W. A. Lal......... ....H227.1
Mr. Oldmixon.................................H227.2
Hampdens, The. Martineau, H..........M385.13
HANCOCK, S. J. Etna Vandemir: a ro-
mance of Kentucky and "the great
uprising."....................................H235.1
Hand and glove. Edwards, A. B..........E261.2
Same...*in* E261.4
Hand and ring. Green, A. K...............G795.3
Hand of Ethelberta. Hardy, T............H272.7
Handsome Humes. Black, W.............B627.8
Handy Andy. Lover, S.....................L910.1
Hannah. Mulock, D. M....................M960.8
Hannah Thurston. Taylor, B.............T238.2
HANOUM, L. (*pseud. of* A. D. Piazzi).
Tragedy in the imperial harem at Con-
stantinople...................................H247.1
Hans of Iceland. Hugo, V.................H895.1
Happiness of being rich. Conscience, H...
....C755.2
Happy boy. Björnson, B..............*in* B625.1 ²
Happy conclusion..........................*in* W750.8
Happy Dodd. Cooke, R. T................C773.1
HARBEN, W. N. Mute confessor..........H255.1
White Marie: a story of Georgian planta-
tion life.......................................H255.2
HARCOURT, A. Jack and Minory: a tale of
Christmas-tide. 55 pp.............*in* T143.20
Hard cash. Reade, C......................R285.11
Same...R285.12
Hard times. Dickens, C................*in* D548.2
Same..*in* D548.2 ²
Same..*in* D548.4
Same..*in* D548.21
Hard woman. Hunt, V.....................H943.1
HARDER, L. A family feud. Tr. by A. L.
Wister...W817.2
HARDING, V. E., *and* Braga, T. Twelve
Portuguese legends. 12 pp.........*in* H496.1
HARDMAN, F. The Great Unknown: a jest
from the German. 41 pp...........*in* T143.15
Major Moss: a campaigning remin-
iscence. 56 pp.......................*in* T143.6
Same..*in* T143.6 ¹
My English acquaintance. 69 pp...*in* T143.4
Same..*in* T143.4 ¹
My friend the Dutchman. 63 pp...*in* T143.3
Same..*in* T143.3 ²
Smuggler's leap: a passage in the Pyre-
nees. 19 pp...........................*in* T143.5
Same..*in* T143.5 ²

HARDY, A. S. But yet a woman..........H268.1
  Passe Rose...................................H268.2
  Wind of destiny.............................H268.3
HARDY, T. Desperate remedies...........H272.3
  Far from the madding crowd.............H272.5
  Group of noble dames......................H272.6
  Hand of Ethelberta.........................H272.7
  A Laodicean.................................H272.11
  Life's little ironies.........................H272.10
  Mayor of Casterbridge.....................H272.12
  Pair of blue eyes...........................H272.13
  Return of the native........................H272.14
  Tess of the d'Urbervilles..................H272.16
  Three strangers............................in S885.2
  To please his wife.........................in S887.1
  Trumpet-major..............................H272.17
  Two on a tower..............................H272.18
  Under the greenwood tree.................H272.19
  Well-beloved................................H272.22
  Wessex tales................................H272.20
  The woodlanders............................H272.21
Hardy Norseman. Lyall, E.................L981.7
HÄRING, G. W. H. See Alexis, W., pseud.
HARLAND, H. (Sidney Luska, pseud.) As
  it was written: a Jewish musician's
  story.......................................H282.1
  Mademoiselle Miss.........................H282.8
  Mrs. Peixada...............................H282.10
  Yoke of the Thorah........................H282.16
HARLAND, M. (pseud. of M. V. H. Ter-
  hune). Alone...... ....H283.1
  At last......................................H283.2
  A battle summer...........................in H283.5
  Empty heart................................H283.3
    Issued also as Husks.
  From my youth up H283.4
  Helen Gardner's wedding-day. (Also)
    A battle summer.........................H283.5
    Issued also as Colonel Floyd's wards.
  Hidden path................................H283.6
  His great self...............................H283.7
  Husbands and homes.......................H283.8
  Jessamine..................................H283.9
  Miriam......................................H283.10
  Moss-side..................................H283.11
  My little love...............................H283.12
  Nemesis.....................................H283.13
  Phemie's temptation.......................H283.14
  Ruby's husband............................H283.15
  Sunnybank..................................H283.16
  True as steel...............................H283.17
  With the best intentions..................H283.18
Harold. Lytton, E. G. E. L. Bulwer-...L998.10

HARRADEN, B. Bird on its journey...in S885.3
  Hilda Strafford.............................H296.2
  Idyl of London. 23 pp..................in S885.6
  In varying moods..........................H296.3
  Ships that pass in the night.............H296.5
HARRINGTON, G. F., pseud. See Baker,
  W. M.
Harrington. Edgeworth, M..........**E235.14
  Same E235.31
HARRIS, J. C. Aunt Fountain's prisoner.
  46 pp....................................in S866.6
  Balaam and his master, and other
    sketches and stories...................H314.1
  Free Joe, and other Georgian sketches...
    ....H314.3
  Mingo, and other sketches in black and
    white...................................H314.5
  Sister Jane, her friends and acquaint-
    ances...................................H314.8
HARRIS, M. C. Frank Warrington........H315.1
  A perfect Adonis...........................H315.2
  Phœbe......................................H315.3
  Richard Vandermarck.....................H315.4
  Rutledge...................................H315.5
  St. Philip's................................H315.6
  The Sutherlands...........................H315.7
  An utter failure............................H315.8
HARRISON, C. C. The Anglomaniacs....H318.1
  Bachelor maid.............................H318.2
  Bar Harbor tales.......................in H318.11
  Belhaven tales. (Also) Crow's nest.
    (And) Una and King David.........H318.4
  Crow's nest..............................in H318.4
  Edelweiss of the Sierras, etc.............H318.5
  Errant wooing.............................H318.6
  Flower de Hundred: the story of a Vir-
    ginia plantation.........................H318.7
  Sweet bells out of tune...................H318.9
  Una and King David ....in H318.4
  Virginia cousin, and Bar Harbor tales...
    ....H318.11
HARRISON, J. Whose fault?................H320.1
HARRISON, Mrs. R. G. K. See Malet, L.,
  pseud.
Harry Bolton's curacy. 48 pp..........in T143.5
  Same ....in T143.5 ¹
Harry Coverdale's courtship and marriage.
  Smedley, F. E.............................S637.4
Harry Harson. Irving, J. T..................I723.2
Harry Heathcote. Trollope, A...........T846.12
Harry Lorrequer, Confessions of. Lever, C...
    ....L658.12
Harry Ogilvie. Grant, J...................G761.20

Harry Racket Scapegrace, Fortunes of.
Smedley, F. E................................S637.1
Harry Richmond, Adventures of. Mere-
dith, G...M559.1
Harsha, *Judge. See* Theamba, I., *pseud.*
HART, J. C. Miriam Coffin; or, the whale-
fishermen....................................H325.1
HARTE, B. Argonauts of North Liberty...
....H327.1
Barker's luck, and other stories.........H327.40
Bell-ringer of Angel's, and other stories...
....H327.2
By shore and sedge...........................H327.3
Clarence...H327.4
Colonel Starbottle's client and other peo-
ple..H327.5
Condensed novels............................H327.6
Same, and stories.............................H327.7
Cressy...H327.8
Crusade of the Excelsior....................H327.9
Devil's Ford.........................*in* H327.23
Drift from Redwood Camp...........*in* H327.27
Drift from two shores........................H327.11
Eastern sketches...................*in* H327.34
First family of Tasajara.....................H327.13
Flip, and, Found at Blazing Star.........H327.14
Found at Blazing Star.............*in* H327.14
Gabriel Conroy.................................H327.15
Heritage of Dedlow Marsh, and other
tales...H327.17
In a hollow of the hills.....................H327.18
In the Carquinez woods....................H327.19
Luck of Roaring Camp, and other
sketches..H327.20
Same, and other stories....................H327.21
Maruja...H327.22
Millionaire of Rough-and-Ready, and
Devil's Ford...................................H327.23
Mrs. Skaggs's husbands, and other
sketches...................................... H327.24
On the frontier................................H327.26
Phyllis of the Sierras, and, A drift from
Redwood Camp...............................H327.27
Sally Dows, etc...............................H327.29
Sappho of Green Springs...................H327.30
Snow-bound at Eagle's......................H327.31
Story of a mine...............................H327.32
Susy...H327.33
Tales of the Argonauts, and Eastern
sketches...H327.34
Same, and other sketches.............H327.34 ²
Thankful Blossom: a romance of the
Jerseys, 1779.................................H327.35

HARTE, B.—*Continued.*
Twins of Table Mountain, and other
stories H327.36
Waif of the plains............................H327.38
Ward of the Golden Gate..................H327.39
HARTLEY, G. W. The factor's shooting.
29 pp......................................*in* T143.20
Master Tommy's experiment: a heather-
burning story. 24 pp..............*in* T143.19
HARTLEY, *Mrs.* M. L. *See* Laffan, M.
HARTNER, E. Severa. Tr. by A. L.
Wister..W817.3
Hartwell farm. Caxton, L................C384.1
Harveys, The. Kingsley, H................K555.2
HASSELT, A. H. C. van. *See* Aveline, A.
d', *pseud.*
HASTINGS, E., *pseud. See* Sherwood, M.
Hated son. Balzac, H. de.........*in* B198.41
Hathercourt. Molesworth, M. L........M719.1
HATTON, J. John Needham's double.....H366.1
Not in society, and other tales...........H366.2
Queen of Bohemia...........................H366.3
Tallants of Barton...........................H366.4
HAUFF, W. Cold heart. 31 pp. Nose,
the dwarf. 21 pp. Severed hand. 10
pp...*in* O983.1
—*ed.* Arabian days' entertainments.....A658.1h
Haunted and the haunters. Lytton, E. G.
E. L. B-................................*in* L998.21
Same...................................*in* L998.25
Haunted Enghenio. 17 pp.............*in* T143.17
Haunted life. Grant, J................*in* G761.10
Hauntings. Lee, V...........................L482.1
HAWKER, M. *See* Falconer, L., *pseud.*
HAWKESWORTH, J. Almoran and Hamet...
....*in* **B232.26
Same.....................................*in* **N938.1
HAWKINS, A. H. *See* Hope, A., *pseud.*
Haworth's. Burnett, F. H................B964.8
HAWTHORNE, J. Another's crime.........H398.1
Archibald Malmaison........................H398.2
Bressant H398.3
Calbot's rival.........................*in* H398 4
Constance, and, Calbot's rival............H398.4
A dream and a forgetting.................H398.5
Fool of nature...............................H398.7
Garth..H398.8
John Parmelee's curse......................H398.10
Kildhurm's oak. (*Also*) A strange friend...
....H398.11
Love is a spirit.............................H398.12
Mrs. Gainsborough's diamonds.........H398.13
Professor's sister............................H398.15

HAWTHORNE, J.—*Continued.*
  Sebastian Strome.............................H398.17
  Sinfire. *(Also)* Douglas Duane. By E.
    Fawcett.......................................H398.18
  Six Cent Sam's..............................H398.19
  Strange friend........................*in* H398.11
HAWTHORNE, N. Ancestral footstep...
  ....*in* H399.3
  Blithedale romance.....................*in* H399.11
  Same...H399.16
  Doctor Grimshawe's secret...............H399.1
  The Dolliver romance, etc................H399.2
  Same...*in* H399.3 ¹
  Same, Fanshawe, and Septimius Felton.
    (Also) The ancestral footstep.......H399.3
  Fanshawe H399.3
  Same, Dolliver romance, etc.........*in* H399.3 ¹
  House of the seven gables................H399.4
  Same, and, The snow image, etc........H399.5
  Marble faun..................................H399.6
    Issued also as Transformation; or, the
    romance of Monte Beni.
  Mosses from an old manse................H399.7
  Our old home, and, Septimius Felton...H399.8
  Scarlet letter...............................H399.10
  Same, and the Blithedale romance.....H399.11
  Septimius Felton......................*in* H399.8
  Same.......................................*in* H399.8
  Same...H399.12
  Snow image, etc.........................*in* H399.5
  Same...H399.13
  Twice-told tales...........................H399.14
  Analytical index to works of H........H399.15
HAY, J. (?) The bread-winners............H412.1
HAY, M. C. Arundel motto H413.1
  For her dear sake..........................H413.2
  Hidden perils. *(Also)* Old Myddelton's
    money H413.3
  Missing.......................................H413.4
  Nora's love test.............................H413.5
  Old Myddelton's money................*in* H413.3
  Squire's legacy..............................H413.6
  Wicked girl...................................H413.7
HAYES, A. A. Denver express. 37 pp..
  ....*in* S884.6
HAYES, H., *pseud. See* Kirk, E. O.
HAYWOOD, E. (Explorabilis, *pseud.*) Betsy
    Thoughtless..............................*in* **N938.13
  Invisible spy............................*in* **N938.23
  Jemmy and Jenny Jessamy........*in* **N938.17
HAZARD, D., *pseud. See* Feuillet, O.
Hazard of new fortunes. 2 vols. Howells,
  W. D...H859.16
Hazel Kirke. Walsh, M...................W226.1

He fell in love with his wife. Roe, E. P....
  ....R699.6
He knew he was right. Trollope, A......T846.13
He that will not when he may. Oliphant,
  M. O. W......................................O475.14
He would be a gentleman. Lover, S.......L910.2
Head of a hundred. Goodwin, M. W......G657.4
Head of Medusa. Fleming, G.............F597.1
Head of the family. Mulock, D. M.......M960.9
Headless horseman. Reid, M.............R357.3
Headlong Hall. Peacock, T. L.............Q356.3
Headsman, The: a tale of doom. 83pp. *in* T143.2
  Same....................................*in* T143.2 ¹
Headsman, The. Cooper, J. F. C777.10
  Same....................................*in* C777.12
HEALY, M. *(Mrs. Bigot)* (Jeanne Mairet,
    pseud.) Lakeville; or, substance and
    shadow.................................... H434.1
  Storm-driven..............................H434.2
Healey. Fothergill, J......................F761.2
Heaps of money. Norris, W. E............N861.5
HEARD, J., *Jr.* Charge for France. 61 pp....
  ....*in* S886.3
HEARN, L. Chita: a memory of Last
    Island......................................H436.1
  Youma: the story of a West-Indian
    slave..H436.3
  Stray leaves from strange literature.....H436.2
    CONTENTS: Stray leaves *(viz)*: The book
    of Thoth. The fountain maiden: legend of
    the South Pacific.—The bird wife: an Esqui-
    maux tradition.—Tales retold from Indian
    and Buddhist literature.—Runes from the
    Kalewala.—Stories from Moslem lands.—
    Traditions retold from the Talmud.
Heart. 81 pp. Tupper, M. F............*in* T928.1
Heart of a mystery. Speight, T. W......S742.3
Heart of it. Stoddard, W. O..............S869.1
Heart of life. Mallock, W. H..............M255.1
Heart of Mid-Lothian. Scott, *Sir* W.....S431.27
  Same....................................*in* **S431.45
Heart of Princess Osra. Hope, A......H791.14
Heart of steel. Reid, C....................R353.6
Heart of the world. Haggard, H. R.....H146.6
Heart stories. Bartlett, T.................B291.1
Hearts. Murray, D. C......................M981.3
Hearts and hands. Reid, C...............R353.3
Hearts and homes. 3 vols. Ellis, S. S..E473.2
Heartsease. Yonge, C. M.................Y555.13
Heather and snow. MacDonald, G......M135.8
Heavenly twins. Grand, S.................G751.1
HECTOR, *Mrs.* A. F. *See* Alexander, *Mrs.*,
  pseud.
Hector O'Halloran, Fortunes of. Maxwell,
  W. H...M465.4

Hector Servadac. Verne, J............V531.22
Hedged in. Phelps, E. S................Q539.8
Hedri. Mathers, H....................M426.1
HEIBERG, C. T. *See* Bernhard, C., *pseud.*
Heidenmauer, The. Cooper, J. F........C777.11
Same................................C777.12
HEIMBURG, W. *(pseud. of B. Behrens).*
Lora: the major's daughter............H467.1
Penniless girl. Tr. by A. L. Wister...W817 4
Heir of Linne. Buchanan, R............*in* B918.7
Heir of Redclyffe. Yonge, C. M........Y555.14
Heir of the ages. Payn, J............Q345.12
Heir to millions. Fawcett, E............F278.8
Heiress of Bruges. Grattan, T. C........G771.1
Heiress of Kilorgan. Sadlier, M. A......S126.3
Heiress of Sweetwater. Randolph, J. T.....
....R193.1
Heirs of Bradley House. Douglas, A. M....
....D734.10
Helen Gardner's wedding-day. Harland,
M.....................................H1283.5
Helen of Glenross. 4 vols. (in 2.) Mar-
tin, H...............................**M381.1
Helen Treveryan. Roy, J................R889.1
Helen's babies. Habberton, J............H1113.5
HELIODORUS. The Ethiopics; or, adven-
tures of Theagenes and Chariclea....
....*in* S657.1
HELM, C. Child and woman..............H478.1
HELME, E. St. Clair of the isles; or, the
outlaws of Barra.....................H479.1
HELPS, *Sir* A. Casimir Maremma........H484.1
Ivan de Biron; or, the Russian court in
the middle of last century............H484.2
Realmah..............................H484.3
HEMINGWAY, P. Gregorio..............*in* S885.1
HENDERSON, F. C. Priscilla Baker, the
freedwoman. 20 pp................*in* H496.1
—*tr.* Dunderviksborg, and other tales,
forming an epitome of modern European literature.....................H496.1

CONTENTS: Henderson, F. C. Priscilla
Baker, the freedwoman.—Zedritz, K. E. The
double wedding at Dunderviksborg.—Kis-
faludy, K. Three at once: farce —Straparola
de Cararaggio, G. F. Salardo.—Pushkin, A.
G. The snow-storm.—Palarik, J. Friendship at the harvest-feast: farce.—Alarcon, P.
A. de. Black eyes.—Van Doosselaeve, T. S.
No happiness without virtue: drama.—Kar-
pinsky, F. Taxes: com.—Eckstein, E.
Cards for four.—Pfleger, G. Revenge.—
Stroobant, E. Rue des Pierres, No. 60: a
Flemish play with a French name.—Harding, V. E., *and* Braga, T. Twelve Portuguese
legends.—Dequet, A. Theodore, conte de la

HENDERSON, F. C.—*Continued.*
vie littéraire.--Milan, N. Amanda: farce.—
Rask, C. E. The storm-bride.—Krypow, *Dr.*
Leka; or reminiscences of a physician.—
Celestin, F. Roza: play.
2d. ed., *containing two additional stories, is
issued as* An epitome of modern European
literature.
HENDERSON, I. Agatha Page............H497.1
The prelate.........................H497.2
Henrietta. Lennox, C................*in* **N938.23
Henrietta, Countess Oscuvor. 69 pp. Treys-
sac de Vergy, P. H................*in* **N938.17
Henrietta Temple. Di-raeli, B............D613.7
HENRY, E. '89; edited from the original
manuscript.........................H521.1
Henry Esmond. Thackeray, W. M........T363.8
Same................................T363.10
Henry Masterton. James, G. P. R........J276.20
Henry of Guise. James, G. P. R..........J276.21
Henry Powers (banker.) Kimball, R. B...
....K492.1
Henry St. John, Gentleman. Cooke, J. E...
....C772.1
Henry Smeaton. James, G. P. R......*in* J276.41
Henry the Eighth, and his court. Mühl-
bach, L.............................M952.9
HENTY, G. A. Curse of Carne's Hold...H527.1
Military sketches and stories. *See* Forbes,
A., *and others.*
HEPBURN, G. *See* Setoun, G., *pseud.*
Her dearest foe. Alexander, *Mrs.*........A374.17
Her fair fame. Fawcett, E................F278.9
Her great ambition. Earle, A. R..........E127.1
Her great idea; and other stories. Walford,
L. B................................W174.4
Her Johnnie. Whyte, V................W629.1
Her lord and master. Marryat, F........M361.4
Her Majesty. Tompkins, E. K............T662.5
Her majesty the queen. Cooke, J. E......C772.6
Her picture. Hamerton, P. G............H215.1
Herb-moon, The. Hobbes, J. O............H682.2
HERBERT, H. W. (Frank Forester, *pseud.*)
The brothers: a tale of the Fronde. 2
vols.................................**H536.1
Chevaliers of France from the crusades to
the marechals of Louis XIV............H536.2
Fair Puritan: an historical romance of
the days of witchcraft................H536.3
Frank Forester's sporting scenes and
characters. 2 vols...................H536.6
Oliver Cromwell.....................H536.4
Roman traitor; or, the days of Cicero,
Cato, and Catiline H536.5
Hereward the Wake. Kingsley, C........K553.3

Heriot's choice. Carey, R. N..............C276.15

Heritage of Dedlow Marsh, and other tales.
     Harte, B.. H327.17

Heritage of Langdale. Alexander, *Mrs*...A374.18

Hermann Agha. Palgrave, W. G..........Q161.1

Hermesenda. Fernandez y Gonzalez, M...F363.1

Hero, A. Mulock, D. M....................M960.10

Heroes of the desert. Manning, A........M283.2

Heroine of '49. Sawtelle, M. P..............S271.1

Herr Paulus. Besant, *Sir* W................B554.15

HERTZKA, T. Freeland: a social anticipa-
tion..H576.1

HERVEY, M. H. Amyas Egerton, cava-
lier.. H579.1

HESELTINE, W. Last of the Plantage-
nets..H584.1

Hesperus. 2 vols. Richter, J. P. F.......R535.3

Hester. Oliphant, M. O. W.................O475.15

Hester Morley's promise. Stretton, H....S915.5

Hester's venture. Roberts, M...............R646.3

HETHRINGTON, W. Seers' cave........*in* W750.3

Hetty. Kingsley, H.............................K555.3

Hetty's strange history. Jackson, H. M....
....J127.2

HEYSE, P. L'Arrabiata. 28 pp. Beppe,
the star gazer. 50 pp. Maria Fran-
cisca. 64 pp...........................*in* S331.1

Children of the world.......................H621.1

The huntsman........................*in* Z767.1 ²

In Paradise. 2 vols.........................H621.2

Laurella...............................*in* H621.3

Same.................................*in* H621.5

Same.................................*in* S331.1

     Issued also as L'Arrabiata.—The fury.

The maiden of Treppi. (*Also*) Laurel-
la H621.3

Romance of the canoness..................H621.4

Tales from the German.....................H621.5

HIBBARD, G. A. As the sparks fly up-
ward. 71 pp...........................*in* S886.4

End of the beginning. 44 pp.........*in* S886.2

Iduna, and other stories....................H624.1

Nowadays, and other stories.............H624.2

HICHENS, R. S. Folly of Eustace, and
other stories......................................H626.3

Hidden masterpiece. 37 pp. Balzac, H.
de...*in* B198.14

Hidden path. Harland, M...................H283.6

Hidden perils. Hay, M. C..................H413.3

Hidden power. Tibbles, T. H..............T552.1

Hide-and-seek. Collins, W................C713.15

HIGGINSON, E. Flower that grew in the
sand, and other stories....................H636.3

HIGGINSON, T. W. Malbone..............H637.1

Monarch of dreams...........................H637.2

High Mills. Saunders, K...................S258.1

Higher law. Maitland, E.....................M231.2

Higher than the church. Hillern, W.
von...H651.4

Highland cousins. Black, W..............B627.9

Highland widow. Scott, *Sir* W.......*in* S431.6

Same...S431.16

Same.................................*in* **S431.55

Hilda Strafford. Harraden, B..............H296.2

HILL, J., (*calling himself Sir J.*) Adventures of Mr. George Edwards, a Cre-
ole.....................................*in* **N938.23

Hill and the valley. Martineau, H......
....*in* **M385.4

HILLERN, W. VON. By his own might...H651.1

Ernestine H651.2
     Issued also as Only a girl.

A graveyard flower..........................H651.3

Higher than the church....................H651.4

Only a girl. Tr. by A. L. Wister......W817.5
     Issued also as Ernestine.

HILLIARD, H. W. De Vane................H654.1

Hills of Shatemuc. Warner, S............W284.3

Hillyars and the Burtons. Kingsley, H....
....K555.4

HILLYER, S. Marable family..............H655.1

Hilt to hilt. Cooke, J. E....................C772.7

HINKSON, K. T. *See* Tynan, K.

His father's son. Matthews, B..............M438.4

His Grace. Norris, W. E....................N861.6

His great self. Harland, M.................H283.7

His honour, and a lady. Cotes, S. J. D....C843.8

His inheritance. Trafton, A................T764.1

His level best, and other stories. Hale, E.
E...H161.5

His little mother, and other tales. Mulock,
D. M..M960.11

His opportunity. Pearson, H. C...........Q362.1

His sombre rivals. Roe, E. P.............R699.7

His vanished star. Craddock, C. E.......C884.5

His young wife. Smith, J. P..............S653.4

Historical mystery. Balzac, H. de.......B198.21

History of a week. Walford, L. B........W174.5

History of Amelia. Fielding, H............F459.2

History of David Grieve. Ward, M. A. A..W261.3

History of Mr. John Decastro and his
brother Bat. 4 vols. Mathers, J., *and*
A solid gentleman, (*pseud.*)..............M427.1

History of Nicholas Muss. Du Bois-Melly,
C...D814.1

History of Pompey the Little. Coventry,
F...**B232.23

History of Rasselas. Johnson, S.............J692.1

History of Samuel Titmarsh and the great
Hoggarty diamond. Thackeray, W.
M.................................*in* T363.7

History of Sir Charles Grandison. Richardson, S.................................R525.4

History of the famous preacher Friar
Gerund de Campazas. 2 vols. Isla,
Father J. F.............................I821.1

History of the life of the late Mr. Jonathan
Wild the Great. Fielding, H..........F459.3

History of Tom Jones, a foundling. Fielding, H.................................F459.4

Hitherto. Whitney, A. D. T.............W617.4

HOBBES, J. O. *(pseud. of* P. W. Craigie.)
The gods, some mortals, and Lord
Wickenham.............................H682.1

The herb-moon..........................H682.2

HOFFMAN, C. F. Greyslaer: a romance of
the Mohawk. 3 vols....................H709.1

HOFFMAN, M. J. Agnes Hilton............H708.1

HOFFMAN, W. Elementary spirit. 31 pp.
Jesuits' church in G. 21 pp. The sand-
man. 26 pp.......................*in* O983.1

Serapion brethren. 2 vols..............H710.1

Weird tales. 2 vols....................H710.3

HOFLAND, B. Reflection: a tale.........H712.1

HOGBIN, A. C. Elsa.....................H715.1

HOGG, J. (Ettrick shepherd, *pseud.*) The
bogle o' the brae. Laidlaws and the
Scots............................*in* Q594.1

Singular letter from southern Africa. 13
pp...............................*in* T143.3

Same...........................*in* T143.3 1

Tales and sketches. 5 vols.............H716.1-5

Hohensteins, The. Spielhagen, F........S755.2

HOLBERG, L., *Freiherr* von. *See* Klimius,
N., *pseud.*

HOLCROFT, T. Road to ruin. 31 pp...*in* M875.1 2

HOLDING, C. B. Reuben: a prince in disguise...................................H727.1

Holiday romance. Dickens, C........*in* D548.29 2

HOLLAND, C. Lure of fame...............H734.1

HOLLAND, J. G. Arthur Bonnicastle.......H735.1

Bay-path: a tale of New England colonial
life...................................H735.2

Miss Gilbert's career..................H735.3

Nicholas Minturn.......................H735.4

Sevenoaks..............................H735.5

Hollands, The. Townsend, V. F..........T751.3

HOLLEY, M. Miss Richards' boy, and
other stories..........................H738.1

HOLLISTER, G. H. Kinley Hollow........H744.1

HOLM, Saxe, *pseud. See* Jackson, H. M.

Holmby House. Melville, G. J. W-......M530.15

Same................................**M530.16

HOLMES, E. Scenes in our parish. 1st and
2d series...........................**H750.1

HOLMES, M. J. Bessie's fortune.........H751.1

Cameron pride..........................H751.2

Château d'Or. *(Also)* Norah, and,
Kitty Craig............................H751.3

Christmas stories......................H751.4

Cousin Maude, and, Rosamond............H751.5

Daisy Thornton, and, Jessie Graham....H751.6

Darkness and daylight..................H751.7

Dora Deane, and, Maggie Miller.........H751.8

Edith Lyle.............................H751.9

Edna Browning..........................H751.10

English orphans........................H751.11

Ethelyn's mistake......................H751.12

Forrest House..........................H751.13

Gretchen...............................H751.14

The homestead on the hillside, and other
tales..................................H751.15

Hugh Worthington.......................H751.16

Jessie Graham......................*in* H751.6

Kitty Craig........................*in* H751.3

'Lena Rivers...........................H751.17

Madeline...............................H751.18

Maggie Miller......................*in* H751.8

Marguerite.............................H751.19

Marian Grey............................H751.20

Meadow Brook...........................H751.21

Mildred................................H751.22

Millbank...............................H751.23

Norah..............................*in* H751.3

Queenie Hetherton......................H751.24

Rector of St. Mark's...............*in* H751.27

Rosamond...........................*in* H751.5

Rose Mather............................H751.25

Tempest and sunshine...................H751.26

West Lawn, and, The rector of St.
Mark's.................................H751.27

HOLMES, O. W. Elsie Venner: a romance of destiny.......................H752.1

Guardian angel.........................H752.2

A mortal antipathy.....................H752.3

HOLST, H. P. Lisette's castles in the air.
24 pp.............................*in* B979.1 3

HOLT, E. S. At ye Grene Griffin........H758.1

Imogen.................................H758.2

In all time of our tribulation.........H758.3

In convent walls.......................H758.4

Joyce Morrell's harvest................H758.5

Lady Sybil's choice....................H758.6

HOLT, E. S.—*Continued.*
　Lord mayor..................................H758.7
　Margery's son.............................H758.8
　Robin Tremayne..........................H758.9
　Sister Rose........................ ....H758.10
　Tangled web.............................H758.11
　Wearyholme H758.12
　Well in the desert. (*Also*)　May Lane.
　　By M. C. M............................H758.13
Holy cross, and other tales.　Field, E......F453.2
Holy rose.　Besant, *Sir* W.................B554.16
HOME, J.　Douglas.　24 pp.............*in* M875.1 ²
Home.　Ellis, S. S.........................E473.3
Home, The.　Bremer, F.....................B836.6
Home again.　MacDonald, G...............M135.9
Home as found.　Cooper, J. F.............C777.13
　Same...............................*in* C777.15
Home influence.　Aguilar, G.................A283.2
Home nook.　Douglas, A. M...............D734.11
Home scenes and heart studies.　Aguilar,
　G..A283.3
Home, sweet home.　Riddell, C. E. L.....R543.7
Homes abroad.　Martineau, H......*in* **M385.12
Homestead on the hillside, and other tales.
　Holmes, M. J............................H751.15
Homeward bound.　Cooper, J. F..........C777.14
　Same..................................C777.15
Homo sum.　Ebers, G.......................E165.8
Honor May.　Bartol, M.....................B292.1
Honorable Peter Stirling.　Ford, P. L....F711.1
Honorable surrender.　Adams, M..........A215.1
Honorine.　88 pp.　Balzac, H. de.....*in* B198.42
HOOD, T.　Tylney Hall.....................H776.1
HOOK, J.　Pen Owen.　3 vols...........**H777.1
HOOK, T.　Cousin Geoffry. *(Also)* Claude
　Stocq: a tale of the sixteenth century.
　(by H. E. F. Reybaud.)..................H781.1
　Cousin William..........................H781.2
　Fathers and sons.........................H781.3
　Gervase Skinner.........................H781.4
　Gilbert Gurney............................H781.5
　Gurney married: a sequel to Gilbert
　　Gurney................................H781.6
　Martha, the gypsy.　20 pp.............*in* H781.9
　Maxwell H781.7
　The parson's daughter....................H781.8
　Passion and principle. *(Also)* Martha,
　　the gypsy..............................H781.9
HOOPER, L. H.　Tsar's window...........H786.1
　Under the tricolor.......................H786.2
Hoosier mosaics.　Thompson, M...........T474.1
Hoosier schoolmaster.　Eggleston, E.....E294.6

HOPE, A.　Alive and yet dead :　some pas-
　sages in the life of a French convict.
　47 pp......................................*in* T143.22
HOPE, A.　(*pseud. of* A. H. Hawkins.)
　Change of air.............................H791.5
　Chronicles of Count Antonio............H791.6
　Comedies of courtship...................H791.8
　Dolly dialogues..........................H791.10
　God in the car............................H791.13
　Heart of Princess Osra..................H791.14
　Indiscretion of the duchess.............H791.15
　Man of mark.............................H791.18
　Philosopher in the apple orchard....*in* S885.2
　Phroso...................................H791.19
　Prisoner of Zenda.......................H791.20
HOPE, T.　Anastasius; or, memoirs of a
　Greek.　3 vols...........................**H790.1
Hope Meredith.　Tabor, E.................T114.2
Hope Mills.　Douglas, A. M...............D734.12
Hopes and fears.　Yonge, C. M...........Y555.15
HOPFFEN, H.　Trudel's ball.　70 pp.　For-
　tunes and fate of little Spangle.　53
　pp..*in* S331.1
HOPKINS, M., *Jr.*　The world's verdict...H793.1
HOPKINS, S., *of Northampton.*　Youth of
　the Old Dominion........................ H795.1
HOPKINS, T.　Nugents of Carriconna.....H796 1
HOPPIN, A.　A fashionable sufferer........H798.1
HOPPUS, M. A. M. *(Mrs. Marks)*　Masters
　of the world.　3 vols....................H799.1
　Story of carnival.........................H799.2
Horace Chase.　Woolson, C. F.............W916.7
Horace Templeton.　Lever, C.............L658.13
HORNADAY, W. T.　Man who became a
　savage H813.4
Hornby mills, and other stories.　Kingsley,
　H...K555.5
HORNUNG, E. W.　Bride from the bush....H816.1
　Irralie's bushranger...................... H816.2
　Unbidden guest..........................H816.3
Horse-shoe Robinson.　Kennedy, J. P...K353.1
Hospital sketches.　Alcott, L. M..........A355.1
Hostages to fortune.　Braddon, M. E......B798.14
Hot plowshares.　Tourgée, A. W..........T727.7
House, The.　Field, E......................F453.1
House at High Bridge.　Fawcett, E......F278.10
House by the medlar tree.　Verga, G......V493.1
House by the works.　Garrett, E............G239.8
House divided against itself.　Oliphant,
　M. O. W...............................O475.16
House of a merchant prince.　Bishop, W.
　H...B622.5
House of cards.　Wolf, A. S................W835.1

House of gentlefolk. Turgénieff, I. S......T936.5
House of Martha. Stockton, F. R.........S866.14
House of Ross, and other tales. Riddle, A.
　G.............. ....R544.1
House of the seven gables. Hawthorne,
　N...H399.4
　Same...H399.5
House of the wolf. Weyman, S. J.........W549.5
House on the marsh. Warden, F......W265.2
House on the moor. Oliphant, M. O. W...
　..O475.17
House on the scar. Thomas, B...............T454.1
House-party. Ouida.........................O934.10
House terrible. Towner, A....................T746.1
Household of Bouverie. Warfield, C. A...W274.5
How a husband forgave. Fawcett, E.....F278.11
How could he help it? Roe, A. S.........R698.1
How they kept the faith. Raymond, G...R269.1
How they lived in Hampton. Hale, E. E...H161.6
How to boil peas..............................*in* T143.11
HOWARD, B. W. *(Mrs. Teufel.)* Aulnay
　Tower..H848.1
　Aunt Serena.....................................H848.2
　Guenn, a wave on the Breton coast......H848.3
　One summer......................................H848.4
　Open door..H848.5
　Tony, the maid..................................H848.6
　—*and* Sharp, W. A fellowe and his wife...H848.7
HOWE, E. W. Man story.....................H855.1
　Moonlight boy...................................H855.2
　Mystery of the locks..........................H855.3
　Story of a country town......................H855.4
HOWE, G. Last slave ship. 66 pp......*in* S886.5
HOWE, M. *(Mrs. Elliott)* San Rosario
　ranch... H857.1
HOWELL, J. The experimenter. The slave...
　...*in* W750.2
　Fortunes of William Wighton.........*in* W750.1
　Legend of Calder moor. Prisoner of war....
　...*in* W750.9
　Major Weir's coach. Sergeant's tales:
　The palantines............................*in* W750.3
　Man-of-war's man..........................*in* W750.8
　Scottish veteran ....*in* W750.6
　Sergeant's tales: John Square's voyage to
　India; Beggar's camp.................*in* W750.4
　Same: Packman's journey to London;
　Imprudent marriage ....*in* W750.5
　Seven years' dearth......................*in* W750.7
HOWELLS, W. D. Annie Kilburn H859.1
　April hopes......................................H859.2
　Chance acquaintance..........................H859.5
　Coast of Bohemia..............................H859.8

HOWELLS, W. D.—*Continued.*
　Character and comment selected from
　(his) novels by M. Macoun..............H859.6
　Day of their wedding......................H859.9
　A day's pleasure, and other sketches...H859.10
　Dr. Breen's practice.......................H859.11
　Fearful responsibility, and other sto-
　ries..H859.13
　Foregone conclusion............ ....H859.14
　Hazard of new fortunes. 2 vols........H859.16
　Imperative duty...............................H859.17
　Indian summer.................................H859.18
　Lady of the Aroostook.....................H859.20
　Landlord at Lion's Head.................H859.34
　Minister's charge; or, the apprenticeship
　of Lemuel Barker.........................H859.21
　Modern instance..............................H859.22
　Parting and a meeting.....................H859.24
　Quality of mercy.............................H859.25
　Rise of Silas Lapham H859.26
　Shadow of a dream..........................H859.27
　Suburban sketches...........................H859.28
　Their wedding journey; with an addi-
　tional chapter on Niagara revisited
　(twelve years after).....................H859.29
　Traveler from Altruria.....................H859.30
　Undiscovered country.......................H859.31
　Woman's reason...............................H859.32
　World of chance..............................H859.33
HOWITT, M., *joint author. See* Howitt, W.
HOWITT, W. John Darbyshire, a primitive
　Quaker.................................*in* J737.1
　Same ....*in* T559.1
　Woodburn Grange.............................H863.1
　—*and* M. Stories of English and foreign
　life..H863.2
Howleglass, the merry jester............*in* R794.1 '
HUBBARD, E. No enemy (but himself)...H874.1
HUBBELL, M. S. Shady side; or, life in a
　country parsonage..........................H875.1
HUBBELL, W. Great Amherst mystery: a
　true narrative of the supernatural....H876.1
Hubbub. Currier, E. C.......................C978.1
Huckleberries gathered from New England
　hills. Cooke, R. T.........................C773.2
HUDSON, W. C. Vivier of Vivier, Long-
　man & Company, bankers.............H886.1
HUET, C. BUSKEN- *See* Busken-Huet, C.
HUGESSEN, *Hon.* E. K. A dramatic effect.
　46 pp.....................................*in* T143.23
Hugh Worthington. Holmes, M. J...H751.16
HUGHES, T. Scouring of the White
　Horse...H894.1
　Tom Brown at Oxford......................H894.2

HUGO, V., *vicomte.* Hans of Iceland.....H895.1
Same. Tr. by A. L. Alger............**H895.1a
Hernani, Dramatic scenes founded on, by
F. Egerton, Earl of Ellesmere......*in* Q594.1
Man who laughs. Tr. by I. F. Hapgood...
....H895.2
Same. Tr. by W. Young...............H895.2y
Issued also as By order of the king.
Les misérables. Tr. by I. F. Hapgood...
....H895.3
Same. Tr. by C. E. Wilbour...........H895.3w
Ninety-three. 2 vols.....................H895.4
Same. Tr. by F. L. Benedict...........H895.4b
Same. Tr. by H. B. Dole..............H895.4d
Notre-Dame de Paris. Tr. by I. F. Hap-
good...H895.5
Toilers of the sea. Tr. by I. F. Hap-
good...H895.6
Huguenot, The. James, G. P. R..........J276.22
Huguenot exiles. Dupuy, E. A...........D945.4
Huguenot family in the English village.
Tytler, S.....................................T997.5
Hulda. Lewald, F...........................W817.8
Humble enterprise. Cambridge, A........C178.3
Humble romance, and other stories. Wil-
kins, M. E...................................W684.3
HUME, F. W. Aladdin in London.......H920.1
HUME, J. F. Five hundred majority.....H921.1
HUMPHREYS, S., *tr.* Peruvian tales...
....*in* **N938.21
Humphry Clinker. Smollett, T. G...
....*in* **N938.19
Same...S666.1
Same. 2 vols.....................**B232.30-1
Hundredth man. 2 vols. Stockton, F. R....
....S866.15
Hungarian tales. 3 vols. Gore, C. G...G666.1
HUNGERFORD, J. The old plantation....H936.1
HUNGERFORD, M. *See* Duchess, *pseud.*
HUNT, *Mrs.* A. *See* Hunt, M. R.
HUNT, H. M. *See* Jackson, H. M.
HUNT, L. Romances of real life. 2 vols...
....H941.1
HUNT, M. R. Barrington's fate...........H942.1
Issued also as Self-condemned.
Leaden casket..............................H942.2
HUNT, V. Hard woman...................H943.1
Maiden's progress.........................H943.2
Husbands and homes. Harland, M........H283.8
HUSSON-FLEURY, J. F. F. *See* Champ-
fleury, *pseud.*
HWA TSIEN KI. Flowery scroll: a Chinese
novel. Tr. by Sir J. Bowring.........H991.1
Hypatia. Kingsley, C....................K553.4

I. D. B. in South Africa. Sheldon, L. V........
....S544.1
I have lived and loved. Forrester, *Mrs.*....F730.5
"I say No." Collins, W....................C713.16
Ia. Couch, A. T. Q.......................C853.5
IBSEN, H. Nora's return: a sequel to "The
doll's house" of Henry Ibsen, by E. D.
Cheney....................................C518.1
Ice desert. Verne, J.......................V531.13
Iceland fishermen. Loti, P.................L883.3
Ida Craven. Cadell, J.....................C122.1
Idalia. Ouida..............................O934.11
Ideala. Grand, S...........................G751.2
Iduna, and other stories. Hibbard, G. A.....
....H624.1
Iermola. Kraszewski, J. I.................K893.1
'Ilâm-en-Nâs. Tr. by A. M. Clerk.........C631.1
Ilka on the hill-top, and other stories.
Boyesen, H. H...........................B791.4
Illustrations of lying. 85 pp. Opie, A...*in* O614.3
Illustrious Dr. Mathéus. Erckmann, E.,
and Chatrian, A........................E654.10
Illustrious Gaudissart. 57 pp. Balzac, H. de
....*in* B198.14
Image of his father. Mayhew H., *and* A.
S...M469.1
Imaginary mistress. 59 pp. Balzac, H. de
....*in* B198.44
Imaginary portraits. Pater, W...........Q295.2
IMMERMANN, K. Wonders in the Spes-
sart. 17 pp.............................*in* O983.1
Immortal, The. Daudet, A.................D238.3
Imogen. Holt, E. S........................H758.2
Impending sword. Yates, E...............Y317.4
Imperative duty. Howells, W. D..........H859.17
Improvisatore. Andersen, H. C...........A544.1
Impudent comedian, and others. Moore,
F. F..M820.5
In a country town. Noble A. L...........N747.2
In a dike shanty. Pool, M. L.............Q821.7
In a hollow of the hills. Harte, B........H337.18
In a house-boat. Mulock, D. M......*in* M960.17
In a north country village. Francis, M.
E...F819.2
In a winter city. Ouida...................O934.12
In all shades. Allen, G....................A425.9
In all time of our tribulation. Holt, E. S...
....H758.3
In black and white. Kipling, R......*in* K575.13
In blue uniform. Putnam, G. I...........Q980.1
In change unchanged. Villari, L.........V722.1
In Colston's days. Marshall, E...........M367.4
In convent walls. Holt, E. S..............H758.4

In deacon's orders, and other stories. Besant, Sir W...............................B554.17
In exile, and other stories. Foote, M. H...F689.5
In extremis. Greenough, S. D.............G815.2
In far Dakota. Locke, M...................L814.1
In far Lochaber. Black, W.................B627.11
In four reigns. Marshall, E.........M367.5
In Glenoran. Fife, M. B...................F469.1
In her earliest youth. Tasma.............T199.1
In His name. Hale, E. E..................H161.7
In homespun. Nesbit, E....................N458.3
In love with the czarina. Jokai, M.........J745.5
In low relief. Roberts, M.................R647.1
In Maremma. Ouida..........................O934.13
In old New England. Butterworth, H...B989.1
In old Quinnebasset. May, S...............M467.1
In old St. Stephens. Drake, J............D761.1
In ole Virginia. Page, T. N...............Q133.6
In Paradise. 2 vols. Heyse, P.............H621.2
In prison and out. Stretton, H............S915.6
In pursuit of happiness. Tolstoi, Count
L. N.......................................T654.4
In quarters with the 25th Dragoons. Winter, J. S............................in W785.1
In search of quiet. Frith, W..............F920.1
In search of the castaways. Verne, J...V531.24
In sight of the goddess. Davis, H. R.....D261.1
In silk attire. Black, W..................B627.12
In the Camargue. Bowles, E................B787.1
In the Carquinez woods. Harte, B......H327.19
In the clouds. Craddock, C. E.............C884.6
In the day of adversity. Burton, J. B...B973.9
In the distance. Lathrop, G. P............L354.3
In the east country. Marshall, E.........M367.6
In the fire of the forge. 2 vols. Ebers,
G..E165.9
In the golden days. Lyall, E..............L981.b
In the heart of the storm. Gray, M......G781.5
In the king's country. Douglas, A. M...
....D734.13
In the middle watch. Russell, W. C.....R968.7
In the midst of alarms. Barr, R...........B269.1
In the olden time. Roberts, M.............R646.5
In the sanctuary. Van der Naillen, A...V238.1
In the Schillingscourt. Marlitt, E......W817.14
In the sixties. Frederic, F...............F852.3
In the "stranger people's" country. Craddock, C. E...............................C884.7
In the Tennessee mountains. Craddock,
C. E.......................................C884.8
In the valley. Frederic, H................F852.4
In the valley of Havilah. Clark, F. T....C592.1
In the valley of Tophet. Nevinson, H.
W..N528.4

In the wake of King James. O'Grady, S....
....O357.2
In the wire-grass. Pendleton, L...........Q398.1
In the year of jubilee. Gissing, G........G535.3
In trust. Douglas, A. M...................D734.14
In varying moods. Harraden, B............H296.3
In war time. Mitchell, S. W...............M681.1
INCHBALD, E. S. Nature and art...in **B232.27
Simple story...........................**B232.28
Independence. Alcott, L. M.............in A355.4
Indian summer. Howells, W. D...........H859.18
Indiana. Sand, G..........................S213.7
Indiscretion of the duchess. Hope, A...H791.15
Inez. Wilson, A. J. E.....................W746.3
Infanta at Presburg. Gore, C. G......in G666.1 3
Infelice. Wilson, A. J. E.................W746.4
Infernal marriage, The. Disraeli, B...in D613.1
Infidel, The. 2 vols. Bird, R. M.........B618.1
Influence. Mackarness, M. A...............M153.1
INGELOW, J. Don John......................I464.1
Fated to be free.......................I464.2
John Jerome............................I464.3
Motto changed..........................I464.4
Off the Skelligs.......................I464.5
Sarah de Berenger......................I464.6
Studies for stories....................I464.7
INGEMANN, B. S. Aged rabbi. All Souls'
Day. Death ship..................in B979.1 3
Doomed house. Secret witness....in B979.1 1
Ingénue. Dumas, A.........................D886.21
Ingham papers. Hale, E. E.................H161.8
Ingo. Freytag, G..........................F895.2
Ingraban. Freytag, G......................F895.3
INGRAHAM, J. H. Pillar of fire; or, Israel
in bondage.............................I543.3
Prince of the house of David...........I543.1
Throne of David........................I543.2
Inheritance. Ferrier, S. E................F391.2
Initial experience, etc. King, C.........K523.15
Initials. Tautphœus, J. M. Freiherrin
von..T229.3
Inner house. Besant, Sir W.........in B554.16
Same...................................B554.19
Innocent. Oliphant, M. O. W...............O475.18
Innocent imposter, etc. Gray, M.........G781.6
Inside. Baker, W. M.......................B169.3
Inside the bar. Melville, G. J. W-...in M530.23
Same................................in **M530.30
Interloper. Peard, F. M...................Q359.6
Interpreter, The. Melville, J. G. W——...M530.17
Same...................................in **M530.9
Into the highways and hedges. Montrésor,
F. F.......................................M811.2

Invaders, and other stories. Tolstoi, *Count*
L. N...T654.5
Invasion, The. Griffin, G....................G851.4
Invasion of France in 1814. Erckmann, E.,
and Chatrian, A............................E654.11
Invisible empire. Tourgée, A. W..........T727.6
Invisible eye. Erckmann, E., *and* Chatrian,
A..*in* E654.2
Invisible lodge. Richter, J. P. F..........R535.4
Invisible spy. Haywood, E........ *in* **N938.23
Involuntary experimentalist. 17 pp.....*in* T143.6
Same..*in* T143.6²
IOTA (*pseud. of* Mrs. M. Caffyn). Yellow
aster..I645.1
Ireland. Martineau, H................*in* **M385.7
Ireland's dream. 2 vols. Lyon, E. D......L990.1
Irene, the missionary. De Forest, J. W...D315.2
Irish idylls. Barlow, J.........................B258.3
Irish fireside stories..........................I686.1
IRON, R., *pseud. See* Schreiner, O.
Iron game. Keenan, H. F...................K267.1
Iron mask. Dumas, A..........................D886.22
Iron master. Ohnet, G........................O383.3
Irralie's bushranger. Hornung, E. W....H816.2
IRVING, J. T. (J. Quod, *pseud.*) The attor-
ney..I723.1
Harry Harson...................................I723.2
IRVING, WASHINGTON. (Geoffrey Crayon,
pseud.) The Alhambra....................I725.1
Bracebridge Hall..............................I725.2
Crayon miscellany No. 3: Legends of the
conquest of Spain........................**I725.4
Sketch-book...................................I725.6
Tales of a traveler.............................I725.7
Wolfert's Roost, and other papers........I725.8
—*joint author. See* Irving, William.
IRVING, WILLIAM, Paulding, J. K., *and*
Irving, W. Salmagundi...................I726.1
Is he Popenjoy? Trollope, A..............T846.14
Is it possible? Van Anderson, H..........V217.1
Is that all? Preston, H. W...................Q927.2
Is this your son, my lord? Gardener, H.
H...G218.1
ISAACS, A. S. Stories from the rabbis......I731.1
ISAACS, J. Maria: a South American
romance I733.1
Isabel of Bavaria. Dumas, A..............D886.23
Ishmaelite, An. Braddon, M. E..........B798.15
ISLA, J. F. History of the famous preacher,
Friar Gerund de Campazas. 2 vols.....I821.1
Island nights' entertainments. Stevenson,
R. L...S848.3
Isle in the water. Tynan, K.............. T987.1

Ismay's children. Laffan, M.................L163.3
It is the fashion. Auer, A. von............A917.1
Italians, The. Elliot, F.......................E465.1
Itinerant house, and other stories. Daw-
son, E. F....................................D271.3
Ivan de Biron. Helps, *Sir* A................H484.2
Ivan Graham. Thompson, L................T473.3
Ivan Ilyitch, and other stories. Tolstoi,
Count L. N..................................T654.6
Ivanhoe. Scott, *Sir* W..............*in* **S431.13
Same S431.28
Ivar the viking. Du Chaillu, P. B..........D826.5
Ivory gate. Besant, *Sir* W.................B554.18
Ixion in heaven. Disraeli, B...........*in* D613.1
JACK *the shepherd, pseud.* Dicky Dawkins;
or, the bookmaker of the outer ring...
16 pp.......................................*in* T143.24
Jack. Daudet, A..............................D238.4
Jack Chaloner. Grant, J.....................G761.21
Jack Hinton. Lever, C........................L658.14
Jack Horner. Tiernan, M. S...............T564.1
Jack Manly. Grant, J..........................G761.22
Jack Sheppard. Ainsworth, W. H.........A297.9
Jack the fisherman. Phelps, E. S.........Q539.9
Jack Tier. Cooper, J. F......................C777.16
Same ....*in* C777.44
Jack's courtship. Russell, W. C............R968.8
JACKSON, H. M. (Saxe Holm, *pseud.*)
Between whiles..............................J127.1
Hetty's strange history......................J127.2
Mercy Philbrick's choice....................J127.3
Ramona.......................................J127.4
Saxe Holm's stories. 1st and 2d ser. 2
vols...J127.5
Zeph...J127.6
Jacob Faithful. Marryat, *Capt.* F.........M362.5
JACOBI, M. P. Martyr to science. 46 pp...
....*in* S884.2
Jacquerie, The. James, G. P. R............J276.23
Jacques Bonneval. Manning, A............M283.3
JAMES, *Mrs.* F. A. P. *See* Warden, F.,
pseud.
JAMES, G. P. R. Agincourt...................J276.1
Aims and obstacles. (*Also*) The fate.
Henry Smeaton. Margaret Graham.
(*And*) Last of the fairies...............J276.41
Ancient régime: a tale. 3 vols............J276.2
Issued also as Castelneau.
Arabella Stuart. 3 vols.................**J276.3
Attila. (*Also*) My aunt Pontypool.....J276.4
Beauchamp. (*Also*) Castle of Ehren-
stein. (*And*) Pequinillo...............J276.5
Bertrand de la Croix; or, the siege of
Rhodes..................................*in* Q594.1

JAMES, G. P. R.—Continued.

Castelneau; or, the ancient régime...**J276.2
    Issued also as The ancient régime.
Castle of Ehrenstein......................in J276.5
The cavalier.......................................J276.7
Charles Tyrrell.................................J276.8
The convict.......................................J276.9
Corse de Leon..................................J276.10
Darnley..J276.11
Delaware; or, the ruined family........J276.12
    Issued also as "Thirty years since."
De l'Orme...J276.13
Desultory man...................................J276.14
Eva St. Clair, and other collected tales...
    ....J276.15
The fate.......................................in J276.41
Forest days.......................................J276.16
Gentleman of the old school............J276.17
The gipsy..J276.18
Gowrie; or, the king's plot...............J276.19
Henry Masterton...............................J276.20
Henry of Guise.................................J276.21
Henry Smeaton: a Jacobite story of the
    reign of George the First............in J276.41
The Huguenot...................................J276.22
The jacquerie....................................J276.23
John Marston Hall............................J276.24
King's highway..................................J276.25
Last of the fairies.........................in J276.41
Leonora d'Orco.................................J276.26
Lord Montagu's page. 3 vols............J276.27
Man at arms.....................................J276.28
Margaret Graham..............................J276.29
Same...in J276.41
Mary of Burgundy; or, the revolt of
    Ghent...J276.30
Morley Ernstein J276.31
My aunt Pontypool.......................in J276.4
Norfolk and Hereford...................in S637.2
Old Dominion...................................J276.32
Pequinillo.....................................in J276.5
Philip Augustus................................J276.33
Richelieu J276.34
Rose d'Albret...................................J276.35
Russell: a tale of the reign of Charles
    II... J276.36
Step-mother......................................J276.37
Ticonderoga; or, the black eagle........J276.38
Whim and its consequences................J276.39
Woodman...J276.40
JAMES, H., Jr. The American J277.1
Aspern papers. (Also) Louisa Pallant.
    (And) Modern warning...................J277.2
Author of Beltraffio. (Also) Pandora.

JAMES, H., Jr.—Continued.

Georgiana's reasons.   Path of duty.
    (And) Four meetings.......................J277.3
Bostonians J277.4
Brooksmith..in J277.8
Collaboration...................................in J277.22
Confidence..J227.5
Embarrassments....................:...........J277.6
Europeans..J277.7
Four meetings...............................in J277.3
Georgina's reasons.......................in J277.3
Lesson of the master. (Also) The mar-
    riages. The pupil. Brooksmith. The
    solution. (And) Sir Edmund Orme....J277.8
The liar...in J277.9
A light man. 47 pp....................... in S884.5
A London life. (Also) The Patagonia.
    The liar. (And) Mrs. Temperly..........J277.9
Lord Beaupré.................................in J277.13
Louisa Pallant.................................in J277.2
The marriages.................................in J277.8
Mrs. Temperly.............. ....in J277.9
Modern warning........... ....in J277.2
The other house......... ....J277.23
Owen Wingrave..............................in J277.22
Pandora..in J277.3
A passionate pilgrim, and other tales...J277.10
The Patagonia.................................in J277.9
Path of duty....................................in J277.3
Pension Beaurepas.........................in J277.17
Point of view.................................in J277.17
Portrait of a lady.............. ....J277.11
Princess Casamassima J277.12
The private life. (Also) Lord Beaupré.
    (And) The visits............................J277.13
The pupil ....in J277.8
Real thing, and other stories.............J277.14
The Reverberator..............................J277.15
Roderick Hudson...............................J277.16
Siege of London. (Also) Pension Beau-
    repas. (And) Point of view J277.17
Sir Edmund Orme...........................in J277.8
The solution...................................in J277.8
Spoils of Poynton............................J277.24
Terminations....................................J277.18
Tragic muse. 2 vols..........................J277.19
The visits.....................................in J277.13
Washington square...........................J277.20
Watch and ward................................J277.21
Wheel of time. (Also) Collaboration.
    (And) Owen Wingrave...................J277.22
James Montjoy. Roe, A. S..................R698.2
James the Second. Ainsworth, W. H...A297.10
JAMISON, C. V. Story of an enthusiast...J327.1

Jan Vedder's wife. Barr, A. E..............B268.12
Jane Eyre. Brontë, C.....................B870.1
Jane Field. Wilkins, M. F..................W684.5
Jane Seton. Grant, J...................G761.23
Jane Sinclair. Carleton, W.................C281.7
Same........................... C281.8
Jane Talbot. Brown, C. B.................B879.3
Janet's repentance. Eliot, G............*in* E426.8
JANSON, K. N. Spell-bound fiddler: a
Norse romance......................J355.2
JANVIER, T. A. (Ivory Black, *pseud.*)
Aztec treasure-house....................J358.1
Color studies, and, A Mexican cam-
paign...............................J358.3
A Mexican campaign..............*in* J358.3
Pancha: a story of Monterey. 39 pp...
...........................*in* S884.10
Stories of old new Spain..... ....J358.6
Uncle of an angel and other stories.....J358.7
Japhet in search of a father. Marryat,
Capt. F............................M362.6
JARBOE, *Mrs.* M. T. *See* Brainerd, T. H.
JARVES, J. J. Kiana: a tradition of Ha-
waii...............................J384.1
JARVIS, T. S. Geoffrey Hampstead........J385.1
Jason Edwards. Garland, H................G233.1
JAUFRE, *Chevalier*. Geoffrey the knight:
a tale of chivalry of the days of King
Arthur.............................J413.1
JAY, H. (*Mrs. Buchanan*). Dark colleen...J421.1
JAY, W. M. L. Shiloh...................J424.1
JEAFFRESON, J. C. Not dead yet J432.1
Jealousy. Sand, G.....................S213.8
Jean Téterol's idea. Cherbuliez, V.........C521.2
Jeanie's quiet life. Tabor, E...............T114.3
JEFFERY, W., *joint author*. *See* Becke, L.
Jemmy and Jenny Jessamy. Haywood, E...
........................*in* **N938.17
JENKIN, *Mrs.* C. *See* Jenkin, H. C.
JENKIN, H. C. Jupiter's daughters........J525.1
Psyche of to-day.....................J525.2
Skirmishing........................J525.3
"Who breaks—pays.".................J525.4
Within an ace.......................J525.5
JENKINS, E. Little Hodge..................J527.1
Paladin of finance....................J527.2
JENNER, G. A philanthropist: a tale of the
vigilance committee at San Francisco.
40 pp.........................*in* T143.24
JENNINGS, H. One of the thirty (pieces of
silver for which Jesus Christ was sold)....
...............................J544.1
JERDAN, W. Sleepless woman..........*in* Q594.1
Jericho road. Habberton, J.................H113.6

JEROME, J. K. John Ingerfield, and other
stories..............................J565.1
Told after supper.....................J565.5
JERROLD, D. St. Giles and St. James J566.2
Story of a feather. (*And*) Cakes and ale..J566.3
Jerry. Elliott, S. B....................E467.2
Jerry the dreamer. Payne, W............Q346.1
"Jess." Haggard, H. R..................H146.7
Jessamine. Harland, M..................H283.9
Jessie Cameron. Butler, *Lady* R..........B985.1
Jessie Graham. Holmes, M. J..........*in* H751.6
Jessie Trim. Farjeon, B. L...............F229.7
JESSOP, G. H. Emergency men.........*in* S885.4
Gerald Ffrench's friends....................J585.1
Judge Lynch.........................J585.2
—*joint author*. *See* Matthews, B.
Jesus Christ in Flanders. 28 pp. Balzac,
H. de..........................*in* B198.33
Same..........................*in* B198.34
Jewel in the lotos. Tincker, M. A........T587.4
JEWETT, S. O. Country by-ways...........J593.3
Country doctor.......................J593.4
Country of the pointed firs................J593.19
Deephaven..........................J593.5
King of Folly island, and other people...J593.7
Life of Nancy.......................J593.8
A marsh island......................J593.9
Mate of the Daylight, and friends ashore...
.............................J593.10
Native of Winby, etc...................J593.11
Old friends and new...................J593.13
Strangers and wayfarers.................J593.15
Tales of New England..................J593.16
White heron, and other stories J593.18
Jews of Barnow. Franzos, K. E............ F837.2
Jill and Jack. Dillwyn, E. A...........D580.1
Jim Skaggs of Skaggsville. Legif, L.......L514.1
Joan. Broughton, R...................B877.4
Joan the maid. Charles, E. R............C476.9
Joe Thompson. Kimber, E...........*in* **N938.12
Johannes Olaf. Wille, E. de..............W698.1
JOHN, E. *See* Marlitt, E., *pseud.*
John. Oliphant, M. O. W................O475.19
John. Woods, K. P......................W895.4
John Andross. Davis, *Mrs.* R. H..........D263.5
John Bodewin's testimony. Foote, M. H....
.............................F689.6
John Brent. Winthrop, T..................W793.3
John Charaxes. Boylston, P..............B793.1
John Dorrien. Kavanagh, J...............K212.6
John Eax. Tourgée, A. W...............T727.8
John Godfrey's fortunes. Taylor, B......T238.3
John Gray. Allen, J. L..................A427.5

John Halifax, Gentleman. Mulock, D.
M..M960.12
John Halsey. Reed, C........................R323.1
John Ingerfield, and other stories. Jerome,
    J. K..J565.1
John Inglesant. Shorthouse, J. H.........S559.3
John Jerome. Ingelow, J....................I464.3
John Law. Ainsworth, W. H............A297.11
John March, southerner. Cable, G. W...C115.7
John Marchmont's legacy. Braddon, M.
    E...B798.16
John Marston Hall. James, G. P. R......J276.24
John Milton and his times. Ring, M....R581.1
John Needham's double. Hatton, J......H366.1
John Paget. Elliott, S. B.....................E467.3
John Parmelee's curse. Hawthorne, J...
    .... H398.10
John Rintoul; or, the fragment of a wreck...
    ....in T143.6
Same...in T143.6 ¹
John Thompson, and other stories. Parr,
    L...Q258.6
John Ward, preacher. Deland, M.........D337.3
John Winter. Garrett, E......................G239.9
John Worthington's name. Benedict, F.
    L...B463.2
JOHNSON, Col. The white fawn: a North
    American story. 10 pp................in J737.1
Same..in T559.1
JOHNSON, H. K. Raleigh Westgate.....J675.1
JOHNSON, S. Rasselas, Prince of Abis-
    sinia.......................................** B232.26
Same......................................in C615.1
Same.. J692.1
Same ....in ** N938.23
JOHNSON, V. W. Fainalls of Tipton......J695.1
    Image of San Donato. 35 pp.......in S884.7
JOHNSTON, C. Chrysal; or, the adventures
    of a guinea. 4 vols. (in 2.)..........J723.1-2
JOHNSTON, H. Doctor Congalton's leg-
    acy..J725.1
JOHNSTON, R. M. Dukesborough tales:
    the chronicles of Mr. Bill Williams...J733.3
    Mr. Absalom Billingslea, and other Geor-
    gian folk. J733.5
    Ogeechee cross-firings.......................J733.7
    Old Mark Langston............................J733.8
    Primes and their neighbors: ten tales of
    middle Georgia.............................J733.9
    Widow Guthrie................................J733.11
JOHNSTONE, C. I. Experiences of Richard
    Taylor. Mrs. Mark Luke..........in J737.1
    Sabbath night's supper. 12 pp......in T559.1

JOHNSTONE, C. I.,—cd. Standard tales by
    standard authors...........................J737.1
    CONTENTS: Johnstone, C. I. Experiences
    of Richard Taylor, Esq. Mrs. Mark Luke.
    Sabbath night's supper.—Fraser, Mrs. The
    cousins.—Nicander, K. A. The renounced
    treasure.—Gore, C. Maid of honour.—Quil-
    linan, E. Rangers of Connaught.--Tieck. L.
    The elves.—Mitford, M. R. Freshwater fish-
    erman.—Crowe, C. Story of Martha Guinnis
    and her son.—Tytler, M. F. The deformed.
    —Johnson, Col. The white fawn.—Howitt,
    W. Johnny Darbyshire.—Lauder, Sir T. D.
    Story of Farquharson of Inverey.
JOKAI, M. Black diamonds..................J745.1
    Eyes like the sea................................J745.3
    Green book.......................................J745.4
    In love with the czarina, etc...............J745.5
    Modern Midas..................................J745.7
    The plague.............................in Z767.1 ¹
    "There is no devil."...........................J745.9
    Timar's two worlds...........................J745.10
Jonathan. Tytler, C. C. F....................T996.1
Jonathan Wild the Great. Fielding, H...F459.3
    Same ....in ** N938.9
JONES, A. I. Beatrice of Bayou Têche.....J767.1
JONES, C. H. Davault's mills.................J774.1
JONES, E. Latter-day saint....................J775.1
JONES, J. B. Rival belles.....................J778.1

    Issued also as Spanglers and tinglers.
    Wild western scenes: adventures of
    Daniel Boone...............................J778.2
JONSON, B. Every man in his humor. 39
    pp...M875.1 ¹
Joost Avelingh. Maartens, M..............M111.6
José and Benjamin. Delitzsch, F...........D355.1
Joseph and his friend. Taylor, B..........T238.4
Joseph Andrews. Fielding, H..........** B232.18
    Same.....................................F459.1
    Same...................................... ** N938.1
Joseph Balsamo. Dumas, A...............D886.30 ²
Joseph in the snow. Auerbach, B..........A918.7
Joseph II. and his court. Mühlbach, L....M952.10
Joseph's coat. Murray, D. C.................M981.5
Joshua. Ebers, G...............................E165.10
Joshua Haggard's daughter. Braddon, M.
    E.. B798.17
Journey from this world to the next.
    Fielding, H....................................in F459.3
    Same.................................in ** N938.12
Journey to the centre of the earth. Verne,
    J...V531.25
Journey to the world underground. Klimius,
    N...K635.1
Joy after sorrow. Riddell, C. E. L........R543.8
Joy of life. Wolf, E.............................W854.3

Joyce. Oliphant, M. O. W...............O475.20
Joyce Morrell's harvest. Holt, E. S......H758.5
JUAN MANUEL, *prince*. Count Lucanor; or, the fifty pleasant stories of Patronio...J912.1
Juana. 82 pp. Balzac, H. de..............B198.41
JUDD, S. Margaret........................J923.1
  Richard Edney and the governor's family...........................J923.2
Judge Lynch. Jessop, G. H............J585.2
Judith Shakespeare. Black, W.......B627.13
JUDSON, *Mrs.* E. C. *See* Chubbuck, E.
Juggernaut. Eggleston, G. C., *and* Marbourg, D.........................E295.2
Julia de Roubigné. Mackenzie, H... **B232.29
Julian. 2 vols. Ware, W.................W273.2
Julius Courtney. Cobban, J. M.........C653.1
JUNCKER, E. (*Mrs. Schmieden*). Margarethe; or, life-problems. Tr. by A. L. Wister.........................W817.7
Jupiter lights. Woolson, C. F.........W916.8
Jupiter's daughters. Jenkin, H. C........J525.1
Kafir stories. Scully, W. C.............S437.1
Kalani of Oahu. Newell, C. M.........N544.1
Kaloolah. Mayo, W. S..................M473.2
Karma. Sinnett, A. P..................S617.1
KARR, A. Visit to the arsenal. 24 pp...*in* R657.1
Kate Beaumont. De Forest, J. W........D315.3
Kate Carnegie. Watson, J...............W339.10
Kate Coventry. Melville, G. J. W-....M530.18
  Same........................**M530.19
Katerfelto. Melville, G. J. W-........M530.20
  Same........................**M530.21
Katharine Lauderdale. 2 vols. Crawford, F. M............................C899.9
Katharine North. Pool, M. L..........Q821.8
Katharine Regina. Besant, *Sir* W......B554.21
  Same........................*in* B554.30
Katharine von Bora. Stein, A.........S819.1
Katharine Walton. Simms, W. G.......S592.9
Kathleen mavourneen. Burnett, F. H..*in* B964.4
Kathleen mavourneen. Mulholland, C...M955.1
Katia. Tolstoi, *Count* L. N..............T654.7
Katie Stewart. Oliphant, M. O. W......O475.21
Katy of Catoctin. Townsend, G. A......T748.2
KAVANAGH, J. Adèle....................K212.1
  Beatrice..............................K212.2
  Bessie...............................K212.3
  Daisy Burns...........................K212.4
  Grace Lee.............................K212.5
  John Dorrien..........................K212.6
  Madeleine: a tale of Auvergne.........K212.7
  Nathalie..............................K212.8
  Queen Mab.............................K212.9
  Rachel Gray...........................K212.10

KAVANAGH. J.—*Continued.*
  Seven years, and other tales..........K212.11
  Silvia................................K212.12
  Sybil's second love...................K212.13
  Two lilies............................K212.14
Kavanagh. Longfellow, H. W...........L853.1
KEARY, A. Castle Daly.................K241.1
  Oldbury...............................K241.2
KEDDIE, H. *See* Tytler, S., *pseud.*
KEELER, R. Gloverson and his silent partners..........................K264.1
Keena Karmody. Kerr, E...............K411.1
KEENAN, H. F. Iron game..............K267.1
  Money-makers..........................K267.2
KEIGHTLEY, S. R. The cavaliers.........K273.1
  Crimson sign..........................K273.2
  Last recruit of Clare's...............K273.6
KELLER, G. The funeral. Clothes make men............................*in* Z767.1 ²
KELLY, H. Memoirs of a Magdalen; or, Louisa Mildmay....................*in* **N938.7
Kellys and the O'Kellys. Trollope, A...
  ....T846.15
KENDALL, M. 'Such is life.'............K333.1
KENEALY, A. Dr. Janet of Harley street...
  ....K334.1
Kenelm Chillingly. Lytton, E. G. E. L. Bulwer-.........................L998.11
Kenilworth. Scott, *Sir* W.............S431.30
  Same...............................S431.31
  Same...............................**S431.32
KENNEDY, J. P. Horse-shoe Robinson: a tale of the Tory ascendency.......K353.1
  Quodlibet.............................K353.2
  Rob of the bowl: a legend of St. Inigoe's.............................K353.3
  Swallow Barn..........................K353.4
KENT, W. C. Vision of Cagliostro. 42 pp.............................*in* T143.5
  Same..............................*in* T143.5 ²
Kentuckian in New York. 2 vols. Neal, J..................................**N341.2
Kentucky cardinal. Allen, J. L.........A427.7
Kentucky colonel. Read, O. P...........R284.2
Kentucky's love. King, E...............K526.2
KENYON, E. C. The stranger-artist......K375.2
—*joint author. See* Soans, R. G.
Kéraban the inflexible. 2 pts. Verne, J...
  ....V531.26
KERR, E. Keena Karmody. (*Also*) Mervyn's meed.........................K411.1
Kerrigan's quality. Barlow, J..........B258.5

KERSLEREN, J. C. VAN. Blue dragoon: a story of circumstantial evidence, from the criminal records of Holland. 38 pp.................................*in* T143.15

KEYSER, A. Exile's romance; or, realities of Australian life............................K445.1

Khaled: a tale of Arabia. Crawford, F. M...C899.10

Kiana. Jarves, J. J...............................K384.1

Kidnapped. Stevenson, R. L.............S848.4

KIELLAND, A. L. Battle of Waterloo. 14 pp.................................*in* V629.1

Siesta...............................*in* M690.1

Tales of two countries....................K473.1

Kildhurm's oak. Hawthorne, J.......H398.11

Kilmeny. Black, W......................B627.15

KIMBALL, R. B. Henry Powers, (banker)..K492.1

Romance of student life abroad........K492.2

KIMBER, E. Joe Thompson........*in* **N938.12

KING, C. An army Portia..............*in* K523.21

Between the lines.........................K523.3

Campaigning with Crook, and stories of army life...................................K523.5

Captain Blake.............................K523.6

The colonel's Christmas dinner, etc.....K523.7

The colonel's daughter; or, winning his spurs...............................K523.8

The deserter, and, From the ranks......K523.9

Dunraven ranch.....................*in* K523.25

Foes in ambush..........................K523.11

From the ranks.........................*in* K523.9

An initial experience, etc..............K523.15

Kitty's conquest.........................K523.17

Laramie...................................K523.18

Marion's faith. Sequel to "The colonel's daughter."...............................K523.19

Soldier's secret. And, An army Portia...
...................................K523.21

Starlight ranch, and other stories of army life on the frontier..............K523.22

Story of Fort Frayne....................K523.12

Tame surrender...........................K523.23

Trumpeter Fred..........................K523.24

Two soldiers. *And*, Dunraven ranch...
....K523.25

Under fire................................K523.26

War-time wooing.........................K523.27

Waring's peril...........................K523.28

KING, CLARENCE. (?) Democracy: an American novel.........................K524.1

KING, E. Gentle savage..................K526.1

Kentucky's love; or, roughing it around Paris.....................................K526.2

KING, G. Balcony stories... ....K527.1

Tales of a time and place...............K527.3

KING, R. A. (Basil, *pseud.*) Passion's slave.....................................K543.1

"Wearing of the green."................K543.2

King and a few dukes. Chambers, R. W...C445.3

King and viking. Smyth, P. G............S667.1

King Arthur. Mulock, D. M............M960.13

King Capital. Sime, W...................S589.2

King Noanett. Stimson, F. J.............S859.3

King of Folly Island, and other people. Jewett, S. O..............................J593.7

King of the conjurors. Borlase, J. S......B735.1

King of the mountains. About, E........A156.1

King of the schnorrers. Zangwill, I.....Z295.5

King of the tigers. Rousselet, L.........R866.2

King of Tyre. Ludlow, J. M.............L945.2

King Solomon's mines. Haggard, H. R...H146.8

King Solomon's wives. Ragged, H......R142.1

King's highway. James, G. P. R........H276.25

Kings in exile. Daudet, A...............D238.5

King's lesson. 13 pp. Morris, W....*in* M877.4

King's men. Grant, R., *and others*......G763.12

King's own. Marryat, *Capt.* F.........M362.7

King's Own Borderers. Grant, J.........G761.24

King's stratagem, and other stories. Weyman, S. J...............................W549.7

King's treasure house. Walloth, W.......W215.1

KINGSBURY, A. *See* Cooley, A. K.

KINGSFORD, J., *pseud. See* Barnard, C.

KINGSLEY, C. Alton Locke, tailor and poet.......................................K553.1

At last: a Christmas in the West Indies....
....K553.2

Hereward the Wake, 'last of the English.'......................................K553.3

Hypatia; or, new foes with an old face...K553.4

Two years ago............................K553.5

Westward ho! or, the voyages of Sir Amyas Leigh in the reign of Queen Elizabeth...............................K553.6

Yeast: a problem.........................K553.7

KINGSLEY, H. Austin Elliot.............K555.1

Geoffry Hamlyn..........................K555.9

The Harveys..............................K555.2

Hetty.....................................K555.3

Hillyars and the Burtons................K555.4

Hornby mills, and other stories.........K555.5

Leighton Court...........................K555.6

Old Margaret.............................K555.7

Ravenshoe................................K555.8

Recollections of Geoffry Hamlyn........K555.9

Silcote of Silcotes......................K555.10

Stretton..................................K555.11

KINGSLEY, M. Puerto de Medina. 37 pp.....................................*in* T143.20
KINGSTON, W. H. G. Count Ulrich......K558.1
KINKEL, G. A family feud. 34 pp...*in* T143.17
Kinley Hollow. Hollister, G. H.........H744.1
Kinsfolk and others. Roberts, M.........R646.6
Kintail Place. Paul, M. A....................Q324.1
KIP, L. Dead marquise...................K572 1
"——mas has come." 29 pp.........*in* S884.9
Under the bells............................K572.2
KIPLING, R. Courting of Dinah Shadd, and other stories.........................K575.2
In black and white.....................*in* K575.13
Life's handicap: being stories of mine own people...............................K575.5
Light that failed.......................K575.6
Man who would be king...............*in* S885.7
Many inventions...........................K575.7
Mine own people...........................K575.8
Issued also—with two exceptions—in collection entitled Life's handicap.
Phantom 'rickshaw, and other tales. (*Also*) Wee Willie Winkie, and other child stories.................................K575.10
Plain tales from the hills.................K575.11
Soldier stories...............................K575.16
Same. (Also) In black and white...K575.13
Story of the Gadsbys. (*Also*) Under the deodars K575.14
Under the deodars...................*in* K575.14
Wee Willie Winkie, and other child stories.................................*in* K575.10
—*and* Balestier, W. The naulahka: a story of west and east...........................K575.15
KIRBY, W. Chien d'Or, the golden dog: a legend of Quebec.....................K582.1
Issued also as The Golden dog.
KIRK, E. O. Better times: stories.........K593.2
Ciphers K593.3
Daughter of Eve...........................K593.4
Queen money...............................K593.6
Sons and daughters......................K593.8
Story of Margaret Kent...................K593.9
Through winding ways......... ....K593.10
KIRKE, E. (*pseud. of* J. R. Gilmore). Mountain-White heroine...............K594.2
KIRKLAND, C. M. (Mrs. M. Clavers,*pseud.*) Forest life. 2 vols...........................K598.1
A new home—who'll follow? or, glimpses of western life.............................K598.2
Western clearings.........................K598.3
KIRKLAND, J. The McVeys.................K597.1
Zury: the meanest man in Spring county K597.2

KIRSCHNER, L. *See* Schubin, O., *pseud.*
Kirsteen. Oliphant, M. O. W...............O475.22
Kismet. Fleming, G............................F597.2
Kissing the rod. Yates, E...................Y317.5
Kit and Kitty. Blackmore, R. D.........B629.8
Kith and kin. Fothergill, J...................F761.3
Kitty Craig. 71 pp. Holmes, M. J...*in* H751.3
Kitty's conquest. King, C...................K523.17
KLEIST, H. VON. Michael Kohlhaas. 66 pp. St. Cecilia. 9 pp...................*in* O983.1
KLIMIUS, N. (*pseud. of* L. *Freiherr* von Holberg). Journey to the world under ground..K635.1
KNAPP, A. One thousand dollars a day; studies in practical economics.........K672.1
Knapsack, The. Edgeworth, M.....*in* E235.18
Knight-errant. Lyall, E...................L981.10
Knight of Gwynne. 2 vols. Lever, C....L658.15
Knight of the nets. Barr, A. E............B268.14
Knight of the nineteenth century. Roe, E. P...R699.9
Knitters in the sun. Thanet, O............T367.4
KNORRING, S. M. Z. *Baroness* VON. The ancestress; or, family pride. 20 pp....
....*in* B979.1 [1]
The peasant and his landlord.............K725.1
KNOWLES, J. S. The wife. 34 pp.....*in* M875.1 [3]
KNOWLTON, J. A. Txleama...................K735.1
KNOX, *Mrs.* A. T. *See* Trafton, A.
KNOX, T. W. Siberian exiles...............K743.1
Kohala of Hawaii. Calhoun, A. R.........C152.1
KOMPERT, L. Silent woman.............*in* M690.1
Kophetua the Thirteenth. Corbett, J.....C790.5
KOROLENKO, V. Blind musician............K845.1
KOSTROMITIN, J. Last day of the carnival....
....K865.1
KOUNS, N. C. Arius the Libyan...........K883.1
KOVALEVSKY, S. Vera Vorontzoff........K887.1
KRASZEWSKI, J. I. The foundling...*in* Z767.1 [2]
Iermola...K893.1
Kriegspiel: the war game. Groome, F. H..G876.1
KRYPOW, *Dr.* Leka; or, reminiscences of a physician. 16 pp.....................*in* H496.1
LABADYE, A. DE. Baron of Hertz: a tale of the Anabaptists..........................L112.1
LABOULAYE, E. (R. Lefebvre, *pseud.*) Abdallah; or, the four-leaved shamrock....
....L124.1
Paris in America...............................L124.2
Labour stands on golden feet. Zschokke, H..Z923.2
LA BRETE, J. DE. My uncle and my curé..L126.1
Lace. Lindau, P...................................L742.1

Laconia. Scribner, J. P.............................S434.1
Ladies' gallery. McCarthy, J., *and* Praed,
R. Campbell-...................................M122.11
Ladies of Lone Leventhorpe. Linskill,
M...................................*in* L981.3
Lad's love. Bates, A.............................B329.4
Lady Adelaide. Wood, E. P...............W874.7
Lady Audley's secret. Braddon, M. E...B798.18
Lady Branksmere. Duchess.................D829.9
Lady-bird. Fullerton, *Lady* G..............F971.3
Lady Car. Oliphant, M. O. W...........O475.24
Lady Hester. Yonge, C. M................Y555.16
Lady Judith. McCarthy, J....................M122.3
Lady Julia Mandeville, History of. Brooke,
F. M...................................**B232.27
Lady Lee's widowhood. Hamley, *Sir* E. B...
....H223.1
Lady Marabout's troubles. Ouida......*in* O934.4
Lady of Fort St. John. Catherwood,
M. H...................................C363.4
Lady of quality. Burnett, F. H............B964.10
Lady of the Aroostook. Howells, W. D...H859.20
Lady of the ice. De Mille, J................D381.6
Lady, or the tiger? and other stories.
Stockton, F. R...................................S866.17
Lady Sybil's choice. Holt, E. S..........H758.6
Lady Wedderburn's wish. Grant, J......G761.25
Lady Willoughby. Manning, A...........M283.4
Lady with the rubies. Marlitt, E.........W817.15
Lady's mile. Braddon, M. E.............B798.19
LAFFAN, M. (*Mrs. MacNabb*). Christy
Carew...................................L163.1
Flitters, Tatters, and the Counsellor, and
other sketches..................................L163.2
Ismay's children...................................L163.3
A singer's story...................................L163.4
Lajla. Friis, J. A...................................F913.1
Lakeville. Healy, M...................................H434.1
Lal. Hammond, W. A...................................H227.1
LAMARTINE, A. DE. Fior d'Aliza.........L217.1
Graziella: a story of Italian love........L217.2
My mother's manuscript.........L217.3
Raphael; or, pages of the book of life at
twenty L217.4
Stone-mason of Saint Point.............L217.5
Lame Jervas. Edgeworth, M.............**E235.6
Same...................................*in* E235.19
LA MOTTE FOUQUÉ, C. A., *Freiherrin* DE.
Castle on the beach. 39 pp........*in* C972.1 ²
LAMOTTE FOUQUÉ, F. H. K., *Freiherr* DE.
Field of terror. Mandrake. Head Mas-
ter Rhenfried and his family......*in* R794.1 ²
Four seasons. Undine. Two captains.
Sintram. Aslauga's knight.............L235.1
Issued also as Undine and other tales.

LA MOTTE FOUQUÉ, F. H. K. DR—*Continued.*
Magic ring: a knightly romance.........L235.2
Minstrel love L235.3
Sintram and his companions.............L235.4
Thiodolf the Icelander L235.5
Undine; or, the water-spirit. 52 pp....*in* S892.14
Same, and other tales.........L235.6
Issued also as Four seasons.
Lamplighter. Cummins, M. S.............C970.2
Lancashire witches. Ainsworth, W. H...A297.12
LANCASTER, A. E. "All's dross but love:"
a strange record of two reincarnated
souls. 64 pp...................................L244.1
Lances of Lynwood. Yonge, C. M......Y555.17
Land at last. Yates, E.........Y317.6
"Land of the sky." Reid, C...........R353.8
Land of the sun. Reid, C...................R353.9
LANDER, M. (*pseud. of* M. W. Lawrence.)
Marion Graham...................................L255.1
LANDERS, J. King Bemba's point.....*in* S885.1
Same...................................*in* T143.19
Story of James Barker: a tale of the
Congo coast. 68 pp...................*in* T143.23
Landlord at Lion's Head. Howells, W.
D...................................H859.34
LANE, E. W., *tr.* Thousand and one
nights; or, the Arabian nights' enter-
tainments. 2 vols...................A658.11
LANG, A. Monk of Fife...................L269.4
—*joint author. See* Haggard, H. R.
LANGBEIN, A. F. E. Albert Limbach.
Hour's instruction in political econ-
omy. Irreconcileable man. Lady's
palfrey. Marianne Richards. Seven
marriages and never a husband...*in* R794.1 ⁴
LANGHORNE, J. Letters between Theo-
dosius and Constantia...............*in* **N938.7
Solyman and Almena. 35 pp..........*in* **N938.2
LANIER, S. Tiger-lilies...................L287.1
Laodiceau, A. Hardy, T...................H272.11
Lapsed, but not lost. Charles, E. R.....C476.10
LA RAMÉE, L. DE. *See* Ouida, *pseud.*
Laramie. King, C...................................K523.18
LA ROCHERE, E. DE. (*pseud. of* E. Du-
theil.) Castle of Roussillon; or, Quercy
in the sixteenth century.................L328.1
Last abbot of Glastonbury. Crake, A. D...
....C888.8
Last day of the carnival. Kostromitin, J...
....K865.1
Last days of Pompeii. Lytton, E. G. E.
L. Bulwer-...................................L998.12
Last incarnation of Vautrin. Balzac, H.
de...................................*in* B198.17

Last love. Ohnet, G............................O383.4
Last mass. 28 pp. Besant, Sir W...*in* B554.16
Last meeting. Matthews, B...............M438.8
Last of the barons. Lytton, E. G. E. L.
Bulwer-...L998.13
Last of the fairies. James, G. P. R.....*in* J276.41
Last of the Macallisters. Barr, A. E....B268.15
Last of the Mohicans. Cooper, J. F...*in* C777.9
Same...C777.17
Last of the Mortimers. Oliphant, M. O.
W. O475.25
Last of the Plantagenets. Heseltine, W...
.... H584.1
Last recruit of Clare's. Keightley, S. R..K273.6
Last sentence. Gray, M........................G781.9
Last tenant. Farjeon, B. L...............F229.10
LASZOUSKI, *Mrs.* E. G. *See* Gerard, E.
Late for the train. 53 pp...............*in* T143.8
Late Mrs. Null. Stockton, F. R.........S866.18
LATHROP, G. P. Afterglow...............L354.1
Echo of passion L354.2
In the distance.................................L354.3
Newport...L354.4
Somebody else.................................L354.5
Two purse-companions. 38 pp......*in* S884.3
—*and* Rideing, W. H. Letter of credit...
....L354.6
LATIMER, E. W. My wife and my wife's
sister..L357.1
Latimer family. Arthur, T. S..............A791.2
Latreaumont. Sue, E.........................S944.2
Latter-day saint. Jones, E.................J775.1
LAUDER, *Sir* T. D. Story of Farquharson
of Inverey. 6 pp.....................*in* J737.1
Same.......................................*in* T559.1
Launcelot Greaves. Smollett, T. G....*in* **N938.9
Laura Everingham. Grant, J..............G761.26
Laurel bush. Mulock, D. M..............M960.14
Laurella. 41 pp. Heyse, P...........*in* I1621.3
Lavengro. Borrow, G.......................B737.1
Lavinia. Ruffini, G............................R923.1
Law and the lady. Collins, W...........C713.18
LAWLESS, *Hon.* E. Chelsea householder...
....L418.1
Grania: the story of an island...........L418.2
Maelcho... ....L418.3
LAWRENCE, G. A. Anteros.................L421.1
Barren honour...................................L421.2
Brakespeare L421.3
Breaking a butterfly..........................L421.4
Issued also as Blanche Ellerslie's ending.
Guy Livingstone.................................L421.5
Maurice Dering.................................L421.6
Sans merci..L421.7

LAWRENCE, *Mrs.* M. W. *See* Lander, M.,
pseud.
Lawton girl. Frederic, H....................F852.5
Lawyer's story. Maitland, J. A...........M232.2
LAZARUS, E. Alide: an episode of Goethe's
life..... ....L431.1
Lazy man's work. Sparhawk, F. C........S736.1
Lazy tour of two idle apprentices. Dick-
ens, C.......................................*in* D548.46
Leaden casket. Hunt, M. R................H942.2
Leafless spring. Schubin, O.................S384.3
Leaguer of Lathom. Ainsworth, W. H...A297.13
Leah. Edwardes, A.............................E254.3
Leah of Jerusalem. Berry, E. P............B534.1
Leal souvenir. Weber, A......................W373.1
LEAN, *Mrs.* F. M. *See* Marryat, F.
Lear of the steppe. 71 pp. Turgénieff, I.
S..*in* T936.11
Leather stocking and silk. Cooke, J. E....C772.8
Leavenworth case. Green, A. K...........G795.4
LE CLERC, M. E. Mistress Beatrice Cope;
or, passages in the life of a Jacobite's
daughter..L462.1
Led-Horse claim. Foote, M. H.............F689.8
LEE, H. Canterbury tales. 2 vols.......L478.1
LEE, M. C. Quaker girl of Nantucket.....L479.1
LEE, S. Canterbury tales....................L481.1
LEE, V. (*pseud. of* V. Paget). Hauntings:
fantastic stories.................................L482.1
Leech club. Owen, G. W....................O972.1
LE FANU, J. S. All in the dark.............L488.1
Guy Deverell.....................................L488.2
Lost name...L488.3
Tenants of Malory..............................L488.4
LEFÈBVRE, *Dr.* R. *See* Laboulaye, E.
LEFFINGWELL, W. B. Manulito............L493.1
LE GALLIENNE, R. Quest of the golden
girl L496.3
Legend of Montrose. Scott, *Sir* W.....*in* S431.7
Same ....*in* S431.12
Same ....*in* **S431.13
Same ....*in* S431.48
Legend of the large mouth, etc..............L510.1
Legends and stories of Ireland. Lover, S...L910.3
Legends of le Détroit. Hamlin, M. C. W...H224.1
Legends of the conquest of Spain. Irving,
W. **I725.4
Legends of the west. Hall, J...............H177.1
LEGIF, L. Jim Skaggs of Skaggsville.....L514.1
LEIGHTON, A. Burgher's tales: House in
Bell's Wynd; Ancient bureau. Law-
yer's tales: Woman with the white
mice. Detective's tales: Chance ques-
tion; Bride of Bell's Tower. Surgeon's

LEIGHTON, A.—*Continued.*

tales: The wager; Diamond eyes; Amateur robbery; Ten of diamonds..*in* W750.11

Contrast of wives. Surgeon's tales: The suicide; Three letters; Glass back. Mike Maxwell and the Gretna Green lovers..................*in* W750.6

Domestic griefs of Gustavus M'Iver. The avenger. Sportsman of Outfieldhaugh. Dominie of St. Fillan's. The heroine. Miser of Newabbey .... *in* W750.10

The Droich. Amateur lawyers. Harden's revenge. Surgeon's tales: The cherry-stone; The henwife; The artist... ....*in* W750.4

Hogmanay. Surgeon's tales: The bereaved; The condemned; The monomaniac. Hume and the governor of Berwick. Bride of Bramblehaugh. Laird Rorieson's will ....*in* W750.9

Kate Kennedy. Prescription; or, the 29th of September. Lord Durie and Christie's Will. Surgeon's tales: The cured ingrate.........................*in* W750.1

Lawyer's tales: Lord Kame's puzzle; Story of Mysie Craig. Burgher's tales: Brownie of the West Bow. Story of Mary Brown. Cradle of Logie. Story of the pelican. Girl forger. Two red slippers. Faithful wife. Romaunt of Sir Peregrine and the Lady Etheline. Legend of Allerley Hall. Legend of Lady Katharine. Ballad of Ailie Faa. Legend of the fair Emergilde. Romaunt of the castle of Weir. Romaunt of St. Mary's Wynd. Legend of Mary Lee. Ballad of age and youth. Legend of Craigullan. Ballad of Rumbollow. Legend of the burning of Mrs. Jamphray. Ballad of Ballogie's daughters. Legend of Dowielee. Ballad of Maid Marion. Ballad of Roseallan Castle. Ballad of the tournay. Ballad of golden counsel. Ballad of matrimony. Song of Rosalie. Ballad of the world's vanity.....................................*in* W750.12

Legend of fair Helen of Kirconnel. The abduction. Christie of the cleek. Romance of the siege of Perth. Caleb Crabbin. Crooked Comyn.........*in* W750.5

Old chronicler's tales: Death of James I.; Death of James III. Surgeon's tales: Case of evidence. Clerical murderer. Mr. Samuel Ramsey Thriven... ....*in* W750.8

LEIGHTON, A.—*Continued.*

Surgeon's tales: Conscience stricken; Somnambulist of Redcleugh. Duncan Schulebred's vision of judgment. Geordie Willison and the heiress of Castle Gower.....................*in* W750.3

Same: Diver and the bell. Royal raid. Maiden feast of Cairnkibbie. Linton lairds.................................*in* W750.2

Trials of Menie Dempster. Roscallan's daughter. Old chronicler's tales: Prince of Scotland. Legend of Holyrood..................................W750.7

Leighton Court. Kingsley, H.............K555.6

Leila. Lytton, E. G. E. L. Bulwer-.......L998.14

Len Gansett. Read, O. P...................R284.2

'Lena Rivers. Holmes, M. J.............H751.17

LENNOX, C. Female Quixote.......*in* **N938.12

Same. 2 vols **B232.24-5

Henrietta...............................*in* **N938.23

Lenox Dare. Townsend, V. F..............T751.4

LENZEN, M. (*Mrs. ten Brink*). Not in their set............................L575.1

Leon Pontifex. Greene, S. P. McL........G812.6

Leon Roch. 2 vols. Perez Galdós, B.....Q438.3

Leonard and Gertrude. Pestalozzi, J. H...Q476.1

Léonie. Lucas, A............................L932.1

Leonora. Edgeworth, M.............*in* **E235.5

Same E235.27

Leonora d'Orco. James, G. P. R..........J276.26

LE SAGE. A. R. Asmodeus; or, the devil on two sticks.........................L622.1

Issued also as Devil on two sticks.

Bachelor of Salamanca. 2 vols...........L622.2

Devil upon two sticks. Prefixed, Asmodeus's crutches, and dialogues between two chimneys of Madrid...........*in* **N938.2

Issued also as Asmodeus.

Gil Blas of Santillane.....................L622.3

Same. ....*in* **N938.4

LESPERANCE, J. The Bastonnais...........L637.1

Less black than we're painted. Payn, J...Q345.13

Lesser bourgeoisie. Balzac, H. de........B198.22

Lesson of the master. James, H., *Jr*......J277.8

Letter-bag of the Great Western. Haliburton, T. C...............................H172.3

Letter of credit. Lathrop, G. P., *and*, Rideing, W. H..............................L354.6

Letter of credit. Warner, S.................W284.4

Letters from Felicia to Charlotte. Collyer, J..................................*in* **N938.23

Letters of a Peruvian princess. Grafigny, F. de.................................*in* **N938.9

Letters of Julia and Caroline, etc. Edgeworth, M..............................*in* **E235.5

Letty Hyde's lovers. Grant, J..............G761.28
LEVER, C. Arthur O'Leary..............L658.1
Barrington..L658.2
Braulcighs of Bishop's Folly L658.3
Charles O'Malley, the Irish dragoon....L658.4
Con Cregan...L658.5
The Daltons..L658.6
Same. (Also) A day's ride................L658.7
Davenport Dunn. 2 vols...................L658.8
A day's ride...............................in L658.7
Same...L658.9
Dodd family abroad. 2 vols............L658.10
Fortunes of Glencore..........................L658.11
Harry Lorrequer...............................L658.12
Hero-worship and its dangers. 26 pp....
....in T143.14
Horace Templeton..........................L658.13
How Frank Thornton was cured. 42 pp...
....in T143.16
Jack Hinton, the guardsman............L658.14
Knight of Gwynne. 2 vols............L658.15
Lord Kilgobbin...............................L658.16
Luttrell of Arran............................L658.17
Martins of Cro' Martin..................L658.18
Maurice Tiernay............................L658.19
The O'Donoghue............................L658.20
     Issued also as Kate O'Donoghue.
One of them....................................L658.21
Rent in a cloud.......................in L658.25
Roland Cashel...............................L658.22
St. Patrick's eve.....................in L658.25
Sir Brook Fossbrooke....................L658.23
Sir Jasper Carew............................L658.24
Some one pays. 24 pp..............in T143.18
That boy of Norcott's. (Also) A rent
   in a cloud, and, St. Patrick's eve....L658.25
Tom Burke of "Ours."......................L658.26
Tony Butler...................................L658.27
What I did at Belgrade. 55 pp......in T143.12
LEVY, A. Romance of a shop.............L668.1
LEWALD, F. (Mrs. Stahr.) The aristo-
   cratic world. 87 pp.; Maid of Oyas.
   16 pp..............................in S331.1
Hulda; or, the deliverer. Tr. by A.
   L. Wister W817.8
LEWES, C. L. Dragon-tree of Telde. 56
   pp...in T143.21
LEWES, Mrs. M. A. E. See Eliot, G., pseud.
Lewey and I. Thomes, W. H..............T465.5
LEWIS, A. Wrong black bag............in S885.2
LEWIS, M. G. Romantic tales...............L675.1
Lewis Aruudel. Smedley, F. E............S637.5
LEYS, J. K. The Lindsays. 3 vols......L685.1

Lha dhu. Carleton, W....................in C281.7
Same ....in C281.8
Liar, The. 66 pp. James, H., Jr......in J277.9
Liberators of Holland. Charles, E. R..in C476.11
Lebrun's lawsuit. 38 pp..................in T143.6
Same..in T143.6 ²
LIDDELL, Mrs. C. C. F.-T. See Tytler,
   C. C. Fraser-
LIE, J. Barque Future; or, life in the far
   north..L716.1
Commodore's daughters....................L716.2
The visionary................................L716.3
Weird tales from northern seas.........L716.4
LIEFDE, J. B. DE. Galama; or, the beg-
   gars. L719.1
     Issued also as The beggars.
Maid of Stralsund: a story of the thirty
   years' war L719.2
Life, etc., of Captain Singleton. Defoe,
   D..D314.3
Life, etc., of Michael Armstrong, the
   factory boy. Trollope, F. M...........T848.1
Life, etc., of Peter Wilkins. Paltock, R...
.... Q183.1
Life, etc., of Private Miles O'Reilly.
   Halpiue, C. G.............................H195.1
Life for a life. Mulock, D M..........M960.15
Life in the East Indies. Thomes, W. H...T465.6
Life in the open air. Winthrop, T......W793.4
Life in the wilds. Martineau, H...in **M385.4
Same................................. M385.14
Life of Colonel Jack. Defoe, D........in D314.3
Life of Nancy. Jewett, S. O................J593.8
Life sentence. Sergeant, A..............S484.3
Life's assize. Riddell, C. E. L..........R543.9
Life's atonement. Murray, D. C.........M981.6
Life's handicap. Kipling, R..............K575.5
Life's little ironies. Hardy, T............H272.10
Lifted veil. Eliot, G....................in E426.9
Light of her countenance. Boyesen, H. H..B791.5
Light that failed. Kipling, R..............K575.6
Lights and shadows of a life. Dahlgren,
   M. V.......................................D130.1
Lights and shadows of Scottish life. Wil-
   son, J......................................W749.1
Lights and shadows of the soul. Drey, S..D778.1
Like Lucifer. Vane, D V249.1
Lilac sunbonnet. Crockett, S. R.........C938.9
Lilith. MacDonald, G M135.10
Lillian Morris, etc. Sienkiewicz, H.......S572.6
Lily and the cross. De Mille, J...........D381.7
Lily of the valley. Balzac, H. de.........B198.23
Limerick gloves. Edgeworth, M....in **E235.6
Same...................................in E235.19

LIN, FRANK, *pseud*. *See* Atherton, G. F.
LINCOLN, J. G. A genuine girl: sequel to
   Marjorie's quest.............................L737.1
   Marjorie's quest...............................L737.2
LINDAU, P. Lace: a Berlin romance.......L742.1
LINDAU, R. All in vain. 42 pp. First
   love. 10 pp. Hans the dreamer.
   94 pp..*in* S331.1
   The philosopher's pendulum. 44 pp...*in* T143.16
Lindsays, The. 3 vols. Leys, J. K......L685.1
Lindsay's luck. Burnett, F. H.............B964.3
   Same...B964.12
Linley Rochford. McCarthy, J...........M122.4
LINSKILL, M. Ladies of Lone Leventhorpe.
   ....*in* L981.3
LINTON, E. L. Ghost of the past. 47
   pp..S887.1
   One too many...................................L761.1
   Patricia Kemball..............................L761.2
   True history of Joshua Davidson, com-
   munist...L761.3
   World well lost................................L761.4
Linwoods, The. 2 vols. Sedgwick, C. M...S448.1
Lion of Flanders. Conscience, H...........C755.3
Lionel Lincoln. Cooper, J. F...............C777.18
   Same.......................................C777.19
List ye landsmen! Russell, W. C.........R968.10
LITCHFIELD, G. D. Little Venice, and
   other stories..................................L776.1
Little barefoot. Auerbach, B...............A918.8
Little Dorrit. Dickens, C..................D548.22
   Same.......................................D548.23
Little Guzzy, and other stories. Habber-
   ton, J..H113.7
Little Hodge. Jenkins, E....................J527.1
"Little Huguenot." Pemberton, M.........Q395.1
Little Irish girl, etc. Duchess.............D829.10
Little journey in the world. Warner,
   C. D...W280.2
Little lady of Lagunitas. Savage, R. H...S265.2
Little Loo. Russell, W. C...................R968.11
Little Make-Believe. Farjeon, B. L....*in* F229.4
Little minister. Barrie, J. M...............B275.5
Little minx. Cambridge, A..................C178.6
Little Miss Muffet. Carey, R. N..........C276.17
Little moorland princess. Marlitt, E....W817.16
Little pilgrim. 72 pp. Oliphant, M. O. W..O475.26
Little regiment, and other episodes of the
   American civil war. Crane, S............C891.4
Little Renault. 48 pp. Catherwood, M.
   H..*in* C363.8
Little room, and other stories. Wynne,
   M. Y...W989.1

Little savage. Marryat, *Capt.* F.........M362.8
   Same...................................*in* M362.21
Little schoolmaster Mark. Shorthouse,
   J. H...S559.4
Little sister. Yardley, J....................Y273.1
Little Tu'penny. Gould, S. B-............G698.6
Little Venice, and other stories. Litch-
   field, G. D...................................L776.1
Little wizard. Weyman, S. J..............W549.9
Living link. De Mille, J....................D381.8
Living or dead. Conway, H.................C767.6
Living too fast. Optic, O...................O625.1
Liza. Turgénieff, I. S......................T936.6
Lizzie Leigh and other tales. Gaskell, E.
   C...G248.2
LLOYD, D. D. Poor Ogla-Moga. 35 pp...
   ....*in* S884.3
LLOYD, J. U. Etidorhpa....................L793.1
Lloyd Pennant. Neville, R.................N525.1
LOCKE, D. R. (Petroleum V. Nasby,
   pseud.) A paper city....................L813.1
LOCKE, M. In far Dakota..................L814.1
Locke Amsden. Thompson, D. P.........T470.3
LOCKHART, J. G. Reginald Dalton......L816.1
   Valerius: a Roman story...................L816.2
LOCKHART, L. W. M. Night with the vol-
   unteers of Strathkinahan. 59 pp...*in* T143.7
   Unlucky Tom Griffin, his love and his
   luck. 82 pp.............................*in* T143.10
LOGAN, O. (*Mrs. Sikes.*) Château Fris-
   sac; or, home scenes in France......L831.1
LOGAN, W. Double-bedded room...*in* W750.3
   Recluse of the Hebrides. Ellen Arun-
   del.....................................*in* W750.5
   Story of Clara Douglas..................*in* W750.2
LOHMANN, F. Mill of the vale. 68 pp...
   ....*in* C972.1 ¹
   The pilgrim. 45 pp. Night on the
   mountain. 42 pp.....................*in* C972.1 ²
Lola. Griffiths, A.........................G855.1
Lombard street mystery. Robertson, M...R652.1
London idylls. Dawson, W. J...........D272.4
London life. James, H., *Jr*..............J277.9
London's heart. Farjeon, B. L.........F229.11
Lone house. Barr, A. E..................B268.16
Lonely life. Blythe, J. A. St. J...........B661.1
LONG, L. A. Apprentices to destiny......L848.1
   Squire of low degree.......................L848.2
LONGFELLOW, H. W. Kavanagh. *(Also)*
   Drift-wood L853.1
LONGSTREET, A. B. Georgia scenes....L857.1
LONGUS. Amours of Daphnis and Chloe.
   87 pp..................................*in* S657.1

Look before you leap. Alexander, *Mrs....* A374.19

Looking backward 2000-1887. Bellamy, E........ ....B437.2

Looking further forward. Michaelis, R...M620.1

Loom and the lugger. Martineau, H...... .... *in* **M385.15

Lora: the major's daughter. Heimburg, W H467.1

LORD, A. E. Days of Lamb and Cole- ridge..L866.1

Lord Beaupré. James, H. *Jr*............*in* J277.13

Lord Brockenhurst. Brydges, *Sir* S. E... ....*in* **B916.2

Lord Harry Bellair. 2 vols. Manning, A M283.5

Lord Hermitage. Grant, J..................G761.29

Lord Kilgobbin. Lever, C.................L658.16

Lord mayor. Holt, E. S.....................H758.7

Lord mayor of London. Ainsworth, W. H..A297.26

Lord Montagu's page. 3 vols. James, G. P. R..J276.27

Lord of himself. Underwood, F. H......U563.2

Lord Ormont and his Aminta. Meredith, G.. M559.7

Lord Roldan. Cunningham, A............C971.1

Lord Vanecourt's daughter. Collins, M....C711.1

Lorenzo. Bresciani, A.......................B842.1

Lorenzo Benoni. Ruffini, G.................R923.2

Lorley and Reinhard. Auerbach, B......A918.9

Lorna Doone. Blackmore, R. D..........B629.9

LORNE, J. G. E. H. D. S. CAMPBELL, *Marquis of.* From shadow to sunlight...L875.1
Who were they? a Maltese apparition. 36 pp...............................*in* T143.20

Lorrimer Littlegood. Smedley, F. E...S637.6

Lost and saved. Norton, C. E. S......NS83.1

Lost casket. Du Boisgobey, F............D816.2

Lost illusions. Balzac, H. de...........B198.24

Lost in a great city. Douglas, A. M......D734.16

Lost inca. Ozollo, *Inca P.*....................O995.1

Lost Lenore. Reid, M.........................R357.4

Lost manuscript. Freytag, G................F895.4

Lost name. Le Fanu, J. S...................L488.3

Lost secret of the Cocos group. 54 pp...*in* T143.13

Lost Sir Massingberd. Payn, J............Q345.14

Lothair. Disraeli, B..........................D613.8

LOTHAR *(pseud.)* Archrogue. Castle Christburg .... *in* R794.1 ²

LOTI, P. *(pseud. of* L. M. J. Viaud). Book of pity and of death............................L883.1
Iceland fishermen.....................L883.3
Phantom from the east L883.4
Rarahu; or, the marriage of Loti.........L883.6

Lotta Schmidt, and other stories. Trollope, A...T846.17

Lottery, The. Edgeworth, M........*in* **E235.6
Same..............................*in* E235.19

LOUGHEAD, F. H. Man from nowhere. (*Also*) Crown of thorns. Santos's brother. (*And*) Sealskin Annie.....L887.1
Man who was guilty....................L887.2

Louis Lambert. Balzac, H. de............B198.25

Louisa Kirkbride. Thébaud, A. J......... T375.1

Louisa of Prussia and her times. Mühl-bach, L.....................................M952.11

Louisa Pallant. James, H. *Jr*..............*in* J277.2

Louisiana. Burnett, F. H....................B964.13

Loukis Laras. Bikelas, D....................B595.1

Love afloat. Sheppard, F. H..................S550.1

Love and liberty. Dumas, A...............D886.27

Love and life. Yonge, C. M................Y555.18

"Love and quiet life." Raymond, W......R273.2

Love in old cloathes, and other stories. Bunner, H. C B942.1

Love in the nineteenth century. Preston, H. W......................................Q927.3

Love in the tropics. White, C. E.........W583.1

Love is a spirit. Hawthorne, J............H398.12

Love-letters of a worldly woman, (etc.) Clifford, L. L..............................C639.5

"Love me little, love me long." Reade, C...................................... R285.19

Love, mystery, and superstition. 42 pp. Opie, A.....................................*in* O614.3

Love of a lady. Thomas, A..................T453.2

Lovel the widower. Thackeray, W. M...*in* T363.5
Same..............................*in* T363.19

LOVELACE, F. Moloch of fashion: a story of London society.........................L898.1

Lovels of Arden. Braddon, M E.........B798.20

LOVER, S. The gridiron...................*in* S885.4
Handy Andy.....................................L910.1
He would be a gentleman; or, treasure trove..L910.2
Issued also as Treasure trove.
Legends and stories of Ireland............L910.3
Rory O'More....................................L910.4

Lovers' Saint Ruth's, and three other tales. Guiney, L. I..................................G964.3

Love's victory. Farjeon, B. L............F229.12

LOWELL, R. T. S. Antony Brade.........L916.1
New priest in Conception bay. 2 vols...L916.2
Story or two from an old Dutch town...L916.3

LOYAL, C., *pseud.* Squatter and the don: a novel of contemporary occurrences in California L923.1

Loyal Ronins. Tamenaga Shunsui......T157.1

Loÿs, Lord Berresford, and other tales. Duchess....................................D829.11

LUBOMIRSKI, S. H. *Prince.* Safar-Hadgi; or, Russ and Turcoman....................L930.1

LUCAS, A. Léonie. *(Also)* Within iron walls: twin-stories of the Franco-German war....................................L932.1

Lucas Garcia, and other stories.........L933.1

Lucia, Hugh, and another. Needell, *Mrs.* J. H..N374.1

Lucien de Rubempré. Balzac, H. de...B198.26

Lucius Davoren. Braddon, M. E........B798.29

Luck is everything. Maxwell, W. H....M465.6

Luck of Barry Lyndon. Thackeray, W. M...T363.14

Luck of Roaring Camp, and other sketches. Harte, B....................................H327.20

Same, and other stories................H327.21

Luck of the Darrells. Payn, J...........Q345.15

Luck of the house. Sergeant, A........S484.4

Lucretia. Lytton, E. G. E. L. Bulwer-..L998.15

LUCY, H. W. Gideon Fleyce..............L943.1

Lucy. Smith, J. P.........................S653.6

Lucy Arden. Grant, J...................G761.30

Lucy Crofton. Oliphant, M. O. W......O475.27

Lucy Howard's journal. Sigourney, L. H....................................S578.1

LUDLOW, J. M. Captain of the Janizaries: a story of the times of Scanderbeg and the fall of Constantinople...............L945.1

King of Tyre...........................L945.2

That angelic woman....................L945.3

Ludovic and Gertrude. Conscience, H...C755.4

LUMSDEN, K. M. How I fell among thieves. 26 pp.....................*in* T143.21

A vendetta. 12 pp...................*in* T143.19

LUNN, *Mrs.* J. C. Shamrock and rose. 3 vols..................................L963.1

Lure of fame. Holland, C................H734.1

LUSKA, S., *pseud. See* Harland, H.

Lutaniste of St. Jacobi's. Drew, C.....D776.1

Luttrell of Arran. Lever, C............L658.17

LYALL, E. *(pseud. of* A. E. Bayly.) Derrick Vaughan, novelist. *(Also)* Ladies of Lone Leventhorpe, by M. Linskill...................................L981.3

Donovan: a modern Englishman......L981.4

Doreen: the story of a singer.........L981.5

Hardy Norseman.......................L981.7

In the golden days....................L981.8

Knight-errant.........................L981.10

We two. (Sequel to Donovan.).........L981.14

Won by waiting........................L981.15

Lydia. Shebbeare, J.................*in* **N938.22

Lyndell Sherburne. Douglas, A. M...D734.18

LYNDON. *(pseud. of* M. A. Bright.) Margaret: a story of life in a prairie home..................................L988.1

LYON, F. D. Ireland's dream. 2 vols...L990.1

LYON, S. For a mess of pottage..........L991.1

LYSTER, A. My treasure. 45 pp......*in* T143.20

LYTTON, E. G. E. L. BULWER- 1 *Baron Lytton.* (Pisistratus Caxton, *pseud.*) Alice; or, the mysteries. (Sequel to "Ernest Maltravers.").................L998.1

Calderon, the courtier................*in* L998.14

The Caxtons............................L998.2

Coming race; or, the new Utopia......L998.3

Same. (Also) Falkland. Zicci. *(And)* Pausanias the Spartan................L998.4

Devereux..............................L998.5

The disowned..........................L998.6

Ernest Maltravers; or, the Eleusinia....L998.7

Eugene Aram...........................L998.8

Falkland..............................*in* L998.4

Godolphin.............................L998.9

Harold: the last of the Saxon kings...L998.10

Haunted and the haunters..........*in* L998.21

Same..............................*in* L998.25

Same..............................*in* T143.5

Same..............................*in* T143.5 *

Issued also as House and the brain.

Kenelm Chillingly.....................L998.11

Last days of Pompeii..................L998.12

Last of the barons....................L998.13

Leila; or, the siege of Granada. *(Also)* Calderon the courtier, and, Pilgrims of the Rhine.........................L998.14

Lucretia; or, the children of night.....L998.15

"My novel." 2 vols....................L998.16

Night and morning.....................L998.17

The Parisians. 2 vols.................L998.18

Paul Clifford.........................L998.19

Pausanias, the Spartan...............*in* L998.4

Same................................L998.20

Same. (Also) Haunted and the haunters. L998.21

Pelham................................L998.22

Pilgrims of the Rhine................*in* L998.14

Rienzi: the last of the Roman tribunes..L998.23

Strange story.........................L998.24

Same, and, Haunted and the haunters..L998.25

What will he do with it?..............L998.26

Zanoni................................L998.27

Zicci.................................*in* L998.4

LYTTON, E. R. Bulwer- *Earl of Lytton.* (Owen Meredith, *pseud.*) Ring of Amasis................................L999.1

M., C. J. Alice Sherwin: a tale of the days of Sir Thomas More.......................M110.1
M., C. M. May Lane: a story of the sixteenth century..........................*in* H758.13
M. or N. Melville, G. J. W-..............M530.22
Same.......................................*in* **M530.21
MAARTENS, M. (*pseud. of* H. Van der Pooten Schwartz). God's fool: a Koopstad story...............................M111.3
Greater glory.........................M111.4
Joost Avelingh......................M111.6
My lady Nobody M111.8
Mabel Lee. Reid, C...................R353.10
Mabel Vaughan. Cummins, M. S.........C970.3
Mabel's progress. Trollope, F. C..........T847.2
Macaria. Wilson, A. J. E................W746.5
MACAULEY, E. Tales of the drama.......M117.1
McCARTHY, J. The dictator................M122.1
Lady Judith...........................M122.3
Linley Rochford.....................M122.4
Maid of Athens.......................M122.5
Maurice Tyrone; or, the fair Saxon....M122.2
Issued also as The fair Saxon.
Miss Misanthrope...........................M122.7
My enemy's daughter.......................M122.8
Red diamonds................................M122.9
Riddle ring...............................M122.10
Waterdale neighbors.......................M122.15
—and Praed, R. Campbell- Ladies' gallery..................................M122.11
"The Right Honourable."................M122.12
MacCarthy More. Sadlier, M. A...........S126.4
McCARTY, L. Gabrielle.....................M123.1
McCLELLAN, Mrs. H. H. See Flemming, H., *pseud.*
McCLELLAND, M. G. Madame Silva. (*Also*) Ghost of Dred Power..........M126.1
Manitou island..........................M126.2
Oblivion M126.3
Princess M126.4
MacDermots of Ballyclorau. Trollope, A...T846.18
MacDONALD, G. Adela Cathcart.........M135.1
Alec Forbes of Howglen....................M135.2
Annals of a quiet neighbourhood.......M135.3
David Elginbrod M135.4
Donal Grant............................M135.5
Elect lady.............................M135.6
Guild court............................M135.7
Heather and snow........................M135.8
Home again.............................M135.9
Lilith................................M135.10
Malcolm..............................M135.11
Marquis of Lossie....................M135.12

MacDONALD, G.—*Continued.*
Mary Marston........................M135.13
Paul Faber, surgeon.......................M135.14
Phantastes M135.15
Same. (*Also*) The portent.............M135.16
The portent: a story of the inner vision of the highlanders, commonly called the second sight.....................*in* M135.16
Same............................M135.17
Robert Falconer........................M135.18
St. George and St. Michael...........M135.19
Seaboard parish. Sequel to "Annals of a quiet neighbourhood."..............M135.20
Sir Gibbie.............................M135.21
Stephen Archer, and other tales......M135.22
There and back........................M135.23
Thomas Wingfold, curate..............M135.24
Vicar's daughter M135.25
Warlock o' Glenwarlock..................M135.26
Weighed and wanting....................M135.27
Wilfrid Cumbermede M135.28
MACDONALD, J. Narrative of prince Charlie's escape. 28 pp...................*in* T143.16
McDONNELL, W. Exeter Hall: a theological romance M136.1
MacDOWALL, C. Queen among queens: a tale of the desert.......................M138.1
McDOWELL, Mrs. K. See Bonner, S.
MacFARLANE, C. Romance of history: Italy..............................M143.1
MacGAHAN, B. E. Xenia Repnina: a story of the Russia of today..........M145.1
McGLASSON, E. W. Diana's livery......M146.1
McINTOSH, M. J. Two pictures............M152.2
MACKARNESS, M. A. Influence..........M153.1
McKAY, J. T. Stella Grayland. 42 pp...*in* S884.7
MACKENZIE, E. (*pseud. of* M. Grogan.) Roua pass; or, Englishmen in the Highlands. 3 vols........................M156.1
MACKENZIE, H. Man of feeling, and, Julia de Roubigné....................**B232.29
MACKENZIE, R. S. Tressilian and his friends...............................M157.1
McKNIGHT, C. Captain Jack, the scout; or, the Indian wars about old Fort Duquesne M158.1
Issued also as Old Fort Duquesne.
McLANDBURGH, F. Automaton ear, and other sketches.....................M159.1
MACLAREN, *Miss.* "Thrust out;" an old legend.............................M160.1
MACLAREN, I., *pseud. See* Watson, J.
MACLAY, A. C. Mito Yashiki: a tale of old Japan M162.1

MACLEAN, H. E. Andromeda............M163.1
McLEAN, S. P. See Greene, S. P. McL.
MACLEOD, F. Washer of the ford......M165.5
Macleod of Dare. Black, W............B627.17
McMANUS, L. Silk of the kine............M167.1
MACNABB, Mrs. M. L. See Laffan, M.
MACNISH, R. The metempsychosis. 59
  pp............in T143.1
  Same............in T143.1 ²
MACOUN, M., comp. Character and com-
  ment selected from the novels of W.
  D. Howells............H859.6
MACQUOID, K. S. At an old chateau......M173.1
  Mère Suzanne, and other stories.........M173.5
  Patty............M173.6
  Rookstone............M173.7
McVeys, The. Kirkland, J............K597.1
Mad Sir Uchtred of the hills. Crockett,
  S. R............C938.10
Mad world and its inhabitants. Cham-
  bers, J............C444.1
Madam. Oliphant, M. O. W............O475.28
Madame Agnes. Dubois, C............D813.1
Madame de Fleury. Edgeworth, M...in **E235.9
  Same............in E235.25
  Same............in E235.34
Madame de Maurescamp. Feuillet, O.....F426.3
Madame de Presnel. Poynter, E. F...... Q892.3
Madame Delphine. Cable, G. W............C115.8
Madame d'Orgevaut's husband. Rabusson,
  H............R117.1
Madame Firmiani. 32 pp. Balzac, H. de...
  ....in B198.1
  Same............in B198.6 ³k
Madame Gosselin. Ulbach, L............U362.2
Madame Jane Junk and Joe. Bornemann,
  M............B736.1
Madame Silva. McClelland, M. G........M126.1
Madame Thérèse. Erckmann, E., and
  Chatrian, A............E654.12
Madcap Violet. Black, W............B627.18
Made or marred. Fothergill, J...........in F761.4
Madeleine. Kavanagh, J............K212.7
Madeleine. Sandeau, J............S214.1
Madeleine Graham. Robinson, J...........R662.3
Madeline. Holmes, M. J............H751.18
Madeline. Opie, A............in O614.1
Madelon. Wilkins, M. E............W684.7
Mademoiselle. Peard, F. M............Q359.8
Mademoiselle Bismarck. Rochefort, H...R674.1
Mademoiselle de La Fayette. Genlis, S. F.
  Comtesse de............**G332.2
Mademoiselle de Mersac. Norris, W. E...N861.7
Mademoiselle Miss. Harland, H...........H282.8

Mademoiselle Mori. Roberts, M............R646.7
Mademoiselle Panache. Edgeworth, M...
  ....in E235.18
Madonna Mary. Oliphant, M. O. W....O475.29
Madonna of the tubs. Phelps, E. S......Q539.10
Maelcho. Lawless, E............L418.3
Magdalen Hepburn. Oliphant, M. O. W..O475.30
Maggie. Crane, S............C891.2
Maggie Miller. Holmes, M. J...........in H751.8
MAGHERINI-GRAZIANI, G. Fioraccio..in M690.1
Magic ring. La Motte Fouqué, F. H. K.
  Freiherr de............L235.2
Magic skin. Balzac, H. de............B198.27
MAGINN, W. Bob Burke's duel with en-
  sign Brady. 39 pp............in T143.2
  Same............in T143.2 ¹
  Story without a tail. 23 pp............in T143.1
  Same............in T143.1 ²
Magnetic man, and other stories. Van
  Zile, E. S............V285.1
Magnhild. Björnson, B............B625.5
Magnum bonum. Yonge, C. M.........Y555.20
MAGRUDER, J. Across the chasm.......M212.1
  Princess Sonia............M212.2
Maid Marian. Peacock, T. L............Q356.4
Maid Marian, and other stories. Seawell,
  M. E............S442.5
Maid of Athens. McCarthy, J............M122.5
Maid of honor. Wingfield, L............W771.2
Maid of Killeena, and other stories. Black,
  W............B627.20
Maid of Orleans. Robinson, J............R662.4
Maid of Sker. Blackmore, R. D.........B629.11
Maid of Stralsund. Liefde, J. B. de......L719.2
Maid, wife, or widow? Alexander, Mrs..A374.20
Maiden and married life of Mary Powell.
  Manning, A............M283.6
Maiden of Treppi. Heyse, P............H621.3
Maiden's progress. Hunt, V............H943.2
MAIDMENT, J. Cateran of Lochloy. Mort-
  lake: a legend of Merton.........in W750.4
  Heir of Inshannock............in W750.6
Main-travelled roads. Garland, H......G233.2
Mainstone's housekeeper. Meteyard, E...M591.1
MAIRET, J., pseud. See Healy, M.
MAITLAND, E. (H. Ainslie, pseud.) By
  and by............M231.1
  Higher law............M231.2
  Pilgrim and the shrine............M231.3
MAITLAND, J. A. Diary of an old doctor...
  ....M232.1
  Lawyer's story............M232.2

MAITLAND, J. A.—*Continued.*
  Old patroon; or, the great Van Broek
    property M232.3
  Sartaroe: a tale of Norway...............M232.4
  The wanderer M232.5
Ma'tre–Cornélius 82 pp. Balzac, H. de
  ....*in* B198.41
Maiwa's revenge. Haggard, H. R.........H146.9
MAJENDIE, *Lady* M. Dita....................M233.1
  A French speculation. 45 pp.........*in* T143.20
  Giannetto...M233.2
  Railway journey. 29 pp...............*in* T143.12
Major and minor. 2 vols. Norris, W. E.....N861.8
Major Max. Townsend, E. W...........*in* T747.1
Maker of moons, etc. Chambers, R. W....C445.5
Making of a man. Baker, W. M............B169.4
Malbone. Higginson, T. W.................H637.1
Malcolm. MacDonald, G....................M135.11
MALET, L. (*pseud. of* R. G. K. Harrison.)
  The carissima...................................M247.1
  Counsel of perfection.......................M247.2
  Mrs. Lorimer...................................M247.3
MALLOCK, W. H. Heart of life...........M255.1
  New Paul and Virginia; or, positivism
    on an island................................M255.2
  New republic...................................M255.3
  Old order changes............................M255.4
  Romance of the nineteenth century.....M255.5
MALOT, H. H. Anie M257.1
Mamelon. Tourgée, A. W................*in* T727.8
Mammon of unrighteousness. Boyesen,
  H. H...B791.6
Mam'zelle Eugénie. Gréville, H..........G838.4
Man and wife. Collins, W.................C713.21
Man as he is not. Bage, R.............**B232.48
Man at arms. James, G. P. R.............J276.28
Man from Mars. Blot, T....................B657.1
Man from nowhere. Loughead, F. H...*in* L887.1
Man in black. Weyman, S. J..............W549.10
Man in the bell. 10 pp...................*in* T143.3
  Same...................................*in* T143.3²
Man of feeling. Mackenzie, H.........**B232.29
Man of honor. Eggleston, G. C..........E295.1
Man of mark. Hope, A....................H791.18
Man of the people. 2 vols. Erckmann,
  E., *and* Chatrian, A......................E654.13
Man of the world. North, W..............N867.1
Man story. Howe, E. W....................H855.1
Man who became a savage. Hornaday,
  W. T...H813.4
Man who laughs. Hugo, V..................H895.2
Man who was guilty. Loughead, F. H...L887.2

Man with seven hearts, and other stories.
  Burrell, A.....................................B969.1
Man with the broken ear. About, E......A156.2
Man without a country, and other tales.
  Hale, E. E.....................................H161.9
Manchester strike. Martineau, H....*in* **M385.7
Manfred. Guerrazzi, F. D...................G934.2
Manitou island. McClelland, M. G......M126.2
MANNING, A. (*Mrs. Rathbone.*) Cherry and
  Violet: a tale of the great plague.....M283.1
  Heroes of the desert: the story of Moffat
    and Livingstone M283.2
  Jacques Bonneval; or, the days of the
    dragonnades M283.3
  Lady Willoughby...............................M283.4
  Lord Harry Bellair. 2 vols.............M283.5
  Maiden & married life of Mary Powell,
    afterwards Mistress Milton............M283.6
  Old Chelsea bun-house...................M283.7
  Faire gospeller, Mistress Anne Askew...
  ....M283.8
  Sower's reward................................M283.9
  Spanish barber. M283.10
MANNING, E. Six months on a slaver...M284.1
Manoeuvring. Edgeworth, M......*in* **E235.9
  Same...E235.22
  Same...................................*in* E235.34
  Same...................................*in* E235.35
"Man's a man for a' that." M286.1
Man's foes. Strain, E. H....................S897.1
Man's will. Fawcett, E.......................F278.12
Mansfield Park. Austen, J..................A933.2
MANTEUFFEL, U. Z. VON. Violetta. (Tr.)
  by A. L. Wister...............................W817.9
Manuel Pereira. Adams, F. C.............A212.1
Manuelita. Wilson, M. C....................W751.1
Manufacturers, The. Edgeworth, M........
  ....*in* **E235.6
  Same...................................*in* E235.20
Manulito. Leffingwell, W. B...............L493.1
Manxman. Caine, H...........................C135.6
Many inventions. Kipling, R...............K575.7
MANZONI, A. The betrothed.............M296.1
  Issued also as Lucia the betrothed.
Marable family. Hillyer, S.................H655.1
Marble faun. Hawthorne, N................H399.6
MARBOURG, D., *joint author. See* Eggles-
  ton, G. C.
Marcella. 2 vols. Ward, M. A. A......W261.5
March hares. Frederic, H...................F852.6
Marchioness of Brinvilliers. Smith, A...S641.3
Marco Visconti. Grossi, T.................G878.1
Margaret. Judd, S............................J923.1
Margaret. Lyndon............................L988.1

Margaret Graham. James, G. P. R......J276.29

Same..............................*in* J276.41

Margaret Maitland, Passages in the life of.
Oliphant, M. O. W..................O475.43

Margaret Moncrieffe. Burdett, C.........B951.1

Margaret Percival. Sewell, E. M........S516.2

Margaret Roper. Stewart, A. M...........S850.1

Margarethe. Juncker, E..................W817.7

Margaret's secret. Brock, F. E. G........B864.4

Margery. 2 vols. Ebers, G...............E165.11

Margery's son. Holt, E. S..............H758.8

Margret Howth. Davis, *Mrs.* R. H.......D263.2

Marguerite. Holmes, M. J...............H751.19

Marguerite de Valois. 2 vols. Dumas, A..D886.29

Maria. Isaacs, J.........................I733.1

Maria Theresa and her fireman. Mühlbach, L............................*in* M952.13

MARIAGER, P. Pictures of Hellas.........M332.1

Mariam. Victor, H.......................V643.1

Marian Grey. Holmes, M. J.............H751.20

Marianela. Perez Galdós, B..............Q438.4

Marie. Andrews, L. H....................A567.1

Marie. Pushkin, A. S....................Q976.1

Marie. Richards, L. E...................R516.3

Marie Antoinette and her son. Mühlbach,
L...................................M952.12

Marion Darche. Crawford, F. M.........C899.11

Marion Graham. Lander, M..............L255.1

Marion Scatterthwaite. Symington, M....S987.1

Marionettes. Gordon, J.................G663.3

Marion's faith. King, C.................K523.19

Marius the epicurean. 2 vols. Pater, W..Q295.3

MARIVAUX, P. C. DE C. DE. Virtuous
orphan.............................*in* **N938.16

Marjorie Daw and other people. Aldrich,
T. B..................................A365.3

Same, and other stories..................A365.4

Marjorie's quest. Lincoln, J. G..........L737.2

Marked "In haste." Roosevelt, B.........R781.1

Market Harborough. Melville, G. J. W-..M530.23

Same..............................*in* **M530.30

Markof, the Russian violinist. Gréville,
H...................................G838.5

MARKS, *Mrs.* M. A. M. H. *See* Hoppus,
M. A. M.

MARLITT, E. (*pseud. of* E. John). At the
councillor's. Tr. by A. L. Wister...W817.10

Bailiff's maid. Tr. by A. L. Wister...W817.11

Countess Gisela. Tr. by A. L. Wister...
...................................W817.12

Gold Elsie. Tr. by A. L. Wister......W817.13

In the Schillingscourt. Tr. by A. L.
Wister..............................W817.14

MARLITT, E.—*Continued.*

Lady with the rubies. Tr. by A. L. Wister...............................W817.15

Little moorland princess. Tr. by A. L.
Wister.............................W817.16

Old mam'selle's secret. Tr. by A. L.
Wister.............................W817.17

Owl's Nest. Tr. by A. L. Wister......W817.18

Second wife. Tr. by A. L. Wister...W817.19

Twelve apostles....................*in* Z767.1 ²

Marm Lisa. Wiggin. K. D................W655.4

MARMONTEL, J. F. Moral tales.........M352.1

Same.............................*in* **N938.6

Marmorne. Hamerton, P. G.............H215.2

Maroon. Reid, M.......................R357.5

Marooned. Russell, W. C...............R968.12

Marquis and merchant. Collins, M......C712.2

Marquis of Carabas. Spofford, H. P.....S762.4

Marquis of Lossie. MacDonald, G.......M135.12

Marriage. Ferrier, S. E................F391.3

Marriage at a venture. Gaboriau, E....G116.6

Marriage by capture. Buchanan, R......B918.8

Marriage contract. Balzac, H. de.......B198.28

Marriages, The. James, H., *Jr...* .....*in* J277.8

Married belle. Smith, J. P.............S653.7

Married by proxy. Dupree, F...........D942.1

MARRYAT, FLORENCE. (*Mrs. Lean.*)
Blindfold..........................M361.1

Gerald Estcourt: his confessions......M361.2

Girls of Feversham.................M361.3

Her lord and master................M361.4

Master passion....................M361.6

Mount Eden M361.7

On circumstantial evidence.........M361.8

Prey of the gods...................M361.9

Scarlet sin........................M361.10

MARRYAT, *Capt.* F. Children of the New
Forest............................M362.1

The dog-fiend; or, Snarleyyow.......M362.2

Frank Mildmay.....................M362.3

Same. (*Also*) Olla podrida.........M362.4

Jacob Faithful.....................M362.5

Japhet in search of a father........M362.6

The king's own....................M362.7

Little Savage......................M362.8

Mission; or, scenes in Africa.......M362.9

Mr. Midshipman Easy...............M362.10

Monsieur Violet in California, Sonora,
and western Texas, Travels of....M362.11

Moonshine ....*in* **M362.26

Newton Forster...................M362.12

Same. (*Also*) Monsier Violet......M362.13

Olla podrida......................M362.14

Same. (*Also*) The pirate, and The Three
cutters...........................M362.28

MARRYAT, *Capt.* F.—*Continued.*
Pacha of many tales........................M362.15
Percival Keene...............................M362.16
Peter Simple.................................M362.17
Phantom ship.................................M362.18
Pirate.................................*in* **M362.26
Same..................................*in* M362.28
Same, and, Three cutters.............. M362.19
Same. *(And)* Moonshine..............**M362.26
The poacher.................................M362.20
Same. *(Also)* Little savage.............M362.21
Poor Jack...................................M362.22
Privateersman...............................M362.23
Rattlin, the reefer M362.24
Settlers in Canada..........................M362.25
Stories of the sea: Pirate; Three cutters;
Moonshine..............................**M362.26
Three cutters........................*in* M362.19
Same.................................*in* **M362.26
Same.................................*in* M362.28
Valerie, an autobiography.................M362.27
Marsena, and other stories of the wartime.
Frederic, H...............................F852.7
MARSH, A. C. Tales of the woods and
fields....................................**M364.1
MARSH, C. L. Opening the oyster........M365.1
Marsh island. Jewett, S. O..................J593.9
MARSHALL, E. Alma; or, the story of a
little music mistress.....................M367.1
Dayspring: a story of the time of Wil-
liam Tyndale.............................M367.2
Escape from the tower......................M367.3
In Colston's days: a story of Old Bristol...
....M367.4
In four reigns, 1785-1842.................M367.5
In the east country with Sir Thomas
Browne M367.6
Master of the musicians...................M367.13
Memories of troublous times M367.7
Now-a-days M367.8
On the banks of the Ouse; or, life in
Olney a hundred years ago.............M367.9
Story of John Marbeck: a Windsor organ-
ist of three hundred years ago........M367.10
Under Salisbury spire in the days of
George Herbert...........................M367.11
Under the Mendips..........................M367.12
Marston. 3 vols. Croly, G.................C944.1
MARTEL DE JANVILLE, S. G. M. A. *Com-
tesse* DE. *See* Gyp, *pseud.*
Martha, the gypsy. 20 pp. Hook, T....*in* H781.9
MARTIN, *Miss—.* Canvassing.............*in* B218.3
MARTIN, H. Helen of Glenross. 4 vols.
(in 2)..................................**M381.1

MARTIN, *Mrs.* H. *See* Martin, M. E.
MARTIN, M. E. "For a dream's sake."...M382.1
MARTIN, T. Bon Gaultier's tales: Country
quarters..............................*in* W750.2
Same: Mrs. Humphrey Greenwood's
tea-party.............................*in* W750.5
Martin Chuzzlewit. Dickens, C.......... D548.24
Same.....................................D548.25
Martin Paz. Verne, J......................V531.27
Same.....................................V531.45
MARTINEAU, H. Berkeley the banker. Pt.
2.......................................M385.1
Charmed sea...............................M385.5
Deerbrook M385.8
Demerara..................................M385.9
The Hampdens..............................M385.13
Illustrations of political economy. 9 vols.
1. Brooke and Brooke farm. Hill and the valley. Life in the wilds...............**M385.4
2. Demerara. Ella of Garveloch. Weal and
woe in Garveloch....................**M385.10
3. Cousin Marshall. Ireland. Manchester
strike..............................**M385.7
4. For each and for all. French wines and
politics. Homes abroad..............**M385.12
5. Berkeley, the banker. Charmed sea......**M385.2
6. The loom and the lugger. Messrs. Vanderput and Snoek.......................**M385.15
7. Cinnamon and pearls. Sowers not reapers.
Tale of the Tyne....................**M385.6
8. Briery creek. Three ages..............**M385.3
9. The Farrers of Budge-Row. Moral of many
fables..............................**M385.11
Life in the wilds.........................M385.14
Messrs. Vanderput and Snoek........M385.16
Sowers not reapers........................M385.17
Weal and woe in Garveloch............M385.18
Martins of Cro' Martin. Lever, C......L658.18
Martyr of Golgotha. 2 vols. Escrich, E.
P..E746.1
Martyrdom of Madeline. Buchanan, R...B918.4
Martyred fool. Murray, D. C.............M981.7
Martyrs of Spain. Charles, E. R........C476.11
Maruja. Harte, B.........................H327.22
MARVEL, IK, *pseud. See* Mitchell, D. G.
Mary Anerley. Blackmore, R. D.........B629.12
Mary Barton, and other tales. Gaskell,
E. C....................................G248.3
Mary Gresley. Trollope, A...............T846.8
Mary Marston. MacDonald, G...........M135.13
Mary Musgrave..... ....*in* S885.1
Mary of Burgundy. James, G. P. R......J276.30
Mary of Lorraine. Grant, J..............G761.31
Mary Ogilvie. Picken, A.................Q594.2
Mary St. John. Carey, R. N.............C276.19
Mary Schweidler, the amber witch. Mein-
hold, J. W..............................M514.1

Marzio's crucifix. Crawford, F. M........C899.12

MASON, A. E. W. Courtship of Morrice Buckler............................M398.3

MASON, T. Adam Dickson..................M412.1

MASSINGER, P. New way to pay old debts. 31 pp....................*in* M875.1 ¹

Master, The. Zangwill, I....................Z295.7

Master Ardick, buccaneer. Costello, F. H C841.3

Master and man. Tolstoi, *Count* L. N.....T654.8

Master Bieland and his workmen. Auerbach, B..............................A918.10

Master craftsman. Besant, *Sir* W.........B554.23

Master Humphrey's clock. Dickens, C...... ....*in* D548.26

Same..*in* D548.29

Same......................................*in* D548.29 ²

Same...... ....*in* D548.33

Master mosaic-workers. Sand, G.........S213.9

Master of Ballantrae. Stephenson, R. L...S848.5

Master of ceremonies. Fenn, G. M........F334.1

Master of Greylands. Wood, E. P.........W874.8

Master of his fate. Barr, A. E..............B268.17

Master of Rathkelly. Smart, H.............S636.5

Master of the magicians. Phelps, E. S., *and* Ward, H. D Q539.19

Master of the musicians. Marshall, E...M367.13

Master passion. Marryat, F.................M361.6

MASTERS, C. Shuttle of fate..............M423.5

Masters of the world. 3 vols. Hoppus, M. A. M............................H799.1

Matchmaker. Walford, L. B..............W174.6

Mate of the Daylight. Jewett, S. O.......J593.10

Mate to mate. Sharkey, T. K.............S530.1

MATHERS, H. (*Mrs. Reeves*). Hedri; or, blind justice. (*Also*) Miss Meredith..M426.1

MATHERS, J., *and* A solid gentleman, (*pseud.*) History of Mr. John Decastro and his brother Bat, commonly called Old Crab. 4 vols....................M427.1

MATHEWS, J. A. Bessie Harrington's venture. M429.1

Mathias Sandorf. Verne, J..................V531.29

Mathilda of Canossa and Yoland of Groningen. Bresciani, A....................B842.2

Matilda. 2 vols. Cottin, S. R.............C848.1

Matrimonial agent. Winterfeld, A. von...W788.1

Matrimony. Norris, W. E....................N861.9

Matter of millions. Green, A. K..........G795.5

Matter of temperament. Stevenson, E. I....S847.3

Matthew Austin. Norris, W. E. N861.10

MATTHEWS, B. His father's son.........M438.4

Last meeting............................M438.8

Memories. 37 pp........................*in* S886.3

MATTHEWS, B.—*Continued.*

Secret of the sea, etc....................M438.10

Story of a story, etc....................M438.11

Tales of fantasy and fact...............M438.12

Venetian glass. 26 pp..................*in* S884.3

Vignettes of Manhattan..................M438.14

With my friends: tales told in partnership......................................M438.16

CONTENTS.—Art and mystery of collaboration.—Documents in the case, (*and*) Seven conversations of Dear Jones and Baby Van Rensselaer (*with H. C. Bunner*).—Edged tools, (*and*) Mated by magic (*with W. H. Pollock*).—One story is good till another is told (*with G. H. Jessop*).—Three wishes (*with F. Anstey*).

—*and* Anstey, F. Three wishes. 53 pp... ....*in* M438.16

—*and* Bunner, H. C. Documents in the case. 54 pp....................*in* S884.1

Same. (*Also*) Seven conversations of Dear Jones and Baby Van Rensselaer... ....*in* M438.16

—*and* Jessop, G. H. One story is good till another is told. 36 pp.........*in* M438.16

—*and* Pollock, W. H. Edged tools: a tale in two chapters. 52 pp. Mated by magic. 36 pp....................*in* M438.16

MATURIN, E. Bianca: a tale of Erin and Italy........ ....M445.1

MATURIN, R. C. Melmoth, the wanderer. 4 vols....................................M446.1

MAUNSELL, W. P. Poisoned chalice...M450.1

MAUPASSANT, G. DE. The Horla. On the river.................. ....*in* M690.1

Odd number: thirteen tales...............M452.1

Pierre and Jean............................M452.2

Who can tell? 19 pp. The drowned man. 11 pp..........................*in* R657.1

Mauprat. Sand, G..........................S213.10

Maureen Dhu. Sadlier, M. A..............S126.5

Maureen's fairing, etc. Barlow, J.........B258.7

Maurice Dering. Lawrence, G. A.........L421.6

Maurice Tiernay. Lever, C.................L658.19

Maurice Tyrone. McCarthy, J..............M122.2

Mavericks..M461.1

MAXWELL, *Lady* C. E. S. STIRLING- *See* Norton, C. E. S.

MAXWELL, *Mrs.* M. E. B. *See* Braddon, M. E.

MAXWELL, P. White woman of Tarras... ....*in* W750.6

MAXWELL, W. H. Adventures of Captain Blake............................M465.1

Bivouac; or, stories of the Peninsular war......................................M465.2

MAXWELL, W. H.—*Continued.*
Captain Blake...................................M465.1
Flood and field................................M465.3
Hector O'Halloran.............................M465.4
Grace Willoughby: a tale of the wars of
   King James...... ....M465.5
Luck is everything............................M465.6
Sports in the Highlands and islands of
   Scotland. Sequel to "Wild sports of
   the west.''....................................M465.7
Stories of the Peninsular war.............M465.8
Stories of Waterloo...........................M465.9
Maxwell. Hook, T.............................H781.7
MAY, S. (*pseud. of* R. S. Clarke). In old
   Quinnebasset.................................M467.1
May. Oliphant, M. O. W...................O475.31
May flower, etc. Stowe, H. B.............S892.3
May Lane. M., C. M...................*in* H758.13
May Martin, and other tales of the Green
   Mountains. Thompson, D. P.........T470.4
MAYHEW, A. S., *joint author. See* May-
   hew, H.
MAYHEW, H., and A. S. Image of his
   father...M469.1
MAYO, *Mrs.* I. F. *See* Garrett, E., *and* R.,
   pseud.
MAYO, W. S. The Berber: a tale of Mo-
   rocco................................... . M473.1
   Issued also as Mountaineer of the Atlas.
Kaloolah; or, journeyings to the Diébel
   Kumri.......................................M473.2
Mayor of Casterbridge. Hardy, T.......H272.12
Mayor of Wind-gap. Banim, M...........B218.3
Meadow Brook. Holmes, M. J...........H751.21
Meadow-grass. Brown, A..................B878.1
MECKLENBURG, A. S. *See* Ring, I., *pseud.*
MEINHOLD, J. W. Mary Schweidler, the
   amber witch.................................M514.1
Melbourne House. Warner, S...........W284.5
MELDRUM, D. S. Rathillet. 57 pp....*in* T143.24
Melincourt. 2 vols. Peacock, T. L.......Q356.5
Mellichampe. Simms, W. G.................S592.10
Melmoth, the wanderer. 4 vols. Maturin,
   R. C...M446.1
MELVILLE, G. J. WHYTE- Black but
   comely.......................................M530.1
Same...............................*in* **M530.32
"Bones and I"; or, the skeleton at
   home.................................. M530.2
Same...............................*in* **M530.35
The Brookes of Bridlemere.................M530.3
Same. (*Also*) Sarchedon.............**M530.4
Cerise: a tale of the last century.........M530.5
Same...............................*in* **M530.16

MELVILLE, G. J. WHYTE—*Continued.*
Contraband; or, a losing hazard.........M530.6
Same. (*Also*) Roy's wife.............**M530.7
Digby Grand...................................M530.8
Same. (*Also*) The interpreter......**M530.9
General Bounce...............................M530.10
Same. (*Also*) Tilbury Nogo........**M530.11
The gladiators: a tale of Rome and
   Judæa......................................M530.12
Same. (*Also*) Good for nothing....**M530.13
Good for nothing.....................*in* **M530.13
Same............................ M530.14
Holmby House.................................M530.15
Same. (*Also*) Cerise...................**M530.16
Inside the bar ....*in* M530.23
Same...............................*in* **M530.30
The interpreter: a tale of the war...*in* **M530.9
Same.................................... M530.17
Kate Coventry.................................M530.18
Same. (*Also*) Rosine.................**M530.19
Katerfelto: a story of Exmoor...........M530.20
Same. (*Also*) M. or N...............**M530.21
M. or N.................................*in* **M530.21
Same.................................... M530.22
Market Harborough. (*Also*) Inside the
   bar........... .... M530.23
Same...............................*in* **M530.30
The queen's Maries: a romance of Holy-
   rood.......................................M530.24
Same. (*Also*) The white rose......**M530.25
Rosine................................... *in* **M530.19
Same.................................... M530.26
Roy's wife...............................*in* **M530.7
Same.................................... M530.27
Sarchedon: a legend of the great queen...
   ....*in* **M540.4
Same.............................. M530.28
Satanella: a story of Punchestown.....M530.29
Same. (*Also*) Market Harborough (*And*)
   Inside the bar...........................**M530.30
Sister Louise.................................M530.31
Same. (*Also*) Black but comely....**M530.32
Tilbury Nogo...........................*in* **M530.11
Same. (*Also*) Scotland and the moors...
   ....M530.33
Uncle John................................... M530. 34
Same. (*Also*) "Bones and I.".....**M530.35
White rose...............................*in* **M530.25
Same.................................... M530.36
MELVILLE, H. Moby-Dick; or, the
   whale........ ....M531.1
Omoo: a narrative of adventures in the
   south seas. Sequel to "Typee."......M531.2
Pierre; or, the ambiguities...............M531.3

MELVILLE, H.—*Continued.*
The refugee......................................M531.4
Typee: a real romance of the south
seas......... ....M531.5
White-Jacket; or, the world in a man-of-
war..M531.6
Member, The. Galt, J.....................G179.3
Same ....*in* G179.6
Member for Paris. Murray, E. C. G.....M982.1
Memoirs, etc., of Adam Graeme of Moss-
gray. Oliphant, M. O. W............O475.32
Memoirs of a cavalier. Defoe, D.........D314.4
Memoirs of a Magdalen. Kelly, H...*in* **N938.7
Memoirs of a millionaire. Ames, L. T...A513.1
Memoirs of a physician. Dumas, A.....D886.30
Memoirs of Barry Lyndon. Thackeray,
W. M......................................T363.10
Same...*in* T363.15
Memoirs of Mr. C. J. Yellowplush. Thack-
eray. W. M...................................T363.16
Memoirs of Sherlock Holmes. Doyle, A.
C......... .... D754.11
Memoirs of two young married women.
Balzac, H. de.............................B198.29
Memories. Müller, F. M.....................M958.1
Memories of troublous times. Marshall,
E......... ....M367.7
Men born equal. Robinson, H. P.........R661.1
Men of the moss-hags. Crockett, S. R..C938.11
Men, women, and ghosts. Phelps, E. S...
....Q539.11
MÉNARD, T. (*pseud.* of J. J. E. Roy.)
Adventures of a casket: an episode of
the invasion of 1814.....................M535.1
MENDÈS, *Mme.* J. G. *See* Gautier, J.
MENGER, R. Countess Loreley..........M544.1
Men's wives. Thackeray, W. M......*in* T363.13
Menshikoff. Aveline, A. d'.................A948.1
Mercedes of Castile. Cooper, J. F.....*in* C777.3
Same...C777.20
Merchant of Antwerp. Conscience, H....C755.5
Merchant of Berlin. Mühlbach, L,......M952.13
Mercy Philbrick's choice. Jackson, H.
M....... ....J127.3
Mère Suzanne, and other stories. Mac-
quoid, K. S.................................. M173.5
MEREDITH, G. Amazing marriage. 2
vols...M559.2
Beauchamp's career.........................M559.3
Diana of the crossways......................M559.4
The egoist: a comedy in narrative......M559.5
Evan Harrington.............................M559.6
Farina...*in* M559.12
Harry Richmond.............................M559.1

MEREDITH, G.—*Continued.*
Lord Ormont and his Aminta............M559.7
One of our conquerors.....................M559.8
Ordeal of Richard Feverel.................M559.9
Rhoda Fleming...............................M559.10
Sandra Belloni...............................M559.11
Issued also as Emilia in England.
Shaving of Shagpat; and, Farina......M559.12
Tragic comedians: a story................M559.13
Vittoria..M559.14
MEREDITH, O., *pseud. See* Lytton, E. R.
Bulwer-
MÉRIMÉE, P. Il viccolo di Madama Lu-
crezia. 34 pp.............................*in* R657.1
Venus of Ille............................ ...*in* G277.5
Merkland. Oliphant, M. O. W............O475.33
Merle's crusade. Carey, R. N............C276.20
Mermaid, The. Dougall, L.................D731.2
MERRIMAN, H. S. (*pseud.* of H. S. Scott.)
Flotsam M571.3
From one generation to another.........M571.4
The sowers....................................M571.7
With edged tools............................M571.9
Merry Chanter. Stockton, F. R..........S866.20
Merry men. Stevenson, R. L..............S848.7
Same, etc....................................S848.6
Merry tales. Twain, M.....................T969.3
Merry tales of the three wise men of
Gotham. Paulding, J. K..............**Q325.2
Mervyn Clitheroe. Ainsworth, W. H...A297.14
Mervyn's meed. Kerr, E..............*in* K411.1
Messrs. Vanderput and Snoek. Mar-
tineau, H.............................*in* **M385.15
Same........ ....M385.16
Meta Holdenis. Cherbuliez, V.............C521.3
Metamorphoses: a tale....................*in* T143.10
Metamorphoses. Apuleius...................A655.1
METEYARD, E. (Silverpen, *pseud.*) Main-
stone's housekeeper.........................M591.1
Metropolitans. Drake, J.....................D761.4
Metzerott, shoemaker. Woods, K. P.....W895.2
Mexican campaign. Janvier, T. A......*in* J358.3
MEYER, K. F. Tempting of Pescara......M612.1
Micah Clarke. Doyle, A. C...............D754.12
Michael Armstrong, Life and adventures
of. Trollope, F. M.......................T848.1
Michael Rudolph. Dupuy, E. A.........D945.5 .
Michael Strogoff. Verne, J...............V531.28
MICHAELIS, R. Looking further forward:
an answer to Looking backward, by E.
Bellamy M620.1
Michael's crag. Allen, G.................A425.11
Mick Tracy, the Irish scripture reader.....M625.1
Middlemarch. Eliot, G.....................E426.4

MIDDLEMORE, *Mrs.* S. G. C. Round a
posada fire: Spanish legends...........M627.1
Midge, The. Bunner, H. C.................B942.2
Midnight sun. Bremer, F.....................B836.7
Mighty atom. Corelli, M.....................C797.7
Mignon. Forrester, *Mrs.*.................... F730.6
MIKOULITCH, V. Mimi's marriage........M636.1
Mildred. Holmes, M. J.....................H751.22
Mildred's cadet. Hamilton, A. K.........H217.1
Miles O'Reilly, Life and adventures of.
Halpine, C. G...............................H195.1
Miles Wallingford. Cooper, J. F.......*in* C777.7
Same..C777.21
Military adventure in the Pyrenees. By a
peninsular medallist. 98 pp........*in* T143.9
Military sketches and stories. Forbes,
A., *and others*.....................................F692.1
Mill and the tavern. Arthur, T. S.........A791.3
Mill mystery. Green, A. K.................G795.6
Mill on the Floss. Eliot, G.................E426.6
MILLARD, F. B. Pretty bandit............M645.5
Millbank. Holmes, M. J.....................H751.23
MILLER, C. H. *See* Miller, J., *pseud.*
MILLER, H. Bill Whyte.................*in* W750.3
The lykewake.......................*in* W750.4
Recollections of Ferguson. Recollections
of Burns......................................*in* W750.1
Scenes and legends of the north of Scot-
land; or, the traditional history of
Cromarty...................................... M648.1
Scottish hunters of Hudson's Bay...*in* W750.6
Tales and sketches............................M648.2
Thomas of Chartres......................*in* W750.9
Widow of Dunskaith. Salmon-fisher of
Udoll. .... *in* W750.2
MILLER, J. (*pseud. of* C. H. Miller). Build-
ing of the city Beautiful.................M649.1
Danites in the Sierras.........................M649.2
Destruction of Gotham......................M649.3
First fam'lies of the Sierras...............M649.4
One fair woman M649.5
Miller of Angibault. Sand, G.............S213.11
MILLET, F. D. A capillary crime, and
other stories..................................M653.1
Yatil. 27 pp.....................................*in* S884.5
Millionaire of Rough-and-Ready. Harte,
B..H327.23
Mills of the gods. Twells, J. H.............T971.1
Mills of Tuxbury. Townsend, V. F.......T751.5
Mimi's marriage. Mikoulitch, V..........M636.1
Mine own people. Kipling, R...............K575.8
Mingo, and other sketches. Harris, J. C...H314.5
Minister's charge. Howells, W. D......H859.21
Minister's wife. *See* Beecher, E. W. B.

Minister's wife. Oliphant, M. O. W..... O475.34
Minister's wooing. Stowe, H. B............S892.4
Minstrel love. La Motte Fouqué, F. H.
K., *Freiherr* de...............................L235.3
Mirage. Fleming, G............................F597.3
Miriam. Harland, M............................H283.10
Miriam Balestier. Fawcett, E............F278.13
Miriam Coffin. Hart, J. C...................H325.1
Miriam's memoirs. Warfield, C. A.......W274.7
Mirza, The. Morier, J..........................M855.6
Misadventure. Norris, W. E...............N861.11
Misérables, Les. Hugo, V...................H895.3
Miser's daughter. Ainsworth, W. H....A297.16
Misfortunes of Elphin. Peacock, T. L....Q356.6
Miss Angel. Thackeray, A. I...............T362.2
Miss Bagg's secretary. Burnham, C. L...B966.5
Miss Bretherton. Ward, M. A. A.........W261.6
Miss Brooks. White, E. O...................W584.2
Miss Carew. Edwards, A. B................E261.3
Same..E261.4
Miss Cheyne of Essilmont. Grant, J....G761.32
Miss Churchill. Reid, C.....................R353.11
Miss Crespigny. Burnett, F. H.........*in* B964.3
Same...B964.14
Miss Defarge. Burnett, F. H.........*in* H113.10
Miss Eaton's romance. Allen, R.........A429.1
Miss Frances Merley. Curran, J. E.......C976.1
Miss Gilbert's career. Holland, J. G.....H735.3
"Miss Lou." Roe, E. P.........................R699.10
Miss Ludington's sister. Bellamy, E......B437.3
Miss Mackenzie. Trollope, A..............T846.19
Miss Marjoribanks. Oliphant, M. O. W......
.... O475.35
Miss Meredith. Mathers, H............*in* M426.1
Miss Misanthrope. McCarthy, J.........M122.7
Miss Molly. Butt, B. M.......................B988.1
Miss Mordeck's father. Gooch, *Mrs.* F.
P...G645.1
Miss Oona McQuarrie. Smith, A...........S642.1
Miss Richards' boy, etc. Holley, M........H738.1
Miss Roberts' lodger. Noble, A. L........N747.3
Miss Stuart's legacy. Steel, F. A...........S813.1
Miss Tommy. Mulock, D. M.............M960.17
Miss Van Kortland. Benedict, F. L......B463.4
Miss Wentworth's idea. Norris, W. E..N861.12
Miss Williamson's divagations. Thack-
eray, A. I...T362.3
Miss Wilton. Warren, C.....................W287.1
Missing. Hay, M. C............................H413.4
Missing bills: an unsolved mystery. 54
pp..*in* T143.16
Mission. Marryat, *Capt.* F..................M362.9
Missionary sheriff. Thanet, O..............T367.7
Mist of error. Dickens, M. A...............D549.1

Mr. Absalom Billingslea, and other Georgian folk. Johnston, R. M...........J733.5

Mr. and Mrs. Morton. Williams, *Dr. and Mrs.* H.................................W721.1

Mr. Barnes of New York. Gunter, A. C...
....G977.9

Mr. C. J. Yellowplush, Memoirs of. Thackeray, W. M.................................T363.16

Mr. Facey Romford's hounds. Surtees, R. S..S962.2

Mr. George Edwards, a Creole. 67 pp. Hill, J..............................*in* **N938.23

Mr. Ghin's dream.............................M678.1

Mr. Gilfil's love-story. Eliot, G.......*in* E426.8

Mr. Isaacs. Crawford, F. M.............C899.13

Mr. Jonathan Wild the Great. Fielding, H...F459.3

Mr. Ledbury and his friend Jack Johnson, Adventures of. Smith, A.............S641.4

Mr. Meeson's will. Haggard, H. R.....H146.10

Mr. Midshipman Easy. Marryat, *Capt.* F.....
....M362.10

Mr. Oldmixon. Hammond, W. A.........H227.2

Mr. Peter Crewitt. Denison, M. A.......D396.1

Mr. Phillips' goneness. Bailey, J. M....B154.1

Mr. Potter of Texas. Gunter, A. C......G977.10

Mr. Scarborough's family. Trollope, A.....
....T846.20

Mr. Smith. Walford, L. B.................W174.7

Mr. Tangier's vacations. Hale, E. E...H161.11

Mr. Tommy Dove, and other stories. Deland, M.....................................D337.5

Mistress and maid. Mulock, D. M....M960.18

Mrs. Armington's ward. Wright, D. T...
....W948.1

Mrs. Arthur. Oliphant, M. O. W.........O475.36

Mistress Beatrice Cope. Le Clerc, M. E...
....L462.1

Mrs. Beauchamp Brown. Austin, J. G...A936.7

Mrs. Beauchamp's vengeance. 50 pp...
....*in* T143.17

Mrs. Cliff's yacht. Stockton, F. R........S866.22

Mrs. Curgenven of Curgenven. Gould, S. B..G698.7

Mistress Dorothy Marvin. Snaith, J. C...S669.3

Mrs. Gainsborough's diamonds. Hawthorne, J..H398.13

Mrs. Geoffrey. Duchess....................D829.12

Mrs. Harold Stagg. Grant, R..............G763.5

Mrs. Herndon's income. Campbell, H...C188.1

Mistress Judith. Tytler, C. C. F..........T996.2

Mrs. Keats Bradford. Pool, M. L........Q821.10

Mrs. Limber's raffle. Butler, W. A........B987.1

Mrs. Lorimer. Malet, L....................M247.3

Mrs. Martin's company, and other stories. Barlow, J.....................................B258.8

Mrs. Mayburn's twins. Habberton, J....H113.8

Mrs. Merriam's scholars. Hale, E. E...H161.10

Mistress of Beech Knoll. Burnham, C. L...B966.6

Mistress of Brae Farm. Carey, R. N.....C276.21

Mistress of Sherburne. Douglas, A. M...D734.35

Mistress of the house. Chamberlain, P. B...C443.1

Mrs. Peixada. Harland, H.................H282.10

Mrs. Skaggs's husbands, and other sketches..
Harte, B..H327.24

Mistress Spitfire. Fletcher, J. S.........F613.3

Mrs. Temperly. 59 pp. James, H., *Jr...in* J277.9

Mrs. Vereker's courier maid. Alexander, *Mrs.*.................................*in* A374.27

Misunderstood. Montgomery, F..........M787.1

MITCHELL, D. G. Doctor Johns. 2 vols...
....M679.1

Dream life: a fable of the seasons.......M679.2

Reveries of a bachelor.....................M679.3

Seven stories, with basement and attic...
....M679.4

MITCHELL, E. P. Ablest man in the world. 28 pp..................................*in* S884.10

The Tachypomp: a mathematical demonstration. 24 pp.....................*in* S884.5

MITCHELL, J. A. Amos Judd............M680.1

That first affair and other sketches......M680.7

MITCHELL, S. W. In war time...........M681.1

Roland Blake.................................M681.2

MITCHELL, W. Two strings to his bow....M682.1

MITFORD, A. B. Tales of old Japan......M683.1

MITFORD, M. R. Freshwater fisherman. 7 pp..*in* J737.1

Same.....................................*in* T559.1

Our village: sketches of rural character and scenery. 2 vols....................M684.1

Tajima.....................................*in* S885.7

Mito Yashiki. Maclay, A. C.............M162.1

Moby-Dick. Melville, H...................M531.1

Model of Christian Gay. Vachell, H. A...
....V118.1

Modern Adam and Eve in a garden. Douglas, A. M.................................D734.19

Modern Agrippa. White, C. E...........W583.2

Modern buccaneer. Boldrewood, R......B687.5

Modern ghosts: selected and translated. Introd. by G. W. Curtis.................M690.1

CONTENTS: Curtis, G. W. Introd.—Maupassant, G. de. The Horla. On the river.
—Kielland, A. L. Siesta.—Alarcón, P. A. de. The tall woman.—Becquer, G. A. Maese Pérez, the organist.—Magheriui-Graziaui, G. Fioraccio.—Kompert, L. The silent woman.

Modern Griselda. 82 pp. Edgeworth,
M...............................*in* **B232.50
Same.................................*in* **E235.2
Same.................................*in* E235.25
Modern instance. Howells, W. D.......H859.22
Modern Magdalene. Woods, V...........W897.1
Modern Mephistopheles. Alcott, L. M...A355.2
Modern Midas. Jókai, M.....................J745.7
Modern Telemachus. Yonge, C. M......Y555.21
Modern warning. James, H., *Jr*......*in* J277.2
Modeste Mignon. Balzac, H. de..........B198.30
Mohawks. Braddon, M. E................B798.23
Mohicans of Paris. Dumas, A............D886.31
Mohun. Cooke, J. E.........................C772.9
MOIR, D. M. Bridal of Borthwick......*in* Q594.1
Divinity student.... ....*in* W750.3
MOLESWORTH, M. L. (Ennis Graham,
pseud.) Hathercourt.....................M719.1
Philippa.................................. M719.2
Molly Bawn. Duchess...................D829.13
Moloch of fashion. Lovelace, F...........L898.1
Monarch of dreams. Higginson, T. W....H637.2
Monarch of Mincing-Lane. Black, W....B627.21
Monastery, The. Scott, *Sir* W.............S431.33
Same.................................S431.34
MONCREIFF, F. The X jewel..............M739.1
MONCREIFF, H. J. *See* Wellwood, H. J.
Moncreiff, *Lord.*
MONCRIEFF, *Mrs.* W. G. SCOTT- An Elie
ruby. 61 pp.....................*in* T143.19
Such pity as a father hath. 46 pp...*in* T143.23
Money-god. Quinton, M. A.................Q995.1
Money-makers. Keenan, H. F............K267.2
Monikins, The. Cooper, J. F...............C777.22
Same...............................*in* C777.46
Monk and knight. 2 vols. Gunsaulus,
F. W.................................G976.1
Monk of Fife. Lang, A.....................L269.4
Monk of the Aventine. Eckstein, E......E195.3
Monsieur le ministre. Claretie, J..........C591.1
Monsieur Lecoq. 2 pts. Gaboriau, E......G116.7
Monsieur Sylvestre. Sand, G............S213.13
Monsieur Violet. Marryat, *Capt.* F...*in* M362.11
Same.................................M362.13
MONTAGUE, C. H. Countess Muta........M759.1
Montezuma's daughter. Haggard, H. R...
....H146.11
Montezuma's gold mines. Ober, F. A......O125.1
MONTGOMERY, F. Misunderstood M787.1
Thwarted; or, ducks' eggs in a hen's
nest.................................M787.2
MONTRÉSOR, F. F. False coin or true?...
....M811.1

MONTRÉSOR, F. F.—*Continued.*
Into the highways and hedges............M811.2
One who looked on..........................M811.3
Worth while.................................M811.6
Moods. Alcott, L. M..........................A355.3
Moondyne. O'Reilly, J. B................O665.1
Moonlight boy. Howe, E. W..............H855.2
Moonshine. 20 pp. Marryat, *Capt.* F...
....*in* **M362.26
Moonstone. Collins, W......................C713.23
Moor of Granada. Guenot, H..............G927.1
MOORE, E. The gamester. 25 pp....*in* M875.1 [2]
MOORE, F. F. Impudent comedian, and
others...................................M820.5
MOORE, G. Vain fortune....................M821.1
MOORE, *Dr.* J. Edward: various views of
human nature, chiefly in England.
2 vols...................................M822.1
Same. 4 vols..........................**M822.2
Zeluco. 2 vols...........................**B232.34-5
MOOREHEAD, W. K. Wanneta, the Sioux...
.... M825.1
Moral of many fables. Martineau, H...
....*in* **M385.11
Moral tales. Marmontel, J. F..............M352.1
Same...............................*in* **N938.6
MORE, H. Coelebs in search of a wife...M835.1
Same. (*Also*) Essays (*And*) Moriana...
.... M835.3
Moriana.................................*in* M835.2
Repository tales...........................M835.4
Shepherd of Salisbury Plain, and other
tales...................................M835.5
More bywords. Yonge, C. M..............Y555.22
More "short sixes." Bunner, H. C.........B942.3
MORELL, *Sir* C., *tr.* Tales of the genii...
....*in* **N938.3
MORFORD, H. Sprees and splashes; or,
droll recollections of town and country..
.... M846.1
MORGAN, *Lady* S. O. Florence Macarthy...
.... M850.1
Wild Irish girl: a national tale. 3 vols...
.... M850.2
Morgan's horror. Fenn, G. M..............F334.2
Moriana. More, H.....................*in* M835.2
MORIER, J. Abel Allnutt.....................M855.1
Ayesha, the maid of Kars...............M855.3
The banished: a Swabian historical tale...
....M855.4
Hajji Baba in England......................M855.5
Hajji Baba in Turkey, etc.................M855.2
The Mirza.................................M855.6
Zohrab the hostage.......................M855.7

MORLEY, F. T. PARKER, *Countess of.*
Dacre: a novel.........................**M864.1
Morley Ashton. Grant, J....................G761.33
Morley Ernstein. James, G. P. R.........J276.31
MORRIS, C. Tales from the dramatists. 3
vols...... ....M875.1
CONTENTS: v. 1: Jonson, B. Every man
in his humor.—Beaumont, F., *and* Fletcher,
J. Philaster; or, love lies bleeding.—Massin-
ger, P. New way to pay old debts.—Otway,
T. Venice preserved.—Centlivre, S. The
busybody.—Farquhar, G. The beaux' stratagem.—Cowley II. The belle's stratagem.
v. 2: Moore, E. The gamester.—Home, J.
Douglas.—Goldsmith, O. She stoops to conquer.—Holcroft, T. Road to ruin.—O'Keefe,
J. Wild oats.—Sheridan, R. B. B. School
for scandal. The rivals.
v. 3: Colman, G. Poor gentleman. Heir
at law.—Morton, T. Speed the plough.—
Tobin, J. The honeymoon.—Knowles, J. S.
The wife.—Sheil, R. L. The apostate.—Tal-
fourd, *Sir* T. N. Ion.
MORRIS, W. Dream of John Ball, and, A
king's lesson..................................M877.4
A king's lesson..........................*in* M877.4
News from nowhere: some chapters from
a Utopian romance.......................M877.1
Roots of the mountains....................M877.5
Story of the glittering plain..............M877.2
Tale of the house of the Wolfings......M877.7
Well at the world's end. 2 vols.........M877.6
Wood beyond the world....................M877.3
MORRISON, A. Child of the Jago........M878.3
That brute Simmons. 13 pp..........*in* S885.6
MORROW, W. C. The ape, the idiot, and
other people................................M883.1
MORSE, L. G. Rachel Stanwood..........M885.1
Mortal antipathy. Holmes, O. W.........H752.3
Mortomley's estate. Riddell, C. E. L....R543.11
MORTON, T. Speed the plough. 30 pp.....
....*in* M875.1 3
Morton House. Reid, C.....................R353.12
Mose Evans. Baker, W. M..................B169.5
Moss-side. Harland, M.....................H283.11
Mosses from an old manse. Hawthorne,
N..H399.7
Mother of a marquise. About, E..........A156.3
Mother's recompense. Aguilar, G.........A283.4
Moths. Ouida...............................O934.14
Motto changed. Ingelow, J................I464.4
MOUHY, C. DE F. *Chevalier* DE. For-
tunate country maid..............*in* **N938.7
MOULTON, L. C. My third book.........M927.1
Some women's hearts......................M927.2
Mount Eden. Marryat, F...................M361.7
Mount Royal. Braddon, M. E............B798.24

Mountain-White heroine. Kirke, E......K594.2
Mountain woman. Peattie, E. W.........Q363.1
Mozart: a biographical romance. Rau,
H...R269.2
Mudfog papers. Dickens, C...............D548.27
MUDFORD, W. First and last. 14 pp......
....*in* T143.2
Same.......................................*in* T143.2 2
Iron shroud. 22 pp.....................*in* T143.1
Same.......................................*in* T143.1 1
MÜGGE, T. Afraja; or, life and love in
Norway..M951.1
MUHAMMED DIYAB Al-Ailidi. 'Ilâm-en-
Nâs: historical tales, etc., of the times
of the early Khalîfahs. Tr. from the
Arabic by Mrs. A. M. Clerk.............C631.1
MÜHLBACH, L. (*pseud. of* C. M. Mundt.)
Andreas Hofer.............................M952.1
Bernthal; or, the son's revenge..........M952.3
Daughter of an empress..................M952.4
Empress Josephine.........................M952.5
Frederick the Great and his court......M952.6
Frederick the Great and his family.....M952.7
Goethe and Schiller.......................M952.8
Henry the Eighth and his court.........M952.9
Joseph II. and his court...................M952.10
Louisa of Prussia and her times.........M952.11
Maria Theresa and her fireman.....*in* M952.13
Marie Antoinette and her son............M952.12
Merchant of Berlin. (*Also*) Maria
Theresa and her fireman...............M952.13
1st story *issued also as* Frederick the Great
and his merchant.
Napoleon and Blücher.....................M952.15
Napoleon and the Queen of Prussia....M952.16
Old Fritz and the new era...... ....M952.17
Prince Eugene and his times.............M952.18
Two life-paths...............................M952.20
MULHOLLAND, C. Kathleen mavourneen....
....M955.1
MULHOLLAND, R. Fair emigrant.........M956.1
MÜLLER, C. (*pseud. of* E. C. W. van Wal-
rée.) The burgomaster's family......M957.1
MÜLLER, F. M. Memories: a story of
German love...............................M958.1
MULLER, O. Charlotte Ackerman........M959.1
Dr. Goethe's courtship....................M959.2
MULOCK, D. M. (*Mrs. Craik.*) About
money and other things.................M960.1
Agatha's husband...........................M960.2
Alice Learmont.........................*in* M960.10
Brave lady...................................M960.4
Bread upon the waters....................M960.5
Same.......................................*in* M960.10

MULOCK, M. D.—*Continued.*
Christian's mistake............................M960.6
Hannah..M960.8
Head of the family.............................M960.9
A hero. (*Also*) Bread upon the waters.
(*And*) Alice Learmont.................M960.10
His little mother, and other tales......M960.11
In a house-boat......................*in* M960.17
John Halifax, Gentleman.................M960.12
King Arthur, not a love story............M960.13
The laurel bush................................M960.14
Life for a life..... ....M960.15
Miss Tommy, and, In a house-boat...M960.17
Mistress and maid...........................M960.18
My mother and I.............................M960.19
A noble life....................................M960.20
The Ogilvies..................................M960.21
Olive..M960.23
Studies from life............................M960.25
Two marriages...............................M960.26
Unkind word, and other stories........M960.27
Will Denbigh, nobleman..................M960.28
Woman's kingdom...........................M960.29
Young Mrs. Jardine..........................M960.30
Mumu. Turgénieff, I. S.....................T936.7
MUNDT, *Mrs.* C. M. See Mühlbach, L.,
pseud.
MUNDT, T. Count Mirabeau.............M965.1
Murad the unlucky. Edgeworth, M...
...................................*in* **E235.6
Same...*in* E235.20
MURFREE, F. N. D. Felicia..............M975.1
MURFREE, M. N. See Craddock, C. E.,
pseud.
MURGER, H. Francine's muff. 11 pp.
Passage of the Red sea. 9 pp....*in* Z767.1 ¹
Scenes from the life of Bohemia M976.1
Murphy's master. Payn, J...................Q345.16
MURRAY, C. A. The prairie-bird..........M980.1
MURRAY, D. C. By the gate of the sea...
.... M981.1
First person singular.......................M981.2
Hearts: queen, knave, and deuce..... ...M981.3
Joseph's coat.................................M981.5
Life's atonement.............................M981.6
Martyred fool................................M981.7
Rainbow gold................................M981.8
Time's revenges.............................M981.9
Val Strange..................................M981.10
"Way of the world."........................M981.11
Weaker vessel...............................M981.12
MURRAY, E. C. G. Member for Paris:
a tale of the second empire.............M982.1

MURRAY, W. H. H. Adirondack tales. v.
1: Story that the keg told me. Story
of the man who didn't know much.
.... M984.1
Murvale Eastman. Tourgée, A. W........T727.9
MUSAEUS, J. K. A. Dumb lover......*in* R794.1 ³
Same. Libussa. Melechsala.........*in* C286.1
Music hath charms. Ferguson, V. M.....F353.1
Musical sketches. Polko, E..................Q770.1
MUSICK, J. R. Columbia: a story of the
discovery of America......................M987.1
Estevan: a story of the Spanish con-
quests..M987.2
St. Augustine: a story of the Huguenots
in America...................................M987.3
Muskingum legends. Powers, S...........Q888.1
MUSSET, A. DE. Story of a white blackbird.
38 pp...............................*in* R657.1
Mute confessor. Harben, W. N...........H255.1
My after-dinner adventures with Peter
Schlemihl. 43 pp.................*in* T143.15
My aunt Margaret's mirror. Scott, *Sir*
W......... .... *in* S431.15
Same..............................*in* **S431.19
Same.............................. *in* S431.51
My aunt Pontypool. James, G. P. R...*in* J276.4
My brother. Brown, V......................B882.1
My brother's keeper. Warner, A. B......W279.2
My brother's wife. Edwards, A. B.....*in* E261.4
My college friends: Charles Russell, the
gentleman-commoner................*in* T143.2
Same..............................*in* T143.2 ²
No. 2: Horace Leicester. 45 pp. No. 3:
W. Wellington Hurst. 43 pp...... *in* T143.3
Same..............................*in* T143.3 ²
My Danish sweetheart. Russell, W. C...
....R968.14
My daughter Elinor. Benedict, F. L..... B463.5
My desire. Warner, S.......................W284.6
My enemy's daughter. McCarthy, J......M122.8
My first love. Riddell, C. E. L............R543.12
My friend Jim. Norris, W. E.............N861.13
My friend the boss. Hale, E. E.........H161.12
My friend the murderer. Doyle, A. C....D754.13
My good friend. Bélot, A..................B452.3
My health. Burnand, F. C.................B963.1
My investment in the far west. 50 pp...
....*in* T143.18
My lady Coquette. Rita....................R598.4
My lady Nicotine. Barrie, J. M......*in* B275.2
Same..B275.7
My lady Nobody. Maartens, M............M111.8
My lady Pokahontas. Cooke, J. E......C772.10
My lady Rotha. Weyman, S. J.......W549.12

My last love. Riddell, C. E. L.........*in* R543.12

My little girl. Besant, *Sir* W., *and* Rice, J.....................................B554.41

My little lady. Poynter, E. F.............Q892.4

My little love. Harland, M.................H283.12

My lord and my lady. Forrester, *Mrs*...F730.7

My mother and I. Mulock, D. M.....M960.19

My mother's manuscript. Lamartine, A. de..L217.3

"My novel." 2 vols. Lytton, E. G. E. L. Bulwer-................................L998.16

My official wife. Savage, R. H...........S265.3

My shipmate Louise. Russell, W. C....R968.15

My sister Jeannie. Sand, G.............S213.14

My third book. Moulton, L. C.............M927.1

My time and what I've done with it. Burnand, F. C....................................B963.2

My trivial life and misfortune. 2 pts. Barter, K..B283.1

My uncle and my curé. La Brète, J. de....L126.1

My uncle Scipio. Theuriet, A...............T415.5

My uncle the curate. Savage, M. W......S264.3

My uncle's garret window. 46 pp. Lewis, M. G......................................*in* L675.1

My wife and I. Stowe, H. B.............S892.5

My wife and my wife's sister. Latimer, E. W..L357.1

My wonderful wife. Corelli, M........*in* C797.15

My young Alcides. Yonge, C. M.......Y555.23

My young master. Read, O. P.............R284.3

Mysteries of Paris. Sue, E.................S944.3

Mysteries of Redgrave Court. 34 pp. Smedley, F. E....................*in* S637.2

Mysteries of the unseen. Campbell, *Sir* G.......................................C187.2

Mysteries of Udolpho. Radcliffe, A. W... ....R125.1

Same. 3 vols...................**B232.45-7

Mysterious disappearance.............*in* W750.8

Mysterious island. Verne, J.............V531.30

Mystery of Edwin Drood. Dickens, C...D548.28

Same..D548.29

Same...*in* D548.50

Mystery of Metropolisville. Eggleston, E...E294.7

Mystery of Mrs. Blencarrow. Oliphant, M. O. W.......................O475.37

Mystery of Orcival. Gaboriau, E.........G116.8

Mystery of the locks. Howe, E. W......H855.3

Mystery of the "Ocean Star," etc. Russell, W. C....................................R968.16

Mystery of the Patrician Club. Vandam, A. D.....................................V224.1

Mystery of Witch-face mountain. Craddock, C. E....................................C884.10

NACHTIGAL, O. *See* Otmar, *pseud.*

Nada the lily. Haggard, H. R...........H146.12

Nadya. Norris, O. M.........................N857.5

Nameless nobleman. Austin, J. G........A936.8

Nancy. Broughton, R......................B877.4

Nancy Noon. Swift, B......................S978.6

Nanon. Dumas, A...........................D886.45

Nantucket scraps. Austin, J. G..........A936.9

Napoleon and Blücher. Mühlbach, L...M952.15

Napoleon and the Queen of Prussia. Mühlbach, L.....................................M952.16

NARES, E. Thinks-I-to-myself: a serioludicro, tragico-comico tale...N226.1

Narka, the nihilist. O'Meara, K.........O552.1

Narrative of Herbert Willis, B. D. 61 pp... ....*in* T143.4

Same...*in* T143.4 '

NASBY, P. V., *pseud. See* Locke, D. R.

Nash, W. G. Century of gossip...........N253.1

Nathalie. Kavanagh, J....................K212.8

NATHUSIUS, M. VON. Elizabeth...........N276.1

Native of Winby, etc. Jewett, S. O........J593.12

Natolian story-teller. 69 pp..............*in* T143.6

Same...*in* T143.6 '

Nature and art. Inchbald, E. S....*in* **B232.27

Nature's serial story. Roe, E. P.........R699.11

Naulahka. Kipling, R., *and* Balestier, W... ....K575.15

Necera. Graham, J. W....................G740.1

NEAL, J. Down-easters, &c. &c. &c. 2 vols...................................**N341.1

Kentuckian in New York. 2 vols....**N341.2

Neal Malone. Carleton, W............*in* C281.7

Near to happiness. Tr. by F. H. Potter....Q866.1

Near to nature's heart. Roe, E. P.....R699.12

Nearer and dearer. Bede, C.............B411.2

NEEDELL, *Mrs.* J. H. Lucia, Hugh, and another.............................N374.1

Passing the love of women............N374.2

Stephen Ellicott's daughter...........N374.3

Vengeance of James Vansittart........N374.4

NEELE, H. Romance of history: England... ....N379.1

Neighbor Jackwood. Trowbridge, J. T...T863.3

Neighbours (and other stories). Bremer, F..B836.8

Neighbours on the green. Oliphant, M. O. W........................O475.38

Nellie Harland. Vance, E. E.............V223.1

Nellie Netterville. Caddell, C. M..........C121.1

Nellie's memories. Carey, R. N...........C276.22

Nelly Kinnard's kingdom. Douglas, A.
M...................................D734.20
Nemesis. Harland, M.................H283.13
Nemesis of faith. Froude, J. A..........F942.1
Nenuphar: a fancy. 48 pp.............*in* T143.18
Nephelé. Bourdillon, F.W.................B769.3
Nero. 2 vols. Eckstein, E.............E195.4
NESBIT, E. In homespun.................N458.3
Never too late to mend. Reade, C......R285.14
Same, etc..........................R285.15
NEVILLE, C. M. Behind the arras........N522.1
NEVILLE, E. Alice Ashland............... N523.1
NEVILLE, R. Lloyd Pennant: a tale of the
west...............................N525.1
NEVINSON, H. W. In the valley of
Tophet............................N528.4
New Antigone. Barry, *Rev. Dr.*-..........B280.1
New Arabian nights. Stevenson, R. L....S848.9
New home—who'll follow? Kirkland, C.
M...................................K598.2
New Magdalen. Collins, W..............C713.24
New Nero. Fawcett, E.................F278.15
New nobility. Forney, J. W.............F727.1
New Paul and Virginia. Mallock, W. H...
.... M255.2
New Penelope. 71 pp. Victor, F. A. F.....V642.1
New priest in Conception bay. 2 vols.
Lowell, R. T. S.....................L916.2
New race. Raimund, G...............W817.22
New republic. Mallock, W. H............M255 3
New tales. Opie, A...................*in* O614.2
New Timothy. Baker, W. M.............B169.6
New waggings of old tales. Bangs, J. K.,
and Sherman, F. D.................B216.1
NEWBY, *Mrs.* C. J. Wondrous strange...N535.1
Newcomes. Thackeray, W. M...........T363.17
NEWELL, C. M. Kalani of Oahu: an his-
torical romance of Hawaii............N544.1
New England nun, and other stories. Wil-
kins, M. E..........................W684.8
NEWMAN, J. H. Callista: a sketch of the
3d century.........................N553.1
Newport. Lathrop, G. P..............L354.4
News from nowhere. Morris, W.........M877.1
Newton Forster. Marryat, *Capt.* F......M362.12
Same...............................M362.13
Next door. Burnham, C. L............B966.8
NICANDER, K. A. Renounced treasure...
.................................*in* J737.1
Same..............................*in* T559.1
Nicholas Minturn. Holland, J. G.........H735.4
Nicholas Nickleby. Dickens, C..........D548.30
Same D548.31

NICHOLLS, *Mrs.* C. B. *See* Brontë, C.
NICHOLS, G. W. The sanctuary: a story
of the civil war....................N618.1
NICHOLSON, J. J. The Blemmertons......N626.1
NICHOLSON, J. S. Dreamer of dreams: a
modern romance................. ....N627.1
Nick of the woods. Bird, R. M..........B618.2
Nicolas Muss, History of. Du Bois-Melly,
C. D814.1
Night and morning. Lytton, E. G. E. L.
Bulwer-........... ....L998.17
Night side of nature. Crowe, C. S.........C953.1
Night-wanderer of an Afghaun fort. 52
pp....................................*in* T143.11
Nightmare Abbey. Peacock, T. L.........Q356.7
Night's adventure in Rome (1830). Ains-
worth, W. H.......................*in* A297.1
Nimble dollar, with other stories. Thomp-
son, C. M..........................T469.5
Nimport. Bynner, E. L................B994.4
Nimrod & Co. Ohnet, G................O383.5
Nina's atonement, and other stories. Reid,
C...................................R353.13
Nine of hearts. Farjeon, B. L...........*in* F229.1
Same...............................F229.13
Ninette. Dempster, C. L...............D389.1
Ninety-three. 2 vols. Hugo, V..........H895.4
NISBET, J. Siege of Damascus. 3 vols...
....**N723.1
Nix's mate. Dawes, R.................D270.1
No alternative. Thomas, A.............T453.3
No enemy (but himself). Hubbard, E...H874.1
"No gentlemen." Burnham, C. L.........B966.9
No laggards we. Raymond, R. W.........R271.1
No name. Collins, W..................C713.25
No new thing. Norris, W. E............N861.14
No quarter! Reid, M..................R357.6
NOBLE, A. L. Eunice Lathrop, spinster...N747.1
In a country town...................N747.2
Miss Roberts' lodgers...............N747.3
NOBLE, L. G. A reverend idol...........N750.1
Noble life. Mulock, D. M..............M960.20
Noble name. Glümer, C. von...........W817.1
Noblesse oblige. Roberts, M...........R646.1
Nobody's fortune. Yates, E............Y317.7
Norah. Holmes, M. J................*in* H751.3
Nora's love test. Hay, M. C...........H413.5
Nora's return. Cheney, E. D.............C518.1
NORDAU, M. Comedy of sentiment......N828.1
Norman Leslie. 2 vols. Fay, T. M...**F282.1
Norman Sinclair. 3 vols. Aytoun, W. E...A990.1
NORRIS, O. M. Nadya: a tale of the
steppes..............................N857.5

Norris, W. E. Bachelor's blunder......N861.1
Baffled conspirators............................N861.2
Bianca..*in* S885.5
Chris..N861.3
Countess Radna.............................N861.4
Heaps of money.................................N861.5
His Grace..N861.6
Mademoiselle de Mersac...................N861.7
Major and minor. 2 vols...................N861.8
Matrimony.......................................N861.9
Matthew Austin...............................N861.10
Misadventure..................................N861.11
Miss Wentworth's idea.....................N861.12
My friend Jim.................................N861.13
No new thing..................................N861.14
The rogue......................................N861.15
Romance of Madame de Chanteloup. 49
  pp...*in* S887.1
St. Ann's.......................................N861.16
Norseman's pilgrimage. Boyesen, H. H...B791.7
North, Christopher, *pseud.* See Wil-
  son, J.
North, W. Man of the world.............N867.1
    Issued also as Slave of the lamp.
North and south. Gaskell, E. C...........G248.5
North country comedy. Edwards, M. B...E267.3
Northanger Abbey. Austen, J.............A933.3
Same..*in* A933.5
Norton, C. E. S. (*Lady Stirling-Max-
  well.*) Lost and saved..................N883.1
Old Sir Douglas.............................N883.2
The wife, and, Woman's reward. 2 vols.
  ....**N883.3
Norwood. Beecher, H. W..................B415.1
Not angels quite. Dole, N. H.............D663.3
Not dead yet. Jeaffreson, J. C............J432.1
Not in society, and other tales. Hatton,
  J. H366.2
Not in their set. Lenzen, M................L575.1
Not like other girls. Carey, R. N........C276.23
Not wisely but too well. Broughton, R...B877.5
Notary's daughter. Donnet, L............D686.1
Notary's nose. About, E...................A156.4
Notre-Dame de Paris. Hugo, V........H895.5
Nott, C. C. Tale of a goblin horse. 48
  pp...*in* S886.3
Nourjahad. 38 pp. Sheridan, F...*in* **N938.23
Novelist's magazine. 23 vols........**N938.1-23
    Contents: 1: Hawkesworth, J. Almoran
    and Hamet.—Fielding, H. Joseph Andrews.
    Amelia.
      2: Langhorne, J. Solyman and Almena.
    —Goldsmith, O. Vicar of Wakefield.—Smol-
    lett, T. G. Roderick Random.—Voltaire, F.
    M. A. de. Zadig.—LeSage, A. R. Devil
    upon two sticks, etc.

Novelist's magazine—*Continued.*
      3: Morell, Sir C., *tr.* Tales of the genii.
    —Fielding, H. Tom Jones.
      4: Smollett, T. G. Gil Blas.—Defoe, D.
    Robinson Crusoe.
      5: Sterne, L. Tristram Shandy.—Gueul-
    lette, T. S. Chinese tales.—Dodd, W. The
    sisters.
      6: Smollett, T. G. Peregrine Pickle.—
    Marmontel, J. F. Moral tales.
      7: Mouhy, C. de F., *Chevalier* de. For-
    tunate country maid.—Kelly, H. Louisa
    Mildmay.—Langhorne, J. Theodosius and
    Constantia.—Smollett, T. G. Ferdinand,
    Count Fathom.
      8: Cervantes Saavedra, M. de. Don
    Quixote.
      9: Sterne, L. Sentimental journey.—Swift,
    J. Gulliver's travels.—Fielding, S. David
    Simple.—Smollett, T. G. Sir Launcelot
    Greaves.—Grafigny, F. de. Letters of a
    Peruvian princess.—Fielding, H. Jonathan
    Wild the Great.
      10-11: Richardson, S. Sir Charles Grandi-
    son.
      12: Lennox, C. Female Quixote.—Field-
    ing, H. Journey from this world to the next.
    —Kimber, E. Joe Thompson.—Paltock, R.
    Peter Wilkins.
      13: Haywood, E. Betsy Thoughtless.—
    Philips, A., *tr.* Thousand and one days: Per-
    sian tales.
      14-15: Richardson, S. Clarissa Harlowe.
      16: Avellaneda, A. F. de. Continuation of
    Don Quixote.—Marivaux, P. C. de C. de.
    Virtuous orphan.
      17: Fenelon, F. de S. de la M. Telemachus.
    —Treyssac de Vergy, P. H. Henrietta, Coun-
    tess Osenvor.—Haywood, E. Jemmy and
    Jenny Jessamy.
      18: Arabian nights' entertainments; tr.
    from the Fr. of M. Galland.
      19: Coventry, F. Pompey the little.—
    Fielding, S. Ophelia.—Gueullette, T. S.
    Tartarian tales.—Smollett, T. G. Humphry
    Clinker.
      20: Richardson, S. Pamela.
      21: Humphreys, S., *tr.* Peruvian tales.—
    Berington, S. Signor Gaudentio di Lucca.—
    Smollett, T. G. Adventures of an atom.—
    Voltaire, F. M. A. de. Sincere Huron.—
    Dorrington, E. English hermit.
      22: Shebbeare, J. Lydia.—Sheridan, F.
    Sidney Bidulph.
      23: Johnson, S. Rasselas, Prince of Abis-
    sinia.—Lennox, C. Henrietta.—Sheridan, F.
    Nourjahad.—Collyer, J. Letters from Felicia
    to Charlotte.—Hill, Sir J. Mr. George Ed-
    wards, a Creole.—Haywood, E. Invisible
    spy.

Now and then. Warren, S..................W293.1
Now-a-days. Marshall, E...................M367.8
Nowadays, and other stories. Hibbard, G.
  A...H624.2
Nugents of Carriconna. Hopkins, T....H796.1

Numa Roumestan. Daudet, A............D238.8
Nun's curse. Riddell, C. E. L............R543.13
Nurse Elisia. Fenn, G. M............F334.3
Nuttie's father. Yonge, C. M............Y555.24
NYE, E. W. Guest at the Ludlow.........N994.1
O. T. Andersen, H. C...................A544.2
"O thou, my Austria!" Schubin, O.....W817.27
Oak-openings. Cooper, J. F............C777.23
Same...... ....C777.24
Oakridge. Smith, J. E...................S652.1
OBER, F. A. Montezuma's gold mines...O125.1
Oblivion. McClelland, M. G............. M126.3
O'BRIEN, F. J. Spider's eye. 24 pp...in S884.3
O'BRIEN, W. When we were boys........O134.1
O'BYRNE, M. L. Court of Rath Croghan...
....O138.1
Occidental sketches. Truman, B. C......T867.1
Occupations of a retired life. Garrett, E...
....G239.10
Ocean tragedy. Russell, W. C............R968.18
O'CONNOR, W. D. The ghost.............O196.1
Same. (Also) Brazen android. (And)
The carpenter.................O196.2
Oddfellows' offering, for 1848. Ed. by J.
L. Ridgely and P. Donaldson........**R546.1
Odd number. Maupassant, G. de.........M452.1
Odd, or even? Whitney, A. D. T..........W617.5
Odd situation. Waterloo, S.................W327.1
Odd women. Gissing, G....................G535.4
O'DONOGHUE, N. P. Unfairly won......O266.1
O'Donoghue, The. Lever, C..............L658.20
O'DOWD, C., pseud. See Lever, C.
OEHLENSCHLAGER, A. Ali and Gulhyndi.
49 pp..........................in O983.1
Off the Skelligs. Ingelow, J..................I464.5
Ogeechee cross-firings. Johnston, R. M..J733.7
Ogilvies. Mulock, D. M....................M960.21
OGLE, ANNIE. (Ashford Owen, pseud.)
Georgy Sandon.............................O353.1
Issued also as Her second love. Lost love.
O'GRADY, S. In the wake of King James..
....O357.2
Red Hugh's captivity: a picture of Ire-
land in the reign of Queen Elizabeth...
....O357.4
Ulrick the ready..............................O357.7
O'HALLORAN, G. B. Master of the "Chry-
solite.".................................in S885.9
O'HARA, A., pseud. See Banim, M.
OHNET, G. Antoinette......................O383.1
Dr. Rameau............. ....O383.2
Iron master...................................O383.3
    Issued also as Claire and the forge master.
    Master of the forges.

OHNET, G.—Continued.
A last love....................................O383.4
Nimrod & Co.................................O383.5
Pierre's soul..................................O383.6
O'KEEFE, J. Wild oats. 35 pp......in M875.1 ²
Old Adam, The. Boyesen, H H............B791.8
Old and new. Sadlier, M. A...............S126.6
Old Chelsea bun-house. Manning, A....M283.7
Old continental. Paulding, J. K..........Q325.3
Old creole days. Cable, G. W.............C115.9
Old curiosity shop. Dickens, C......in D548.31
Same...D548.33
Same...D548.35
Old doctor. Cheney, J. V..................C519.2
Old Dominion. James, G. P. R...........J276.32
Old English baron. Reeve, C.........**B232.22
Old friends and new. Jewett, S. O......J593.13
Old Fritz and the new era. Mühlbach, L...
....M952.17
Old gentleman's teetotum. 46 pp......in T143.2
Same................................in T143.2 ²
Old Goriot. Balzac, H. de..................B198.31s
Old helmet. Warner, S.....................W284.7
Old Kaskaskia. Catherwood, M. H......C363.6
Old Kensington. Thackeray, A. I.........T362.4
Old Lady Mary. Oliphant, M. O. W....O475.40
Old maid. Balzac, H. de.................in B198.18
Old maids and burglars in paradise. Phelps,
E. S...Q539.12
Old maids' club. Zangwill, I..............Z295.9
Old mam'selle's secret. Marlitt, E......W817.17
Old man Savarin, and other stories.
Thomson, E. W.............................T482.1
Old manor house. 2 vols. Smith, C. T...
....**B232.36-7
Old Margaret. Kingsley, H................K555.7
Old Mark Langston. Johnston, R. M....J733.8
Old Mortality. Scott, Sir W..........in **S431.4
Same.............................in S431.9
Same.............................in S431.10
Same.............................in S431.35
Same.............................in S431.46
OLD MOUNTAINEER, pseud. See Scribner,
J. P.
Old Myddelton's money. Hay, M. C.....H413.3
Old Olaf. 46 pp. Thoresen, M.........in G622.1
Old, old story. Carey, R. N...............C276.24
Old order changes. Mallock, W. H......M255.4
Old patroon. Maitland, J. A...............M232.3
Old plantation. Hungerford, J............H936.1
Old Saint Paul's. Ainsworth, W. H....A297.18
Old Sir Douglas. Norton, C. E. S.........N883.2
Old ways and new. Roseboro', V.......R798.1

Old woman who lived in a shoe. Douglas, A. M..................D734.21
Oldbury. Keary, A..................K241.2
Oldtown folks. Stowe, H. B..................S892.6
OLIPHANT, F. R. Grateful ghosts. 81 pp..................in T143.24
OLIPHANT, L. Altiora Peto..................O474.1
The brigand's bride..................in S885.5
Same..................in T143.19
Piccadilly..................O474.2
Tender recollections of Irene Magilli-cuddy..................O474.3
Same..................in T143.7
OLIPHANT, M. O. W. Adam Graeme of Mossgray..................O475.32
Agnes..................O475.1
At his gates..................O475.2
Beleaguered city..................O475.3
Brownlows..................O475.5
Carita..................O475.6
Country gentleman..................O475.7
Cuckoo in the nest..................O475.8
Curate in charge..................O475.9
Doctor's family..................in O475.51
For love and life..................O475.11
Golden rule. 40 pp..................in S887.1
Greatest heiress in England..................O475.12
He that will not when he may..................O475.14
Hester..................O475.15
House divided against itself..................O475.16
House on the moor..................O475.17
Innocent..................O475.18
John: a love story..................O475.19
Joyce..................O475.20
Katie Stewart..................O475.21
Kirsteen: the story of a Scotch family seventy years ago..................O475.22
Lady Car..................O475.24
Last of the Mortimers..................O475.25
Little pilgrim. 72 pp..................O475.26
Lucy Crofton..................O475.27
Madam..................O475.28
Madonna Mary..................O475.29
Magdalen Hepburn..................O475.30
Margaret Maitland of Sunnyside..................O475.43
May..................O475.31
Merkland; or, self-sacrifice..................O475.33
Minister's wife..................O475.34
Miss Marjoribanks..................O475.35
Mrs. Arthur..................O475.36
Mystery of Mrs. Blencarrow..................O475.37
Neighbours on the green..................O475.38
Old Lady Mary..................O475.40
Ombra..................O475.41

OLIPHANT, M. O. W.—Continued.
Open door; and, The portrait: two stories of the seen and the unseen..................O475.42
Perpetual curate..................O475.44
Phœbe, junior..................O475.45
The portrait..................in O475.42
Primrose path..................O475.47
Quiet heart..................O475.48
Salem chapel..................O475.50
Same. (Also) The doctor's family...O475.51
Secret chamber. 50 pp..................in T143.7
Son of his father..................O475.53
Son of the soil..................O475.54
Squire Arden..................O475.55
Whiteladies..................O475.59
Who was lost and is found..................O475.60
Wizard's son..................O475.61
Young Musgrave..................O475.63
—and Aldrich, T. B. Second son........O475.52
Olive. Mulock, D. M..................M960.23
Olive Lacey. Argyle, A..................A695.2
OLIVER, P. Charley Kingston's aunt....O483.1
Oliver Cromwell. Herbert, H. W.........H536.4
Oliver Ellis. Grant, J..................G761.34
Oliver Twist. Dickens, C..................in D548.23
Same..................D548.37
Same..................D548.38
Same..................D548.39
Olivia Delaplaine. Fawcett, E...........F278.14
Olla podrida. Marryat, Capt. F........in M362.4
Same..................M362.14
Same..................M362.28
OLNEY, E. W. See Kirk, E. O.
Olympe de Clèves. 2 vols. Dumas, A....D886.33
O'Mahony, The. Conyngham, D. P......C770.1
Ombra. Oliphant, M. O. W..................O475.41
O'MEARA, K. Narka, the nihilist........O552.1
Omega. Flammarion, C..................F581.1
Omnia vanitas. Forrester, Mrs..................F730.8
Omoo. Melville, H..................M531.2
On both sides. Baylor, F. C..................B359.2
On both sides of the sea. Charles, E. R...C476.12
On circumstantial evidence. Marryat, F...M361.8
On guard. Thomas, A..................in T453.4
On land and sea. Thomes, W. H..........T465.7
On Newfound river. Page, T. N..........Q133.8
On the banks of the Ouse. Marshall, E...M367.9
On the edge of the storm. Roberts, M.....R646.8
On the eve. Turgénieff, I. S..................T936.8
On the face of the waters. Steel, F. A....S813.3
On the frontier. Harte, B..................H327.26
On the heights. 2 vols. Auerbach, B.....A918.11
On the heights of Himalay. Van der Naillen, A..................V238.2

On the offensive. Putnam, G. I............Q980.2
On the point. Dole, N. H...............D663.4
On the verge. Shirley, P...................S558.1
On the Wallaby track. 20 pp..........*in* T143.24
Once again. Forrester, *Mrs*...............F730.12
One day. Björnson, B....................*in* B625.2
One fair woman. Miller, J...............M649.5
One maid's mischief. Fenn, G. M.........F334.4
One of our conquerors. Meredith, G....M559.8
One of the Duanes. Hamilton, A. K.....H217.2
One of the family. Payn, J............Q345.17
One of "The six hundred." Grant, J....G761.35
One of the thirty. Jennings, H............J544.1
One of them. Lever, C...................L658.21
"One of three." Fothergill, J...............F761.4
One of us. Schubin, O....................S384.4
One summer. Howard, B. W.............H848.4
One thousand dollars a day. Knapp, A...K672.1
One too many. Linton, E. L............L761.1
One who looked on. Montrésor, F. F.....M811.3
One woman's two lovers. Townsend, V.
  F. T751.7
One year. Peard, F. M...................Q359.10
Only a clod. Braddon, M. E..............B798.26
Only a fiddler. Andersen, H. C...........A544.3
Only a girl. Hillern, W. von..............W817.5
Only an ensign. Grant, J...................G761.36
Only girls. Townsend, V. F...............T751.6
Only human. Winter, J. S..............W785.12
Only one. French, H. W..................F874.2
Only the governess. Carey, R. N........C276.25
Open door. Howard, B. W................H848.5
Open door. 54 pp. Oliphant, M. O. W...O475.42
Open question. De Mille, J..............D381.9
Open verdict. Braddon, M. E.............B798.28
Opening a chestnut burr. Roe, E. P....R699.13
Opening the oyster. Marsh, C. L........M365.1
Ophelia. Fielding, S.................*in* **N938.19
OPIE, A. Works. 3 vols.................O614.1-3

> CONTENTS: 1: Madeline. Adeline Mowbray. Simple tales.
> 2: Tales of real life. New tales.
> 3: Temper. Woman's love. Wife's duty. Two sons. Opposite neighbour. Love, mystery and superstition. After the ball. False or true. Confessions of an odd-tempered man. Illustrations of lying.

Opinions of a philosopher. Grant, R.....G763.7
Opportunity. Seemüller, A. M............S453.1
Opposite neighbour. 21 pp. Opie, A...*in* O614.3
OPTIC, O. (*pseud. of* W. T. Adams.) Living too fast....................O625.1
  Three millions.......................O625.3
    Issued also as Way of the world.
  Way of the world....................O625.3
    Issued also as Three millions.

Orange blossoms. Arthur, T. S............A791.4
ORAQUILL, *pseud. See* Bornemann, M.
Ordeal of Richard Feverel. Meredith,
  G M559.9
O'REILLY, B. Two brides...................O663.1
O'REILLY, J. BOYLE. Moondyne: a story
  from the under-world O665.1
—*joint author. See* Grant, R., *and others.*
Oriental pearl. Dorsey, A. H.............D718.2
Original belle. Roe, E. P. R699.14
Orley Farm. Trollope, A..................T846.22
Ormond. Brown, C. B....................B879.4
Ormond. Edgeworth, M...................E235.32
  Same. 2 vols.................*in* **E235.14-15
Orphan's trials. Bennett, E.................B471.3
Orthodox. Gerard, D......................G356.1
OSBORNE, D. Spell of Ashtaroth.........O813.1
Osborne of Arrochar. Douglas, A. M...D734.22
OSBOURNE, L., *joint author. See* Stevenson, R. L.
Osego chronicles. Sleight, M. B...........S632.2
OSWALD, E. (*pseud. of* Mrs. B. Schulze-
  Smidt.) Vain forebodings. Tr. by
  A. L. Wister......................... W817.20
Oswald Cray. Wood, E. P................ W874.10
Othello the second. Robinson, F. W......R660.3
Other girls. Whitney, A. D. T............W617.6
Other house. James, H., *Jr*...............J277.23
Other people's money. Gaboriau, E......G116.9
Other things being equal. Wolf, E...... W854.1
Othmar. Ouida...........................O934.15
OTMAR (*pseud. of* O. Nachtigal). Horseshoe on the church door. Jacob Nimmernüchtern. Lora: the goddess of love. Knights' cellar in the Kyffhäusen. Peter Klaus the goatherd...
  ....*in* R794.1 [2]
OTWAY, T. Venice preserved. 20 pp...
  ....*in* M875.1 [1]
Otto the knight, and other trans-Mississippi stories. Thanet, O.................T367.5
Ought we to visit her? Edwardes, A.....E254.4
OUIDA (*pseud. of* L. de La Ramée). Ariadne: the story of a dream.............O934.1
  Beatrice Boville, and other stories.......O934.2
  Bébée; or, two little wooden shoes......O934.3
  Cecil Castlemaine's gage, Lady Marabout's troubles, and other stories......O934.4
  Chandos.............................O934.5
  Dog of Flanders......................*in* S885.3
  Don Gesualdo........................*in* O934.10
  Folle-farine..........................O934.6
  Friendship............................ O934.8

OUIDA (*pseud. of* L. de La Ramée).—*Continued.*
A house-party. (*Also*) Don Gesualdo.
(*And*) A rainy June.....................O934.10
Idalia................................O934.11
In a winter city.......................O934.12
In Maremma............................O934.13
Lady Marabout's troubles...........*in* O934.4
Leaf in the storm. 49 pp..........*in* S885.10
Moths.............. ....O934.14
Othmar.................................O934.15
Pascarel...............................O934.28
Princess Napraxine.....................O934.16
Puck....................................O934.17
A rainy June.......................*in* O934.10
Same...................................O934.18
Randolph Gordon, and other stories...O934.19
Signa................................. O934.20
Strathmore.............................O934.21
Syrlin.................................O934.22
Tricotrin..............................O934.23
Two offenders..........................O934.24
Under two flags........................O934.25
Village commune........................O934.26
Wanda, Countess von Szalras...........O934.27
Our Bessie. Carey, R. N...............C276.26
Our Christmas in a palace. Hale, E. E...H161.13
Our forefathers. Freytag, G...........F895.2-3
Our mutual friend. Dickens, C.........D548.40
Our new crusade. Hale, E. E...........H161.14
Our old home. Hawthorne, N............H399.8
Our own set. Schubin, O...............S384.5
Our refugee household. Clack, L.......C583.1
Our village. 2 vols. Mitford, M. R......M684.1
Out of debt out of danger. Edgeworth,
    M.............................*in* **E235.6
Same..............................*in* E235.19
Out of due season. Sergeant, A.........S484.7
Out of step. Pool, M. L................Q821.12
Out of the foam. Cooke, J. E...........C772.11
Out of the wreck. Douglas, A. M........ D734.23
Outcast. Reade, W. W...................R286.1
Overland tales. Clifford, J............C638.1
Ovingdean Grange. Ainsworth, W. H...A297.19
OWEN, A., *pseud. See* Ogle, A.
OWEN, G. W. Leech club; or, the mysteries of the Catskills.....................O972.1
OWEN, *Mrs.* J. A. After shipwreck.......O974.1
OWEN, R. D. Beyond the breakers........O976.1
Owen Tudor. Robinson, J...............R662.5
Owen Wingrave. James, H., *Jr*.......*in* J277.22
Owl's Nest. Marlitt, E................W817.18

OXENFORD, J., *and* Feiling, C. A., *trs.*
Tales from the German.....................O983.1
    CONTENTS: Göthe, J. W. v. New Paris.—Hauff, W. Cold heart. Nose, the dwarf. Severed hand.—Hoffmann, E. T. W. Elementary spirit. Jesuits' church in G—. The sandman.—Immermann, K. L. Wonders in the Spessart.—Kleist, H. v. Michael Kohlhass. St. Cecilia; or, the power of music.—Musæus, J. K. A. Libussa.—Oehlenschläger, A. Ali and Gulhyndi.—Richter, J. P. F. The moon.—Schiller, J. C. F. v. Criminal from lost honour.—Tieck, L. The Klausenburg.—Van der Velde, C. F. Axel.—Zschokke, H. Alamontade.
Oxonians. Beazley, S....................B386.1
OZOLLO, *Inca* P. Lost inca..............O995.1
P—, P. *Count.* The conspirator. 2 vols...Q110.1
PAALZOW, H. W. VON. Citizen of Prague...Q111.1
Pacha of many tales. Marryat, *Capt.* F...M362.15
Pactolus Prime. Tourgée, A. W.........T727.10
Pagans. Bates, A........................B329.6
PAGE, T. N. Burial of the guns..........Q133.1
    Elsket. Q133.4
In ole Virginia; or, Marse Chan, and
    other stories........................Q133.6
Marse Chan: a tale of old Virginia. 36
    pp.............................*in* S884.9
    Issued also as In ole Virginia.
No Haid Pawn. 42 pp...............*in* S886.6
On Newfound river.....................Q133.8
Pastime stories.........................Q133.9
Run to seed. 46 pp...............*in* S886.4
Page of the duke of Savoy. 2 vols. Dumas,
    A.................................D886.34
PAGET, V. *See* Lee, V., *pseud.*
PAIN, B. Stories and interludes...........Q144.1
Pair of blue eyes. Hardy, T.............H272.13
Paladin of finance. Jenkins, E.......... J527.2
PALGRAVE. W. G. Hermann Agha......Q161.1
PALTOCK, R. (R. S., *pseud.*) Peter Wilkins.............................*in* **N938.12
    Same Q183.1
Pamela. Richardson, S.............*in* **N938.20
    Same...............................R525.2
    Same. 4 vols.......................**R525.3
Pan Michael. Sienkiewicz, H............S572.9
Pandora. 78 pp. James, H., *Jr*.......*in* J277.3
Pandour and his princess: an Hungarian
    sketch. 64 pp......................*in* T143.5
    Same..............................*in* T145.5
Panglima Muda. Wildman, R............W674.1
Paper city. Locke, D. R................L813.1
Paragreens on a visit to the Paris Universal
    Exhibition. Ruffini, G.............R923.3
Parasite. Doyle, A. C..................D754.15

PARDOE, J. The will. 52 pp...........*in* S637.2
Paris in America. Laboulaye, E............L124.2
Parisians. 2 vols. Lytton, E. G. E. L.
     Bulwer-....................................... L998.18
PARKER, F. T., *Countess of Morley. See*
     Morley, *Countess of.*
PARKER, G. Adventurer of the north....Q240.1
     Pierre and his people.........................Q240.6
     Pomp of the Lavilettes.....................Q240.17
     Romany of the snows.......................Q240.7
     Seats of the mighty............................Q240.9
     Trail of the sword...........................Q240.11
     Translation of a savage....................Q240.12
     The trespasser................................Q240.13
     When Valmond came to Pontiac........Q240.15
PARR, L. Adam and Eve....................Q258.1
     Bluebell of Red-neap......................Q258.2
     Dorothy Fox...................................Q258.5
     John Thompson, and other stories......Q258.6
     Robin..Q258.7
Parsonage of Mora. Bremer, F.............B836.11
Parson's daughter. Hook, T................H781.8
Parson's proxy. Hamilton, K. W.........H219.1
Part of the property. Whitby, B W579.3
Parting and a meeting. Howells, W. D..H859.24
Partisan. Simms, W. G....................S592.11
Partisan leader. Tucker, B................T891.1
PARTON, S. P. W. *See* Fern, F., *pseud.*
Passages from the diary of a late physician.
     Warren, S.................................... W293.2
Passages in the life of Mrs. Margaret Mait-
     land of Sunnyside. Oliphant, M. O.
     W..O475.43
Passages in the life of the faire gospeller...
     Manning, A.....................................M283.8
Pascarel. Ouida.............................O934.28
Passe Rose. Hardy, A. S.....................H268.2
Passing the love of women. Needell, *Mrs.*
     J. H...N374.2
Passion and principle. Hook, T...........H781.9
Passion in the desert. 20 pp. Balzac, H. de
     ....*in* B198.14
     Same....................................*in* B198.34
Passionate pilgrim, and other tales. James,
     H., *Jr*..J277.10
Passion's slave. King, R. A..................K543.1
Paste or diamonds. Tinseau, L. de........T592.1
Pastels of men. 2d ser. Bourget, P.........B772.6
Pastime stories. Page, T. N..................Q133.9
Patagonia, The. 82 pp. James, H., *Jr*...J277.9
PATER, W. Gaston de Latour: an unfin-
     ished romance...............................Q295.1
     Imaginary portraits..........................Q295.2
     Marius the epicurean: his sensations and
     ideas. 2 vols...................................Q295.3

PATERSON, A. Son of the plains...........Q296.1
PATERSON, W. R. *See* Swift, B., *pseud.*
Pathfinder. Cooper, J. F....................C777.25
Path of duty. James, H., *Jr*...............*in* J277.3
Patience Barker. White, C. E.........*in* W583.2
Patience Strong's outings. Whitney, A.
     D. T..W617.7
PATRICIA, *pseud.* Blanche Carey...........Q314.1
Patricia Kemball. Linton, E. L............L761.2
Patriot and tory. Wright, J. McN.......W951.1
Patronage. 2 vols. Edgeworth, M...**E235.12-13
     Same....................................E235.28-30
Patty. Macquoid, K. S.....................M173.6
Patty's perversities. Bates, A.............B329.7
PAUL, M. A. Kintail Place: a tale of revo-
     lution..Q324.1
Paul and Christina. Barr, A. E.........B268.18
Paul and Virginia. Saint-Pierre, J. H. B.
     de...*in* G625.3
     Same...S149.1
Paul and Virginia of a northern zone.
     Drachmann, H..................................D757.1
Paul Clifford. Lytton, E. G. E. Bulwer-...
     ....L998.19
Paul Faber, surgeon. MacDonald, G.....M135.14
Paul Patoff. Crawford, F. M..............C899.14
PAULDING, J. K. Dutchman's fireside.....Q325.1
     Merry tales of the three wise men of
     Gotham....................................**Q325.2
     Old continental; or, the price of liberty....
     .... Q325.3
     Puritan and his daughter.................**Q325.4
     Tales of the good woman...................Q325.5
     —*joint author. See* Irving, William.
Pauline. Walford, L. B......................W174.8
Pauline Seward. 2 vols. Bryant, J. D.......B915.1
Pausanias, the Spartan. Lytton, E. G. E.
     L. Bulwer-..................................*in* L998.4
     Same...L998.20
     Same...L998.21
PAYN, J. At her mercy......................Q345.1
     A beggar on horseback.....................Q345.2
     Best of husbands.............................Q345.3
     Bred in the bone.............................Q345.4
     Issued also as Like father, like son.
     Burnt million.................................Q345.5
     By proxy.......................................Q345.6
     Canon's ward.................................Q345.7
     Carlyon's year................................Q345.8
     Faithful retainer ....*in* S885.5
     Found dead....................................Q345.9
     Gwendoline's harvest......................Q345.10
     Halves....................................*in* Q345.11
     Heir of the ages..............................Q345.12

PAYN, J.—*Continued.*
Less black than we're painted............Q345.13
Lost Sir Massingberd....................Q345.14
Luck of the Darrells......................Q345.15
Murphy's master.........................Q345.16
One of the family........................Q345.17
Prince of the blood.....................Q345.18
Rebecca's remorse. 43 pp...........*in* S887.1
What he cost her........................Q345.19
PAYNE, W. Jerry the dreamer.............Q346.1
Paz. 86 pp. Balzac, H. de..........*in* B198.1
Peace in the house. 42 pp. Balzac, H. de...
....*in* B198.28
Same.................................*in* B198.44
Peace Pelican, spinster. Smith, J. P......S653.8
PEACOCK, T. L. Crotchet Castle Q356.1
Gryll Grange. 2 vols...................Q356.2
Headlong Hall.........................Q356.3
Maid Marian...........................Q356.4
Melincourt. 2 vols....................Q356.5
Misfortunes of Elphin..................Q356.6
Nightmare Abbey.......................Q356.7
Peak and prairie. Fuller, A..............F965.1
PEARD, F. M. Castle and town Q359.1
Catherine...............................Q359.2
An interloper...........................Q359.6
Mademoiselle: a story of the siege of
Paris.................................Q359.8
One year..............................Q359.10
Rose-garden..........................Q359.12
Thorpe Regis.........................Q359.14
Unawares............................ Q359.16
Winter story.........................Q359.18
Pearl of Orr's island. Stowe, H. B........S892.8
Pearl-powder. Edwardes, A................E254.6
PEARSON, H. C. His opportunity.........Q362.1
Peasant and his landlord. Knorring, S.
M. *Freifrau* von......................K725.1
Peasantry, The. Balzac, H. de...........B198.35s
PEATTIE, E. W. Mountain woman........Q363.1
PECK, G. W. (Cantell A. Bigly, *pseud.*)
Aurifodina; or, adventures in the gold
region...............................**Q366.1
PECK, W. H. Stone-cutter of Lisbon....Q367.1
Peculiar. Sargent, E....................S245.1
PEEKE, M. B. Zenia, the vestal...........Q373.1
Peep o' day. Banim, J., *and,* M.........B217.6
Peerless Cathleen. Agnew, C............A273.1
Peg Woffington. Reade, C..............R285.21
Same................................R285.22
Peggy Thornhill. Damant, M D155.1
Pelham. Lytton, E. G. E. L. Bulwer-....L998.22
Pemaquid. Prentiss, E. P................Q916.1
PEMBER, P. Y. Southern woman's story..Q394.1

PEMBERTON, M. "Little Huguenot."...Q395.1
Puritan's wife.........................Q395.6
Pemberton. Peterson, H................Q485.1
Pembroke. Wilkins, M. E..............W684.10
Pen Owen. 3 vols. Hook, J...........**H777.1
Pendennis. Thackeray, W. M..........T363.11
PENDLETON, E. Virginia inheritance...Q397.1
PENDLETON, L. In the wire-grass........Q398.1
Sons of Ham..........................Q398.2
Wedding garment......................Q398.3
Pendower. Filleul, M..................F485.1
Penelope's English experiences. Wiggin,
K. D.............................*in* W655.3
Penelope's suitors. Bynner, E. L..........B994.5
Penniless girl. Heimburg, W............W817.4
Pennimans, The. Fuller, G. A...........F967.1
PENNOT, *Rev.* P., *pseud. See* Round, W.
M. F.
Pennycomequicks, The. Gould, S. B.-...G698.9
Pennyroyal and mint. Swett, S..........S975.3
Penruddocke. Aïdé, H.................A288.3
Pension Beaurepas. 83 pp. James, H.,
Jr..............................*in* J277.17
People at Pisgah. Sanborn, E. W........S198.1
People we pass. Ralph, J................R163.4
Pepita Ximenez. Valera, J..............V162.4
PEPPERGRASS, P. (*pseud. of* J. Boyce.)
Shandy M'Guire: a story of the north
of Ireland..........................Q424.1
The spae wife: a story of the reign of
Elizabeth............................Q424.2
Pequinillo. James, G. P. R............*in* J276.5
Percival Keene. Marryat, *Capt.* F....M362.16
Père Goriot. Balzac, H. de............B198.31
Peregrine Pickle. Smollett, T. G...*in* **N938.6
Same................................S666.2
PERELAER, T. H. Baboe Dalima; or, the
opium fiend.........................Q437.1
PEREZ GALDOS, B. Court of Charles IV.:
a romance of the Escorial.............Q438.2
Doña Perfecta.........................Q438.1
Leon Roch: a romance. 2 vols..........Q438.3
Marianela............................Q438.4
Perfect Adonis. Harris, M. C............H315.2
Perico the sad.........................Q440.1
Perilous secret. Reade, C...............R285.23
Periwinkle. Gray, A...................G778.1
PERKINS, F. B. Devil-puzzlers, and other
sketches.............................Q448.1
Scrope; or, the lost library..............Q448.2
Perlycross. Blackmore, R. D...........B629.14
Perpetual curate. Oliphant, M. O. W...O475.44
PERRY, A. The schoolmaster's trial......Q462.1

PERRY, B. Broughton house................Q463.1
Commonest possible story. 19 pp...*in* S886.2
Plated city.............................Q463.4
Persis Yorke. Christian, S..............C555.1
Personal recollections of Joan of Arc.
   Twain, M..........................T969.4
Persuasion. Austen, J................*in* A933.3
Same..*in* A933.7
Peruvian princess, Letters of. Grafigny,
   F. de.............................*in* **N938.9
Peruvian tales. Tr. from the orig. Fr. by
   S. Humphreys.................*in* **N938.21
PESTALOZZI, J. H. Leonard and Ger-
   trude.............................Q476.1
Peter and Polly. Douglas, M..........D735.1
Peter Ibbetson. Du Maurier, G..........D887.1
Peter of the castle. Banim, J..........B217.3
Peter Schlemihl. Chamisso, A. de........C449.1
Peter Simple. Marryat, *Capt.* F..........M362.17
Peter Wilkins. Paltock, R...........*in* **N938.12
Same.......................................Q183.1
PETERKIN, A. The parsonage: My father's
   fireside..........................*in* W750.3
PETERSON, H. Pemberton; or, one hun-
   dred years ago...................Q485.1
"Petrel" and "The Black Swan.".......*in* S885.9
Petrie estate. Brown, H. D.............B880.1
Peveril of the Peak. Scott, *Sir* W...*in* **S431.23
Same.....................................S431.36
Same.....................................S431.37
PFLEGER, GUSTAV. Revenge. 8 pp...*in* H496.1
Phantasmion. Coleridge, S. H...........C693.1
Phantastes. MacDonald, G.............M135.15
Same...................................M135.16
Phantom from the east. Loti, P.........L883.4
Phantom regiment. Grant, J..........G761.37
Phantom 'rickshaw, and other tales. Kip-
   ling, R.........................K575.10
Phantom ship. Marryat, *Capt.* F.........M362.18
Phantoms of the foot-bridge. Craddock,
   C. E...........................C884.13
Phaulcon the adventurer. Dalton, W...D152.1
PHELPS, E. S. (*Mrs. Ward*). Beyond
   the gates........................Q539.1
Doctor Zay..............................Q539.2
Donald Marcy...........................Q539.3
Fourteen to one........................Q539.4
Friends: a duet.........................Q539.5
Gates ajar.............................Q539.6
Gates between..........................Q539.7
Hedged in..............................Q539.8
Jack the fisherman.....................Q539.9
Madonna of the tubs...................Q539.10
Men, women, and ghosts................Q539.11

PHELPS, E. S. (*Mrs. Ward*).—*Continued.*
Old maids, and burglars in paradise...Q539.12
Sealed orders..........................Q539.13
Silent partner.........................Q539.14
Singular life..........................Q539.15
Story of Avis..........................Q539.16
Supply at Saint Agatha's...............Q539.17
Zerviah Hope. 36 pp... ....*in* S884.8
—*and* Ward, H. D. Come forth..........Q539.18
Master of the magicians................Q539.19
Phemie Keller. Riddell, C. E. L........R543.14
Phemie Millar. 3 vols. (in 2.) Tytler, S...T997.6
Phemie's temptation. Harland, M......H283.14
Philip. Cutler, M. C....................C989.1
Philip, Adventures of. Thackeray, W.
   M................................T363.1
Philip and his wife. Deland, M..........D337.7
Philip Augustus. James, G. P. R........J276.33
Philip Nolan's friends. Hale, E. E....H161.15
Philip Rollo. Grant, J.................G761.38
Philippa. Molesworth, M. L.............M719.2
PHILIPS, A., *tr.* Thousand and one days:
   Persian tales..................*in* **N938.13
Philistines. Bates, A..................B329.8
PHILLPOTTS, E. Folly and fresh air......Q565.1
Philosopher's baby.....................*in* T143.7
Philothea. Child, L. M.................C536.1
Phineas Finn. Trollope, A..............T846.23
Phineas Redux. Trollope, A.............T846.24
Phœbe. Harris, M. C....................H315.3
Phœbe, junior. Oliphant, M. O. W......O475.45
Phroso. Hope, A........................H791.19
Phyllis. Duchess.......................D829.15
Phyllis. Gaskell, E. C.................G248.6
Phyllis of the Sierras. Harte, B..........H327.27
PIAZZI, *Mme.* A. D. *See* Hanoum, L.,
   pseud.
Piccadilly. Oliphant, L................O474.2
PICHLER, C. Count of Barcelona. 29
   pp..............................*in* C972.1¹
Picked up in the streets. Schobert, H..W817.24
PICKEN, A. Deer-stalkers of Glenskiach:
   a highland legend. Eisenbach. Three
   Kearneys.......................*in* C594.1
Mary Ogilvie...........................Q594.2
—*ed.* Club-book: being original tales...Q594.1
   CONTENTS: Cunningham, A. Gowden
   Gibbie. –Egerton, F., *Earl of Ellesmere.*
   Dramatic scenes, founded on Victor Hugo's
   tragedy of Hernani. –Galt, J. Book of life.
   Fatal whisper. Haddad-Ben-Ahab. The
   painter. Unguarded hour.—Hogg, J. Bogle
   o' the brae. Laidlaws and the Scotts.—
   James, G. P. R. Bertrand de la Croix. –
   Jerdan, W. Sleepless woman.—Moir, D M.

PICKEN, A.—*Continued.*
Bridal of Borthwick.—Picken, A. Deer-
stalkers of Glenskinch. Eisenbach. Three
Kearneys.—Power, T. Gipsy of the Abruzzo.
—Ritchie, L. Cheaterie packman.

PICKERING, E. The grumbler..............Q595.2
Pickwick papers. Dickens, C............D548.42
Same..D548.44
Picture of Las Cruces. Reid, C..........R353.14
Pictures of country life. Cary, A..........C332.2
Pictures of Hellas. Mariager, P..........M332.1
PIERCE, G. A., *and* WHEELER, W. A.
Dickens dictionary.....................D548.55
PIERCE, H. C. Curse of Everleigh........Q616.1
Pierre. Melville, H..............................M531.3
Pierre and his people. Parker, G.........Q240.6
Pierre and Jean. Maupassant, G. de.......M452.2
Pierre Grassou. 25 pp. Balzac, H. de...
....*in* B198.42
Pierre's soul. Ohnet, G.........................O383.6
Pierrette. Balzac, H. de...... ....B198.32
PIERSON, E. D. Vagabond's honor........Q624.1
Pietro Ghisleri. Crawford, F. M.....C899.15
Pilgrim and the shrine. Maitland, E...M231.3
Pilgrims of the Rhine. Lytton, E. G. E.
L. Bulwer-.............................*in* L998.14
Pilgrim's progress. Bunyan, J............B943.1
Pillar of fire. Ingraham, J. H................I543.3
Pillars of the house. 2 vols. Yonge, C. M....
....Y555.27
Pilot. Cooper, J. F............................C777.26
Same..C777.27
Pilot Fortune. Reeves, M. C. L., *and*
Read, E..R332.1
Pine needles. Warner, S.....................W284.8
Pink and white tyranny. Stowe, H. B...S892.9
Pioneers. Cooper, J. F.........................C777.28
Pique. Ellis, S. S.................................E473.4
Pirate. Marryat, *Capt.* F....................M362.19
Same...............................*in* **M362.26
Same..............................*in* M362.28
Pirate. Scott, *Sir* W...................*in* S431.24
Same.......................... *in* **S431.32
Same..S431.38
Same.................................*in* S431.43
Pirate gold. Stimson, F. J....................S859.5
Plain tales from the hills. Kipling, R...K575.11
Plan of campaign. 2 vols. Robinson, F.
M...R659.1
Plated city. Perry, B............................Q463.4
Play-actress. Crockett, S. R................C938.14
Play of fate. Bjursten, H.....................B626.1
Played out. Thomas, A.........................T453.4
Playing the mischief. De Forest, J. W....D315.5

Playing with fire. Grant, J..............G761.39
Pleasant Waters. Claytor, G..............C622.1
Pleasures of old age. Souvestre, E.........S729.3
Plébiscite. Erckmann, E., *and* Chatrian,
A..E654.14
Ploughed. Walford, L. B.................... W174.9
Ploughed under. Theamba, I..............T374.1
Poacher. Marryat, *Capt.* F..... ....M362.20
Same..M362.21
POE, E. A. Prose tales. 1st–2d ser. 2 vols...
.... Q743.1
Same. 1st–3d ser. 3 vols..............Q743.2-4
Poet and merchant. Auerbach, B.........A918.12
Poganuc people. Stowe, H. B.............S892.10
Point of honor. Edwardes, A...............E254.7
Point of view. 71 pp. James, H., *Jr*....*in* J277.17
Poison tree. Chatterjee, B. C...............C495.1
Poisoned chalice. Maunsell, W. P........M450.1
Polikouchka. 70 pp. Tolstoi, *Count* L. N..T654.9
Polish Jew, and other tales. Erckmann,
E., *and* Chatrian, A......................E654.15
POLKO, E. Musical sketches.............Q770.1
POLLOK, R. Tales of the covenanters...Q777.1
Pomona's travels. Stockton, F. R........S866.25
Pomp of the Lavilettes. Parker, G......Q240.17
Pompey the little. 77 pp. Coventry, F....
....*in* **B232.23
Same.................................*in* **N938.19
PONTOPPIDAN, H. Emanuel...............Q818.1
POOL, M. L. Dally..............................Q821.4
In a dike shanty.................................Q821.7
Katharine North................................Q821.8
Mrs. Keats Bradford Q821.10
Out of step..Q821.12
Roweny in Boston............................Q821.14
Two Salomes....................................Q821.15
Poor folk. Dostoyevsky, F. M..............D724.2
Poor gentleman. Conscience, H...........C755.6
Poor Jack. Marryat, *Capt.* F.............. M362.22
Poor Miss Finch. Collins, W...............C713.27
Poor relation. Soans, R. G., *and* Kenyon,
E. C...S676.1
Poor scholar, and other tales. Carleton,
W...C281.9
Popanilla. Disraeli, B....................*in* D613.1
Poppaea. Gordon, J............................G663.4
Port Tarascon. Daudet, A...................D238.9
Portent. MacDonald, G...................*in* M135.16
Same..M135.17
PORTER, D. D. Arthur Merton............Q844.1
PORTER, J. Scottish chiefs................Q846.1
Thaddeus of Warsaw.......................Q846.2

PORTER, L. B. *See* Ross, A., *pseud*.

PORTER, W. O. (Sir E. Seaward, *pseud*.) Sir Edward Seaward's narrative of his shipwreck, and consequent discovery of certain islands in the Caribbean sea...Q849.1

Portia. Duchess........ ....D829.16

Portrait. Oliphant, M. O. W...........*in* O475.42

Portrait of a lady. James, H., *Jr*........J277.11

POSTEL, K. *See* Sealsfield, C., *pseud*.

POTTER, F. H., *tr*. Near to happiness...Q866.1

Potter's thumb. Steel, F. A.................S813.2

Pottleton legacy. Smith, A........ ....S641.5

Pound of cure. Bishop, W. H.............B622.7

POUSHKIN, A. S. *See* Pushkin, A. S.

POUVILLON, E. Césette: a story of peasant life in the south of France.........Q880.1

Poverty Corner. Fenn, G. M.............F334.5

POWER, T. Gipsy of the Abruzzo......*in* Q594.1

POWERS, S. Muskingum legends.........Q888.1

POYNTER, E. F. Among the hills.........Q892.1

Ersilia................ ....Q892.2

Madame de Presnel...........................Q892.3

My little lady....................................Q892.4

PRAED, R. CAMPBELL— Christina Chard...
....Q897.1

"December roses.".........................Q897.2

Romance of a châlet.........................Q897.3

—*joint author. See* McCarthy, J.

Prairie. Cooper, J. F...................C777.29

Prairie-bird. Murray, C. A.............M980.1

Prairie folks. Garland, H.....................G233.3

PRATT, C. A. Book of martyrs.............Q901.2

Pratt portraits. Fuller, A.....................F965.2

Pray you sir, whose daughter? Gardener, H. H...................................G218.2

Preacher and the king. Bungener, L.....B941.1

Precaution. Cooper, J. F.....................C777.30

Same....................................C777.31

Prelate. Henderson, I.......................H497.2

Premier and his wife. 39 pp.............*in* T143.6

Same...............................*in* T143.6 1

Premier and the painter. Zangwill, I...Z295.11

Premiums paid to experience. Garrett, E....................................G239.11

PRENTISS, E. P. Pemaquid: a story of old times in New England....................Q916.1

PRESCOTT, E. L. Apotheosis of Mr. Tyrawley...Q918.1

PRESCOTT, H. E. *See* Spofford, H. P.

Present problem. Bolton, S. K...........B694.1

President's daughters. Bremer, F.........B836.12

Same. Pt. 2.........................B836.12 2

PRESTON, H. W. Aspendale...............Q927.1

Is that all?...................................Q927.2

Love in the nineteenth century.........Q927.3

Pretty bandit. Millard, F. B.............M1645.5

Pretty Miss Bellew. Gift, T.............G458.2

Pretty Mrs. Gaston, etc. Cooke, J. E....C772.12

Pretty Polly Pemberton. Burnett, F. H..*in* B964.4

Same...B964.17

Pretty sister of José. Burnett, F. H......B964.18

Prey of the gods. Marryat, F.............M361.9

Price she paid. Benedict, F. L.............B463.6

Pride and prejudice. Austen, J.............A933.4

Same...A933.5

Pride of life. Scott, *Lady* J.............S425.1

Priest and the Huguenot. 2 vols. Bungener, L..................................B941.2

PRIME, W. C. Among the northern hills...
....Q942.1

Prime minister. Trollope, A.............T846.25

Primes and their neighbors. Johnston, R. M....................................J733.9

Primrose path. Oliphant, M. O. W......O475.47

PRINCE, H. C. Story of Christine Rochefort....................................Q944.1

Transatlantic chatelaine...................Q944.4

Prince, The. Cockton, H C666.1

Prince Eugene and his times. Mühlbach, L...M952.18

Prince Fortunatus. Black, W.............B627.23

Prince of India. 2 vols. Wallace, L......W191.3

Prince of the blood. Payn, J.............Q345.18

Prince of the house of David. Ingraham, J. H. I543.1

Prince Otto. Stevenson, R. L.............S848.10

Prince Serebryani. Tolstoi, *Count* A......T653.1

Princess. McClelland, M. G.............M1126.4

Princess Aline. Davis, R. H.............D264.10

Princess Amélie: a fragment of autobiography..Q947.1

Princess Casamassima. James, H., *Jr*..J277.12

Princess of Montserrat. Drysdale, W.....D808.1

Princess Napraxine. Ouida.................O934.16

Princess Nourmahal. Sand, G.............S213.15

Princess of Brunswick-Wolfenbüttel. Zschokke, H..................................Z923.3

Princess of Thule. Black, W.............B627.24

Princess Oghérof. Gréville, H.............G838.7

Princess Sonia. Magruder, J.............M1212.2

Princess Tarakonava. Danilevski, G. P...D187.1

PRIOR, H. L. Expiated.....................Q948.1

Prisoner of Zenda. Hope, A.............H791.20

Prisoners of conscience. Barr, A. E......B268.23

Prisons of air. Conway, M. D.............C768.1

Private life. James, H., *Jr*....................J277.13
Private Miles O'Reilly, Life, etc., of. Hal-
    pine, C. G..H1195.1
Privateersman. Marryat, *Capt.* F........M362.23
Probation. Fothergill, J.....................F761.6
Proctor's tithe. Alcock, D..............*in* A354.2
Prodigal in love. Wolf, E.................. W854.2
Professor. Brontë, C....................BS70.2
Same....BS70.3
Professor's sister. Hawthorne, J...........H398.15
Prophet of the Great Smoky mountains...
    Craddock, C. E.........................C884.14
Prose tales. 1st–2d ser. 2 vols. Poe, E. A..Q743.1
Same. 1st–3d ser. 3 vols................ Q743.2-4
Prosper. Cherbuliez, V......................C521.4
PROTHERO, H. The misogynist. 11 pp....
    .... *in* T143.19
Provost, and other tales. Galt, J...........G179.4
Prudence Palfrey. Aldrich, T. B............A365.6
Prue and I. Curtis, G. W....................C979.1
Prusias. 2 vols. Eckstein, E...............E195.5
Prussian vase. Edgeworth, M.........*in* E235.17
Psyche of to-day. Jenkin, H. C.............J525.2
Publicans and sinners. Braddon, M. E...B798.29
Puck. Ouida....................................O934.17
PULSZKY, F. A., *and* T. Tales and tradi-
    tions of Hungary. 3 vols................Q972.1
Pupil. James, H., *Jr*....................*in* J277.8
Purchase of the north pole. Verne, J...V531.32
Puritan and his daughter. Paulding, J.
    K...**Q325.4
Puritan Bohemia. Sherwood, M............S553.8
Puritan pagan. Gordon, J...................G663.5
Puritan's wife. Pemberton, M................Q395.6
Purse, The. 48 pp. Balzac, H. de...*in* B198.6 ²k
Same..................................*in* B198.16
Pushed by unseen hands. Gardener, H.
    H..G218.3
PUSHKIN, A. S. Marie: a story of Russian
    love...Q976.1
    Russian romance.............................Q976.2
    Snow-storm. 12 pp. ....*in* H496.1
Put yourself in his place. Reade, C......R285.26
Same..R285.27
PUTNAM, G. I. In blue uniform............Q980.1
    On the offensive............................Q980.2
Q., *pseud. See* Couch, A. T. Q.
Quabbin. Underwood, F. H..................U563.3
Quadroon. Reid, M..........................R357.7
Quaker girl of Nantucket. Lee, M. C...L479.1
Quality of mercy. Howells, W. D......H859.25
Queechy. Warner, S..........................W284.9
Queen among queens. MacDowall, C...M138.1

Queen Mab. Kavanagh, J....................K212.9
Queen Money. Kirk, E. O...................K593.6
Queen of Bohemia. Hatton, J.............H366.3
Queen of hearts. Collins, W..............C713.28
Queen of Sheba. Aldrich, T. B............A365.7
Queen Titania. Boyesen, H. H.............B791.9
Queenhoo-Hall. 4 vols. Strutt, J......**S929.1
Queenie Hetherton. Holmes, M. J......H751.24
Queenie's whim. Carey, R. N.............C276.28
Queens. Emery, E. B.........................E537.1
Queen's cadet, and other tales. Grant, J...
    ....G761.40
Queen's Maries. Melville, G. J. W-...M530.24
Same.................................... **M530.25
Queen's necklace. Dumas, A..............D886.35
QUEIROS, E. DE Dragon's teeth.......... ..Q993.1
Quentin Durward. Scott, *Sir* W......*in* S431.10
Same.................................. ....S431.39
Same................................. ....**S431.40
Quest of the absolute. Balzac, H. de.....B198.2s
Quest of the golden girl. Le Gallienne,
    R...L496.3
Question. Ebers, G.........................E165.12
Question of honor. Reid, G...............R353.15
Question of love. Combe, T................C729.1
Quicksands. Streckfuss, A.................W817.29
Quicksands of Pactolus. Vachell, H. A..V118.3
Quiet heart. Oliphant, M. O. W.........O475.48
Quiet life. Burnett, F. H..................B964.19
Quiet Miss Godolphin. 53 pp. Garrett, E.
    and R.......................................G239.12
QUILLINAN, E. Rangers of Connaught.....
    ....*in* J737.1
    Same.....................................*in* T559.1
QUINTON, M. A. Money-god: a tale of the
    third century..............................Q995.1
Quintus Claudius. 2 vols. Eckstein, E...E195.6
Quits. Tautphoeus, J. M. *Freiherrin* von...
    ....T229.4
Quixstar. Taylor, E.........................T240.2
"Quo vadis." Sienkiewicz, H............S572.10
Quodlibet. Kennedy, J. P..................K353.2
R., E., *tr.* Chateau Morville.............R110.1
Rabbi and priest. Goldsmith, M..........G624.1
RABUSSON, H. Madame d'Orgevaut's hus-
    band...R117.1
Rachel Gray. Kavanagh, J.................K212.10
Rachel Noble's experience. Edwards, B..E263.1
Rachel Stanwood. Morse, L. G...........M885.1
RADCLIFFE, A. W. Mysteries of Udol-
    pho.......... ....R125.1
    Same. 3 vols......................**B232.45-7
    Romance of the forest.....................R125.2
    Same. 2 vols.......................**B232.43-4

Radical. Galt, J...................................G179.5
Same......................................in G179.6
Raffles Haw. Doyle, A. C..................D754.16
RAGGED, H. King Solomon's wives......R142.1
Raiders. Crockett, S. R.....................C938.16
Railroad and the churchyard, (etc). 54
     pp. Björnson, B........................in G622.1
Railway junction; or, the romance of Lady-
     bank. 59 pp.........................in T143.10
RAIMUND, G. (pseud. of B. Friedrich.)
     From hand to hand. Tr. by A. L.
     Wister..................................W817.21
     New race. Tr. by A. L. Wister........W817.22
Rainbow gold. Murray, D. C..............M981.8
Rainy June. Ouida..........................in O934.10
Same...O934.18
Rajah's heir.................................R161.1
Raleigh Westgate. Johnson, H. K.........J675.1
RALPH, J. Alone in China, and other
     stories.................................R163.1
     People we pass.........................R163.4
Ralph the bailiff, etc. Braddon, M. E...B798.30
Ralph the heir. Trollope, A..............T846.26
Ralph Wilton's weird. Alexander, Mrs....
     ....A374.23
Ralstons. 2 vols. Crawford, F. M......C899.16
Rambling story. Clarke, M. C-...........C599.2
Ramona. Jackson, H. M.,..................J127.4
RANDOLPH, J. T. Heiress of Sweetwater...R193.1
Randolph Gordon, etc. Ouida...........O934.19
Rangers. Thompson, D. P..................T470.5
Rangers and regulators. Reid, M........R357.8
Raphael. Lamartine, A. de................L217.4
Rarahu. Loti, P...............................L883.6
RASK, E. C. Storm-bride. 4 pp..........H496.1
RASPE, R. E. Adventures of Baron Mün-
     chausen. Illus. by G. Doré.........**R226.1
Rasselas, History of. Johnson, S......**B232.26
Same....................................J692.1
Same........................in **N938.23
RATHBONE, Mrs. M. A. M. See Manning,
     A.
Rattlin, the reefer. Marryat, Capt. F...M362.24
RAU, H. Beethoven: a biographical ro-
     mance.............................R239.1
     Mozart: a biographical romance........R239.2
Ravellings from the web of life. Green-
     way, Grandfather.........................G816.1
Ravenshoe. Kingsley, H....................K555.8
RAYMOND, G. How they kept the faith: a
     tale of the Huguenots of Languedoc...
     ....R269.1
RAYMOND, R. W. No laggards we.......R271.1

RAYMOND, W. (Tom Cobbleigh, pseud.)
     Gentleman Upcott's daughter.........R273.1
     "Love and quiet life."......................R273.2
     Tryphena in love...........................R273.3
Raymonde. Theuriet, A.....................T415.6
READ, E., joint author. See Reeves, M.
     C. L.
READ, O. P. Kentucky colonel............R284.1
     Len Gansett................................R284.2
     My young master..........................R284.3
READE, C. Box tunnel....................in S885.2
     Christie Johnstone........................R285.2
     Same.................................in R285.21
     Same.................................in R285.22
     Cloister and the hearth...................R285.4
     Course of true love never did run
        smooth.................................R285.7
     Same. (Also) Singleheart and Double-
        face.....................................R285.8
     Good stories...............................R285.9
     Griffith Gaunt.............................R285.10
     Hard cash................................R285.11
     Same. (Also) Wandering heir. 2 vols...
        ....R285.12
     It is never too late to mend..............R285.14
     Same, etc................................R285.15
     "Love me little, love me long.".......R285.19
     Peg Woffington. (Also) Christie John-
        stone, and other stories.................R285.21
     Same. (Also) Christie Johnstone.
        (And) Singleheart and Doubleface..R285.22
     Perilous secret...........................R285.23
     Put yourself in his place.................R285.26
     Same. (Also) White lies...............R285.27
     A simpleton................................R285.28
     Same. (Also) Wandering heir........R285.29
     Singleheart and Doubleface............in R285.8
     Same.................................in R285.22
     Terrible temptation.......................R285.30
     Wandering heir...........................in R285.12
     Same.................................in R285.29
     White lies...............................in R285.27
     Same.....................................R285.31
     Woman-hater............................R285.32
     —and Boucicault, D. Foul play........R285.33
READE, W. W. The outcast.................R286.1
Reading party in the long vacation. 63 pp...
     ....in T143.2
     Same.................................in T143.2 ¹
Ready money Mortiboy. Besant, Sir W.,
     and Rice, J..............................B554.42
Real folks. Whitney, A. D. T............W617.8
Real issue. White, W. A...................W589.5

Real lady. Garrett, E....................*in* G239.5
Real thing, and other stories. James, H.,
   Jr................................J277.14
Realmah. Helps, *Sir* A....................H484.3
Rebel queen. Besant, *Sir* W..............B554.26
Rebellious heroine. Bangs, J. K...........B216.3
Recalled to life. Allen, G.............A425.12
Recollections of Geoffry Hamlyn. Kings-
   ley, H............................K555.9
Recruit, The. 21 pp. Balzac, H. de...*in* B198.41
Rector of St. Marks. Holmes, M. J...*in* H751.27
Rector's home. Giberue, A...............G445.1
Rector's wife. Stretton, J................S916.1
Red as a rose is she. Broughton, R.........B877.6
Red badge of courage. Crane, S............C891.3
Red cockade. Weyman, S. J..............W549.14
Red Court farm. Wood, E. P............W874.11
Red diamonds. McCarthy, J................M1122.9
Red Hugh's captivity. O'Grady, S........O357.4
Red Inn. 48 pp. Balzac, H. de.........*in* B198.41
Red men and white. Wister, O............W818.1
Red republic. Chambers, R. W.........C445.6
Red Rover. Cooper, J. F...............*in* C777.27
   Same..............................C777.32
Red rowans. Steel, F. A..................S813.4
Redbank. Cowles, M. L..................C875.1
Redgauntlet. Scott, *Sir* W..............S431.41
   Same.............................**S431.42
   Same.............................S431.43
Reds of the midi. Gras, F.................G767.1
Redskins. Cooper, J. F................*in* C777.5
   Same..............................C777.33
REED, C. (*pseud. of* R. U. Collins). John
   Halsey the anti-monopolist.............R323.1
REED, T. B. Sir Ludar...................R326.1
Reed shaken with the wind. Faithfull,
   E...................................F174.1
REEDER, A. P. Around the golden deep:
   a romance of the Sierras................R327.1
REEVE, C. Old English baron.........**B232.22
REEVES, *Mrs.* H. M. *See* Mathers, H.
REEVES, M. C. L., *and* Read, E. Pilot
   Fortune................................R332.1
Reflection. Hofland, B.....................H712.1
Reflections of a married man. Grant, R...G763.9
Reform. Galt, J..........................G179.6
Refugee. Melville, H.....................M531.4
Refugees. Doyle, A. C...................D754.17
Regent's daughter. Dumas, A............D886.36
Regicides. Cogswell, F. H................C677.5
Regimental legends. Winter, J. S.......W785.13
   Same..............................*in* W785.1
Reginald Archer. Seemüller, A. M........S453.2
Reginald Dalton. Lockhart, J. G........L816.1

REICHENBACH, M. VON. (*pseud. of* V.
   Gräfin Bethusy-Huc.) The Eichhofs.
   Tr. by A. L. Wister...................W817.23
REID, C. (*pseud. of* F. C. F. Tiernan).
   After many days......................R353.1
   Bonny Kate R353.2
   Daughter of Bohemia.................R353.3
   Ebb-tide, and other stories R353.4
   Gentle belle..........................R353.5
   Heart of steel........................R353.6
   Hearts and hands.....................R353.7
   "Land of the sky.".....................R353.8
   Land of the sun: vistas Mexicanas......R353.9
   Mabel Lee............................R353.10
   Miss Churchill........................R353.11
   Morton House.........................R353.12
   Nina's atonement, and other stories..R353.13
   Picture of Las Cruces.................R353.14
   Question of honor.....................R353.15
   Summer idyl R353.16
   Valerie Aylmer........................R353.17
REID, M. Child wife.....................R357.1
   Free Lances..........................R357.2
   Headless horseman....................R357.3
   Lost Lenore R357.4
   The maroon...........................R357.5
   No quarter R357.6
   The quadroon........................R357.7
      Issued also as Love's vengeance.
   Rangers and regulators...............R357.8
   White gauntlet R357.9
Release. Yonge, C. M... ....Y555.26
Remarkable history of Sir Thomas Upmore.
   Blackmore, R. D.....................B629.15
Remember the Alamo. Barr, A. E......B268.19
Rent in a cloud. Lever, C........ ...*in* L658.25
Repository tales. More, H..............M835.4
Reprinted pieces, Dickens, C.........*in* D548.29 ²
   Same..............................*in* D548.35
   Same .... D548.35 ²
   Same..............................D548.46
Reproach of Annesley. Gray, M.........G781.12
Republic without a president, etc. Ward,
   H. D.................................W258.1
Reputed changeling. Yonge, C. M....Y555.28
Residuary legatee. Stimson, F. J..........S859.7
Resolution. Roe, A. S...................R698.3
Return of the native. Hardy, T...........H272.14
Reuben: a prince in disguise. Holding,
   C. B.................................H727.1
Reverberator. James, H., *Jr*...............J277.15
Reverend idol. Noble, L. G..............N750.1
Reveries of a bachelor. Mitchell, D. G....M679.3
Revolt of man. Besant, *Sir* W............B554.27

Revolution in Tanner's lane. Rutherford, M..............R975.1
REYBAUD, H. E. F. Claude Stocq.....*in* H781.1
Reynard the fox: numerous authors and editions..............*in* R794.1 ³
REYNOLDS, B., *pseud. See* Sheppard, E. S.
Rhoda Fleming. Meredith, G..............M559.10
Rhona. Forrester, *Mrs*..............F730.9
RHOSCOMYL, O. Battlement and tower....R478.1
For the white rose of Arno R478.5
RICE, J., *joint author. See* Besant, *Sir* W.
Rich husband. Riddell, C. E. L..............R543.15
Rich Miss Riddell. Gerard, D..............G356.2
Richard Edney and the governor's family. Judd, S..............J923.2
Richard Feverel, Ordeal of. Meredith, G..............*M559.9
Richard Hurdis. Simms, W. G..............S592.12
Richard Vandermarck. Harris, M. C....H315.4
RICHARDS, L. E. Marie..............R516.3
RICHARDSON, B. W. Son of a star: a romance of the second century..........R521.1
RICHARDSON, O. Dissolved pledge...*in* W750.10
Physiognomist's tales..............*in* W750.4
Rothesay fisherman..............*in* W750.3
Schoolfellows. Sea-storm..............*in* W750.6
Story of Tom Bertram. Angler's tales..............*in* W750.8
Tom Duncan's yarn. Meeting at St. Boswell's..............*in* W750.5
Two sailors. Restored son..............*in* W750.7
RICHARDSON, S. Clarissa Harlowe........R525.1
Same. 2 vols..............**N938.14-15
Same. 8 vols..............**B232.1-8
Pamela..............**N938.20
Same..............R525.2
Same. 4 vols..............**R525.3
Sir Charles Grandison..............R525.4
Same..............**N938.10-11
Same. 7 vols..............**B232.9-15
Richelieu. James, G. P. R..............J276.34
RICHTER, J. P. F. Campaner Thal, and other writings..............R535.1
Flower, fruit, and thorn pieces. 2 vols...R535.2
Hesperus. 2 vols..............R535.3
Invisible lodge..............R535.4
The moon. 8 pp..............*in* O983.1
Schmelzle's journey to Flætz. Life of Quintus Fixlein..............*in* C286.2
Titan: a romance. 2 vols..............R535.5
Ricketicketack. Conscience, H..........*in* C755.2

RIDDELL, C. E. L. (G. F. Trafford, *pseud.*)
Austin Friars..............R543.1
City and suburb R543.2
The earl's promise..............R543.3
Far above rubies..............R543.4
Forewarned, forearmed..............*in* R543.5
Frank Sinclair's wife, and Forewarned, forearmed..............R543.5
George Geith of Fen Court..............R543.6
Home, sweet home..............R543.7
Joy after sorrow..............R543.8
Life's assize..............R543.9
Mortomley's estate..............R543.11
My first love, and My last love..........R543.12
The nun's curse..............R543.13
Phemie Keller..............R543.14
Rich husband..............R543.15
Ruling passion..............R543.16
Too much alone..............R543.18
World in the church..............R543.19
RIDDELL, *Mrs.* J. H. *See* Riddell, C. E. L.
RIDDLE, A. G. House of Ross, and other tales..............R544.1
Riddle ring. McCarthy, J..............M122.10
Ride for life. 30 pp..............*in* T143.17
RIDEING, W. H., *joint author. See* Lathrop, G. P.
RIDGE, W. P. Second opportunity of Mr. Staplehurst..............R545.1
RIDGELY, J. L., *and* Donaldson, P., *eds.* Odd-fellows' offering, for 1848. Illus...............**R546.1
Rienzi. Lytton, E. G. E. L. Bulwer-....L998.23
Rifle, rod, and gun in California. Van Dyke, T. S..............V248.1
RIGGS, *Mrs.* K. D. *See* Wiggin, K. D.
Right at last and other tales. Gaskell, E. C..............G248.7
Right Honourable, The. McCarthy, J. *and,* Praed, R. C-..............M122.12
Right knock. Van Anderson, H..........V217.2
Right one. Schwartz, M. S..............S408.5
Righted wrong. Yates, E..............Y317.8
RILEY, J. W. Sketches in prose, and occasional verses..............R573.3
RING, I. (*pseud. of* A. S. Mecklenburg,) Furugaard. The snowball.........*in* V629.1
RING, M. John Milton and his times.....R581.1
Ring of Amasis. Lytton, E. R. Bulwer-...L999.1
RIPLEY, E. McH. From flag to flag: a woman's adventures in the south during the war, in Mexico, and in Cuba..............R589.1
Rise of Iskander. Disraeli, B.........*in* D613.4

Rise of Silas Lapham. Howells, W. D..H859.26
RITA. (pseud. of E. M. J. von Booth.)
Daphne.................................R598.1
Faustine...............................R598.2
Fragoletta............................R598.3
My lady Coquette...................R598.4
RITCHIE, Mrs. A. I. T. See Thackeray,
A. I.
RITCHIE, L. Cheaterie packman.........in Q594.1
Romance of history: France.......R610.1
Rival belles. Jones, J. B...............J778.1
Rivals. Griffin, G...................G851.5
RIVERS, G. R. R. Governor's garden...R622.1
RIVES, A. (Princess Troubetskoy.) Bar-
bara Dering............................R623.1
Brother to dragons, and other old-time
tales..................................R623.2
Roanoke of Roanoke Hall. Bell, M......B434.1
Rob of the bowl. Kennedy, J. P..........K353.3
Rob Roy. Scott, Sir W...............S431.44
Same..........................**S431.45
Same................................S431.46
ROBB, J. S. Swamp doctor's adventures in
the south-west.......................R631.1
Issued also as Odd leaves from the life of a
Louisiana "swamp doctor"
Robber baron of Bedford Castle. Foster,
A. J., and Cuthell, E. E................F754.2
Robbery under arms. Boldrewood, R....B687.7
Robert; or, the influence of a good mother,
and other stories...................R639.1
Robert Atterbury. Brainerd, T. H.........B814.2
Robert Elsmere. Ward, M. A. A.........W261.8
Robert Falconer. MacDonald, G......M135.18
Robert Greathouse. Swift, J. F..........S977.1
Robert Helmont. Daudet, A.............D238.10
Robert Ord's atonement. Carey, R. N..C276.29
Robert Urquhart. Setoun, G.............S495.4
ROBERTS, C. G. D. Earth's enigmas.....R643.1
Forge in the forest...................R643.3
ROBERTS, MARGARET. Atelier du Lys...R646.1
Issued also as Noblesse oblige.
Child of the revolution..............R646.2
Hester's venture....................R646.3
In the olden time....................R646.5
King Billy of Ballarat................in S885.7
Kinsfolk and others.................R646.6
Mademoiselle Mori..................R646.7
Noblesse oblige....................R646.1
Issued also as Atelier du Lys.
On the edge of the storm...........R646.8
ROBERTS, M. In low relief: a Bohemian
transcript.........................R647.1

ROBERTSON, H. How the Derby was won.
77 pp...............................in S886.6
ROBERTSON, M. M. By a way she knew
not..................................R651.1
Two Miss Jean Dawsons.............R651.2
ROBERTSON, M. Lombard street mystery...............................R652.1
Robin. Parr, L.......................Q258.7
Robin Tremayne. Holt, E. S...........H758.9
ROBINS, E. P., tr. Tales of to-day and
other days.........................R657.1
CONTENTS: Musset, A. de. Story of a
white blackbird.—Karr, A. Visit to the
arsenal.—Gautier, T. Thousand and second
night.—Mérimée, P. Il viccolo di Madama
Lucrezia.—Coppée, F. Barrel organ.—Bour-
get, P. Case of conscience.—Maupassant, G.
de. Who can tell? Drowned man.—Claretie,
J. The cigarette.—Zola, E. Attack on the
mill.
ROBINSON, A. D. G. See Douglas, M.,
pseud.
ROBINSON, A. M. F. (Mrs. Darmesteter.)
Goneril...............................in S885.5
ROBINSON, F. A. and WALL, G. A. The
disk: a tale of two passions...........R658.1
ROBINSON, F. M. Plan of campaign: a
story of the fortune of war. 2 vols...R659.1
Woman of the world. 3 vols.........R659.2
ROBINSON, F. W. Anne Judge, spinster.
3 vols.............................R660.1
Christie's faith......................R660.2
Minions of the moon................in S885.2
Othello the second.................R660.3
Slaves of the ring..................R660.4
A woman's ransom..................R660.5
ROBINSON, H. P. Men born equal.........R661.1
ROBINSON, J. Gold-worshippers.......R662.2
Madeleine Graham..................R662.3
Maid of Orleans....................R662.4
Owen Tudor........................R662.5
Westminster Abbey; or, the days of the
reformation.........................R662.6
Whitefriars; or, the days of Charles the
Second.............................R662.7
Whitehall; or, the days of Charles the
First...............................R662.8
Robinson Crusoe. Defoe, D.........in D314.5
Same................................in **N938.4
Same. 2 vols.....................**B232.16-17
ROCHE, R. M. Children of the abbey...R673.1
ROCHEFORT, V. H., Marquis de Rochefort-
Lucay. Mademoiselle Bismarck......R674.1
Rock ahead. Yates, E.................Y317.9
Rock scorpions......................in S885.9

Roderick Hudson. James, H., *Jr*.........J277.16
Roderick Hume. Bardeen, C. W...........B245.1
Roderick Random. Smollett, T. G..*in* **N938.2
Same...S666.3
Rodman the keeper. Woolson, C. F......W916.9
Rodney Stone. Doyle, A. C.................D754.19
ROE, A. S. How could he help it?........R698.1
Issued also as Give me thine heart.
James Montjoy; or, I've been thinking...R698.2
Issued also as I've been thinking.
Resolution; or, the soul of power R698.3
Star and the cloud................................R698.4
ROE, E. P. Barriers burned away........R699.1
Day of fate....................................R699.2
Earth trembled................................R699.3
Face illumined R699.4
From jest to earnest..........................R699.5
He fell in love with his wife..............R699.6
His sombre rivals.............................R699.7
Knight of the nineteenth century.......R699.9
"Miss Lou.".....................................R699.10
Nature's serial story.........................R699.11
Near to nature's heart.......................R699.12
Opening a chestnut burr...................R699.13
Original belle.................................R699.14
Taken alive, and other stories...........R699.15
What can she do?............................R699.16
Without a home..............................R699.17
Young girl's wooing.........................R699.18
ROE, E. R. Belteshazzar: a romance of
Babylon...R700.1
Dr. Caldwell; or, the trail of the serpent..R700.2
Roger Berkeley's probation. Campbell,
H.......................................C188.2
Roger Hunt. Woolley, C. P.................W913.1
ROGERS, M. Waverley dictionary: an alpha-
betical arrangement of all the charac-
ters in Sir W. Scott's Waverley novels,
etc.................................. **S431.58
ROGERS, R. C. Will o' the Wasp........R728.1
Rogue. Norris, W. E........................N861.15
Rogue's daughter. Sergeant, A.............S484.9
ROHLFS, *Mrs.* A. K. G. *See* Green, A. K.
Roland Blake. Mitchell, S. W............M681.2
Roland Cashel. Lever, C...................L658.22
Roland Yorke. Wood, E. P...............W874.12
Roman singer. Crawford, F. M..........C899.17
Roman traitor. Herbert, H. W...........H536.5
Romance at the antipodes. Douglass, *Mrs.*
R. D...................................D737.1
Romance of a châlet. Praed, R. C-.......Q897.3
Romance of a mummy. Gautier, T.......G277.3
Romance of a poor young man. Feuillet,
O..F426.4

Romance of a shop. Levy, A..............L668.1
Romance of a transport. Russell, W. C...R968.20
Romance of an honest woman. Cherbu-
liez, V......................................C521.5
Romance of Dollard. Catherwood, M. H...C363.7
Romance of history: England. Neele, H..N379.1
France. Ritchie, L.........................R610.1
India. Caunter, H.........................C374.1
Italy. MacFarlane, C.....................M143.1
Spain. Trueba y Cosio, T. de............ T866.1
Romance of Jenny Harlowe, etc. Russell,
W. C..R968.21
Romance of Judge Ketchum. Vachell,
H. A......................................V118.2
Romance of old court-life in France.
Elliot, F....................................E465.2
Romance of perfume lands. Clifford, F. S..C637.1
Romance of student life abroad. Kimball,
R. B..K492.2
Romance of the canoness. Heyse, P......H621.4
Romance of the forest. Radcliffe, A. W...R125.2
Same. 2 vols...............................**B232.43-4
Romance of the moors. Caird, M.........C136.1
Romance of the nineteenth century. Mal-
lock, W. H................................M255.5
Romance of the revolution. Bunce, O. B..B940.1
Romance of two worlds. Corelli, M......C797.9
Romance of war. Grant, J.................G761.41
Romances of real life. 2 vols. Hunt, L....H941.1
Romances of the east. Gobineau, J. A.,
Comte de..................................G575.1
Romantic tales. Lewis, M. G..............L675.1
Romany Rye. Borrow, G...................B737.2
Romany of the snows. Parker, G.........Q240.7
Romola. Eliot, G............................E426.7
Rookstone. Macquoid, K. S...............M173.7
Rookwood. Ainsworth, W. H..............A297.20
ROOSEVELT, B. *(Mrs. Macchetta).* Marked
"In haste.".................................R781.1
Roots of the mountains. Morris, W.......M877.5
Rory O'More. Lover, S.....................L910.4
Rosamond. Holmes, M. J..............*in* H751.5
Rosanna. Edgeworth, M ....*in* **E235.6
Same..................................*in* E235 19
Rosaura: a tale of Madrid. 70 pp......*in* T143.5
Same.................................*in* T143.5 1
ROSCOE, T., *tr.* German novelists: tales
selected. 4 vols...........................R794.1
CONTENTS: v. 1: Reynard the fox, numer-
ous authors and eds. of it.—Howleglass, the
merry jester.—Doctor Faustus.
v. 2: Popular traditions: Otmar. Local
popular traditions from the south side of the
Hartz; from the Golden Green; from the north
side of the Hartz.—Gottschalck, C. F. Witch-
dance on the Brocken. Meadow dance. Devil's

ROSCOE, T.—*Continued.*
fight in Goslar cathedral. Mouse tower. Castle spectre of Scharzfeld. Kingdom of Heaven. Monastery. Devil stones. Notburga. Ritter Bodo. Lion fight. Unlucky miser of Questenberg. Miraculous fish. Prudent princess. Devil's mill.—Eberhardt, (—) The bet. Treachery its own betrayer.—Büsching, J. G. G. Count Walter and the Lady Helgunda. Assassination of the Empress of Tartary in 1240.—Grimm, J. L., and W. K. Specimens from the Kinder und Haus Märchen.—Lothar. Arch rogue. Castle Christburg.—Lamotte Fouqué, ⸗. H. K., *Baron* de. Field of terror. The mandrake.

    v. 3: Popular tales: Musaeus, J. A. Dumb lover.—Schiller, F. The apparitionist. Sport of destiny. The criminal. Fraternal magnanimity. Walk among the linden trees.

    v. 4: German novels: Tieck, L. Love magic, some centuries ago. Faithful Eckart and the Tannenhäuser, pts. 1-2. Auburn Egbert.—Langbein, A. F. Marianne Richards. Seven marriages, and never a husband. Irreconcileable man. Albert Limbach. Hour's instruction in political economy. Lady's palfrey.—Engel, M. E. Anti-speculator. Toby Witt. Lady Elizabeth Hill.

Rose d'Albret. James, G. P. R............J276.35
Rose-garden. Peard, F. M................Q359.12
Rose Mather. Holmes, M. J............H751.25
Rose of Disentis. Zschokke, H.............Z923.4
Rose of Dutcher's Coolly. Garland, H....G233.4
Rose with a hundred leaves. Barr, A. E...B268.20
ROSEBORO', V. Old ways and new........R798.1
Rosecroft. Round, W. M. F.... ....R860.2
Rosery Folk. Fenn, G. M...................F334.6
Rosine. Melville, G. J. W-..........*in* **M530.19
  Same..M530.26
ROSS, A. (*pseud. of* L. B. Porter.) Speaking of Ellen............ .....R823.1
Ross-shire Buffs, etc. Grant, J............G761.42
ROSSETTI, C. G. Commonplace, and other short stories..................................R829.1
Roua pass. 3 vols. Mackenzie, E..........M156.1
Roué, The. Beazley, S.........................B386.2
ROUND, W. M. F. (Rev. P. Pennot, *pseud.*)
  Achsah: a New England life study...R860.1
  Rosecroft.... ....R860.2
Round a posada fire. Middlemore, S. G. C.......................................M627.1
Round the moon. Verne, J...........*in* V531.16
  Same......................................V531.33
Round the red lamp. Doyle, A. C....D754.18
Round the world in eighty days. Verne, J..................................V531.5
ROUSE, A. L. Stephen Vane's trust......R863.1
ROUSSELET, L. King of the tigers........R866.2
Roweny in Boston. Pool, M. L..........Q821.14

Roxy. Eggleston, E............................E294.8
ROY, G. For her sake: a tale of life in Ireland...............................R888.1
ROY, J. Helen Treveryan...................R889.1
ROY, J. J. E. *See* Ménard, T., *pseud.*
Roy and Viola. Forrester, *Mrs.*.........F730.10
Royal gentleman. Tourgée, A. W........T727.11
Royal Highlanders. Grant, J.............G761.43
Royal regiment, and other novelettes. Grant, J.....................................G761.44
ROYCE, J. Feud of Oakfield creek: a novel of California life..................R890.1
Roy's wife. Melville, G. J. W-......*in* **M530.7
  Same..................... M530.27
Ruby Grey. 3 vols. Dixon, W. H........D621.2
Ruby's husband. Harland, M...........H283.15
Rudder Grange. Stockton, F. R..........S866.27
Rudder Grangers abroad and other stories. Stockton, F. R..............................S866.28
Rudin. Turgénieff, I. S.....................T936.9
RUFFINI, G. Lavinia...........................R923.1
  Lorenzo Benoni.................................R923.2
  The Paragreens on a visit to the Paris Universal Exhibition......................R923.3
  Issued also as Dear experience.
Ruling passion. Riddell, C. E. L........R543.16
Rumor. Sheppard, E. S...................S549.4
Runaway Browns. Bunner, H. C..........B942.4
Running the blockade. Thomes, W. H...T465.8
Running the gauntlet. Yates, E.........Y317.10
Rupert Godwin. Braddon, M. E.........B798.31
RUSSELL, *Col.* Coincidences?? 49 pp................................*in* T143.23
RUSSELL, C. W. Fall of Damascus......R960.1
RUSSELL, W. C. Extraordinary adventure of a chief mate...........................*in* S885.9
  Flying Dutchman; or, the death ship...R968.3
  Frozen pirate...................................R968.4
  Golden Hope...................................R968.5
  In the middle watch....... ....R968.7
  Jack's courtship.............................R968.8
  List ye landsmen!...........................R968.10
  Little Loo.....................................R968.11
  Marooned......................................R968.12
  Memorable swim. 49 pp.............*in* S887.1
  My Danish sweetheart.....................R968.14
  My shipmate Louise........................R968.15
  Mystery of the "Ocean Star," etc......R968.16
  Ocean tragedy................................R968.18
  Romance of a transport...................R968.20
  Romance of Jenny Harlowe, etc........R968.21
  Sailor's sweetheart........................R968.22
  Sea queen.....................................R968.23
  Strange elopement.........................R968.24

RUSSELL, W. C.—*Continued.*
Tragedy of Ida Noble........................R968.25
Wreck of the Corsaire..... ....R968.27
Wreck of the "Grosvenor."............R968.28
Russell. James, G. P. R....................J276.36
Russian proprietor and other stories. Tolstoi, *Count* L. N............................T654.10
Russian romance. Pushkin, A. S.........Q976.2
Ruth Hall. Fern, F..............................F361.1
RUTHERFORD, M. (*pseud. of* W. H. White.) Revolution in Tanner's lane...
....R975.1
Rutledge. Harris, M. C.....................H315.5
Ruy Blas. Ed. by H. L. Williams........W723.1
S., H. C. Who painted the great Murillo de la Merced? 88 pp...................*in* T143.9
S., J., *of Dale, pseud. See* Stimson, F. J.
S., R., *pseud. See* Paltock, R.
Sabina Zembra. Black, W..................B627.27
Sable cloud. Adams, N......................A216.1
SACHER-MASOCH, L. VON. The sledgeride...................................*in* Z767.11
Sacrifice. Green, W. S........................G798.1
Sacristan's household. Trollope, F. E...T847.3
Sad fortunes of the Rev. Amos Barton. Eliot, G..................................*in* E426.8
SADLIER, *Mrs.* J. *See* Sadlier, M. A.
SADLIER, M. A. Con O'Regan............S126.1
Confederate chieftains....................S126.2
Heiress of Kilorgan.........................S126.3
MacCarthy More: the fortunes of an Irish chief in the reign of Queen Elizabeth...................................S126.4
Maureen Dhu: a tale of the Claddagh of Galway.....................................S126.5
Old and new..................................S126.6
Safar-Hadgi. Lubomirski, S. H., *Prince*..L930.1
SAFFORD, M. J., *tr.* True daughter of Hartenstein..................................S128.1
Sailor's sweetheart. Russell, W. C......R968.22
St. Ann's. Norris, W. E....................N861.16
St. Augustine. Musick, J. R..............M987.3
St. Clair of the isles. Helme, E.........H479.1
St. Elmo. Wilson, A. J. E.................W746.6
St. George and St. Michael. MacDonald, G.................................M135.19
St. Giles and St. James. Jerrold, D.......J566.2
Saint James's. Ainsworth, W. H.........A297.21
St. John's eve and other stories. Gogol, N. V..G613.1
ST. JOHNSTON, A. South sea lover........S143.1
St. Katherine's by the tower. Besant, *Sir* W...B554.28

St. Leon. 4 vols. Godwin, W............G592.2
St. Martin's eve. Wood, E. P............W874.14
St. Martin's summer. Brewster, A. H. M...
....B848.1
Saint Michael. Werner, E.................W817.33
St. Olave's. Tabor, E.........................T114.4
St. Patrick's eve. Lever, C............*in* L658.25
St. Philip's. Harris, M. C...................H315.6
SAINT-PIERRE, B. DE. Paul and Virginia..
....*in* G625.3
Same...S149.1
Same..*in* S892.14
St. Ronan's well. Scott, *Sir* W.....*in* **S431.40
Same..S431.47
Same...S431.48
St. Simon's niece. Benedict, F. L.........B463.7
SAINTINE, X. B. (*pseud. of* J. X. Boniface.) Picciola. 86 pp...........*in* S892.14
Solitary of Juan Fernandez; or, the real Robinson Crusoe.........................S142.1
Saints and sinners. Cherbuliez, V........C521.6
SALA, G. A. Dead men tell no tales, but live men do...................................S159.1
Seven sons of mammon...... ....S159.2
Salathiel, the immortal. Croly, G.........C944.2
Salem. Castleton, D. R.....................C353.1
Salem chapel. Oliphant, M. O. W......O475.50
Same...O475.51
Sally Dows, etc. Harte, B..................H327.29
Salmagundi. Irving, W., Paulding, J. K., *and* Irving, W...............................I726.1
Salome Shepard, reformer. Winslow, H. M...W780.1
Salt master of Lüneburg. Wolff, J.......W857.2
SALTER, F. Assunta Howard, and other stories..S177.1
SALTUS, E. Truth about Tristrem Varick.
....S180.1
Salvage...S182.1
Sam Lawson's Oldtown fireside stories. Stowe, H. B.................................S892.11
Samuel Brohl and Company. Cherbuliez, V...C521.7
Samuel Titmarsh and the great Hoggarty diamond. Thackeray, W. M.....*in* T363.7
Same...T363.12
Same...T363.13
Same..*in* T363.15
SANBORN, F. W. People at Pisgah S198.1
Sanctuary. Nichols, G. W...................N618.1
SAND, G. (*pseud. of* A. L. A. D. Dudevant.) Antonia...S213.1
The bagpipers..................................S213.2

SAND, G.—*Continued.*
Consuelo. Tr. by F. Robinson............S213.4
Same. Tr. by F. H. Potter. 4 vols.....S213.4p
Countess of Rudolstadt: sequel to "Consuelo."..S213.5
Fadette...S213.6
Issued also as Fanchon the cricket Little Fadette.
Indiana...S213.7
Jealousy; or, Teverino.........................S213.8
The marriage. 10 pp. The cabbage. 13 pp....................................*in* Z767.1 ¹
Master mosaic-workers.........................S213.9
Mauprat...S213.10
Miller of Angibault..............................S213.11
Monsieur Sylvestre..............................S213.13
My sister Jeannie..................................S213.14
Princess Nourmahal..............................S213.15
Snow man..S213.16
Spiridion... S213.17
Tower of Percemont..............................S213.18
Sand. Gally, J. W..................................G178.1
SANDEAU, J. Last of an old family...*in* Z767.1 ²
Madeleine: a story of French love.......S214.1
Sandra Belloni. Meredith, G...............M559.11
San Rosario ranch. Howe, M...............H857.1
San Salvador. Tincker, M. A...............T587.5
Sans merci. Lawrence, G. A................L421.7
Sant' Ilario. Crawford, F. M................C899.18
Santos's brother. Loughead, F. H.....*in* L887.1
Sappho. Daudet, A................................D238.11
Sappho of Green Springs. Harte, B......H327.30
Saracen. 4 vols. (in 2.) Cottin, S. R...**C848.2
Saracinesca. Crawford, F. M................C899.19
Sarah de Berenger. Ingelow, J.............I464.6
Sarchedon. Melville, G. J. W.......*in* **M530.4
Same..M530.28
SARGENT, E. Peculiar: a tale of the great transition S245.1
Sartaroe. Maitland, J. A......................M232.4
Satauella. Melville, G. J. W................M530.29
Same...**M530.30
Satanstoe. Cooper, J. F..............*in* C777.24
Same..C777.34
Saucy Arethusa. Chamier, F................C448.2
SAUNDERS, J. Guy Waterman. 3 vols..S257.1
SAUNDERS, K. High Mills.....................S258.1
SAVAGE, M. J. Bluffton.........................S263.1
SAVAGE, M. W. Bachelor of the Albany...S264.1
Falcon family; or, young Ireland....... S264.2
My uncle, the curate S264.3
SAVAGE, R. H. For life and love..........S265.1
Little lady of Lagunitas.....................S265.2
My official wife S265.3
SAVIDGE, E. C. American in Paris........S267.1

SAWTELLE, M. P. Heroine of '49..........S271.1
Saxe Holm's stories. 2 vols. Jackson, H. M..J127.5
Say and seal. Warner, S., *and* A. B.,.....W284.12
Scandal in Bohemia. Doyle, A. C. ..*in* D754.21
Scapegoat. Caine, H...........................C135.9
Scarlet letter. Hawthorne, N.............. H399.10
Same.. H399.11
Scarlet poppy, and other stories. Spofford, H. P......................................S762.5
Scarlet sin. Marryat, F.......................M361.10
Scenes and characters. Yonge, C. M...Y555.29
Scenes and legends of the north of Scotland. Miller, H...............................M1648.1
Scenes from the life of Bohemia. Murger, H..M976.1
Scenes in our parish. Holmes, E.......**H750.1
Scenes of clerical life. Eliot, G........... E426.8
Same..E426.10
SCHAYER, J. Story of two lives. 32 pp.*in* S884.10
SCHEFFEL, J. V. VON. Ekkehard. 2 vols...S317.1
SCHICK, L., *pub.* Masterpieces of German fiction...S331.1
CONTENTS: Lindau, R. Hans the dreamer. All in vain. First love.—Lewald, F. The aristocratic world. Maid of Oyas.—Eckstein, E. Visit to the lockup. Boarding school girls. Against the stream.—Wilbrandt, A. Pilot captain.—Heyse, P. L'Arrabiata. Beppe, the star gazer. Maria Francisca.—Hopfen, H. Trudel's ball. Fortunes and the fate of little Spangle.
SCHILLER, J. C. F. VON. The apparitionist. Sport of destiny. The criminal. Fraternal magnanimity. Walk among the linden trees.........................*in* R794.1 ³
Criminal from lost honour. 17 pp...*in* O983.1
SCHMEIDEN, E. J. *See* Juncker, E., *pseud.*
SCHNABEL, L. Voegele's marriage, and other tales..S357.1
SCHOBERT, H. Picked up in the streets. Tr. by A. L. Wister......................W817.24
SCHOOLCRAFT, *Mrs.* H. R. *See* Schoolcraft, M. H.
SCHOOLCRAFT, M. H. Black gauntlet: a tale of plantation life in South Carolina...... ....S372.1
Schoolmaster's trial. Perry, A............Q462.1
SCHREINER, O. (Ralph Iron, *pseud.*) Dream life and real life.....................S378.1
Dreams..S378.2
Story of an African farm........ ....S378.3
Trooper Peter Halket of Mashonaland..S378.4

SCHUBIN, O. (*pseud. of* L. Kirschner.)
  Countess Erika's apprenticeship. Tr.
  by A. L. Wister.............................W817.25
Erlach Court. Tr. by A. L. Wister...W817.26
"Gloria victis!".....................................S384.2
A leafless spring............. ....S384.3
"O thou, my Austria!" Tr. by A. L.
  Wister..W817.27
One of us..S384.4
Our own set............... ....S384.5
SCHULTZ, J. Story of Colette.................S387.3
SCHULZE–SMIDT, B. *See* Oswald, E.,
  pseud.
SCHWARTZ, H. V. *See* Maartens, M.,
  pseud.
SCHWARTZ, M. S. Birth and education...S408.1
  Gerda; or, the children of work.........S408.2
  Gold and name......... ....S408.3
  Guilt and innocence............................S408.4
  Right one..S408.5
  Son of the organ-grinder.....................S408.6
  Two family mothers.............................S408.7
Scots Brigade. Grant, J......................G761.45
SCOTT, H. S. *See* Merriman, H. S., *pseud.*
SCOTT, *Lady* J. Pride of life.................S425.1
SCOTT, M. Cruise of the Midge S428.1
  Tom Cringle's log...............................S428.2
SCOTT, *Mrs.* O. W. Gilead Guards........S429.1
SCOTT, *Sir* W. The abbot: sequel to The
  monastery........ ....S431.1
Same...*in* S431.34
Anne of Geierstein...............................S431.2
Same...................................*in* **S431.21
The antiquary.......................................S431.3
Same. (*Also*) Black dwarf. (*And*) Old
  Mortality...**S431.4
The betrothed: a tale of the crusaders..S431.5
Same....................................*in* **S431.42
Same. (*Also*) Highland widow........S431.6
Black dwarf.................................*in* **S431.4
  Same...................................*in* S431.48
Same. (*Also*) Legend of Montrose...S431.7
Same. (*Also*) Old Mortality............S431.9
Same. (*And*) Quentin Durward......S431.10
Bride of Lammermoor.........................S431.11
Same...S431.48
Same. (*Also*) Legend of Montrose...S431.12
Same. (*And*) Ivanhoe.................**S431.13
Castle Dangerous................................S431.14
Same.....................................*in* **S431.19
Same.....................................*in* S431.37
Same.....................................*in* S431.49
Count Robert of Paris.........................S431.17

SCOTT, *Sir* W.—*Continued.*
Same. (*Also*) Castle Dangerous. My
  Aunt Margaret's mirror. Tapestried
  chamber. (*And*) Death of the laird's
  Jock...**S431.19
Death of the laird's Jock...............*in* S431.15
Same......................................*in* **S431.19
Same......................................*in* S431.51
Fair maid of Perth...............................S431.20
Same......................................*in* S431.31
Same. (*Also*) Anne of Geierstein..**S431.21
Fortunes of Nigel.................................S431.22
Same. (*Also*) Peveril of the peak..**S431.23
Same. (*Also*) Pirate.....................S431.24
Guy Mannering....................................S431.25
Same......................................*in* **S431.53
Heart of Mid-Lothian..........................S431.27
Same......................................*in* **S431.45
Highland widow.......................*in* S431.6
Same......................................*in* **S431.55
Same. (*Also*) Two drovers. The sur-
  geon's daughter. (*And*) My aunt
  Margaret's mirror, etc....................S431.16
Ivanhoe......................' ... *in* **S431.13
Same...S431.28
Kenilworth...S431.30
Same. (*Also*) Fair maid of Perth....S431.31
Same. (*Also*) The pirate.............**S431.32
Legend of Montrose ....*in* S431.7
Same...................................... *in* S431.12
Same.......................................*in* **S431.13
Same......................................*in* S431.48
The monastery.....................................S431.33
Same. (*Also*) The abbot.................S431.34
My aunt Margaret's mirror, etc......*in* S431.15
Same....................................... *in* **S431.19
Same......................................*in* S431.51
Old Mortality............................*in* **S431.4
Same......................................*in* S431.9
Same......................................*in* S431.10
Same...S431.35
Same ....*in* S431.46
Peveril of the Peak....................*in* **S431.23
Same...S431.36
Same. (*Also*) The surgeon's daughter.
  (*And*) Castle Dangerous..............S431.37
The pirate..................................*in* S431.24
Same.. .... *in* **S431.32
Same.. .... *in* S431.38
Same..*in* S431.43
Quentin Durward. . . ..*in* S431.10
Same...S431.39
Same. (*Also*) St. Ronan's well....**S431.40

SCOTT, *Sir* W.—*Continued.*
Redgauntlet..S431.41
Same. *(Also)* Betrothed. *(And)* The
talisman...............................**S431.42
Same. *(Also)* The pirate................S431.43
Rob Roy.......................................S431.44
Same. *(Also)* Heart of Mid-Lothian..**S431.45
Same. *(Also)* Old Mortality..........S431.46
St. Ronan's well.......................*in* **S431.40
Same.......................................S431.47
Same. *(Also)* Black dwarf. Legend of
Montrose. *(And)* Bride of Lammer-
moor......................................S431.48
Surgeon's daughter...................*in* S431.16
Same.....................................*in* S431.37
Same.....................................*in* **S431.55
Same. *(Also)* Castle Dangerous......S431.49
Tales of my landlord.
  1st ser. Black dwarf, and Old Mortality.
  2d ser. Heart of Mid-Lothian.
  3d ser. Bride of Lammermoor, and Legend
  of Montrose.
  4th ser. Count Robert of Paris, and Castle
  Dangerous.
Tales of the crusaders.
  Betrothed. Talisman.
The talisman.......................*in* **S431.42
Same.......................................S431.50
Same. *(Also)* Two drovers. *(And)*
My aunt Margaret's mirror, etc......S431.51
Tapestried chamber...................*in* S431.15
Same.......................................*in* **S431.19
Same.......................................*in* S431.51
Two drovers............................*in* S431.16
Same.......................................*in* S431.51
Same.......................................*in* **S431.55
Same. *(Also)* My aunt Margaret's
mirror. Tapestried chamber. *(And)*
Death of the laird's Jock.............S431.15
Wandering Willie's tale. 33 pp.......*in* S885.8
Waverley..................................S431.52
Same. *(Also)* Guy Mannering......**S431.53
Woodstock................................S431.54
Same. *(Also)* Highland widow. Two
drovers. *(And)* Surgeon's daughter..
....**S431.55
Waverley dictionary: an alphabetical
arrangement of all the characters in
(his) Waverley novels, with descriptive
analysis of each character, and illustra-
tive selections from the text, by M.
Rogers..................................**S431.58
Waverley novels index and glossary..**S431.56
Key with index of principal characters,
by H. Grey.............................S431.57

Scottish cavalier. Grant, J................G761.46
Scottish chiefs. Porter, J................Q846.1
Scottish soldiers of fortune. Grant, J...G761.47
Scouring of the White Horse. Hughes,
T...H894.1
Scout. Simms, W. G......................S592.13
SCRIBNER, J. P. (An old mountaineer,
pseud.) Laconia; or, legends of the
White mountains and Merry Meeting
bay.......................................S434.1
Scripture club of Valley Rest. Habber-
ton, J...................................H113.9
Scrope. Perkins, F. B...................Q448.2
SCUDDER, H. E. Stories and romances...S436.1
SCULLY, W. C. Ghamba.................*in* S885.1
Kafir stories.............................S437.1
Sea fight................................*in* W750.10
Sea lions. Cooper, J. F.................C777.35
Same.....................................C777.36
Sea queen. Russell, W. C...............R968.23
Sea skirmish............................*in* W750.10
Seaboard parish. MacDonald, G.........M135.20
Sealed lips. Du Boisgobey, F............D816.4
Sealed orders. Phelps, E. S............Q539.13
SEALSFIELD, C. (*pseud* of K. Postel.) Ad-
ventures in Texas......................*in* T143.3
Same...................................*in* T143.3 ¹
Sealskin Annie. Loughead, F. H......*in* L887.1
Sealskin cloak. Boldrewood, R.........B687.8
Seamy side. Besant, *Sir* W., *and* Rice, J...
....B554.43
Search for Basil Lyndhurst. Carey, R.
N..C276.31
Season-ticket. Haliburton, T. C........H172.4
Seats of the mighty. Parker, G.........Q240.9
SEAWARD, *Sir* E., *pseud. See* Porter, W.
O.
SEAWELL, M. E. Berkeleys and their
neighbors..............................S442.1
Children of destiny.....................S442.2
Maid Marian and other stories.........S442.5
Sprightly romance of Marsac............S442.6
Strange, sad comedy...................S442.7
Throckmorton.........................S442.8
Virginia cavalier.......................S442.11
Sebastian Strome. Hawthorne, J........H398 17
Second book of tales. Field, E..........F453.3
Second opportunity of Mr. Staplehurst.
Ridge, W. P............................R545.1
Second son. Oliphant, M. O. W., *and*
Aldrich, T. B..........................O475.52
Second to none. Grant, J...............G761.48
Second wife. Marlitt, E.................W817.19

SECONDTHOUGHTS, S., *Schoolmaster, pseud.*
  See Kennedy, J. P.
Secret dispatch. Grant, J.................G761.49
Secret of Fontaine-la-Croix. Field, M...F455.1
Secret of the Lamas: a tale of Thibet.....S446.1
Secret of the sea, &c. Matthews, B.....M438.10
Secrets of the Princesse de Cadignan. 90
  pp. Balzac, H. de..................*in* B198.19
Secret passion. Williams, R. F....*in* **W726.1
SEDGWICK, C. M. The Linwoods; or,
  "sixty years since" in America. 2
  vols.......................................S448.1
SEEMÜLLER, A. M. Opportunity..........S453.1
  Reginald Archer........................S453.2
SEGRAVE, A., *pseud. See* Hamerton, P. G.
'Self or bearer.' Besant, *Sir* W........*in* B554.30
Semi-detached house. Eden, E............E221.1
SENIOR, W., *joint author. See* Francillon,
  R. E.
Sense and sensibility. Austen, J..........A933.6
  Same..A933.7
Sensitive plant. Gerard, E., *and* D......G357.1
Sentimental journey. 58 pp. Sterne, L...
  ....*in* C615.1
  Same...................................*in* **N938.9
Sentimental Tommy. Barrie, J. M........B275.8
Septimius Felton. Hawthorne, N.....*in* H399.3
  Same......................................*in* H399.8
  Same...H399.12
Seraphita. Balzac, H. de....................B198.33
Serapion brethren. 2 vols. Hoffman, W...
  ....H710.1
Serapis. Ebers, G.............................E165.13
SERGEANT, A. Christine.............S484.1
  Life sentence............................S484.3
  Luck of the house......................S484.4
  Out of due season.....................S484.7
  Rogue's daughter......................S484.9
  Surrender of Margaret Ballarmine.....S484.10
SERRAO, T. Brushes and chisels.........S488.1
Seth's brother's wife. Frederic, H........F852.8
SETOUN, G. (*pseud. of* G. Hepburn.)
  Robert Urquhart.........................S495.4
  Sunshine and haar......................S495.6
Settlers in Canada. Marryat, *Capt.* F...M362.25
Seven daughters. Douglas, A. M........D734.24
Seven sons of mammon. Sala, G. A......S159.2
Seven stories, with basement and attic.
  Mitchell, D. G.............................M679.4
Seven years, and other tales. Kavanagh,
  J...K212.11
Sevenoaks. Holland, J. G....................H735.5
1791: a tale of San Domingo. Gilliam, E.
  W..G480.1

Severa. Hartner, E........................W817.3
SEVERANCE, M. S. Hammersmith: his
  Harvard days.............................S498.1
Severed hand. Du Boisgobey, F..........D816.2
SEWELL, E. M. Glimpse of the world...S516.1
  Margaret Percival........................S516.2
Sforza. Astor, W. W.........................A858.1
Shabby genteel story. Thackeray, W. M...
  ....*in* T363.2
Shadow of a crime. Caine, H.............C135.10
Shadow of a dream. Howells, W. D...H859.27
Shadow of Hampton Mead. Van Loon,
  E..V261.1
Shadow of the door. 60 pp.........*in* T143.14
Shadow of the sword. Buchanan, R.....B918.5
Shadows on the snow. Farjeon, B. L....F229.14
Shady side. Hubbell, M. S.................H875.1
Shakespeare and his friends. Williams,
  R. F..**W726.1
Shall I win her? Grant, J.................G761.50
Shamrock and rose. 3 vols. Lunn, *Mrs.*
  J. C...L963.1
SHAND, A. I. Mr. Cox's protégé......*in* T143.23
  Wrecked off the Riff coast............*in* T143.12
Shandon bells. Black, W...................B627.29
Shandy M'Guire. Peppergrass, P........Q424.1
SHAPLEY, R. R. Solid for Mulhooly: a
  sketch of municipal politics............S529.1
  Issued also as I'm fur 'em.
SHARKEY, T. K. Mate to mate............S530.1
SHARP, W. Children of tomorrow........S531.1
  Gypsy Christ, and other tales..........S531.4
  —*joint author. See* Howard, B. W.
Shaving of Shagpat. Meredith, G......M559.12
SHAW, W. J. Solomon's story.............S537.1
She. Haggard, H. R........................H146.13
She-wolves of Machecoul. 2 vols. Du-
  mas, A......................................D886.37
SHEBBEARE, J. Lydia..............*in* **N938.22
SHIEL, R. L. The apostate. 25 pp....*in* M875.1³
SHELDON, L. V. I. D. B. in South Africa....
  ....S544.1
SHELLEY, M. W. Frankenstein; or, the
  modern Prometheus....................S545.1
Shepherd of Salisbury Plain, and other
  tales. More, H.........................M835.5
SHEPPARD, E. S. (E. Berger, Mme. Kinkel,
  B. Reynolds, *pseuds.*) Charles Auches-
  ter..S549.1
  Counterparts; or, the cross of love........S549.2
  Rumor..S549.4
SHEPPARD, F. H. Love afloat: a story of
  the American navy.....................S550.1
Sherburne cousins. Douglas, A. M......D734.25

Sherburne house. Douglas, A. M........D734.26
Sherburne romance. Douglas, A. M.....D734.27
SHERIDAN, F. Nourjahad. 38 pp...*in* **N938.23
  Sidney Bidulph.....................*in* **N938.22
SHERIDAN, R. B. B. School for scandal,
  28 pp. The rivals. 32 pp........*in* M875.1 ⁷
Sherlock Holmes, Adventures of. Doyle,
  A. C............................D754.1
Sherlock Holmes, Memoirs of. Doyle,
  A. C............................D754.11
SHERMAN, F. D., *joint author. See* Bangs,
  J. K.
SHERWOOD, M. (Elizabeth Hastings,
  pseud.) Experiment in altruism.......S553.3
Puritan Bohemia.......................S553.8
Shiloh. Jay, W. M. L...................J424.1
SHINN, M. W. Young Strong of "The
  Clarion." 46 pp...................*in* S884.9
"Ship ahoy!" Fenn, G. M..............F334.7
SHIPPEN, E. Thirty years at sea: story
  of a sailor's life...................S557.1
Ships that pass in the night. Harraden, B..H296.5
SHIRLEY, P. (*pseud. of* A. L. Townsend).
  On the verge: a romance of the cen-
  tennial...........................S558.1
Shirley. Brontë, C....................B870.4
"Short sixes." Bunner, H. C.............B942.5
Shorter stories. Balzac, H. de...........B198.34
SHORTHOUSE, J. H. Blanche, Lady
  Falaise...........................S559.1
  Countess Eve.....................S559.2
  John Inglesant....................S559.3
  Little schoolmaster Mark..............S559.4
  Sir Percival.......................S559.5
  Teacher of the violin, and other tales....S559.6
SHREVE, T. H. Drayton: a story of Amer-
  ican life...........................S561.1
Shuttle of fate. Masters, C.............M423.5
Siberian exiles. Knox, T. W.............K743.1
SIDNEY, *Sir* P. Countess of Pembroke's
  Arcadia...........................S569.1
Sidney. Deland, M....................D337.9
Sidney Bidulph. Sheridan, F.....*in* **N938.22
Sidonie. Daudet, A....................D238.12
Siege baby. Winter, J. S.............*in* W785.1
Siege of Damascus. 3 vols. Nisbet, J... **N723.1
Siege of London. James, H., *Jr*........J277.17
SIENKIEWICZ, H. Children of the soil.... S572.3
  The deluge: an historical novel of Poland,
  Sweden, and Russia. Sequel to "With
  fire and sword." 2 vols..............S572.4
  Lillian Morris, etc..................S572.6
  Pan Michael. Sequel to "The deluge."..S572.9

SIENKIEWICZ, H.—*Continued.*
  "Quo vadis:" a narrative of the time of
  Nero.............................S572.10
  With fire and sword: an historical novel
  of Poland and Russia................S572.12
  Without dogma....................S572.13
  Yanko the musician, and other stories..S572.15
Sights and insights. 2 vols. Whitney,
  A. D. T...........................W617.9
Sigismund Fatello. 87 pp.............*in* T143.4
  Same............................*in* T143.4 ⁷
Sign of the four. Doyle, A. C......... ...D754.20
  Same............................D754.21
Signa. Ouida.........................O934.20
Signing the contract. Finley, M..........F513.2
Signor Gaudentio di Lucca. Berington,
  S..............................*in* **N938.21
Signor Monaldini's niece. Tincker, M. A..T587.6
SIGOURNEY, L. H. Lucy Howard's
  journal...........................S578.1
Sigrid. Thoroddsen, J. T...............T516.1
SIKES, *Mrs.* O. L. *See* Logan, O.
Silas Marner. Eliot, G.............*in* E426.8
  Same............................E426.9
Silcote of Silcotes. Kingsley, H..........K555.10
Silence of Dean Maitland. Gray, M....G781.14
Silent partner. Phelps, E. S.............Q539.14
Silhouettes of American life. Davis, *Mrs.*
  R. H.............................D263.3
Silk of the kine. McManus, L...........M167.1
Silver pitchers. Alcott, L. M............A355.4
Silvia. Kavanagh, J..................K212.12
SIME, W. Boulderstone................S589.1
  King capital.......................S589.2
SIMMS, W. G. Beauchampe. Sequel to
  Charlemont........................S592.1
  Border beagles: a tale of Mississippi.....S592.2
  Charlemont: a tale of Kentucky..........S592.3
  Confession........................S592.4
  Damsel of Darien..................**S592.5
  Eutaw............................S592.6
  The forayers.......................S592.7
  Guy Rivers: a tale of Georgia............S592.8
  Katharine Walton...................S592.9
  Mellichampe: a legend of the Santee..S592.10
  The partisan: a romance of the revolu-
  tion.............................S592.11
  Richard Hurdis.....................S592.12
  The scout; or, the black riders of Con-
  garee.......................... ....S592.13
  Southward ho!.....................S592.14
  Vasconselos.......................S592.15
  Wigwam and the cabin...............S592.16
    Issued also as Life in America.
  The Yemasee: a romance of Carolina..S592.18

Simple adventures of a memsahib. Cotes,
S. J. D..C843.14
Simple story. Inchbald, E. S..........**B232.28
Simple tales. Opie, A.....................in O614.1
SIMPLETON, *Maj., pseud.* Civil-service re-
form; or, the postmaster's revenge.....S612.1
Simpleton. Reade, C.....................R285.28
Same... ......R285.29
Sincere Huron. 35 pp. Voltaire, F. M.
A. de..............................in **N938.21
Sinfire. Hawthorne, J....................H398.18
Singer from the sea. Barr, A. E..........B268.22
Singer's story. Laffan, M...................L163.4
Singleheart and Doubleface. Reade, C...
....in R285.8
Same.....................................in R285.22
SINGLETON, *Mrs.* M. M. L. *See* Fane, V.,
pseud.
Singular life. Phelps, E. S Q539.15
Singularly deluded. Grand, S.............G751.3
SINNETT, A. P. Karma........................S617.1
Sintram and his companions. La Motte-
Fouqué, F. H. K. *Freiherr* de.....in L235.1
Same..L235.4
Same................................... in L235.6
Sir Andrew Wylie of that ilk. Galt, J...G179.7
Sir Brooke Fosbrooke. Lever, C.........L658.23
Sir Charles Grandison, History of. Rich-
ardson, S...................................R525.4
Same. 2 vols.........................**N938.10-11
Same. 7 vols..........................**B232.9-15
Sir Edmund Orme. James, H., *Jr*.....in J277.8
Sir Edward Seaward's narrative of his
shipwreck. Porter, W. O..............Q849.1
Sir George Tressady. 2 vols. Ward, M.
A. A......................................W261.9
Sir Gervase Grey. 3 vols. (in 2.) Gordon,
Mrs...... ....G662.1
Sir Gibbie. MacDonald, G................M135.21
Sir Godfrey's grand-daughters. Carey, R.
N...C276.32
Sir Harry Hotspur of Humblethwaite.
Trollope, A...................................T846.27
Sir Jasper Carew. Lever, C.................L658.24
Sir Jasper's tenant. Braddon, M. E....B798.32
Sir Ludar. Reed, T. B.............. ....R326.1
Sir Mark. Brown, A. R.......................B881.5
Sir Percival. Shorthouse, J. H.............S559.5
Sir Rohan's ghost. Spofford, H. P.......S762.6
Sister Jane. Harris, J. C....................H314.8
Sister Louise. Melville, G. J. W.-.......M530.31
Same............... ....**M530.32
Sister of a saint, and other stories. Chan-
ning, G. E............... ....C458.1

Sister Rose. Holt, E. S.....................H758.10
Sister Saint Sulpice. Valdés, A. P......V145.6
Sisters. Dodd, W........................in **N938.5
Sisters. Ebers, G..............................E165.14
Sister's story. Craven, P. de la F.........C898.4
Six Cent Sam's. Hawthorne, J...........H398.19
Six months on a slaver. Manning, E.....M284.1
Six of one by half a dozen of the other.
Stowe, H. B., *and others*...............S892.15
Six to one. Bellamy, E......................B437.4
Six years ago. Grant, J......................G761.51
Sketch-book. Irving, W....................I725.6
Sketches by Boz. Dickens, C..........in D548.44
Same... ...D548.47
Same.................................. ....D548.48
Same. Pt. 2..............................in D548.3
Sketches in prose, and occasional verses.
Riley, J. W.................................R573.3
Sketches of Irish character. Hall, A. M..H179.1
Skirmishing. Jenkin, H. C.................J525.3
Slain by the Doones, and other stories.
Blackmore, R. D...........................B629.16
Slaver's adventures on sea and land.
Thomes, W. H...............................T465.9
Slaves of the ring. Robinson, F. W......R660.4
SLEIGHT, M. B. Flag on the mill.........S632.1
Osego chronicles................................S632.2
SLICK, SAM, *pseud. See* Haliburton, T. C.
Slip in the fens................... ....S633.1
Small house at Allington. Trollope, A...T846.28
SMART, H. At fault............................S636.1
Belles and ringers.............................S636.2
Breezie Langton: a story of 'fifty-two to
'fifty-five....................... ....S636.3
Courtship in 1720 and in 1860: romances
of two centuries...............................S636.4
Master of Rathkelly...........................S636.5
SMEDLEY, F. E. Fortunes and misfor-
tunes of Harry Racket Scapegrace...S637.1
Fortunes of the Colville family. (*Also*)
Seven tales ed. by F. E. Smedley.....S637.2
Frank Fairlegh; or, scenes from the life
of a private pupil...........................S637.3
Harry Coverdale's courtship and mar-
riage................................ ....S637.4
Lewis Arundel.................................S637.5
Lorrimer Littlegood...........................S637.6
Tom Racquet, and his three maiden
aunts.......................................S637.7
—ed. Seven tales..........................in S637.2

SMEDLEY, M. B. A very woman. 32 pp...
....*in* S637.2

SMITH, A. Adventures of Mr. Ledbury and his friend Jack Johnson............S641.4
Armourer of Paris: a romance of the 15th century...................*in* S641.2
Fortunes of the Scattergood family. (*Also*) The armourer of Paris.........S641.2
Marchioness of Brinvilliers, the poisoner of the seventeenth century...... ....S641.3
Pottleton legacy: a story of town and country life...........................S641.5
Struggles and adventures of Christopher Tadpole at home and abroad............S641.1

SMITH, ALEXANDER. Miss Oona McQuarrie............ ....S642.1

SMITH, C. T. Old manor house. 2 vols...
....**B232.36-7

SMITH, F. H. Colonel Carter of Cartersville.................................S647.2
Day at Laguerre's and other days.......S647.3
Espero Gorgoni, gondolier. 38 pp...*in* S886.1
Gentleman vagabond and some others..S647.5
Tom Grogan....................................S647.8

SMITH, H. *See* Stretton, H., *pseud.*

SMITH, J. Dalbroom folks. 2 vols........S651.1

SMITH, J. E. Oakridge.......................S652.1

SMITH, J. F. Story of May Darling..*in* W750.5

SMITH, J. P. (Christabel Goldsmith, *pseud.*)
Blossom-bud and her genteel friends...
....S653.1
Courting and farming....................S653.3
His young wife.............................S653.4
Lucy..S653.6
Married belle............................. S653.7
Peace Pelican, spinster......... ....S653.8
Ten old maids..............................S653.9
Widow Goldsmith's daughter.............S653.10
The widower. (*Also*) A true account of some brave frolics at Craigenfels....S653.11

SMITH, M. P. W. (P. Thorne, *pseud.*)
Great match, and other matches........S655.1

SMITH, R., *tr.* Greek romances of Heliodorus, Longus, and Achilles Tatius, comprising The Ethiopics; or, adventures of Theagenes and Chariclea; The pastoral amours of Daphnis and Chloe; and The loves of Clitopho and Leucippe.................... ....S657.1

SMITH, W. H. Evolution of "Dodd."...S664.1

SMOLLETT, T. G. Adventures of an atom. 83 pp.....................*in* **N938.21

SMOLLETT, T. G.—*Continued.*
Expedition of Humphry Clinker.....
....*in* **N938.19
Same...S666.1
Same. 2 vols...........................**B232.30-1
Ferdinand Count Fathom............*in* **N938.7
Humphry Clinker...................*in* **N938.19
Same...S666.1
Same. 2 vols...........................**B232.30-1
Launcelot Greaves.....................*in* **N938.9
Peregrine Pickle.........................*in* **N938.6
Same...S666.2
Roderick Random.....................*in* **N938.2
Same...S666.3

Smoke. Turgénieff, I. S....................T936.10
SMYTH, P. G. King and viking: a tale of the Danish invasion of Ireland......S667.1
Wild rose of Lough Gill: a tale of the Irish war in the seventeenth century...
....S667.2
SNAITH, J. C. Mistress Dorothy Marvin..S669.3
Snare of the fowler. Alexander, *Mrs*...A374.25
Snarleyyow. Marryat, *Capt.* F............M362.2
Snob papers. Welcker, A...................W442.1
Snow-bound at Eagle's. Harte, B.........H327.31
Snow image, and other twice-told tales. Hawthorne, N..........................*in* H399.5
Same...H399.13
Snowing-up of Strath Lugas. 24 pp.....*in* T143.6
Same..*in* T143.6²
Snow man. Sand, G........................S213.16
SOANS, R. G., *and* KENYON, E. C.. Poor relation.....................................S676.1
Social departure. Cotes, S. J. D...........C843.16
Social strugglers. Boyesen, H. H........B791.10
Society in search of truth. Clark, J. F.....C594.1
Society's verdict..............................S678.1
Soldier and a gentleman. Cobban, J. M...C653.2
Soldier stories. Kipling, R..................K575.16
Soldier's secret. King, C....................K523.21
Soldiers three. Kipling, R...................K575.13
Solid for Mulhooly. Shapley, R. R.......S529.1
Solitary of Juan Fernandez. Sairtine, X. B.......................................S142.1
Solomon's story. Shaw, W. J...............S537.1
Solution. James, H., *Jr*................*in* J277.8
Solyman and Almena. 35 pp. Langhorne, J.....................................*in* **N938.2
Some one else. Croker, B. M...............C943.1
Some women's hearts. Moulton, L. C...M927.2
Somebody else. Lathrop, G. P.............L354.5
Somebody's Ned. Freeman, *Mrs.* A. M...F855.1
Somebody's neighbors. Cooke, R. T.......C773.3
SOMERS, F., *pseud. See* Chambers, J.

Something occurred. Farjeon, B. L......F229.15
Son of a star. Richardson, B. W..........R521.1
Son of Hagar. Caine, H.....................C135.12
Son of his father. Oliphant, M. O. W...O475.53
Son of Issachar. Brooks, E. S.............B875.1
Son of the organ-grinder. Schwartz, M.
    S..S408.6
Son of the plains. Paterson, A............Q296.1
Son of the soil. Oliphant, M. O. W.......O475.54
Sons and daughters. Kirk, E. O..........K593.8
Sons and fathers. Edwards, H. S.........E265.2
Sons of Belial. Westall, W.................W522.1
Sons of Ham. Pendleton, L................Q398.2
Sons of the soil. Balzac, H. de...........B198.35
Sooner or later. Brooks, S.................B874.2
Soprano. Barnard, C........................B259.1
Sorrows of Satan. Corelli, M.............C797.11
Sorrows of Werther. Goethe, J. W. v...in G599.2
    Same...**G599.3
Soul of Lilith. Corelli, M..................C797.12
Soul of the bishop. Winter, J. S........W785.14
South sea lover. St. Johnston, A.........S143.1
Southern woman's story. Pember, P. Y..Q394.1
SOUTHEY, C. A. Devereux Hall. 56 pp..in T143.1
    Same.....................................in T143.1²
    La petite Madelaine. 69 pp.........in T143.2
    Same.....................................in T143.2¹
Southlanders: expedition to the interior
    of New Holland..........................S727.1
Southward ho! Simms, W. G...............S592.14
SOUVESTRE, E. Brittany and La Vendée...S729.1
    Chamois-hunter............................S729.2
    Pleasures of old age......................S729.3
Sowers. Merriman, H. S....................M571.7
Sowers not reapers. Martineau, H...in **M385.6
    Same.......................................M385.17
Sower's reward. Manning, A...............M283.9
Spaewife. Peppergrass, P..................Q424.2
Spanish barber. Manning, A..............M283.10
Spanish brothers. Alcock, D..............A354.4
SPARHAWK, F. C. Lazy man's work......S736.1
Speaking of Ellen. Ross, A................R823.1
SPEARS, J. R. Port of missing ships. 46
    pp.......................................in S886.5
SPECHT, E. E. H. Alfrieda: a novel......S741.1
SPEIGHT, T. W. Heart of a mystery......S742.3
Spell-bound fiddler. Janson, K. N.........J355.2
Spell of Ashtaroth. Osborne, D............O813.1
SPELLING, T. C. Won on a silver basis....S743.1
Spendthrift. Ainsworth, W. H...........A297.22
Sphinx's children and other people's.
    Cooke, R. T................................C773.4
Sphynx in Aubrey parish. Chamberlain,
    N. H......................................C442.1

SPIELHAGEN, F. Hammer and anvil......S755.1
    The Hohensteins...........................S755.2
    The storm.............................in Z767.1 ¹
    Through night to light....................S755.3
    What the swallow sang....................S755.4
Spinoza. Auerbach, B......................A918.13
Spiridion. Sand, G.......................S213.17
Spirit of an Illinois town. Catherwood,
    M. H......................................C363.8
Spirit-rapper. Brownson, O. A............B885.1
Spirite. Gautier, T.........................G277.4
Spiritual Quixote. 2 vols. Graves, R..**B232.32-3
Splendid spur. Couch, A. T. Q............C853.8
SPOFFORD, H. P. The amber gods and
    other stories..............................S762.1
    Azarian...................................S762.2
    Marquis of Carabas S762.4
    Mount of sorrow. 24 pp.............in S884.2
    Scarlet poppy, and other stories.........S762.5
    Sir Rohan's ghost.........................S762.6
    Thief in the night.........................S762.7
Spoil of office. Garland, H................G233.5
Spoils of Poynton. James, H., Jr.........J277.24
Sports in the highlands, etc., of Scotland.
    Maxwell, W. H............................M465.7
SPRAGUE, M. A. Earnest trifler...........S766.1
Sprees and splashes. Morford, H.........M846.1
Sprightly romance of Marsac. Seawell,
    M. E. S442.6
Spring floods. Turgénieff, I. S...........T936.11
Springhaven. Blackmore, R. D...........B629.17
Spy. Cooper, J. F.........................C777.37
Squatter and the don. Loyal, C..........L923.1
Squatter's dream. Boldrewood, R........B687.9
Squire Arden. Oliphant, M. O. W......O475.55
Squire of low degree. Long, L. A.........L848.2
Squire of Sandal-Side. Barr, A. E......B268.21
Squire Trevlyn's heir. Wood, E. P.....W874.13
Squire's legacy. Hay, M. C..............H413.6
Squirrel Inn. Stockton, F. R.............S866.29
STAHL-HOLSTEIN, A. L. G. N. Baronne de.
    Corinne; or, Italy.........................S778.1
STAHR, F. L. See Lewald, F.
Standard tales by standard authors. Ed.
    by Mrs. C. I. Johnstone..................J737.1
Standish of Standish. Austin, J. G......A936.12
Stanley Thorn. Cockton, H................C666.2
STANNARD, Mrs. H. E. V. P. See Winter,
    J. S., pseud.
Star and the cloud. Roe, A. S.... ....R698.4
Star-chamber. Ainsworth, W. H.........A297.23
Stark Munro letters. Doyle, A. C........D754.22
Starlight Ranch, and other stories. King,
    C..K523.22

Start in life, etc. Balzac, H. de............B198.36
States general (1789). Erckmann, E. *and*
  Chatrian, A................................E654.16
  Same..E654.17
Steadfast. Cooke, R. T......................C773.5
Steam house. Pt. 1. Verne, J...........V531.35 ¹
  Same. Pt. 2.................................V531.35 ²
  Same. 2 pts. (in 1)....................V531.35
STEBBINS, S. B. Annals of a baby....S811.1
STEEL, F. A. On the face of the waters...
  ....S813.3
  Miss Stuart's legacy.....................S813.1
  The potter's thumb........................S813.2
  Red rowans...................................S813.4
Steel hammer. Ulbach, L...................U362.3
STEIN, A. Katharine von Bora, Dr. Mar-
  tin Luther's wife......... ....S819.1
Stella Rae. Burch, H. E....................B947.1
Step aside. Dunning, C......................D924.1
Step-mother. James, G. P. R............J276.37
Stephen Archer, and other tales. MacDon-
  ald, G...M135.22
Stephen Dane. Douglas, A. M..........D734.28
Stephen Ellicott's daughter. Needell, *Mrs.*
  J. H...N374.3
STEPHENS, C. A. Young Moll's Peevy.
  14 pp.......................................*in* S884.10
STEPHENS, R. Cruciform mark.............S835.1
STEPHENSON, *Mrs.* E. T. *See* Tabor, E.
Stephen Vane's trust. Rouse, A. L........R863.1
STEPNIAK, *pseud.* Career of a nihilist.....S838.1
  Female nihilist. 24 pp....................S838.2
STERNDALE, R. A. Afghan knife...........S839.1
STERNE, L. Sentimental journey. 58 pp....
  ....*in* C615.1
  Same....................................*in* **N938.9
  Story of my uncle Toby, etc...............S840.1
  Tristram Shandy......................*in* **N938.5
  Same...S840.2
STEVENSON, E. I. Matter of tempera-
  ment...S847.3
STEVENSON, F. V., *joint author. See* Steven-
  son, R. L.
STEVENSON, R. L. Black arrow: a tale
  of the two Roses..........................S848.1
  David Balfour. (Sequel to Kidnapped)..S848.2
  Dr. Jekyll and Mr. Hyde..............*in* S848.7
  Same...S848.11
  Fables...S848.18
  Island nights' entertainments............S848.3
  Kidnapped: adventures of David Balfour
    in the year 1791.........................S848.4
  Lodging for the night. 33 pp.......*in* S885.10
  Markheim...............................*in* S885.3

STEVENSON, R. L.—*Continued.*
  Master of Ballantrae.........................S848.5
  Merry men, and other tales and fables....S848.6
  Merry men. (*Also*) Dr. Jekyll and Mr.
    Hyde...................................... .....S848.7
  New Arabian nights.........................S848.9
  Prince Otto..................................S848.10
  Strange case of Dr. Jekyll and Mr.
    Hyde. 80 pp.........................*in* S848.7
  Same...S848.11
  Thrawn Janet. 19 pp..................*in* S885.8
  Treasure island..............................S848.12
  Weir of Hermiston: an unfinished
    romance...................................S848.13
  —*and* Osbourne, L. Ebb tide..............S848.14
  The wrecker..................................S848.15
  Wrong box....................................S848.16
  —*and* F. V. The dynamiter.................S848.17
STEWART, E. M. Cloister legends; or, con-
  vents and monasteries in the olden
  time..S851.1
STEWART, A. M. Margaret Roper...........S850.1
Stickit minister. Crockett, S. R..........C938.17
STIFTER, A. Balloon ascent (and) The
  heath.....................................*in* Z767.1 ¹
STIMSON, F. J. (J. S. of Dale, *pseud.*) Crime
  of Henry Vane: a study with a moral..S859.1
  Guerndale: an old story....................S859.2
  King Noanett.................................S859.3
  Mrs. Knollys. 21 pp ....*in* S884.2
  Pirate gold..................................S859.5
  Residuary legatee..........................S859.7
  —*joint author. See* Grant, R., *and others.*
STINDE, J. Buchholz family: sketches of
  Berlin life. 2 vols....................S860.1
  Frau Wilhelmine: concluding part of
    The Buchholz family.......... ....S860.2
STIRLING, M. C. Ghost of Morcar's
  Tower. 25 pp.........................*in* T143.21
STITZEL, *Mrs.* H. V. What came of it.
  (*Also*) Waifs and estrays................S862.1
STOCKTON, F. R. Adventures of Captain
  Horn...S866.1
  Amos Kilbright, with other stories........ S866.2
  Ardis Claverden..............................S866.3
  Casting away of Mrs. Lecks and Mrs.
    Aleshine.....................................S866.5
  Chosen few short stories....................S866.6
  Christmas wreck and other stories........S866.7
  The Dusantes. Sequel to "Casting away
    of Mrs. Lecks and Mrs. Aleshine."...S866.10
  Great war syndicate.........................S866.12
  House of Martha..............................S866.14
  Hundredth man. 2 vols...................S866.15

STOCKTON, F. R.—*Continued.*
Lady, or the tiger? and other stories...S866.17
Late Mrs. Null..............................S866.18
Merry Chanter.............................S866.20
Mrs. Cliff's yacht. (Sequel to Adven-
  tures of Capt. Horn.)................S866.22
Pomona's travels.........................S866.25
Rudder Grange.............................S866.27
Rudder Grangers abroad, and other
  stories...................................S866.28
Squirrel Inn...............................S866.29
Stories of the three burglars............S866.30
Story teller's pack.......................S866.31
Transferred ghost. 19 pp...........*in* S884.2
Watchmaker's wife and other stories...S866.32
STOCKTON, L. Kirby's coals of fire. 12
  pp...*in* S884.7
STODDARD, W. O. Heart of it: a romance
  of east and west..........................S869.1
STODDARD, E. D. Osgood's predicament.
  36 pp.....................................*in* S884.8
Temple House..............................S868.1
Stolen white elephant, etc. Twain, M...T969.5
Stone-cutter of Lisbon. Peck, W. H......Q367.1
Stone-mason of Saint Point. Lamartine,
  A. de.......................................L217.5
Stories and interludes. Pain, B...........Q144.1
Stories and romances. Scudder, H. E....S436.1
Stories by American authors. vols. 1-10.
  10 vols...................................S884.1-10
    CONTENTS: 1: Taylor, B. Who was she?
    —Matthews, B., *and* Bunner, H. C. Docu-
    ments in the case.—Bishop, W. H. One of
    the thirty pieces.—Davis, *Mrs.* R. H. Ba-
    lacchi brothers.—Webster, A. F. Operation
    in money.
      2: Stockton, F. R. Transferred ghost.—
    Jacobi, M. P. Martyr to science.—Stimson,
    F. J. Mrs. Knollys.—Eddy, J. Dinner
    party.—Spofford, H. P. Mount of sorrow.—
    Tincker, M. A. Sister Sylvia.
      3: O'Brien, F. J. Spider's eye.—Burnett,
    F. H. Story of the Latin quarter.—Lath-
    rop, G. P. Two purse-companions.—Lloyd,
    D. D. Poor Ogla-Moga.—Thaxter, C.
    Memorable murder.—Matthews, B. Venetian
    glass.
      4: Brooks, N. Lost in the fog.—Bun-
    ner, H. C. Love in old cloathes.—DeForest,
    J. W. Inspired lobbyist.—Foote, M. H.
    Friend Barton's concern.—Willis, N. P. Two
    buckets in a well.—Woolson, C. F. Miss
    Grief.
      5: James, H. Light man.—Millet, F. D.
    Yatil.—Benjamin, P. End of New York.—
    Arnold, G. Why Thomas was discharged.—
    Mitchell, E. P. The Tachypomp.
      6: Champney, E. W. Heartbreak 'cameo.
    —Fairfax, L. R. Misfortunes of bro' Thomas

Stories by American authors—*Continued.*
    Wheatley.—Frederic, H. Brother Sebastian's
    friendship.—Hayes, A. A. Denver express.—
    Webster, A. F. Miss Eunice's glove.—White,
    C. H. Village convict.
      7: Thanet, O. The bishop's vagabond.
    —Dellamy, E. Lost.—Stockton, L. Kirby's
    coals of fire.—Floyd, M. Passages from the
    journal of a social wreck.—McKay, J. T.
    Stella Grayland.—Johnson, V. W. Image of
    San Donato.
      8: DeForest, J. W. Brigade commander.
    —Beers, H. A. Split-zephyr.—Phelps, E. S.
    Zerviah Hope.—Adee, A. A. Life-magnet.—
    Stoddard, E. D. Osgood's predicament.
      9: Page, T. N. Marse Chan.—Gage, C.
    S. Mr. Bixby's Christmas visitor.—White, C.
    H. Eli.—Shinn, M. W. Young Strong of
    "The Clarion."—Coffin, R. F. How old
    Wiggins wore ship.—Kip, L. "——mas has
    come."
      10: Janvier, T. A. Pancha.—Mitchell,
    E. P. Ablest man in the world.—Stephens,
    C. A. Young Moll's Peevy.—DeKay, C.
    Manmat'ha.—Boyesen, H. H. A daring fic-
    tion.—Schayer, J. Story of two lives.

Stories by English authors: Africa.........S885.1
    CONTENTS: Doyle, A. C. Mystery of
    Sasassa Valley.—Haggard, R. H. Long odds.
    —Landers, J. King Bemba's point.—Scully,
    W. C. Ghamba.—Mary Musgrave.—Heming-
    way, P. Gregorio.

England...............................S885.2
    CONTENTS: Reade, C. Box tunnel.—Rob-
    inson, F. W. Minions of the moon.—
    Edwards, A. B. Four-fifteen express.—
    Lewis, A. Wrong black bag.—Hardy, T.
    Three strangers.—Collins, W. Mr. Lismore
    and the widow.—Hope, A. Philosopher in
    the apple orchard.

France...............................S885.10
    CONTENTS: Stevenson, R. L. Lodging for
    the night.—Ouida. Leaf in the storm.—Col-
    lius, W. Terribly strange bed.—Stretton, H.
    Michel Lorio's cross.—Weyman, S. J. Peril-
    ous amour.

Germany, etc...........................S885.3
    CONTENTS: Harraden, B. Bird on its
    journey.—Winter, J. S. Koosje: a study of
    Dutch life.—Ouida. Dog of Flanders.—
    Stevenson, R. L. Markheim.—Black, W.
    Queen Tita's wager.

Ireland...............................S885.4
    CONTENTS: Lover, S. The gridiron.—Jes-
    sop, G. H. Emergency man.—Barlow, J.
    Lost recruit.—Banim, J. Rival dreamers.—
    Carleton, W. Neal Malone.—The banshee.

Italy.................................S885.5
    CONTENTS: Payn, J. Faithful retainer.—
    Norris, W. E. Bianca.—Robinson, A. M. F.
    Goneril.—Oliphaut, L. Brigand's bride.—
    Trollope, A. Mrs. General Talboys.

Stories by English authors—*Continued*.

London.................................S885.6
CONTENTS: Barrie, J. M. Inconsiderate waiter.—Anstey, F. Black poodle.—Morrison, A. That brute Simmons.—Zangwill, I. Rose of the Ghetto.—Harraden B. Idyl of London.—Couch, A. T. Q. The omnibus.—Corelli, M. Hired baby.

The Orient.............................S885.7
CONTENTS: Kipling, R. Man who would be king.—Mitford, M. R. Tajima.—Douglas, R. K. Chinese girl graduate.—Beaumont, M. Revenge of her race.—Roberts, M. King Billy of Ballarat.—Syrett, N. Thy heart's desire.

Scotland...............................S885.8
CONTENTS: Barrie, J. M. Courting of T'nowhead's Bell.—Crockett, S R. "The heather lintie."—Maclaren, I. Doctor of the old school.—Scott, *Sir* W. Wandering Willie's tale.—Aytoun, W. E. Glenmutchkin railway.—Stevenson, R. L. Thrawn Janet.

The sea................................S885.9
CONTENTS: Russell, W. C. Extraordinary adventure of a chief mate.—Besant, *Sir* W. Quarantine island.—Rock scorpions.—O'Halloran, G. B. Master of the "Chrysolite." —"Petrel" and "The Black Swan."—Allen, G. Melissa's tour.—Vanderdecken's message home.

Stories from Scribner. 6 vols.

Army, Stories of the...................S886.3
CONTENTS: Matthews, B. Memories.—Heard, J., *Jr.* Charge for France.—Armstrong, L. Sergeant Gore.—Nott, C. C. Tale of a goblin horse.

Italy, Stories of......................S886.1
CONTENTS: Smith, F. H. Espero Gorgoni, gondolier.—Sullivan, T. R. Anatomist of the heart.—A'Becket, J. J. Song of the comforter.—Channing, G. E. House on the hilltop.

New York, Stories of...................S886.2
CONTENTS: Eliot, A. From four to six.—Perry, B. Commonest possible story.—Hibbard, G. A. End of the beginning.—Wood, J. S. Puritan ingénue.—Wharton, E. Mrs. Manstey's view.

Railway, Stories of the................S886.4
CONTENTS: Hibbard, G. A. As the sparks fly upward.—Davison, C. S. How I sent my aunt to Baltimore.—Page, T. N. Run to seed.—Gordon, A. C. Flandroe's mogul.

Sea, Stories of the....................S886.5
CONTENTS: Spears, J. R. Port of missing ships.—Blunt, M. Fate of the Georgiana.—Carryl, C. E. Captain Black.—Howe, G. Last slave ship.

South, Stories of the..................S886.6
CONTENTS: Page, T. N. No Haid Pawn.—Robertson, H. How the Derby was won.—Harris, J. C. Aunt Fountain's prisoner. —Davis, *Mrs.* R. H. Tirar y Soult.

Stories from the rabbis. Isaacs, A. S......I731.1

Stories in black and white..............S887.1
CONTENTS: Norris, W. E. Romance of Madame de Chantcloup.—Russell, W. C. Memorable swim.—Hardy, T. To please his wife.—Linton, E. L. Ghost of the past.—Payn, J. Rebecca's remorse.—Barrie, J. M. Is it a man?—Oliphant, M. O. W. Golden rule.—Allen, G. General Passavant's will.

Stories of a sanctified town. Furman, L. S.................................F986.1

Stories of a western town. Thanet, O....T367.6

Stories of English and foreign life. Howitt, W. *and* Howitt, M.............H863.2

Stories of old new Spain. Janvier, T. A..J358.6

Stories of Provence. Daudet, A..........D238.13

Stories of the foothills. Graham, M. C...G741.1

Stories of the Peninsular war. Maxwell, W. H...........................M465.8

Stories of the three burglars. Stockton, F. R.................................S866.30

Stories of Waterloo. Maxwell, W. H...M465.9

Storm-driven. Healy, M.................H434.2

Stormy waters. Buchanan, R.............B918.6
Same..................................B918.7

STORY, W. W. Modern magician. 66 pp.. ....*in* T143.13

Story of a country town. Howe, E. W...H855.4

Story of a feather. Jerrold, D. W.......J566.3

Story of a mine. Harte, B...............H327.32

Story of a modern woman. Dixon, E. H... ....D619.1

Story of a story, etc. Matthews, B......M438.11

Story of an African farm. Schreiner, O..S378.3

Story of an enthusiast. Jamison, C. V....J327.1

Story of an honest man. About, E.......A156.5

Story of Antony Grace. Fenn, G. M.....F334.8

Story of Avis. Phelps, E. S.............Q539.16

Story of Bessie Costrell. Ward, M. A. A... ....W261.10

Story of carnival. Hoppus, M. A. M....H799.2

Story of Christine Rochefort. Prince, H. C.................................Q944.1

Story of Colette. Schultz, J............S387.3

Story of Dan. Francis, M. E............F819.1

Story of Elizabeth. Thackeray, A. I....T362.5

Story of Fort Frayne. King, C..........K523.12

Story of Gisli the outlaw. Tr. by G. W. Dasent...............................**D229.1

Story of Hannah. Dawson, W. J.........D272.7

Story of Helen Davenant. Fane, V.......F211.1

Story of Ida. Francesca...............F815.1

Story of Jael. Gould, S. Baring-......*in* F229.3

Story of John Marbeck. Marshall, E....M367.10

Story of Kennett. Taylor, B............T238.5

Story of Margaret Kent. Kirk, E. O....K593.9

Story of my uncle Toby. Sterne, L.........S840.1
Story of the Gadsbys. Kipling, R......K575.14
Story of the glittering plain. Morris, W...
....M877.2
Story of the man who didn't know much.
Murray, W. H. H.....................*in* M984.1
Story of Tonty. Catherwood, M. H......C363.9
Story or two from an old Dutch town.
Lowell, R. T. S.....................L916.3
Story-teller's pack. Stockton, F. R......S866.31
Story that the keg told me. Murray, W.
H. H..................................*in* M984.1
STOWE, H. B. Agnes of Sorrento.........S892.1
Dred: a tale of the great dismal swamp...
....S892.2
Issued also as Nina Gordon.
The Mayflower, and miscellaneous
writings.................................S892.3
Minister's wooing........................S892.4
My wife and I............................S892.5
Oldtown folks............................S892.6
Pearl of Orr's Island.....................S892.8
Pink and white tyranny...................S892.9
Poganuc people..........................S892.10
Sam Lawson's Oldtown fireside stories....
....S892.11
Issued also as Oldtown fireside stories.
Uncle Tom's cabin.......................S892.12
We and our neighbors. (Sequel to "My
wife and I.")...........................S892.13
—ed. Library of famous fiction: embrac-
ing the nine standard masterpieces of
imaginative literature...................S892.14
CONTENTS: Bunyan, J. Pilgrim's progress.
—DeFoe, D. Robinson Crusoe.—Goldsmith,
O. Vicar of Wakefield.—Swift, J. Gulliver's
travels.—St. Pierre, B. de. Paul and Vir-
ginia.—Cottin, S. R. Elizabeth; or, the
exiles of Siberia.—Saintine, X. B. Picciola.—
Beckford, W. Vathek.—La Motte-Fouqué, F.
H. K. de. Undine.—Forster, E., *tr.* Tales
from the Arabian nights' entertainments.
—*and others.* Six of one by half a dozen
of the other.............................S892.15
STRAIN, E. H. Man's foes.................S897.1
Stranded ship. Davis, L. C................D262.1
Strange adventures of a phaeton. Black,
W.......................................B627.31
Strange case of Dr. Jekyll and Mr. Hyde.
Stevenson, R. L...................*in* S848.7
Same...................................S848.11
Strange disappearance. Green, A. K.....G795.7
Strange elopement. Russell, W. C.......R968.24
Strange friend. Hawthorne, J.........*in* H398.11
Strange, sad comedy. Seawell, M. E.....S442.7

Strange story. Lytton, E. G. E. L. B-...L998.24
Same...................................L998.25
Strange surprising adventures of the ven-
erable Gooroo Simple. Besche, C. G...
....B555.1
Strange true stories of Louisiana. Cable,
G. W..................................C115.11
Strange world. Braddon, M. E...........B798.34
Stranger-artist. Kenyon, E. C............K375.2
Strangers and pilgrims. Braddon, M. E...
....B798.35
Strangers and wayfarers. Jewett, S. O...J593.15
Strangers at Lisconnel. Barlow, J.........B258.9
STRAPAROLA *de Cararaggio*, G. F. Sal-
ardo. 10 pp...........................*in* H496.1
Strathmore. Ouida......................O934.21
Stray leaves from a passing life, and other
stories..................................S913.1
Stray leaves from strange literature.
Hearn, L...............................H436.2
Stray pearls. Yonge, C. M..............Y555.30
STRECKFUSS, A. Castle Hohenwald. Tr.
by A. L. Wister.........................W817.28
Quicksands. Tr. by A. L. Wister.....W817.29
Too rich. Tr. by A. L. Wister.........W817.30
Street and the flower. Wagner, H., *and*
Bunyan, E. T...........................W133.1
STRETTON, H. Bede's charity.............S915.1
Brought home...........................S915.2
Crew of the "Dolphin."...................S915.3
David Lloyd's last will....................S915.4
Hester Morley's promise.................S915.5
In prison and out........................S915.6
Michel Lorio's cross. 29 pp..........*in* S885.10
Through a needle's eye...................S915.8
STRETTON, J. Rector's wife...............S916.1
Issued also as Valley of a hundred fires.
Stretton. Kingsley, H.....................K555.11
Strife. Wallace, *Mrs.* E. D................W188.1
Strife and peace. Bremer, F............*in* B836.6
Same..............................*in* B836.10
Strike at Tivoli mills. Arthur, T. S......A791.5
Stronger will. Green, E. E...............G796.3
Struggle for the right.....................S927.1
Struggles, etc., of Christopher Tadpole.
Smith, A................................S641.1
STRUTT, E. Chances and changes......**S928.1
Curate and the rector.....................S928.2
STRUTT, J. Queenhoo-hall, and, Ancient
times, a drama. 4 vols.... ....**S929.1
STUART, R. McE. Carlotta's intended....S932.1
Golden wedding, and other tales.........S932.2
Studies for stories. Ingelow, J..............I464.7
Studies from life. Mulock, D. M.........M960.25

Study in scarlet. Doyle, A. C......... *in* D754.16
Study of woman. 11 pp. Balzac, H. de....
.....................................*in* B198.44
STURGIS, J. Accomplished gentleman....S935.1
After twenty years, etc.......................S935.3
Disappointing boy. 15 pp............*in* T143.17
Thraldom S935.4
Suburban sketches. Howells, W. D......H859.28
Successful man. Gordon, J.................. G663.7
Successors to the title. Walford, L. B...W174.13
'Such is life.' Kendall, M.................. K333.1
SUDERMANN, H. Dame care...............S943.5
The wish...S943.1
SUE, E. Arthur...................................S944.1
Mysteries of Paris............................S944.3
The temptation...................................S944.4
Latreaumont: romance of the days of
Louis XIV...................................S944.2
Wandering Jew...................................S944.5
SUE-SAND, ALEXANDER, *fils, pseud. See*
Hamley, *Sir* E. B.
SULLIVAN, A. Winifred, countess of
Nithsdale.................................**S950.1
SULLIVAN, J. W. Tenement tales of New
York...S951.1
SULLIVAN, T. R. Anatomist of the heart.
73 pp...................................*in* S886.1
Day and night stories.......................S952.1
Sultanetta. Dumas, A..................*in* D886.4
Summer idyl. Reid, C......................R353.16
Summer in Arcady. Allen, J. L.........A427.9
Summer in Leslie Goldthwaite's life. Whit-
ney, A. D. T.................................W617.10
Sun-maid. Grant, M. M.....................G762.1
Sunnybank. Harland, M...................H283.16
Sunrise. Black, W..........................B627.33
Sunshine and haar. Setoun, G.............S495.6
Superior to circumstances. Blackall, E. L..B628.1
Supply at St. Agatha's. Phelps, E. S.....Q539.17
Surgeon's daughter. Scott, *Sir* W....*in* S431.16
Same.................................*in* S431.37
Same.................................*in* S431.49
Same.................................*in* **S431.55
Surgeon's stories. *See* Topelius, Z.
Surly Tim, and other stories. Burnett,
F. H.................................... B964.21
Surrender of Margaret Bellarmine. Ser-
geant, A S484.10
Surry of Eagle's Nest. Cooke, J. E.....C772.14
SURTEES, R. S. "Ask mamma.".........S962.1
Mr. Facey Romford's hounds.............S962.2
Susan Fielding. Edwardes, A............. E254.8
Susy. Harte, B..............................H327.33

Sutherlands. Harris, M. C...................H315.7
SUTTNER, A. G. VON. Djambek the Geor-
gian: a tale of modern Turkey.........S967.1
SUTTNER, B., *Baroness* VON. "Ground
arms!"...S966.1
Suwanee river tales. Bonner, S.............B716.2
Swallow Barn. Kennedy, J. P............. K353.4
Swamp doctor's adventures in the south-
west. Robb, J. S............................R631.1
Sweet bells out of tune. Harrison, C. C....H318.9
Sweet Mace. Fenn, G. M....................F334.9
SWETT, S. Pennyroyal and mint...........S975.3
SWIFT, B. (*pseud. of* W. R. Paterson).
Nancy Noon.....................................S978.6
SWIFT, J. F. Robert Greathouse...........S977.1
SWIFT, JONATHAN. Gulliver's travels..*in* C615.1
Same.................................*in* **N938.9
Same.................................*in* S892.14
Same................................. S976.1
Issued also as Travels into several remote
nations of the world.
Sword of Damocles. Green, A. K.........G795.8
Sybil. Disraeli, B..............................D613.10
Same...D613.11
Sybil's second love. Kavanagh, J........ K212.13
SYDNEY, E. W. *See* Tucker, B., *pseud.*
Sydney sovereign, and other tales. Tasma....
....T199.2
Sydnie Adriance. Douglas, A. M........D734.29
SYLVA, C. (*pseud. of* Elizabeth, *Queen of
Roumania*). Edleen Vaughan.........S985.1
Sylvester night's adventure. Zschokke, H..Z923.5
Sylvester Sound. Cockton, H.............C666.3
Sylvestres. Edwards, M. B................E267.4
Sylvia's lovers. Gaskell, E. C.............G248.8
Sylvie's betrothed. Gréville, H............ G838.8
SYMINGTON, C. *See* Symington, M., *pseud.*
SYMINGTON, M. (*pseud. of* C. Syming-
ton). Marion Scatterthwaite...........S987.1
Synnöre Solbakken. Björnson, B.........B625.6
SYRETT, N. Thy heart's desire.........*in* S885.7
Syrlin. Ouida O934.22
T., M. A. *See* Tincker, M. A.
TABOR, E. (*Mrs. Stephenson.*) Eglantine..
....T114.1
Hope Meredith..................................T114.2
Jeanie's quiet life.............................T114.3
St. Olave's.......................................T114.4
TADEMA, *Miss* L. A. Wings of Icarus...T121.1
Taken alive, and other stories. Roe, E.
P...R699.15
Taken at the flood. Braddon, M. E......B798.36
Taking the Bastile. Dumas, A..........D886.2

Tale of a lonely parish. Crawford, F. M...

....C899.20

Tale of a physician. Davis, A. J..........D260.1

Tale of the house of the Wolfings. Mor-
ris, W...M877.7

Tale of the Tyne. Martineau, H...*in* **M385.6

Tale of two cities. Dickens, C..........*in* D548.4

Same..*in* D548.48

Same...D548.49

Same...D548.50

Tales and novels. 18 vols. Edgeworth,
M.. ... .E235.16-32

Tales and sketches. 5 vols. Hogg, J...H716.1-5

Tales and sketches. Miller, H..............M648.2

Tales and traditions of Hungary. 3 vols.
Pulzsky, F. A., *and* T....................Q972.1

Tales before supper. Gautier, T., *and*
Mérimée, P......................................G277.5

Tales from the Ægean. Bikélas, D........B595.2

Tales from Blackwood. 12 vols. (in 6)...
....T143.1-6

CONTENTS: 1: Aytoun, W. E. Glenmutchkin railway.—Vanderdecken's message
home.—Floating beacon.—Colonna the
painter.—Lockhart, J. G. Napoleon.—Hamley, E. B. Legend of Gibraltar.—Mudford,
W. Iron shroud.

2: Hamley, E. B. Lazaro's legacy.—
Maginn, W. Story without a tail.—Faustus
and Queen Elizabeth.—Aytoun, W. E. How
I became a yeoman.—Southey, C. A. Devereux Hall.—Macnish, R. The metempsychosis.—College theatricals.

3: Reading party in the long vacation.—
Ferguson, *Sir* S. Father Tom and the pope.—
Southey, C. A. La petite Madelaine.—Maginn,
W. Bob Burke's duel with ensign Brady.
—Headsman.—Galt, J. Wearyful woman.

4: Aytoun, W. E. How I stood for the
Dreepdaily burghs.—Mudford, W. First
and last.—Duke's dilemma: a chronicle of
Niesenstein.—Old gentleman's teetotum.—
"Woe to us when we lose the watery wall."
—My college friends: Charles Russell, the gen-
tleman commoner.—Hughes, J. Magic lay
of the one-horse chay.

5: Sealsfield, C. Adventures in Texas;
abr. from the Ger. by F. Hardman.—Aytoun,
W. E. How we got possession of the Tuileries.—Lockhart, J. G. Captain Paton's
lament.—Arbouville, S. d'. Village doctor.—
Hogg, J. Singular letter from southern
Africa.

6: Hardman, F. My friend the Dutch-
man.—My college friends: No. 2: Horace
Leicester; No. 3: Mr. W. Wellington Hurst.—
Aytoun, W. E. Emerald studs.—Arbouville,
S. d'. Christine. From the Fr. by F. Hard-
man.—Man in the bell.

7: Hardman, F. My English acquaintance.—Doubleday, T. Murderer's last night.—

Tales from Blackwood—*Continued.*
Narration of......Herbert Willis, *B. D.*—The
wags.—Ferguson, *Sir* S. Wet wooing.—Ben-
na-Groich.

8: Aytoun, W. E. Surveyor's tale.
—Forrest-Race romance.—Edwards, C. Di
Vasari: a tale of Florence.—Sigismund Fa-
tello.—The boxes.

9: Rosaura: a tale of Madrid.—Adventure in the north-west territory.—Harry Bolton's curacy.—Florida pirate.—The pandour
and his princess.—The beauty draught.

10: Antonio di Carara.—Fatal repast.—
Kent. W. C. Vision of Cagliostro.—First and
last kiss.—Hardman, F. Smuggler's leap.—
Lyttou, E. G. E. L. B- Haunted and the
haunters.—The duelists.

11: Natolian story-teller.—First and last
crime.—John Rintoul.—Hardman, F. Major
Moss.—The premier and his wife.

12: Tickler among the thieves!—Bridegroom of Barna.—Involuntary experimentalist.—Lebrun's lawsuit. — Snowing-up of
Strath Lugas.—Few words on social philosophy.

Same. 12 vols..........................T143.1'-6'

Same. 2d ser. 12 vols.................T143.7-18

CONTENTS: 1: Oliphant, L. Tender recollections of Irene Macgillicuddy.—Walford, L.
B. Nan: a summer scene.—Bells of Botreaux.—Hamley, E. B. Recent confessions
of an opium eater. Shakespeare's funeral.—
Lockhart, L. W. M. A night with the volunteers of Strathkinahan.—The philosopher's
baby.—Oliphant, M. O. W. Secret chamber.

2: Chesney, C. C. Battle of Dorking.—
Late for the train.—Aytoun, W. E. Congress
and the Agapedome. Raid of Arnaboll.—
Neaves, *Lord.* Maga's birthday. How to
make a pedigree.—Francillon, R. E. Grace
Owen's engagement.

3: S., H. C. Who painted the great
Murillo de la Merced?—J-nes, *Mr.* A
parochial epic.—Military adventure in the
Pyrenees.—Allardyce, A. Pundrapore resi-
dency.—Falsely accused: a criminal trial in
Nürnberg, 1760.—Witch-Hampton Hall.

4: A railway junction.—Metamorphoses: a
tale.—Cheape, D. Betsy Brown.—Hamley,
E. B. Last French hero.—Lockhart, L. W.
M. Unlucky Tom Griffin.—Wilson, A. Spectre of Milaggio.

5: Autobiography of a joint-stock company
(limited).—Walford, L. B. Bee or Beatrix.—
Night-wanderer of an Afghaun fort.—Macleod, N. Ayrshire curling song.—Hamley,
C. Light on the hearth.—How to boil peas.—
—Keene, H. G. Clive's dream before the
battle of Plassey.

6: Lever, C. What I did at Belgrade.—
Shaud, A. I. Wrecked off the Riff coast.
Dollie, and the two Smiths.—Majendie, *Lady*
M. Railway journey.—Francillon, R. E.
Dog without a tail.—Hamley, C. Wassail.

7: Cousin John's property.—Story, W. W.
A modern magician.—Allardyce, A. Edgar

Tales from Blackwood, 2d ser.—*Continued.*
Wayne's escape.—Lost secret of the Cocos group.—Two Mrs. Scudamores.—Bates's tour.

8: Devil's frills: a Dutch illustration of the water cure.—Francillon, R. E. Story of Eulenburg.—Shadow of the door.—W., F. Wreck of the Strathmore.—Lever, C. Hero-worship and its dangers.—Annie and her master.—W., H. D. A feuilleton.

9: Greg, P. Guy Neville's ghost.—Hard-man, F. Great unknown.—Easter trip of two ochlophobists.—Aytoun, W. E. Rapping the question.—My after-dinner adventure with Peter Schlemihl.—Aunt Ann's ghost story.—Moir, G. Blue dragoon: a story of circumstantial evidence from the criminal records of Holland.—Winchilsea, *Earl of.* Lord Hatton: a tale of castle Cornet in Guernsey.

10: Missing bills: an unsolved mystery.—Cheadle, W. B. My hunt of the silver fox.—Macdonald, J. (?) Narrative of Prince Charlie's escape.—Fenian alarm.—Lindau, R. Philosopher's pendulum.—Walford, L. B. Lady Adelaide.—Witcherley ways: a Christmas tale.—Lever, C. How Frank Thornton was cured.—Walker, A. L. In life and death.—Cause worth trying.

11: Haunted Enghenio.—Veley, M. Milly's first love.—Mrs. Beauchamp's vengeance.—Kinkel, G. Family feud.—Sturgis, J. Disappointing boy.—Wyatt, T. Cottage by the river.—Ride for life.—W. Sketch from Babylon.—R., W. J. M. Eugine-driver to his engine (*and*) Coachman of the "Skylark."

12: Francillon, R. E. Left-handed Elsa.—Great earthquake at Lisbon.—Lever, C. Some one pays.—Hamley, E. B. Sir Tray: an Arthurian idyl.—Whittlebridge.—Nenuphar: a fancy.—Whist at our club.—My investment in the far west.—King, H. Brown's peccadillo.

Same. 3d ser. 6 vols.................T143.19-24
CONTENTS: 1: Bourgonef.—Clifford, *Mrs.* W. K. Thomas.—Oliphant, L. Brigand's bride; a tale of southern Italy.—Prothero, H. The misogynist.—Boyle, F. A fetish city.—Ferguson, *Sir* S. Gascon O'Driscol.—Moncrieff, *Mrs.* W. G. S- An Elie ruby.—Gould, S. B- Alexander Nesbitt, ex-schoolmaster.—Landers, J. King Bemba's point.—Lumsden, K. M. A vendetta.—Hartley, G. W. Master Tommy's experiment.—Douglas, R. K. Matrimonial fraud.

2: Majendie, *Lady* M. A French speculation.—Wellwood, *Lord.* Rufus Hickman of St. Botolph's.—Alexis, W. Hans Preller: a legend of the Rhine falls.—Kingsley, M. Puerto de Medina.—Harcourt, A. Jack and Minory.—Lyster, A. My treasure.—Lorne, *Marquess of.* Who were they? a Maltese apparition.—Douglas, R. K. Within his danger: a tale from the Chinese.—Hartley, G. W. Factor's shooting.—Hamley, W. G. A magnetic mystery.

Tales from Blackwood, 3d ser.—*Continued.*
3: Dellenbaugh, F. S. Singular case.—Bradley, M. Pentock.—Lewes, C. L. Dragon-tree of Telde.—Gould, S. B- Last words of Joseph Barrable.—Lumsden, K. M. How I fell among thieves.—Burton, *Mrs* M. E. Fiddlers three.—Stirling, M. C. Ghost of Morcar's Tower.—Blackie, J. S. Ancrum Moor: a historical ballad.

4: Hamley, W. G. Medium of last century.—Hope, A. Alive and yet dead: some passages in the life of a French convict.—Gray, M. An unexpected fare.—W., T. P. Reminiscence of a march.—Burton, *Mrs.* Don Angelo's stray sheep.—Douglas, R. K. The twins.—Bradley, A. G. The doctor: an old Virginia fox-hunter.—Johnstone, H. Enchanted bridle: a legendary ballad.

5: Moncrieff, *Mrs.* W. G. S- Such pity as a father hath.—Russell, *Col.* Coincidences??—Bird, *Capt.* Dead man's vengeance.—Landers, J. Story of James Barker: a tale of the Congo coast.—Shand, A. I. Mr. Cox's protégé.—Hugessen, E. K- A dramatic effect.—Cushing, P. A bud that lived.—Coleridge, S. Daniel Fosqué.—Wellwood, *Lord.* Great unloaded.

6: Cowper, F. Christmas eve on a haunted hulk.—Dicky Dawkins; or, the bookmaker of the outer ring. By Jack the shepherd.—Dziewicki, M. H. Airy nothing.—Bent, M. Chapter from an unknown life.—Bradley, A. G. Mar'se Dab after the war: a Virginia reminiscence.—Cumming, C. F. G. "Unfathomed mysteries."—Jenner, G. A philanthropist: a tale of the vigilance committee at San Francisco.—Oliphant, F. R. Grateful ghosts.—Buckland, C. T. Pickle of salt: a tale of the Indian monopoly.—On the Wallaby track.—Meldrum, D. S. Rathillet.

Tales from the dramatists. 3 vols. Morris, C................................M875.1
Tales from the German. Heyse, P........H621.5
Tales from the German. Tr. by J. Oxenford and C. A. Feiling....................O983.1
Tales from two hemispheres. Boyesen, H. H....................................B791.11
Tales of a time and place. King, G......K527.3
Tales of a traveller. Irving, W............I725.7
Tales of all countries. Trollope, A......T846.30
Tales of fantasy and fact. Matthews, B...................................M438.12
Tales of Flemish life. Conscience, H.....C755.7
Tales of New England. Jewett, S. O.....J593.16
Tales of old Flanders. Conscience, H....C755.8
Tales of old Japan. Mitford, A. B.........M683.1
Tales of other days. Akerman, J. Y......A314.1
Tales of real life. Opie, A. ....*in* O614.2
Tales of soldiers and civilians. Bierce, A...................................B588.1
Tales of the Argonauts. Harte, B.......H327.34

Tales of the borders. 24 vols (in 12).
Wilson, J. M., *and others*............W750.1-12
Tales of the Caucasus. Dumas, A.......D886.4
Tales of the covenanters. Pollok, R......Q777.1
Tales of the drama. Macauley, E.........M117.1
Tales of the genii. Tr. by Sir C. Morell...
....*in* **N938.3
Tales of the good woman. Paulding, J.
K...Q325.5
Tales of the Maine coast. Brooks, N......B868.6
Tales of the Munster festivals. Griffin,
G...G851.6
Same. 2d ser.....................................G851.7
Tales of the southern border. Webber, C.
W...W371.2
Tales of the woods and fields. Marsh, A.
C...**M364.1
Tales of today and other days. Tr. by E.
P. Robins.......................................R657.1
Tales of two countries. Kielland, A. L...K473.1
TALFOURD, *Sir* T. N. Ion. 32 pp...*in* M875.1 [3]
Talis qualis: tales of the jury-room. Grif-
fin, G...G851.8
Talisman. Scott, *Sir* W...............*in* **S431.42
Same...S431.50
Same....S431.51
Tallants of Barton. Hatton, J.............H366.4
Tame surrender. King, C................K523.23
TAMENAGA SHUNSUI. Loyal Ronins.....T157.1
Tancred. Disraeli, B.....................D613.12
Tangled tale. Carroll, L..................C319.1
Tangled web. Holt, E. S.................H758.11
Tapestried chamber. Scott, *Sir* W...*in* S431.15
Same....*in* **S431.19
Same...*in* S431.51
Taquisara. 2 vols. Crawford, F. M.....C899.23
Taras Bulba. Gogol, N. V................G613.2
Tartarian tales. Gueulette, T. S....*in* **N938.19
Tartarin of Tarascon. Daudet, A........D238.14
Tartarin on the Alps. Daudet, A........D238.15
TASMA (*pseud. of* J. Fraser). In her earli-
est youth......................................T199.1
Sydney sovereign, and other tales.......T199.2
Uncle Piper of Piper's Hill: an Australian
novel..T199.3
TAUTPHŒUS, J. M. *Freiherrin* VON. At
odds..T229.1
Cyrilla..T229.2
The initials....................................T229.3
Quits..T229.4
Tavernicus. Gore, C..................*in* G666.1 [2]
TAYLOR, B. Beauty and the beast, and
tales of home..................................T238.1
Hannah Thurston: a story of American
life...T238.2

TAYLOR, B.—*Continued.*
John Godfrey's fortunes...................T238.3
Joseph and his friend: a story of Penn-
sylvania..T238.4
Story of Kennett.............................T238.5
Who was she? 45 pp....................*in* S884.1
TAYLOR, E. Blindpits: a story of Scottish
life..T240.1
Quixstar..T240.2
TAYLOR, M. Confessions of a thug........T244.1
TCHERNUISHEVSKY, N. G. Vital question;
or, what is to be done....................T251.1
Tchitchikoff's journeys. 2 vols. Gogol,
N. V...G613.3
Teacher of the violin. Shorthouse, J. H...S559.6
Telemachus. Fenelon, F. de S. de la M...
....F332.1
Same........................................*in* **N938.17
Temper. Opie, A.........................*in* O614.3
Tempest and sunshine. Holmes, M. J...
....H751.26
Temple House. Stoddard, E. D...........S868.1
Temptation. Sue, E........................S944.4
Tempting of Pescara. Meyer, K. F......M612.1
Ten old maids. Smith, J. P................S653.9
Ten tales. Coppée, F........................C785.2
Ten thousand a year. Warren, S........W293.3
Ten times one is ten. Hale, E. E........H161.16
Tenant of Wildfell Hall. Brontë, A......B869.1
Tenants of Malory. Le Fanu, J. S........L488.4
Tender recollections of Irene Magillicuddy.
Oliphant, L....................................O474.3
Tenement tales of New York. Sullivan,
J. W...S951.1
TENNEY, E. P. Agamenticus............T298.1
TERHUNE, *Mrs.* M. V. H. *See* Harland,
M., *pseud.*
Terminations. James, H., *Jr*............J277.18
Terrible temptation. Reade, C..........R285.30
Tess of the d'Urbervilles. Hardy, T....H272.16
TEUFEL, *Mrs.* B. W. H. *See* Howard, B.
W.

THACKERAY, A. I. (*Mrs. Ritchie.*) Blue-
beard's keys and other stories.........T362.1
From an island.............................*in* T362.5
Fulham Lawn..............................*in* T362.2
Miss Angel. (*Also*) Fulham Lawn...T362.2
Miss Williamson's divagations............T362.3
Old Kensington...............................T362.4
Story of Elizabeth. (*Also*) Two hours.
(*And*) From an island..................T362.5
Two hours..................................*in* T362.5
Village on the cliff, and other stories and
sketches..T362.6

THACKERAY, W. M. (Mr. M. A. Titmarsh, pseud.) Adventures of Philip.........T363.1
Same. Prefixed, Shabby genteel story...
....T363.2
Barry Lyndon.......................in T363.10
Same...T363.14
Same. (Also) History of Samuel Titmarsh and the great Hoggarty diamond. (And) Burlesques............T363.15
Book of snobs................................T363.3
Same.......................................in T363.13
Burlesques.......................................T363.4
Same.......................................in T363.12
Same.......................................in T363.15
Catherine. (Also) Lovel the widower. Denis Duval. Ballads. Wolves and the lamb. Critical reviews. (And) Little travels and roadside sketches...T363.5
Christmas books...............................T363.6
Denis Duval.......................in T363.5
Same. (Also) History of Samuel Titmarsh and the great Hoggarty diamond........T363.7
Fitzboodle papers.................in T363.16
Henry Esmond..............................T363.8
Same. (Also) Memoirs of Barry Lyndon......................................T363.10
History of Samuel Titmarsh and the great Hoggarty diamond.............in T363.7
Lovel the widower.................in T363.5
Same.......................................in T363.19
Luck of Barry Lyndon.....................T363.14
Same. (Also) History of Samuel Titmarsh and the great Hoggarty diamond. (And) Burlesques............T363.15
Memoirs of Mr. C. J. Yellowplush...
....in T363.12
Same. (Also) Fitzboodle papers, etc...T363.16
Men's wives.......................in T363.13
The Newcomes.............................T363.17
Pendennis.....................................T363.11
Samuel Titmarsh and the great Hoggarty diamond....................................T363.7
Same. (Also) Memoirs of Mr. C. J. Yellowplush. (And) Burlesques...T363.12
Same. (Also) Men's wives. (And) Book of snobs.............................T363.13
Shabby genteel story.................in T363 2
Vanity fair: a novel without a hero...T363.18
Same. (Also) Lovel the widower....T363.19
The Virginians..............................T363.20
Yellowplush papers........................T363.21
Thaddeus of Warsaw. Porter, J............Q846.2
Thalia. Bayle, A...........................B358.1

THANET, O. (pseud. of A. French.) The bishop's vagabond. 42 pp..........in S884.7
Expiation..................................T367.3
Knitters in the sun........................T367.4
Missionary sheriff..........................T367.7
Otto the knight and other trans-Mississippi stories..............................T367.5
Stories of a western town.................T367.6
Thankful Blossom. Harte, B..............H327.35
That angelic woman. Ludlow, J. M......L945.3
That beautiful wretch. Black, W.........B627.35
That boy of Norcott's. Lever, C.........L658.25
That first affair, and other sketches. Mitchell, J. A...............................M680.7
That Frenchman! Gunter, A. C...........G977.11
That husband of mine. Denison, M. A...D396.2
That lass o' Lowrie's. Burnett, F. H.....B964.11
That queer girl. Townsend, V. F..........T751.8
That stick. Yonge, C. M.....................Y555.31
That wild wheel. Trollope, F. E...........T847.4
THAXTER, C. A memorable murder. 35 pp...............................in S884.3
THEAMBA, I. (pseud. of Judge Harsha). Ploughed under: the story of an Indian chief..T374.1
THÉBAUD, A. J. Louisa Kirkbride: a tale of New York................................T375.1
Their wedding journey. Howells, W. D...H859.29
Thelma. Corelli, M.........................C797.13
Theo. Burnett, F. H.....................in B964.3
THEODOLI, L. Marchesa. Under pressure..T388.1
Theodora Kantakuzenos. 47 pp.......in C972.1 ¹
Theodosius and Constantia. Langhorne, J...............................in **N938.7
Theophilus, and others. Dodge, M. M...D645.1
There and back. MacDonald, G.........M135.23
"There is no devil." Jókai, M...............J745.9
There's nothing in it. Bidwell, J.........B585.1
THEURIET, A. All alone....................T415.1
Angèle's fortune............................T415.2
Godson of a marquis.......................T415.4
My uncle Scipio.............................T415.5
Raymonde.....................................T415.6
Young Maugars..............................T415.7
Thief in the night. Spofford, H. P.........S762.7
Thinks-I-to-myself. Nares, E..............N226.1
Thiodolf the Icelander. La Motte Fouqué, F. H. K. Freiherr de.....................L235.5
Thirty years ago. 2 vols. Dunlap, W.....D921.1
Thirty years at sea. Shippen, E...........S557.1
This mortal coil. Allen, G..................A425.14
This son of Vulcan. Besant, Sir W., and Rice, J.......................................B554.44

THIUSEN, I., *pseud.* The Diothas; or, a
far look ahead..............................T449.1

THOMAS, A. (*Mrs. Cudlip*). Called to
account................................T453.1
Love of a lady........................T453.2
No alternative.......................... T453.3
On guard ....*in* T453.4
Played out. (*Also*) On guard...........T453.4

THOMAS, B. House on the scar: a tale of
south Devon.............................T454.1

Thomas Wingfold, curate. MacDonald,
G...M135.24

THOMES, W. H. Belle of Australia........ T465.1
The bushrangers.........................T465.2
Gold hunter's adventures; or, life in
Australia.................................. T465.3
Gold hunters in Europe...................T465.4
Lewey and I: sequel to "On land and
sea."...T465.5
Life in the East Indies.......................T465.6
On land and sea; or, California in 1843,
'44 and '45.............................T465.7
Running the blockade.......................T465.8
Slaver's adventures on sea and land.....T465.9
Whaleman's adventures in the Sandwich
Islands and California...................T465.10

THOMPSON, C. M. Nimble dollar, with
other stories...............................T469.5

THOMPSON, D. P. The Green mountain
boys...T470.1
Locke Amsden; or, the schoolmaster...T470.3
May Martin, and other tales of the
Green mountains.........................T470.4
The rangers; or, the tory's daughter...T470.5

THOMPSON, L. Ivan Graham: a story of
the medical mission to the Jews in
Russia.......................................T473.3

THOMPSON, M. Hoosier mosaics...........T474.1

THOMSON, E. W. Old man Savarin, and
other stories..............................T482.1

THOMSON, G. Lost heir of the house of
Elphinstone ....*in* W750.10

THORESEN, M. Old Olaf. 46 pp......*in* G622.1

Thorn in the nest. Finley, M............F513.3

THORNE, P., *pseud. See* Smith, M. P. W.

Thorny path. 2 vols. Ebers, G..........E165.15

THORODDSEN, J. T. Sigrid: an Icelandic
love story...................................T516.1
Issued also as Lad and lass.

THORPE, B., *ed.* Yule-tide stories.........T518.1

Thorpe Regis. Peard, F. M.................Q359.14

Those extraordinary twins. Twain, M..*in* T969.6

Thoughts on bores. Edgeworth, M..*in* E235.31

Thousand and one days: Persian tales. Tr.
by A. Phillips.........................*in* **N938.13

Thousand and one nights. *See* Arabian
nights' entertainments.

Thraldom. Sturgis, J......................S935.4

Three ages. Martineau, H............*in* **M385.3

Three brides. Yonge, C. M...............Y555.32

Three clerks. Trollope, A.................T846.31

Three courses and a dessert. Illus. by G.
Cruikshank................................T531.1

Three crosses. 8 pp.......................*in* V629.1

Three cutters. Marryat, *Capt.* F...*in* M362.19
Same..................... ....*in* **M362.26
Same......................................*in* M362.28

Three days. Cooper, S. W.................C778.1

Three fates. Crawford, F. M..............C899.21

Three feathers. Black, W..................B627.36

Three generations. Emery, S. A..........E538.1

Three Graces. Duchess....................D829.18

Three guardsmen. Dumas, A.............D886.39

Three millions ! Optic, O.................O625.3

Three musketeers. 2 vols. Dumas, A.......
....D886.39

Three scouts. Trowbridge, J. T...........T863.4

Three Spaniards. Walker, G..............W180.1

Throckmorton. Seawell, M. E...........S442.8

Throne of David. Ingraham, J. H........I543.2

Through a needle's eye. Stretton, H....S915.8

Through night to light. Spielhagen, F...S755.3

Through one administration. Burnett, F.
H...B964.22

Through winding ways. Kirk, E. O....K593.10

"Thrust out." Maclaren, *Miss*............M160.1

Thurlston tales. 2 vols. Gillies, R. P...
....**G481.1

Thwarted. Montgomery, F.................M787.2

TIBBLES, T. H. Hidden power: a secret
history of the Indian ring...............T552.1

Tickler among the thieves. 96 pp......*in* T143.6
Same....................................*in* T143.6 ²

Ticonderoga. James, G. P. R..............J276.38

TIECK, L. The elves, tr. by T. Carlyle...
....*in* J737.1
Same. The goblet....................*in* C286.2
Same, with other stories and sketches...T559.1
    CONTENTS: Tieck, L. The elves.—John-
stone, C. I. Sabbath night's supper.—Fraser,
Mrs. The cousins.—Nicander, K. A. Renounced treasure.—Gore, C. G. Maid of
honour.—Quillinan, E. Rangers of Connaught.—Mitford, M. R. Freshwater fisherman.—Crowe, C. Story of Martha Guinnis and her son.—Tytler, M. Fraser- The
deformed.—Johnson, *Col.* White fawn: a
North American story.—Howitt, W. Johnny
Darbyshire.—Lauder, *Sir* T. D. Story of
Farquharson of Inverey.

TIECK, L.—*Continued.*
Fair-haired Eckbert. Trusty Eckart.
The Runenburg..........................*in* C286.1
The Klausenburg. 30 pp..............*in* O983.1
Love magic. Faithful Eckart and the
    Tannenhäuser, Pt. 1. Tannenhäuser,
    Pt. 2. Auburn Egbert.............*in* R794.1 [4]
The pictures. 65 pp..................*in* C972.1 [2]
TIERNAN, *Mrs.* F. C. *See* Reid, C., *pseud.*
TIERNAN, M. S. Jack Horner.............T564.1
Tiger-lilies. Lanier, S...................L287.1
Tigers and traitors. Verne, J............V531.35 [2]
Tigranes. Franco, J. J....................F825.1
Tilbury Nogo. Melville, G. J. W-.......M530.33
Same..*in* **M530.11
Timar's two worlds. Jokai, M.......... .....J745.10
Times of alchemy. Topelius, Z.............T673.6
Times of battle and of rest. Topelius, Z...T673.2
Times of Charles XII. Topelius, Z........T673.3
Times of Frederick I. Topelius, Z.........T673.4
Times of Gustaf Adolf. Topelius, Z.......T673.1
Times of Linnæus. Topelius, Z.............T673.5
Time's revenges. Murray, D. C............M981.9
TINCKER, M. A. Aurora.....................T587.1
By the Tiber.............................T587.2
Jewel in the lotos.........................T587.4
San Salvador............................T587.5
Signor Monaldini's niece...................T587.6
Sister Sylvia. 32 pp.....................*in* S884.2
Two coronets............................T587.7
Winged word, etc.........................T587.8
Tinkling cymbals. Fawcett, E...........F278.16
TINSEAU, L. DE. Paste or diamonds.
    (*Also*) Fontluce........................T592.1
Tinted Venus. Anstey, F...................A625.7
TISSOT, V. *and* AMÉRO, C. Escaped from
    Siberia...................................T616.1
Titan. 2 vols. Richter, J. P. F............R535.5
Tithe-proctor. Carleton, W................C281.10
TITMARSH, *Mr.* M. A., *pseud. See* Thack-
    eray, W. M.
To call her mine. Besant, *Sir* W.........B554.30
To leeward. Crawford, F. M...............C899.22
To the bitter end. Braddon, M. E........B798.37
TOBIN, J. The honeymoon. 27 pp...*in* M875.1 [3]
TODKILL, A., *pseud. See* Cooke, J. E.
Toilers of Babylon. Farjeon, B. L.........F229.16
Toilers of the sea. Hugo, V................H895.6
Toinette. Tourgée, A. W..................T727.11
Told after supper. Jerome, J. K............J565.5
TOLDERBUND, H. Grandmother's scissors.
    11 pp...................................*in* V629.1
TOLSTOI, *Count* A. Prince Serebryani:
    times of Ivan the Terrible and of the
    conquest of Siberia.....................T653.1

TOLSTOI, *Count* L. N. Anna Karénina...T654.1
Childhood, boyhood, youth...............T654.2
The cossacks: a tale of the Caucasus
    in 1852..................................T654.3
In pursuit of happiness.....................T654.4
The invaders, and other stories............T654.5
Iván Ilyitch, and other stories............T654.6
Katia.....................................T654.7
Master and man...........................T654.8
Polikouchka. (*Also*) Two generations,
    and other stories........................T654.9
Russian proprietor, and other stories....T654.10
Two generations.........................*in* T654.9
War and peace. 3 pts. in 6 vols........T654.11
Where love is, there God is also. 17 pp..T654.12
Tom Bowling. Chamier, F..................C448.3
Tom Brown at Oxford. Hughes, T........H894.2
Tom Burke of "Ours." Lever, C.........L658.26
Tom Cringle's log. Scott, M................S428.2
Tom Grogan. Smith, F. H.................S647.8
Tom Jones. Fielding, H....................F459.4
Same.....................................*in* **N938.3
Same. 3 vols.............................**B232.19-21
Tom Racquet. Smedley, F. E...............S637.7
To-morrow. Edgeworth, M..........*in* **E235.7
Same.....................................*in* E235.20
TOMPKINS, E. K. Broken ring. T662.1
Her majesty..............................T662.5
Tompkins and other folks. Deming, P...D382.2
Tony Butler. Lever, C.....................L658.27
Tony, the maid. Howard, B. W..........H848.6
Too curious. Goodman, E. J...............G653.1
Too much alone. Riddell, C. E. L......R543.18
Too rich. Streckfuss, A...................W817.30
TOPELIUS, Z. Surgeon's stories. 6 cycles...
    ....T673.1-6
    1st cycle. Times of Gustaf Adolf.
    Issued also as Gustaf Adolf and the thirty
    years' war.
    2d cycle. Times of battle and rest.
    3d cycle. Times of Charles XII.
    4th cycle. Times of Frederick I.
    5th cycle. Times of Linnæus.
    6th cycle. Times of alchemy.
TOURGÉE, A. W. (H. Churton, *pseud.*)
Black ice.................................T727.1
Bricks without straw.....................T727.2
Button's inn.............................T727.3
Figs and thistles.........................T727.4
Fool's errand............................T727.5
Same, with part 2: Invisible empire...T727.6
Hot plowshares..........................T727.7
Invisible empire..........................T727.6
    Pt. 1 *issued also as* Fool's errand.
John Eax, and Mamelon; or, the south

TOURGÉE, A. W.—*Continued.*
without the shadow..........................T727.8
Mamelon..............................*in* T727.8
Murvale Eastman............................T727.9
Pactolus Prime............................T727.10
A royal gentleman..........................T727.11
Issued also as Toinette.
Toinette: a tale of transition............T727.11
Issued also as A royal gentleman.
With Gauge & Swallow, attorneys.....T727.12
Tower of London. Ainsworth, W. H...A297.24
Tower of Percemont. Sand, G.............S213.18
Towhead. Greene, S. P. McL..............G812.9
Town and country. Adams, J. S...........A213.1
TOWNER, A. The house terrible............T746.1
TOWNSEND, *Mrs.* A. L. *See* Shirley, P.,
pseud.
TOWNSEND, E. W. "Chimmie Fadden,"
Major Max, and other stories...........T747.1
Daughter of the tenements..................T747.2
TOWNSEND, G. A. Entailed hat; or, Patty
Cannon's times..............................T748.1
Katy of Catoctin...........................T748.2
TOWNSEND, V. F. But a Philistine.......T751.1
Darryll Gap................................T751.2
The Hollands...............................T751.3
Lenox Dare.................................T751.4
Mills of Tuxbury...........................T751.5
Only girls.................................T751.6
One woman's two lovers.....................T751.7
That queer girl............................T751.8
A woman's word, and how she kept it..T751.9
TRACY, L. Final war.......................T761.3
Tracy's ambition. Griffin, G............*in* G851.5
Same.....................................G851.9
TRAFTON, A. (*Mrs. Knox*). His inherit-
ance.......................................T764.1
Tragedy in the imperial harem at Constan-
stinople. Hanoum, L......................H247.1
Tragedy of Ida Noble. Russell, W. C....R968.25
Tragedy of Pudd'nhead Wilson. Twain,
M..T969.6
Tragic comedians. Meredith, G.........M559.13
Tragic muse. 2 vols. James, H., *Jr*.....J277.19
Tragic tales. 2 vols. Brydges, *Sir* S. E...**B916.2
Trail of the sword. Parker, G.............Q240.11
Traits and stories of the Irish peasantry.
Carleton, W............................C281.11
Same. 4 vols.............................C281.13
Same. 5 vols.............................**C281.12
Transatlantic chatelaine. Prince, H. C....Q944.4
Translation of a savage. Parker, G.........Q240.12
Travel, war, and shipwreck. Gillmore,
P..G482.1

Traveler from Altruria. Howells, W. D..H859.30
Treasure island. Stevenson, R. L.........S848.12
TREBOR (*pseud. of* R. S. Davis). As it may
happen: a story of American life and
character..................................T785.1
Tremaine. Ward, R. P.....................**W262.2
Trespasser. Parker, G....................Q240.13
Tressilian and his friends. Mackenzie,
R. S......................................M157.1
TREVSSAC DE VERGY, P. H. Henrietta,
Countess Osenvor. 69 pp........*in* **N938.17
Trial. Yonge, C. M.......................Y555.33
Trials of life. 2 vols. Grey, E. C......**G842.3
Trials of Raissa. Gréville, H.............G838.9
Tribulations of a Chinaman in China.
Verne, J..................................V531.1
Tricotrin. Ouida.........................O934.23
Trilby. Du Maurier, G....................D887.2
Tristram Shandy. Sterne, L..........*in* **N938.5
Same.....................................S840.2
Tristrem Varick, Truth about. Saltus, E...
....S180.1
Tritons. Bynner, E. L....................B994.6
TROLLOPE, A. Barchester Towers.........T846.1
Belton estate..............................T846.2
The Bertrams...............................T846.3
Can you forgive her?.......................T846.4
Castle Richmond............................T846.5
Doctor Thorne..............................T846.7
Eustace diamonds...........................T846.9
Framley parsonage..........................T846.10
Golden Lion of Granpere....................T846.11
Harry Heathcote of Gangoil: a tale of
Australian bush-life.....................T846.12
He knew he was right.......................T846.13
Is he Popinjoy?............................T846.14
Kellys and the O'Kellys....................T846.15
Lotta Schmidt and other stories...........T846.17
Macdermots of Ballycloran..................T846.18
Mary Gresley, and other tales.............T846.8
Miss Mackenzie.............................T846.19
Mr. Scarborough's family...................T846.20
Mrs. General Talboys....................*in* S885.5
Orley Farm.................................T846.21
Phineas Finn, the Irish member............T846.23
Phineas Redux..............................T846.24
Prime minister.............................T846.25
Ralph the heir.............................T846.26
Sir Harry Hotspur of Humblethwaite...
....T846.27
Small house at Allington...................T846.28
Tales of all countries.....................T846.30
Three clerks...............................T846.31

TROLLOPE, A.—*Continued.*
La Vendée...................................T846.32
Vicar of Bullhampton...................T846.33
The warden..............................T846.34
Way we live now.........................T846.35
TROLLOPE, F. E. Anne Furness..........T847.1
Mabel's progress........................T847.2
Sacristan's household: a story of Lippe-
Detmold.................................T847.3
That wild wheel.........................T847.4
TROLLOPE, F. M. Life and adventures of
Michael Armstrong, the factory boy..T848.1
Trooper Peter Halket of Mashonaland.
Schreinier, O...........................S378.4
Troublesome daughters. Walford, L. B...
....W174.14
TROWBRIDGE, J. T. Coupon bonds, and
other stories..........................T863.1
Cudjo's cave............................T863.2
Neighbor Jackwood.......................T863.3
Three scouts............................T863.4
Trowel or the cross, and other stories.
Bischoff, J. F. K.......................B621.1
True as steel. Harland, M...............H283.17
True daughter of Hartenstein, tr. from the
German by M. J. Safford.................S128.1
True history of Joshua Davidson, com-
munist. Linton, E. L....................L761.3
True riches. Coppée, F..................C785.3
TRUEBA Y COSIO, T. DE. Romance of his-
tory: Spain.............................T866.1
TRUMAN, B. C. Occidental sketches......T867.1
Trumpet-major. Hardy, T.................H272.17
Trumpeter Fred. King, C.................K523.24
Trumps. Curtis, G. W....................C979.2
Truth about Tristrem Varick. Saltus, E...
....S180.1
Truth-tellers. Winter, J. S.............W785.16
Tryphena in love. Raymond, W............R273.3
Tsar's window. Hooper, L. H.............H786.1
Tubber Derg, and other tales. Carleton,
W.......................................C281.14
TUCKER, B. (*pseud of* E. W. Sydney).
The partisan leader: a novel of the
origin and struggles of the Southern
Confederacy.............................T891.1
TUPPER, M. F. King Veric: a scene of the
Romans in Britain. 12 pp...........*in* S637.2
The twins, and Heart....................T928.1
TURGENEF, I. S. *See* Turgénieff, I. S.
TURGENEV, I. S. *See* Turgénieff, I. S.
TURGÉNIEFF, I. S. Annals of a sports-
man....................................T936.1
Annouchka..............................T936.2

TURGÉNIEFF, I. S.—*Continued.*
Ass'ya.............................*in* T936.12
Diary of a superfluous man........*in* T936.7
Dimitri Roudine........................T936.3
Fathers and sons.......................T936.4
Issued also as Fathers and children.
House of gentlefolk....................T936.5
A Lear of the steppe. 71 pp......*in* T936.11
Liza; or, "a nest of nobles.".........T936.6
Mumu; and, The diary of a superfluous
man...................................T936.7
The nihilist......................*in* Z767.1 ²
On the eve.............................T936.8
Rudin..................................T936.9
Smoke: a Russian novel.................T936.10
Spring floods. *(Also)* A Lear of the
steppe................................T936.11
An unfortunate woman, and Ass'ya....T936.12
Virgin soil............................T936.13
Tutor's secret. Cherbuliez, V...........C521.8
TUTTIET, M. G. *See* Gray, M., *pseud.*
TWAIN, M. (*pseud. of* S. L. Clemens.)
American claimant......................T969.1
Same, and other stories and sketches...T969.8
Connecticut Yankee in King Arthur's
court.................................T969.2
Merry tales............................T969.3
Personal recollections of Joan of Arc...T969.4
Stolen white elephant, etc.............T969.5
Those extraordinary twins.........*in* T969.6
The tragedy of Pudd'nhead Wilson, and,
Those extraordinary twins.............T969.6
—*and* Warner, C. D. Gilded age: a tale of
today.................................T969.7
'Twas in Trafalgar's bay, and other stories.
Besant, *Sir* W., *and* Rice, J.........B554.45
TWELLS, J. H. Mills of the gods.........T971.1
Twenty thousand leagues under the sea.
Verne, J..............................V531.38
Twenty years after. Dumas, A............D886.40
Twice taken. Hall, C. W.................H174.1
Twice-told tales. Hawthorne, N..........H399.14
Twins. Tupper, M. F.....................T928.1
Twins of Table Mountain, and other stories.
Harte, B..............................H327.36
Two admirals. Cooper, J. F..............C777.38
Same.............................*in* C777.41
Two baronesses. Andersen, H. C..........A544.4
Two bites at a cherry, etc. Aldrich, T. B...A365.9
Two brides. O'Reilly, B.................O663.1
Two brothers. Balzac, H. de.............B198.37
Two by tricks. Yates, E.................Y317.11
Two captains. 50 pp. La Motte Fouqué,
F. H. K. *Freiherr* de.............*in* L235.1
Same.............................*in* L235.6

Two chiefs of Dunboy. Froude, J. A......F942.2
Two coronets. Tincker, M. A............... T587.7
Two destinies. Collins, W..................C713.31
Two Dianas. Dumas, A.....................D886.41
Two drovers. Scott, *Sir* W............... ... S431.15
Same.. *in* S431.16
Same..*in* S431.51
Same..............................*in* **S431.55
Two family mothers. Schwartz, M. S.....S408.7
Two generations. Tolstoï, *Count* L. N..*in* T654.9
Two guardians. Yonge, C. M..............Y555.34
Two hours. Thackeray, A. I.............*in* T362.5
Two life-paths. Mühlbach, L..............M952.20
Two lilies. Kavanagh, J.................K212.14
Two marriages. Mulock, D. M..........M950.26
Two Miss Jean Dawsons. Robertson, M.
M..R651.2
Two Mrs. Scudamores. 98 pp.........*in* T143.13
Two modern women. Wells, K. G........W454.1
Two of us. Halsey, C...................... H196.1
Two offenders. Ouida....................O934.24
Two on a tower. Hardy, T..............H272.18
Two penniless princesses. Yonge, C. M..Y555.35
Two pictures. McIntosh, M. J.............M152.2
Two runaways and other stories. Ed-
wards, H. S..............................E265.1
Two Salomes. Pool, M. L.................Q821.15
Two sides of the shield. Yonge, C. M..Y555.36
Two soldiers. King, C....................K523.25
Two sons. 31 pp. Opie, A...............*in* O614.3
Two strings to his bow. Mitchell, W.....M682.1
Two years ago. Kingsley, C.............K553.5
Txleama. Knowlton, J. A.................K735.1
Tylney Hall. Hood, T....................H776.1
TYNAN, K. (*Mrs. Hinkson.*) Isle in the
water.....................................T987.1
Way of a maid.............................T987.2
Typee. Melville, H......................M531.5
Typhaines Abbey. Gobineau, J. A., *comte*
de.......................................G575.2
TYTLER, C. C. FRASER- (*Mrs. Liddell*).
Jonathan..................................T996.1
Mistress Judith............................T996.2
TYTLER, M. FRASER- The deformed. 10
pp..*in* J737.1
Same.....................................*in* T559.1
TYTLER, S. (*pseud. of* H. Keddie). A bub-
ble fortune...............................T997.7
Citoyenne Jacqueline......................T997.1
Days of yore. 2 vols......................T997.2
Duchess Frances. 2 vols..................T997.3
Garden of women...........................T997.4
Huguenot family in the English village..T997.5
Phemie Millar. 3 vols. (in 2)............T997.6

Tzigány, The. 58 pp. Gore, C. G......*in* G666.1 *
Uarda. 2 vols. Ebers, G..................E165.16
Ubaldo and Irene. 2 vols. Bresciani, A...B842.3
ULBACH, L. For fifteen years. Sequel to
"The steel hammer."......................U362.1
Madame Gosselin............................U362.2
Steel hammer...............................U362.3
Ulrich the Ready. O'Grady, S............O357.2
Una and King David. Harrison, C. C...*in* H318.4
Unawares. Peard, F. M....................Q359.16
Unbidden guest. Hornung, E. W........H816.3
Uncle John. Melville, G. J. W-..........M530.34
Same....................................**M530.35
Uncle Max. Carey, R. N..................C276.34
Uncle of an angel, and other stories. Jan-
vier, T. A...............................J358.7
Uncle Piper of Piper's Hill. Tasma........T199.3
Uncle Tom's cabin. Stowe, H. B......... S892.12
Uncloseted skeleton. Hale, L. P., *and*
Bynner, E. L............................H162.1
Uncommercial traveler. Dickens, C...*in* D548.17
Same.....................................*in* D548.39
Same........................ ....D548.51
Same...................................... ...D548.52
Same.................................. ......D548.54
Unconscious comedians. 96 pp. Balzac,
H. de....................................*in* B198.19
Uncrowned king. Grier, S. C.............G848.5
Under fire. King, C......................K523.26
Under pressure. Theodoli, L. *Marchesa*....T388.1
Under Salisbury spire. Marshall, E.....M367.11
Under side of things. Bell, L...............B433.1
Under Slieve-ban. Francillon, R. E......F817.1
Under the bells. Kip, L....................K572.2
Under the deodars. Kipling, R......*in* K575.14
Under the greenwood tree. Hardy, T...H272.19
Under the man-fig. Davis, M. E. M......D265.5
Under the Mendips. Marshall, E.........M367.12
Under the red dragon. Grant, J.........G761.52
Under the red flag. Braddon, M. E.......B798.38
Under the red robe. Weyman, S. J.....W549.16
Under the southern cross. Alcock, D....A354.5
Under the tricolor. Hooper, L. H........H786.2
Under two flags. Ouida....................O934.25
Underground city. Verne, J..............V531.39
UNDERWOOD, F. H. Cloud-pictures......U563.1
Lord of himself...........................U563.2
Quabbin...................................U563.3
Undine. 96 pp. La Motte Fouqué F. H.
K. *Freiherr* de.........................*in* L235.1
Same....................................*in* L235.6
Undiscovered country. Howells, W. D..H859.31
Unfairly won. O'Donoghue, N. P........O266.1
Unfortunate woman. Turgénieff, I. S...T936.12

Unkind word, and other stories. Mulock, D. M..............M960.27
Unknown to history. Yonge, C. M......Y555.37
Unofficial patriot. Gardener, H. H........G218.4
Unto the third and fourth generation. Campbell, H..............................C188.3
Unveiling a parallel.....................U617.1
Upper berth. Crawford, F. M............C899.24
Ups and downs. Hale, E. E...........H161.17
UPWARD, A. Crown of straw.............U688.3
Urania. Flammarion, C...................F581.2
Ursula. Balzac, H. de....................B198.38
Ursule Mirouët. Balzac, H. de..........B198.38s
Urith. Gould, S. B-........................G698.11
Usurper. Gautier, J.........................G276.1
Utter failure. Harris, M. C...............H315.8
VACHELL, H. A. Model of Christian Gay: a study of life in California.............V118.1
Quicksands of Pactolus....................V118.3
Romance of Judge Ketchum...............V118.2
Vagabond heroine. Edwardes, A.........E254.9
Vagabond tales. Boyesen, H. H.........B791.12
Vagabondia. Burnett, F. H..............B964.23
Vagabonds. Woods, M. I,..................W896.1
Vagabond's honor. Pierson, E. D........Q624.1
Vagrant wife. Warden, F.................W265.3
Vain forebodings. Oswald, E...........W817.20
Vain fortune. Moore, G.....................M821.1
Val Strange. Murray, D. C..............M981.10
VALDÉS, A. P. The grandee..............V145.3
Sister Saint Sulpice........................V145.6
Vale of cedars. Aguilar, G..............A283.5
Valentine M'Clutchy. Carleton, W......C281.15
Valentine, the countess. Detlef, K......D481.1
Valentine Vox, Life, etc. of. Cockton, H..................................C666.4
VALERA, J. Commander Mendoza........V162.1
Don Braulio................................V162.2
Doña Luz.....................................V162.3
Pepita Ximenez.............................V162.4
Valerie. Marryat, Capt. F................M362.27
Valerie Aylmer. Reid, C..................R353.17
Valerie's fate. Alexander, Mrs...........A374.27
Valerius. Lockhart, J. G..................L816.2
VAN-ANDERSON, H. Is it possible?......V217.1
Right knock..................................V217.2
Van Bibber and others. Davis, R. H...D264.12
VANCE, E. E. Nellie Harland.............V223.1
VANDAM, A. D. Mystery of the Patrician Club...V224.1
Vanderdecken's message home..........in S885.9
Same..in T143.1
Same..in T143.1 ¹

VAN DER NAILLEN, A. In the sanctuary...................................V238.1
On the heights of Himalay................V238.2
VAN DER VELDE, C. F. Axel. 21 pp..in O983.1
VAN DYKE, T. S. Flirtation Camp; or, the rifle, rod, and gun in California...V248.1
Issued also as Rifle rod and gun in California.
VANE, D. Like Lucifer.....................V249.1
Vanished diamond. Verne, J.............V531.40
Vanity fair. Thackeray, W. M...........T363.18
Same..T363.19
VAN LOON, E. Shadow of Hampton Mead......................................V261.1
VAN ZILE, E. S. Magnetic man, and other stories.............................V285.1
Vasconselos. Simms, W. G.............S592.15
Vashti. Wilson, A. J. E.................W746.7
Vathek. Beckford, W.....................B396.1
VEITCH, S. F. F. The dean's daughter..V429.1
VELEV, M. Milly's first love. 79 pp...................................in T143.17
Vendée, La. Trollope, A.................T846.32
Vendetta. Corelli, M.....................C797.15
Venetia. Disraeli, B......................D613.11
Same..D613.13
Venetian June. Fuller, A.................F965.3
Venetians. Braddon, M. E...............B798.39
Vengeance of a Jew. Guenot, C.........G926.1
Vengeance of James Vansittart. Needell, Mrs. J. H.................................N374.4
Venus of Ille. Mérimée, P...............in G277.5
Vera Vorontzoff. Kovalevsky, S.........K887.1
Verbena Camellia Stephanotis, and other stories. Besant, Sir W..............B554.32
Verdant Green, Adventures of. Bede, C..B411.1
Verdugo, El. 15 pp. Balzac, H. de...in B198.34
Same..in B198.41
Vere of "Ours." Grant, J................G761.53
VERGA, G. House by the medlar-tree....V493.1
VERNE, J. Adventures of a Chinaman in China......................................V531.1
Issued also as Tribulations of a Chinaman.
Adventures of Captain Hatteras. (2 pts.)................................V531.2
Adventures of three Englishmen and three Russians in southern Africa..........V531.3
Archipelago on fire.......................V531.4
Around the world in eighty days.........V531.5
Issued also as Tour of the world in eighty days.
At the north pole...........................V531.6
Issued also as Adventures of Captain Hatteras, pt. 1. English at the north pole. Journey to the north pole. Voyages, etc., of Captain Hatteras.

VERNE, J.—*Continued.*

Blockade runners..............................V531.7
Same.................................*in* V531.15
Castle of the Carpathians...................V531.8
Child of the cavern..........................V531.39
Clipper of the clouds........................V531.9
The cryptogram..........................*in* V531.19
Demon of Cawnpore......................V531.35
Same.................................*in* V531.35 1
Desert of ice.................................V531.13
  Issued also as Adventures of Captain Hatteras, pt. 2. Field of ice. Ice desert.
Dick Sands, the boy captain..............V531.11
English at the north pole................V531.12
  Issued also as Adventures of Captain Hatteras, pt. 1. At the north pole. Journey to the north pole. Voyages and adventures of Captain Hatteras.
Field of ice...................................V531.13
  Issued also as Adventures of Captain Hatteras, pt. 2. Desert of ice. Ice desert.
Five weeks in a balloon.....................V531.14
Floating city, and Blockade runners..V531.15
From the earth to the moon, direct,
  and, A trip round it.....................V531.16
The fur country. 2 pts.....................V531.17
Giant raft....................................V531.19
Godfrey Morgan: a Californian mystery...................................V531.20
Green ray: a romance of the Scottish
  Highlands................................V531.21
Hector Servadac............................V531.22
Ice desert....................................V531.13
  Issued also as Adventures of Captain Hatteras, pt. 2. Desert of ice. Field of ice.
In search of the castaways.................V531.24
  Issued also as Voyage around the world.
Journey to the center of the earth......V531.25
Kéraban the inflexible......................V531.26
Martin Paz...................................V531.27
Same.................................*in* V531.45
Mathias Sandorf.............................V531.29
Michael Strogoff, the courier of the czar....
  ....V531.28
Mysterious island...........................V531.30
Purchase of the north pole................V531.32
Round the moon: a sequel to "From the
  earth to the moon."................*in* V531.16
Same.......................................V531.33
Round the world in eighty days..........V531.5
  Issued also as Tour of the world in 80 days.
Steam house. Pt. 1: Demon of Cawnpore.....................................V531.35 1
Same. Pt. 2. Tigers and traitors...V531.35 2
Same. 2 pts.............................*in* V531.35
Tigers and traitors.................... *in* V531.35

VERNE, J.—*Continued.*

Same......................................V531.35 2
Tribulations of a Chinaman in China....V531.1
  Issued also as Adventures of a Chinaman.
20,000 leagues under the sea.............V531.38
Underground city; or, the child of the
  cavern...................................V531.39
  Issued also as Child of the cavern.
Vanished diamond..........................V531.40
Voyage round the world...................V531.24
Same. 3 pts.: 1. South America. 2.
  Australia. 3. New Zealand.........V531.41-3
  Issued also as In search of the castaways.
Winter in the ice, and other stories.....V531.44
Wreck of the Chancellor. *(Also)* Martin Paz..V531.45
Verner's pride. Wood, E. P..............W874.15
Vernon's aunt. Cotes, S. J. D.............C843.20
Veronica. Zschokke, H...................Z923.6
Vestal; or, a tale of Pompeii..............V583.1
Vestigia. Fleming, G.....................F597.4
Vesty of the Basins. Greene, S. P. McL...
  ....G812.11
Veva. Conscience, H.....................C755.9
VIAUD, L. M. J. *See* Loti, P., *pseud.*
Vicar of Bullhampton. Trollope, A....T846.33
Vicar of Tours. Balzac, H. de.........*in* B198.32
Vicar of Wakefield. Goldsmith, O....
  ....*in* **B232.23
Same......................................G625.1
Same......................................G625.2
Same......................................G625.3
Same.................................*in* **N938.2
Vicar's daughter. MacDonald, G........M135.25
Vicar's people. Fenn, G. M...............F334.11
VICARY, J. F., *comp.* A stork's nest......V629.1
  CONTENTS: Etlar, C. Priest's lamb. Repaid. White stone. Aunt Bodil. What a woman never forgets. A masquerade. Who can one depend on? Whitsuntide at Tibirke. —Three crosses.—Tolderbund, H. Treasure of Kjœrsholm. Olufsburg. — Gloersen, K. Mighty hunter.—Goldschmidt, M. A. Wind as a post office.—Kielland, A. L. Battle of Waterloo. — Bögh, E. Story of a story. Young Jens Jensen. A patient.—Ring, I. Furugaard. The snowball.—Ragnhild.
Vice Versâ. Anstey, F....................A625.9
VICTOR, F. A. F. New Penelope and
  other stories, etc........................V642.1
VICTOR, H. (?) Mariam; or, twenty-one
  days. V643.1
Victor La Tourette. Warriner, E. A......W295.1
Victor's laurel. Crake, A. D..............C888.10
Victory Deane. Griffith, C................G853.2

Victory of the vanquished. Charles, E. R.....................................C476.14

Vignettes of Manhattan. Matthews, B...M438.14

VIGNY, A. V. *Comte de.* Cinq-mars; or, a conspiracy under Louis XIII..........V688.1

Vikram and the vampire. Ed. by R. F. Burton..................................B974.1

Villa on the Rhine. 2 vols. Auerbach, B.....................................A918.14

Village commune. Ouida....................O934.26

Village innkeeper. Conscience, H....*in* C755.8

Same....................C755.10

Village on the cliff, and other stories, etc. Thackeray, A. I.................T362.6

Village rector. Balzac, H. de............B198.40

Village tragedy. Woods, M. L...........W896.2

Village watch-tower. Wiggin, K. D......W655.6

VILLARI, L. In change unchanged.......V722.1

Villette. Brontë, C....................B870.5

VINCE, H. S. As Avon flows...........V767.1

Vineta, the phantom city. Werner, E...W492.3

Violet Jermyn. Grant, J................G761.54

Violetta. Manteuffel, U. Z. v...........W817.9

Violin obligato, and other stories. Crosby, M.....................................C949.1

Virgin soil. Turgénieff, I. S..........T936.13

Virginia Bohemians. Cooke, J. E......C772.15

Virginia cavalier. Seawell, M. E......S442.11

Virginia comedians. Cooke, J. E......C772.16

Virginia cousin. Harrison, C. C.......H318.11

Virginia inheritance. Pendleton, E....Q397.1

Virginians. Thackeray, W. M..........T363.20

Virginians in Texas. Baker, W. M....B169.7

Virtuous orphan. Marivaux, P. C. de C. de...........................*in* **N938.16

Visionary. Lie, J......................L716.3

Visits. James, H., *Jr*...........*in* J277.13

Vital question. Tchernuishevsky, N. G....T251.1

Vittoria. Meredith, G.................M559.14

Viva. Forrester, *Mrs*.................F730.11

Vivian. Edgeworth, M.......*in* **E235.10

Same....................E235.23

Same....................*in* E235.35

Vivian Grey. Disraeli, B.............D613.14

Vivian the beauty. Edwardes, A......E254.10

Vivier, of Vivier, Longman & Company, bankers. Hudson, W. C.............H886.1

Vixen. Braddon, M. E.................B798.40

Voegele's marriage, and other tales. Schnabel, L.............................S357.1

VOLCKHAUSEN, A. VON. Why did he not die? Tr. by A. L. Wister.............W817.31

VOLTAIRE, F. M. A. DE. Sincere Huron. 35 pp......................*in* **N938.21

Zadig. 41 pp.......................*in* **N938.2

VOSMAER, C. The amazon...............V968.1

Voyage of discovery. Aidé, H.........A288.4

Voyage round the world. Verne, J.....V531.24

Same. 3 vols....................V531.41-3

W. Sketch from Babylon. 97 pp.....*in* T143.17

W., A. B. *See* Wood, A. B.

W., F. Wreck of the Strathmore. 64 pp.........................*in* T143.14

W., H. D. A feuilleton. 18 pp.......*in* T143.14

W., T. P. Reminiscence of a march. 14 pp.........................*in* T143.22

WAGNER, H., *and* BUNYAN, R. T. Street and the flower.................W133.1

Wags, The. 31 pp.................*in* T143.4

Same.........................*in* T143.4 [1]

Waif of the plains. Harte, B.........H327.38

Waiting for the verdict. Davis, *Mrs.* R. H.....................................D263.4

Waiting race. Yates, E................Y317.12

Waking dream. 10 pp.............*in* B979.1 [1]

Waldfried. Auerbach, B..............A918.15

WALFORD, L. B. Baby's grandmother...W174.1

Bee or Beatrix. 63 pp...........*in* T143.11

Cousins........................W174.2

Dick Netherby...................W174.3

Her great idea, and other stories........W174.4

History of a week................W174.5

Lady Adelaide. 33 pp...........*in* T143.16

Matchmaker....................W174.6

Mr. Smith.......................W174.7

Nan: a summer scene. 65 pp....*in* T143.7

Pauline.........................W174.8

Ploughed.......................W174.9

Successors to the title............W174.13

Troublesome daughters...........W174.14

WALKER, A. L. In life and in death: a page of family history. 30 pp....*in* T143.16

WALKER, G. Three Spaniards...........W180.1

WALL, G. A., *joint author. See* Robinson, E. A.

WALLACE, *Mrs.* E. D. Strife: a romance of Germany and Italy.................W188.1

WALLACE, *Gen.* L. Ben-Hur: a tale of the Christ....................W191.1

The fair god: a tale of the conquest of Mexico......................W191.2

Prince of India. 2 vols..........W191.3

WALLOTH, W. King's treasure house: a romance of ancient Egypt...........W215.1

WALPOLE, H. Castle of Otranto....*in* **B232.22

Same.........................W218.1

WALRÉE, E. C. W. VAN. *See* Müller, C., *pseud.*

WALSH, M. Hazel Kirke....................W226.1

Wanda. Ouida................................O934.27

Wanderer. Maitland, J. A.......... ....M232.5

Wandering heath. Couch, A. T. Q...... C853.10

Wandering heir. Reade, C.............*in* R285.12

Same..*in* R285.29

Wandering Jew. Sue, E S944.5

Wandering Willie's tale, and others. Illus. by G. Cruikshank..........................W245.1

Wanderings of Persiles and Sigismunda. Cervantes Saavedra, M. de...............C419.4

Wanneta, the Sioux. Moorehead, W. K...M825.1

Wanted—a pedigree. Finley, M............F513.4

War and peace. 3 pts. in 6 vols. Tolstoï, *Count L. N* T654.11

War of women. 2 vols. Dumas, A......D886.45

War-time wooing. King, C.................K523.27

WARBURTON, E. B. G. Darien; or, the merchant prince. 3 vols................W254.1

WARD, *Mrs.* E. S. P. *See* Phelps, E. S.

WARD, H. D. Republic without a president, etc...............................W258.1

—*joint author. See* Phelps, E. S.

WARD, *Mrs.* H. *See* Ward, M. A. A.

WARD, M. A. A. History of David Grieve.............. ....W261.3

Marcella. 2 vols W261.5

Miss Bretherton..........................W261.6

Robert Elsmere..........................W261.8

Sir George Tressady. 2 vols............W261.9

Story of Bessie Costrell.................W261.10

WARD, R. P. De Vere; or, the man of independence...........................W262.1

Tremaine; or, the man of refinement... ....**W262.2

Ward of the Golden Gate. Harte, B...H327.39

WARDEN, F. (*pseud.* of F. A. P. James). At the world's mercy...................W265.1

House on the marsh......................W265.2

Vagrant wife...............................W265.3

Warden. Trollope, A......................T846.34

WARE, W. Aurelian; or, Rome in the third century. (Sequel to Zenobia.) 2 vols....................................W273.1 *Issued also as* Probus.

Julian; or, scenes in Judea. 2 vols.....W273.2

Zenobia; or, the fall of Palmyra........W273.3

WARFIELD, C. A. Cardinal's daughter. Sequel to "Ferne Fleming."..........W274.1

Double wedding..... ....W274.2

Ferne Fleming...........................W274.3

Household of Bouverie...................W274.5

WARFIELD, C. A.—*Continued.* Miriam's memoirs. Sequel to "Monfort Hall."..................................W274.7 *Issued also as* Romance of Beauseincourt.

Waring's peril. King, C...................K523.28

Warlock o' Glenwarlock. MacDonald, G.. ....M135.26

WARNER, A. B. (Amy Lothrop, *pseud.*) Dollars and cents........................W279.1

My brother's keeper.....................W279.2

—*joint author. See* Warner, S.

WARNER, C. D. Golden house.............W280.1

Little journey in the world..............W280.2

—*joint author. See* Twain, M.

WARNER, S. (E. Wetherell, *pseud.*) Daisy. Sequel to "Melbourne house."........W284.1

Diana....................................W284.2

Hills of the Shatemuc............. ......W284.3

Letter of credit..........................W284.4

Melbourne house.........................W284.5

My desire................................W284.6

Old helmet...............................W284.7

Pine needles.............................W284.8

Queechy.................................W284.9

Wide, wide world........................W284.10

—*and* A. B. Gold of Chickaree. (Sequel to.. Wych Hazel.)..........................W284.11

Say and seal............................W284.12

Wych Hazel.............................W284.13

WARREN, C. Miss Wilton.................W287.1

WARREN, S. Now and then..............W293.1

Passages from the diary of a late physician..............................W293.2

Ten thousand a year.....................W293.3

WARRINER, E. A. Victor La Tourette..W295.1

Was it love? Bourget, P..................B772.9

WASHBURN, W. T. Fair Harvard.........W315.1

Washer of the ford. Macleod, F..........M165.5

Washington square. James, H., *Jr*......J277.20

Watch and ward. James, H., *Jr*.........J277.21

Watchmaker's wife, and other stories. Stockton, F. R.........................S866.32

Water ghost and others. Bangs, J. K.....B216.4

Water-Witch. Cooper, J. F................C777.39

Same...................................C777.41

Waterdale neighbors. McCarthy, J.....M122.15

WATERLOO, S. An odd situation.........W327.1

Waterloo. Erckmann, E., *and* Chatrian, A....................................E654.19

WATSON, H. B. M. Galloping Dick......W338.1

WATSON, J. (Ian Maclaren, *pseud.*.) Beside the bonnie brier bush.............W339.2

Days of auld lang syne..................W339.5

Doctor of the old school. 31 pp......*in* S885.8

Kate Carnegie...........................W339.10

Waverley. Scott, *Sir* W......................S431.52
Same.......................................**S431.53
Waverley dictionary. Rogers, M......**S431.58
Waverley novels, Key to the. Grey, H...S431.57
Waverley novels. Index and glossary....
Scott, *Sir* W...............................**S431.56
Way of a maid. Tynan, K.................T987.2
"Way of the world." Murray, D. C......M981.11
Way of the world. Optic, O.................O625.3
Way they loved at Grimpat. Esler, E. R..E763.5
Way we live now. Trollope, A............T846.35
Ways of the hour. Cooper, J. F........*in* C777.31
Same.......................................C777.40
We and our neighbors. Stowe, H. B.....S892.13
We girls. Whitney, A. D. T................W617.11
We two. Lyall, E.............................L981.14
Weaker vessel. Murray, D. C.............M981.12
Weal and woe in Garveloch. Martineau,
H..................................*in* **M385.10
Same.......................................M385.18
Wealth and welfare. 2 vols. Gotthelf, J...G685.1
"Wearing of the green." King, R. A....K543.2
Wearyholme. Holt, E. S...................H758.12
Weavers and weft. Braddon, M. E......B798.41
Web of gold. Woods, K. P.................W895.3
WEBER, A. Leal souvenir...................W373.1
WEBBER, C. W. Tales of the southern
border..W371.2
WEBSTER, A. Miss Eunice's glove. 27
pp..................................*in* S884.6
Operation in money. 30 pp............*in* S884.1
Wedding garment. Pendleton, L.........Q398.3
Wee wifie. Carey, R. N....................C276.35
Wee Willie Winkie, and other child sto-
ries. Kipling, R.......................*in* K575.10
Weighed and wanting. MacDonald, G..M135.27
Weir of Hermiston. Stevenson, R. L....S848.13

Weird tales. 2 vols. Hoffmann, W.........H710.3
Weird tales from northern seas. Lie, J...L716.4
WELCKER, A. Snob papers: a humorous
novel..W442.1
Well at the world's end. 2 vols. Mor-
ris, W..M877.6
Well-beloved. Hardy, T... ....H272.22
Well in the desert. Holt, E. S............H758.13
Wellfields. Fothergill, J....................F761.7
WELLS, H. G. Wheels of chance.......W453.5
WELLS, K. G. Two modern women......W454.1
WELLWOOD, H. J. MONCREIFF, *Lord.*
Great unloaded. 16 pp.............*in* T143.23
Rufus Hickman of St. Botolph's. 44
pp..................................*in* T143.20
Wenderholme. Hamerton, P. G...........H215.3

Wept of Wish-Ton-Wish. Cooper, J. F..*in* C777.19
Same.......................................C777.42
WERNER, E. (*pseud. of* E. Bürstenbinder).
At a high price.............................W492.1
Issued also as No surrender. Price he paid.
Banned and blessed. Tr. by A. L.
Wister..W817.32
"Good luck!"................................W492.2
Issued also as Success and how he won it.
Saint Michael. Tr. by A. L. Wister...W817.33
Vineta, the phantom city.................W492.3
Issued also as Under a charm.
Wessex tales. Hardy, T....................H272.20
WEST, M. A born player.................W519.1
West Lawn. Holmes, M. J.............H751.27
WESTALL, W. Sons of Belial............W522.1
WESTBURY, H. "Acte."...................W523.1
Western clearings. Kirkland, C. M......K598.3
Westminster Abbey. Robinson, J........R662.6
Westward ho! Kingsley, C...............K553.6
Wetherel affair. De Forest, J. W..........D315.6
WETHERELL, E., *pseud. See* Warner, S.
WETTERBERGH, C. A. *See* Adam, *Uncle,*
pseud.
WEYMAN, S. J. From the memoirs of a
minister of France........................W549.3
Gentleman of France.....................W549.4
House of the wolf..........................W549.5
King's stratagem, and other stories...W549.7
Little wizard.................................W549.9
Man in black................................W549.10
My lady Rotha..............................W549.12
Perilous amour. 29 pp.............*in* S885.10
Red cockade................................W549.14
Under the red robe.........................W549.16
Whaleman's adventures in the Sandwich
Islands and California. Thomes, W.
H...T465.10
WHARTON, E. Mrs. Manstey's view. 30
pp..................................*in* S886.2
What came of it. Stitzel, *Mrs.* H. V......S862.1
What can she do? Roe, E. P.............R699.16
What dreams may come. Atherton, G. F...
....A868.3
What he cost her. Payn, J.................Q345.19
What necessity knows. Dougall, L......D731.3
What the swallow sang. Spielhagen, F...S755.4
What will he do with it? Lytton, E. G. E.
L. Bulwer-.................................L998.26
What's bred in the bone. Allen, G......A425.16
Wheel of fire. Bates, A....................B329.10
Wheel of time. James, H., *Jr*............J277.22
WHEELER, W. A., *joint author. See*
Pierce, G. A.
Wheels of chance. Wells, H. G.........W453.5

WHEELWRIGHT, J. T. Bad penny......W566.2
  Child of the century........................W566.1
—joint author. See Grant, R., and others.
When a man's single. Barrie, J. M......B275.9
When Charles the First was king.
  Fletcher, J. S..............................F613.4
When Valmond came to Pontiac. Parker,
  G..Q240.15
When we were boys. O'Brien, W........O134.1
Where love is, there God is also. 17 pp.
  Tolstoi, Count L. N.....................T654.12
Where the battle was fought. Craddock,
  C. E................................... C884.16
Whim and its consequences. James, G.
  P. R..J276.39
Whimsical wooing. Barrili, A. G...........B276.2
Whirl asunder. Atherton, G. F............A868.4
WHISHAW, F. Boyar of the terrible......W576.3
Whist at our club. 22 pp.................in T143.18
WHITBY, B. Awakening of Mary Fen-
  wick..W579.1
  Part of the property.......................W579.3
WHITE, A. L. Doctor Hildreth............W582.1
WHITE, C. E. Love in the tropics........W583.1
  Modern Agrippa. (Also) Patience
  Barker.......................................W583.2
WHITE, C. H., pseud. See Chaplin, H. W.
WHITE, E. O. Coming of Theodora......W584.1
  Miss Brooks..................................W584.2
  Winterborough...............................W584.3
WHITE, R. G. Fate of Mansfield Humph-
  reys.. W587.1
WHITE, W. A. Real issue....................W589.5
WHITE, W. H. See Rutherford, M., pseud.
White aprons. Goodwin, M. W............G657.1
White as snow. Garrett, E. and R......G239.13
White birches. Eliot, A.......................E425.1
White cockade. Grant, J....................G761.55
White company. Doyle, A. C.............D754.25
White gauntlet. Reid, M.....................R357.9
White heather. Black, W....................B627.38
White heron, and other stories. Jewett,
  S. O..J593.18
White islander. Catherwood, M. H......C363.11
White-Jacket. Melville, H...................M531.6
White lies. Reade, C....................in R285.27
  Same...R285.31
White Marie. Harben, W. N..............H255.2
White rose. Melville, G. J. W-........... M530.36
  Same..............................in **M530.25
White slaves of monopolies W590.1
White Wings. Black, W.....................B627.39
White friars. Robinson, J...................R662.7
Whitehall. Robinson, J..................... R662.8

Whiteladies. Oliphant, M. O. W........O475.59
Whites and the blues. 2 vols. Dumas, A..D886.47
WHITNEY, A. D. T. Bonnyborough......W617.1
  Faith Gartney's girlhood..................W617.2
  Gayworthys..................................W617.3
  Hitherto: a story of yesterdays...........W617.4
  Odd, or even?..................... ....W617.5
  Other girls....................................W617.6
  Patience Strong's outings.................W617.7
  Real folks....................................W617.8
  Sights and insights. 2 vols..............W617.9
  Summer in Leslie Goldthwaite's life..W617.10
  We girls: a home story. (Sequel to "Sum-
  mer in Leslie Goldthwaite's life.")..W617.11
Whittlebridge. 53 pp.....................in T143.18
WHITTY, E. M. Friends of Bohemia;
  or, phases of London life. 2 vols....W627.1
"Who breaks—pays." Jenkin, H. C.........J525.4
Who was lost and is found. Oliphant,
  M. O. W....................................O475.60
Whom Kathie married. Douglas, A. M...D734.32
Whose fault? Harrison, J...................H320.1
Why did he not die? Volckhausen, A. v....
  ....W817.31
WHYTE, V. Her Johnnie..................W629.1
WICHERT, E. Green gate. Tr. by A. L.
  Wister............... ....W817.34
Wicked girl. Hay, M. C....................H413.7
Wide, wide world. Warner, S...........W284.10
Widow Goldsmith's daughter. Smith, J.
  P..S653.10
Widow Guthrie. Johnston, R. M........J733.11
Widower. Smith, J. P......................S653.11
Wieland. Brown, C. B.....................B879.5
Wife, The. Norton, C. E. S..............**N883.3
Wife's duty. Opie, A....................in O614.3
Wife's engagement ring. Arthur, T. S...A791.6
WIGGIN, K. D. (Mrs. Riggs.) Cathedral
  courtship. (Also) Penelope's English
  experiences......... ....W655.3
  Marm Lisa....................................W655.4
  Village watch-tower...... ....W655.6
Wigwam and the cabin. Simms, W. G..S592.16
WILBRANDT, A. VON. Fridolin's mys-
  tical marriage...... ....W665.1
  Pilot captain. 69 pp...................in S331.1
Wild and weird. Campbell, Sir G.......C187.3
Wild ass's skin. Balzac, H. de........B198.27s
Wild Irish girl. 3 vols. Morgan, Lady
  S. O..M850.2
Wild rose of Lough Gill. Smyth, P. G..S667.2
Wild times. Caddell, C. M.................C121.2
Wild western scenes. Jones, J. B......J778.2
Wildgoose Lodge. Carleton, W.........in C281.7

WILDMAN, R. Panglima Muda.........W674.1
Wilfrid Cumbermede. MacDonald, G..M135.28
Wilhelm Meister's apprenticeship. Göthe,
    J. W. v..............................G599.4
Wilhelm Meister's apprenticeship and
    Travels. 2 vols. Göthe, J. W. v...G599.4¹⁻²
Wilhelm Meister's travels. Göthe, J. W.
    ....G599.5
Same.....................in G599.4²
WILKINS, G. Body and soul............**W683.1
WILKINS, M. E. Humble romance, and
    other stories...........................W684.3
Jane Field................................W684.5
Madelon...................................W684.7
New England nun, and other stories...W684.8
Pembroke.................................W684.10
Will, The. Edgeworth, M............in **E235.6
Same..........................in E235.19
Will Denbigh, Nobleman. Mulock, D.
    M......................................M960.28
Will o' the Wasp. Rogers, R. C.........R728.1
WILLE, E. DE. Johannes Olaf...........W698.1
WILLIAMS, C. Military sketches and
    stories. See Forbes, A., and others.
WILLIAMS, Dr. and Mrs. H. Mr. and
    Mrs. Morton...........................W721.1
WILLIAMS, H. L., ed. Ruy Blas; or, the
    king's rival: founded on the drama
    by V. Hugo............................W723.1
WILLIAMS, R. F. Shakespeare and his
    friends. (Also) Secret passion. (And)
    Youth of Shakespeare.............**W726.1
WILLIS, N. P. Two buckets in a well.
    25 pp................................in S884.4
Willy Reilly and his dear Coleen bawn.
    Carleton, W..........................C281.16
WILSON, A. Spectre of Milaggio. 46
    pp..................................in T143.10
WILSON, A. J. E. At the mercy of
    Tiberius..............................W746.1
Beulah....................................W746.2
Inez: a tale of the Alamo...............W746.3
Infelice..................................W746.4
Macaria..................................W746.5
St. Elmo................................W746.6
Vashti; or, "until death us do part."..W746.7
WILSON, J. Dominie and the souter..in W750.7
WILSON, J. (Christopher North, pseud.)
    Lights and shadows of Scottish life..W749.1
WILSON, J. M. Bill Stanley. Archy Arm-
    strong. Guidwife of Coldingham.
    Leaves from the diary of an aged
    spinster. Laidley worm of Spindle-
    ton's Heugh. Sabbath wrecks...in W750.3

WILSON, J. M.—Continued.
The cripple. Sir Patrick Hume: a tale
    of the house of Marchmont. Charles
    Lawson. First-foot. I canna be
    fashed...............................in W750.5
Dominie's class. Smuggler. Red Hall;
    or, Berwick in 1296. Reuben Purves.
    We'll have another.................in W750.6
First and second marriage. Leaves from
    the life of Alexander Hamilton. Say-
    ings and doings of Peter Paterson.
    Trials and triumphs................in W750.10
Judith the Egyptian. Poor scholar.
    Broken heart. Doom of Soulis. The
    bride. Henpecked man............in W750.4
The orphan. Tibby Fowler. Death of
    the Chevalier de la Beauté. Widow's
    ae son. Twin brothers. Edmund and
    Helen. Hermit of the hills. The
    siege.................................in W750.12
Prodigal son. The seeker. Ups and
    downs. The procrastinator......in W750.11
Recollections of a village patriarch.
    Grizel Cochrane. Squire Ben. The
    leveller. Perseverance. Irish reaper....
    ....in W750.8
Roger Goldie's narrative. Unbidden
    guest. Simple man is the beggar's
    brother. The fugitive. Willie Wastle's
    account of his wife................in W750.9
The unknown. Lottery Hall. Coven-
    anting family. Polwarth on the green.
    The festival. Order of the garter: a
    story of Wark Castle..............in W750.7
Vacant chair. Faa's revenge. Midside
    Maggy. Wife or the wuddy. Adopted
    son. My black coat; or, the breaking
    of the bride's china................in W750.1
Whitsome tragedy. Royal bridal. Soli-
    tary of the cave. The fair.........in W750.2
—and others. Tales of the borders and of
    Scotland. 12 vols................W750.1-12
    CONTENTS: 1: Wilson, J. M. Vacant
    chair. Faa's revenge. Midside Maggie. A
    wife or the wuddy. Adopted son. My black
    coat.—Leighton, A. Kate Kennedy. Pre-
    scription. Lord Duric and Christie's Will.
    Surgeon's tales: The cured ingrate.—Miller,
    H. Recollections of Ferguson. Recollections
    of Burns.—Campbell, A. Disasters of Johnny
    Armstrong. Countess of Wistonbury. Don-
    ald Gorm.—Gillespie, T. Professor's tales:
    Mountain storm; Fair maid of Cellardykes;
    Convivialists; Phillips Grey.—Howell, J.
    Fortunes of William Wighton.
    2: Miller, H. Widow of Dunskaith.
    Salmon-fisher of Udoll.—Wilson, J. M. Whit-

WILSON, J. M., and others—*Continued.*

some tragedy. Royal bridal. Solitary of the cave. The fair.—Leighton, A. Surgeon's tales: Diver and the bell. Royal raid. Maiden feast of Cairnkibbie. Linton lairds. —Campbell, A. Autobiography of Willie Smith. Rival nightcaps. Monk of St. Anthony. The katheran. Monks of Dryburgh. — Gillespie, T. Professor's tales: Pheebe Fortune; Early recollections of a son of the hills; Suicide's grave.—Howell, J. The experimenter. The slave.—Bethune, A. Young laird.—Martin, T. Bon Gaultier's tales: Country quarters.—Logan, W. Story of Clara Douglas.

3: Wilson, J. M. Bill Stanley. Archy Armstrong. The guidwife of Coldingham. Leaves from the diary of an aged spinster. Laidley worm of Spindletou's Heugh. Sabbath wrecks.—Leighton, A. Surgeon's tales: Conscience stricken; Somnambulist of Redcleugh. Duncan Schulebred's vision of judgment. Geordie Willison, and the heiress of Castle Gower.—Campbell, A. Rattling, roaring Willie. Highland boy. Snowstorm of 1825.—Miller, H. Bill Whyte.—Gillespie, T. Professor's tales: Last of the pedlars.—Logan, W. Double-bedded room.—Howell, J. Major Weir's coach. Sergeant's tales: The palantines.—Moir, D. M. Divinity student.—Richardson, O. Rothesay fisherman.—Guilty, or not guilty.—Peterkin, A. The parsonage: My father's fireside.—Hetherington, W. Seer's cave.

4: Wilson, J. M. Judith the Egyptian. Poor scholar. Broken heart. Doom of Soulis. The bride. Henpecked man.—Leighton, A. The Droich. Amateur lawyers. Harden's revenge. Surgeon's tales: The cherry-stone; The hen-wife; The artist.—Miller, H. The lykewake.—Campbell, A. Penny wedding. Good man of Dryfield. Leein Jamie Murdiston. Duncan M'Arthur.—Gillespie, T. Professor's tales: Family incidents; Home and the gipsy maid; The return.—H., J. Laird of Darnick Tower.—Maidment, J. Cateran of Lochloy. Mortlake: a legend of Merton.—Howell, J. Serjeant's tales: John Square's voyage to India; Beggar's camp.—Richardson, O. Physiognomist's tale.

5: Wilson, J. M. The cripple. Sir Patrick Hume: a tale of the house of Marchmont. Charles Lawson. The first foot. I canna be fashed.—Leighton, A. Legend of fair Helen of Kirconnel. The abduction. Christie of the cleek. Romance of the siege of Perth. Caleb Crabbin. Crooked Comyn.—Richardson, O. Tom Duncan's yarn. Meeting at St. Boswell's.—Gillespie, T. Professor's tales: Three brethren; Mistake rectified; Dura Den; Peat-casting time; The medal.—Campbell, A. Laird of Lucky's How. Chatelard. —Howell, J. Serjeant's tales: Packman's journey to London; Imprudent marriage. —Martin, T. Bon Gaultier's tales: Mrs. Humphrey Greenwood's tea-party.—Logan, W. Recluse of the Hebrides. Ellen Arun-

WILSON, J. M., and others—*Continued.*

del.—Smith, J. F. Story of May Darling.—Conolly, M. F. Tales of the east neuk of Fife: Castle of Crail; Legend of the church of Abercrombie; Romance of the May.—Bethune, J. Bewildered student.

6: Wilson, J. M. Dominie's class. The smuggler. Red Hall; or, Berwick in 1296. Reuben Purves. We'll have another.—Leighton, A. Contrast of wives. Surgeon's tales: The suicide; Three letters; Glass back. Mike Maxwell and the Gretna Green lovers. —Gillespie, T. Professor's tales: Social man; The wedding.—Campbell, A. Two comrades. The surtout. The mosstrooper. The forger. —Bethune, A. Ghost of Howdycraigs. Ghost of Gairyburn.—Richardson, O. Schoolfellows. Sea-storm. — Miller, H. Scottish hunters of Hudson's Bay.—Maidment J. Heir of Iushannock.—Howell, J. Scottish veteran.—Maxwell, P. White woman of Tarras.

7: Wilson, J. M. The unknown. Lottery Hall. Covenanting family. Polwarth on the green. The festival. Order of the Garter: a story of Wark Castle.—Leighton, A. Trials of Menie Dempster. Roseallan's daughter. Old chronicler's tales: Prince of Scotland. Legend of Holyrood.—Gillespie, T. Professor's tales: Natural history of idiots; The enthusiast; Trees and burns; Kirkyards.—Campbell, A. Floshend inn. The dream. Retribution. Skean dhu.—Wilson, J. Dominie and the souter: Dominie's courtship; Souter's wedding. — Richardson, O. Two sailors. Restored son.—Howell, J. Seven years' dearth.

8: Wilson, J. M. Recollections of a village patriarch. Grizel Cochrane. Squire Ben. The leveller. Perseverance. Irish reaper.—Leighton, A. Old chronicler's tales: Death of James I.; Death of James III. Surgeon's tales: Case of evidence. Clerical murderer. Mr. Samuel Ramsay Thriven.—Campbell, A. Curate of Govan. Countess of Cassilis. Grace Cameron.—Gillespie, T. Gleanings of the covenant. 1-9: Grandmother's narrative; Covenanter's march; Peden's farewell sermon; Persecution of the M'Michaels; Rescue at Enterkin; Fatal mistake; Bonny Mary Gibson; Eskdalemuir story; Douglas tragedy. —Richardson, O. Story of Tom Bertram. Angler's tale.—The cottar's daughter.—Bethune, A. The warning.—Battle of Dryffe Sands.—Happy conclusion.—Howell, J. Man-of-war's man.—Mysterious disappearance.

9: Wilson, J. M. Roger Goldie's narrative. Unbidden guest. Simple man is the beggar's brother. The fugitive. Willie Wastle's account of his wife.—Leighton, A. Hogmanay. Surgeon's tales: The bereaved; The condemned; The monomaniac. Hume and the governor of Berwick. Bride of Bramblehaugh. Laird Rorieson's will.—Gillespie, T. Gleanings of the covenant. 10-17: Sergeant Wilson; Helen Palmer; Cairny cave of Gavin Muir; Porter's Hole; James Renwick; Old

WILSON, J. M., and others—*Continued.*
Ishel Kirk; The curlers; Violated coffin.—Campbell, A. The recluse. A highland tradition. Foundling at sea. The assassin The stone-breaker.—Conolly, M. F. Tales of the east neuk of Fife: Robbery at Pittenweem and the Porteous mob; Story of Charles Gordon and Christina Cunningham.—Howell, J. Legend of Caldermoor. Prisoner of war. —Miller, H. Thomas of Chartres.

10: Leighton, A. Domestic griefs of Gustavus M'Iver. The avenger. Sportsman of Outfieldhaugh. Dominie of St. Fillan's. The heroine. Miser of New-abbey.—Wilson, J. M. First and second marriage. Leaves from the life of Alexander Hamilton. Sayings and doings of Peter Paterson. Trials and triumphs.—Richardson, O. Dissolved pledge. —Campbell, A. Hawick spate. Lord of Hermitage. Curse of Scotland. Barley bannock.—Gillespie, T. Gleanings of the covenant. 18-23: Kinaldy; Trials of the Rev. Samuel Austin; John Goran's narrative; "Old Bluntie;" Thomas Harkness of Lockerben; Shoes reversed.—Sea fight.—Thomson, G. Lost heir of the house of Elphinstone.—Sea skirmish.

11: Leighton, A. Burgher's tales: House in Bell's Wynd; Ancient bureau. Lawyer's tales: Woman with the white mice. Detective's tales: Chance question; Bride of Bell's Tower. Surgeon's tales: The wager; Diamond eyes; Amateur robbery; Ten of diamonds.—Wilson, J. M. Prodigal son. The seeker. Ups and downs. The procrastinator.—Gillespie, T. Gleanings of the covenant: Early days of a friend of the covenant.—Campbell, A. Merchant's daughter. Doctor Dobbie. Lady Rae.—David Lorimer.—The convict.

12: Leighton, A. Lawyer's tales: Lord Kames's puzzle; Story of Mysie Craig. Burgher's tales: Brownie of the West Bow. Story of Mary Brown. Cradle of Logie. Story of the pelican. Girl forger. Two red slippers. Faithful wife. Romaunt of Sir Peregrine and the Lady Etheline. Legend of Allerley Hall. Legend of the Lady Katharine. Ballad of Ailie Faa. Legend of the fair Emergilde. Romaunt of the castle of Weir. Romaunt of St. Mary's Wynd. Legend of Mary Lee. Ballad of age and youth. Legend of Craigullan. Ballad of Rumbollow. Legend of the burning of Mrs. Jamphray. Ballad of Ballogie's daughters. Legend of Dowielee. Ballad of Maid Marion. Ballad of Roseallan Castle. Ballad of the tournay. Ballad of golden counsel. Ballad of matrimony. Song of Rosalie. Ballad of the world's vanity.—Wilson, J. M. The orphan. Tibby Fowler. Death of the Chevalier de la Beauté. Widow's ae son. Twin brothers. Edmund and Helen. Hermit of the hills. The siege.—Gillespie, T. Gleanings of the covenant: Last scrap.—G., *Rev.* W. Farewell to a place on the borders.

WILSON, M. C. Manuelita: the story of San Xavier del Bac.....................W751.1
Wind of destiny. Hardy, A. S.............H268.3
Window in Thrums. Barrie, J. M.........B275.10
Windsor Castle. Ainsworth, W. H...... A297.25
Wing and Wing. Cooper, J. F............ C777.43
Same...C777.44
Wing of Azrael. Caird, M...................C136.2
Winged word. Tincker, M. A.............T587.8
WINGFIELD, L. Curse of Koshiu: a chronicle of old Japan..........................W771.1
Maid of honor: a tale of the dark days of France....................................W771.2
Wings of Icarus. Tadema, *Miss* L. A.....T121.1
Winifred Bertram. Charles, E. R........C476.15
Winifred countess of Nithsdale. Sullivan, A...................................... **S950.1
WINSLOW, H. M. Salome Shepard, reformer..W780.1
WINTER, J. S. (*pseud. of* H. E. V. Stannard). Army tales: Bootles' baby; Siege baby; In quarters with the 25th Dragoons; Calvary life; Regimental legends..................................W785.1
Aunt Johnnie.....................................W785.2
Beautiful Jim of the Blankshire Regiment.................................... W785.3
Bootles' baby..... ....*in* W785.1
Calvary life.................................*in* W785.1
Dinna forget.....................................W785.5
Every inch a soldier..........................W785.7
Garrison gossip.................................W785.9
Grip... W785.10
In quarters with the 25th Dragoons..*in*W785.1
Koosje: a study of Dutch life...........*in* S885.3
Only human............... ....W785.12
Regimental legends..................*in* W785.1
Same..W785.13
Siege baby...................................*in* W785.1
Soul of the bishop.............................W785.14
Truth-tellers......................................W785.16
Winter in the ice and other stories. Verne, J...................................... V531.44
Winter story. Peard, F. M.................Q359.18
Winterborough. White, E. O.............W584.3
WINTERFELD, A. VON. Matrimonial agent..W788.1
WINTHER, R. W. C. F. The confessional. 12 pp..................................*in* B979.1
WINTHROP, T. Cecil Dreeme.............W793.1
Edwin Brothertoft...............................W793.2
John Brent... W793.3
Life in the open air, and other papers....W793.4
Wise woman. Burnham, C. L.............B966.14

WISEMAN, N. P. S. *Cardinal.* Fabiola; or, the church of the catacombs......W814.1

Wish, The. Sudermann, H..................S943.1

WISTER, A. L., tr. At the councillor's, by E. Marlitt.......................W817.10

Bailiff's maid, by E. Marlitt...........W817.11

Banned and blessed, by E. Werner...W817.32

Castle Hohenwald, by A. Streckfuss...W817.28

Countess Erika's apprenticeship, by O. Schubin..............................W817.25

Countess Gisela, by E. Marlitt.........W817.12

The Eichhofs,by M. von Reichenbach.W817.23

Erlach Court, by O. Schubin...........W817.26

Family feud, by L. Harder................W817.2

From hand to hand, by G. Raimund..W817.21

Gold Elsie, by E. Marlitt.................W817.13

Green gate, by E. Wichert................W817.34

Hulda, by F. Lewald.......................W817.8

In the Schillingscourt, by E. Marlitt..W817.14

Lady with the rubies, by E. Marlitt...W817.15

Little moorland princess, by E. Marlitt..............................W817.16

Margarethe, by E. Juncker...............W817.7

New race, by G. Raimund.................W817.22

Noble name, by C. v. Glümer...........W817.1

"O thou, my Austria!" by O. Schubin..W817.27

Old mam'selle's secret, by E. Marlitt..W817.17

Only a girl, by W. von Hillern..........W817.5

Owl's nest, by E. Marlitt.................W817.18

Penniless girl, by W. Heimburg.........W817.4

Picked up in the streets, by H. Schobert..............................W817.24

Quicksands, by A. Streckfuss...........W817.29

Saint Michael, by E. Werner...........W817.33

Second wife, by E. Marlitt................W817.19

Severa, by B. Hartner.....................W817.3

Too rich, by A. Streckfuss................W817.30

Vain forebodings, by E. Oswald........W817.20

Violetta, by U. Z. von Manteuffel......W817.9

Why did he not die? by A. von Volckhausen..............................W817.31

WISTER, O. Red men and white.........W818.1

Witch of Jamestown. Bowyer, J. T......B788.1

Witch of Melton hill......................W820.1

Witch of Prague. Crawford, F. M......C899.26

Witcherly ways: a Christmas tale. 47 pp..............................*in* T143.16

Witch-hampton Hall: five scenes in the life of its last lady. 87 pp...........*in* T143.9

Witch's head. Haggard, H R............H146.14

With edged tools. Merriman, H. S......M571.9

With fire and sword. Sienkiewicz, H...S572.12

With fortune made. Cherbuliez, V......C521.10

With Gauge & Swallow, attorneys. Tourgée, A. W..............................T727.12

With harp and crown. Besant, *Sir* W. and Rice, J..............................B554.46

With my friends. Matthews, B...........M438.16

With the best intentions. Harland, M...H283.18

With the immortals. Crawford, F. M....C899.27

With the procession. Fuller, H. B........F968.3

Within an ace. Jenkin, H. C.............J525.5

Within an inch of his life. Gaboriau, E..G116.11

Within iron walls. Lucas, A............*in* L932.1

Without a home. Roe, E. P..............R699.17

Without dogma. Sienkiewicz, H.........S572.13

Witness to the deed. Fenn, G. M........F334.12

Wives of men of genius. Daudet, A......D238.16

Wizard. Haggard, H. R..................H146.15

Wizard's son. Oliphant, M. O. W.......O475.61

WOLF, A. S. House of cards.............W853.1

WOLF, E. Joy of life......................W854.3

Other things being equal................W854.1

Prodigal in love..........................W854.2

Wolf at the door..........................W856.1

Wolfret's Roost, and other papers. Irving, W..............................I725.8

WOLFF, J. Fifty years, three months, two days: a tale of the Neckar valley.....W857.1

Salt master of Lüneburg.................W857.2

Woman-hater. Reade, C..................R285.32

Woman in white. Collins, W.............C713.34

Woman intervenes. Barr, R..............B269.2

Woman of honor. Bunner, H. C...........B942.6

Woman of Shawmut. Carpenter, E. J....C295.1

Woman of the world. 3 vols. Robinson, F. M..............................R659.2

Woman the stronger. Hagg, W. J........H145.1

Woman's courier. Yeoman, W. J.........Y463.5

Woman's friendship. Aguilar, G.........A283.6

Woman's heart. Alexander, *Mrs*........A374.28

Woman's inheritance. Douglas, A. M...D734.34

Woman's kingdom. Mulock, D. M......M960.29

Woman's love. 34 pp. Opie, J..........*in* O614.3

Woman's ransom. Robinson, F. W......R660.5

Woman's reason. Howells, W. D........H859.32

Woman's reward. 2 vols. Norton, C. E. S..............................**N883.3

Woman's word, and how she kept it. Townsend, V. F...........................T751.9

Won and not one. Blackall, E. L........B628.2

Won by waiting. Lyall, E.................L981.15

Won on a silver basis. Spelling, T. C....S743.1

Wondrous strange. Newby, *Mrs.* C. J....N535.1

WOOD, A. B. Cupid on crutches; or, one summer at Narragansett Pier..........W873.1

WOOD, C. D. *See* Dunning, C., *pseud.*
WOOD, E. P. Bessy Rane......................W874.1
The Channings...............................W874.2
Dene Hollow.................................W874.3
East Lynne.................................W874.4
Edina...W874.5
Elster's folly...............................W874.6
Lady Adelaide..............................W874.7
    Issued also as The castle's heir. Out of the
    deep.
Master of Greylands.....................W874.8
Oswald Cray...............................W874.10
Red Court farm...........................W874.11
Roland Yorke. Sequel to "The Chan-
    nings."..................................W874.12
St. Martin's Eve..........................W874.14
Squire Trevlyn's heir....................W874.13
    Issued also as Trevlyn Hold.
Verner's pride.............................W874.15
WOOD, *Mrs.* H. *See* Wood, E. P.
WOOD, J. S. Puritan ingénue. 71 pp...*in* S886.2
WOOD, R. A. *See* Cushing, P., *pseud.*
Wood beyond the world. Morris, W.....M877.3
Woodburn Grange. Howitt, W............H863.1
Woolen Clara. Conscience, H............C755.2
Same..*in* C755.8
Woodlanders. Hardy, T.................H272.21
Woodman. Glouvet, J. de................G564.1
Woodman. James, G. P. R...............J276.40
WOODS, K. P. From dusk to dawn......W895.1
John: a tale of King Messiah............W895.4
Metzerott, shoemaker......................W895.2
Web of gold..................................W895.3
WOODS, M. L. The vagabonds............W896.1
Village tragedy.............................W896.2
WOODS, V. Modern Magdalene...........W897.1
Woodstock. Scott, *Sir* W...............S431.54
Same......................................**S431.55
Wooed and married. Carey, R. N.......C276.36
Wooing o't. Alexander, *Mrs*............A374.29
WOOLLEY, C. P. Roger Hunt............W913.1
WOOLSEY, S. C. *See* Coolidge, S., *pseud.*
WOOLSON, C. F. Anne.....................W916.1
Castle Nowhere: lake-country sketches...
    ....W916.2
Dorothy, and other Italian stories......W916.3
East Angels.................................W916.4
For the major...............................W916.5
Front yard, and other Italian stories....W916.6
Horace Chase...............................W916.7
Jupiter lights...............................W916.8
Miss Grief. 35 pp.......................*in* S884.4
Rodman the keeper.......................W916.9
Word only a word. Ebers, G............E165.17

Work. Alcott, L. M.......................A355.5
World in the church. Riddell, C. E. L....R543.19
World of chance. Howells, W. D........H859.33
World we live in. Crawfurd, O...........C900.1
World well lost. Linton, E. L.............L761.4
World went very well then. Besant, *Sir*
    W..B554.33
World's desire. Haggard, H. R. *and*
    Lang, A....................................H146.17
World's verdict. Hopkins, M., *Jr*......H793.1
Wormwood. Corelli, M....................C797.16
Worth while. Montrésor, F. F..........M811.6
Wreck of the Chancellor. Verne, J.....V531.45
Wreck of the Corsaire. Russell, W. C..R968.27
Wreck of the "Grosvenor." Russell, W.
    C...R968.28
Wrecked in port. Yates, E...............Y317.13
Wrecker. Stevenson, R. L. *and* Osbourne,
    L..S848.15
Wright, D. T. Mrs. Armington's ward...W948.1
WRIGHT, J. McN. Patriot and tory: a tale
    of the revolution.......................W951.1
WRIGHT, S. A. Crimson star............W953.1
Wrong box. Stevenson, R. L. *and*
    Osbourne, L..............................S848.16
Wuthering heights. Brontë, E............B871.1
Same...B871.2
Wyandotté. Cooper, J. F..................C777.45
Same...C777.46
WYATT, T. ? Cottage by the river. 56
    pp...*in* T143.17
Wych Hazel. Warner, S. *and* A. B.....W284.13
WYLDE, K. A dreamer.....................W982.1
Wyllard's weird. Braddon, M. E....B798.42
Wyncote. Erskine, *Mrs.* T...............E735.1
WYNNE, M. Y. Little room, and other
    stories.......................................W989.1
X jewel. Moncreiff, F.....................M739.1
Xenia Repnina. MacGahan, B. E........M145.1
Xénie's inheritance. Gréville, H........G838.10
Yanko the musician, and other stories.
    Sienkiewicz, H............................S572.15
YARDLEY, J. Little sister.................Y273.1
YATES, E. Black sheep....................Y317.1
Broken to harness..........................Y317.2
Dr. Wainwright's patient..................Y317.3
Impending sword............................Y317.4
Kissing the rod.............................Y317.5
Land at last.................................Y317.6
Nobody's fortune...........................Y317.7
Righted wrong..............................Y317.8
Rock ahead..................................Y317.9
Running the gauntlet......................Y317.10
Two, by tricks..............................Y317.11

YATES, E.—*Continued.*
Waiting race....................Y317.12
Wrecked in port................Y317.13
Yellow flag....................Y317.14
Year at Poplar Row. Elliuwood, M......E464.1
Year one of the republic—1793. Erck-
mann, E. *and* Chatrian, A.............E654.20
Same.........................E654.21
Yeast. Kingsley, C.............K553.7
Yekl. Cahan, A.................C131.1
Yellow aster. Iota.............I645.1
Yellow flag. Yates, E..........Y317.14
Yellow Frigate. Grant, J.......G761.56
Yellow snake. Bishop, W. H.....B622.9
Yellowplush papers. Thackeray, W. M...
....T363.21
YELVERTON, T. Zanita: a tale of the Yo-
semite.........................Y436.1
Yemassee. Simms, W. G..........S592.18
YEOMAN, W. J. A woman's courier: a tale
of the famous forty conspiracy of 1696..
....Y463.5
Yoke of the Thorah. Harland, H.......H282.16
Yolande. Black, W..............B627.43
YONGE, C. M. Armourer's prentices.....Y555.1
Beechcroft.....................Y555.2
Bye-words......................Y555.39
Caged lion.....................Y555.3
Castle builders................Y555.4
Chantry House..................Y555.5
Chaplet of pearls..............Y555.6
Clever woman of the family.....Y555.7
Daisy chain....................Y555.8
Danvers papers............*in* Y555.16
Disturbing element.............Y555.9
Dove in the eagle's nest.......Y555.10
Dynevor Terrace................Y555.11
Grisly Grisell.................Y555.12
Heartsease.....................Y555.13
Heir of Redclyffe..............Y555.14
Hopes and fears................Y555.15
Lady Hester, and, Danvers papers....Y555.16
Lances of Lynwood..............Y555.17
Love and life..................Y555.18
Magnum bonum...................Y555.20
Modern Telemachus..............Y555.21
More bywords...................Y555.22
My young Alcides: a faded photo-
graph..........................Y555.23
Nuttie's father................Y555.24
Pillars of the house. 2 vols...Y555.27
The release....................Y555.26
Reputed changeling.............Y555.28
Scenes and characters..........Y555.29

YONGE, C. M.—*Continued.*
Stray pearls...................Y555.30
That stick.....................Y555.31
Three brides...................Y555.32
The trial: more links of the daisy
chain..........................Y555.33
Two guardians: or, home in this
world..........................Y555.34
Two penniless princesses.......Y555.35
Two sides of the shield........Y555.36
Unknown to history: a story of the cap-
tivity of Mary of Scotland.....Y555.37
Young stepmother...............Y555.38
Youma. Hearn, L................H436.3
YOUNG, J. D. Adrift: a story of Niagara...Y693.1
Young doctor. Conscience, H ......*in* C755.4
Young duke. Disraeli, B........D613.15
Same.........................D613.16
Young girl's wooing. Roe, E. P.....R699.18
Young maids and old. Burnham, C. L....B966.15
Young Maugars. Theuriet, A.....T415.7
Young Mrs. Jardine. Mulock, D. M....M960.30
Your money or your life. Carpenter, E...C294.1
Young Musgrave. Oliphant, M. O. W....O475.63
Young stepmother. Yonge, C. M....... Y555.38
Youth of Jefferson. Cooke, J. E.........C772.17
Youth of Shakespeare. Williams, R. F....
................................*in* **W726.1
Youth of the Old Dominion. Hopkins,
S............................. H795.1
Yule-tide stories. Ed. by B. Thorpe.......T518.1
Z., Z. Drama in Dutch..........Z111.1
Zachary Phips. Bynner, E. L....B994.7
Zadig. 41 pp. Voltaire, F. M. A. de....
................................*in* **N938.2
Zadoc Pine, and other stories. Bunner,
H. C...........................B942.7
ZANGWILL, I. Children of the Ghetto....Z295.1
Ghetto tragedies...............S295.3
King of schnorrers.............Z295.5
The master.....................Z295.7
Old maids' club................Z295.9
Premier and the painter........Z295.11
Rose of the Ghetto. 22 pp......*in* S885.6
Zanita. Yelverton, T...........Y436.1
Zanoni. Lytton, E. G. E. L. Bulwer-...L998.27
Zanthon. Doran, J..............D693.1
ZEDRITZ, K. E. Double wedding at Dun-
derviksborg. 58 pp...........*in* H496.1
Zelda's fortune. Francillon, R. E.........F817.2
Zeluco. 2 vols. Moore, J.............**B232.34-5
Zenia, the vestal. Peeke, M. B............Q373.1
Zenobia. Ware, W...............W273.3
Zeph. Jackson, H. M............J127.6

Zicci. Lytton, E. G. E. L. Bulwer-.....*in* L.998.4

ZIMMERN, H., *and* A. Half-hours with foreign novelists. 2 vols..................Z767.1

CONTENTS: 1: Sand, G. The marriage. The cabbage.—Murger, H. Francine's muff. Passage of the Red Sea.—Auerbach, B. The axe.—Busken-Huet, C. Gitje. Saturday at the Hague. Along the churchyard.—Stifter, A. Balloon ascent. The heath.—Farina, S. Separation.—Daudet, A. Indret. The vice. Machines.—Spielhagen, F. The storm.—Sacher-Masoch, L. v. Sledge-ride.—Flygare-Carlén, E. Smugglers.—Cherbuliez, V. L'idée de Jean Téterol.—Hackländer, F. W. Volunteer.—Jokai, M. The plague.
2: Turgénieff, I. The nihilist.—Freytag, G. German professor.—Caballero, F. Old and the new.—Feuillet, O. Julia de Trécœur. —Krasewski, J. I. Foundling.—Marlitt, E. Twelve apostles.—Bjornson, B. The betrothal. The wedding.—Balzac, H. de. A Cretin village. A Breton town.—Heyse, P. The huntsman.—Gaboriau, E. Amateur detective.—

ZIMMERN, H. and A.—*Continued.*

Keller, G. The funeral. Clothes make men. —Bosboom-Toussaint, A. L. G. Major Frances.—Sandeau, J. Last of an old family.

Zohrab the hostage. Morier, J.............M855.7

ZOLA, E. Attack on the mill. 51 pp...
...................................*in* R657.1

Zoroaster. Crawford, F. M.................C899.29

ZSCHOKKE, H. Alamontade. 53 pp...
...................................*in* O983.1

Goldmaker's village...........................Z923.1

Labour stands on golden feet..............Z923.2

Princess of Brunswick-Wolfenbüttel and other tales...................................Z923.3

Rose of Disentis..................................Z923.4

Sylvester night's adventure.................Z923.5

Veronica: or, the free court of Aarau....Z923.6

Zury. Kirkland, J............................K597.2

www.ingramcontent.com/pod-product-compliance
Lightning Source LLC
Chambersburg PA
CBHW021127020726
47500CB00003B/965